SUCKING DEAD

BOOKS 4-6

ANDIE M. LONG

This book is a work of fiction. Names, characters, places, and incidents are either the product of the author's imagination or are used fictitiously, and any resemblance to actual persons, living or dead, events or locales is entirely coincidental.

No part of this book may be reproduced or transmitted in any form or by any means, electronic or mechanical, including photocopying, recording or by any information storage and retrieval system without the written permission of the author, except for the use of brief quotations in a book review.

Copyright © 2022 by Andrea Long.
All rights reserved.
Cover design by Tammy
Formatting by Tammy

SUCK IT UP

CHAPTER ONE

Ginny

"Can I have a Glenlivet and your phone number?" the puffy-faced vampire at the bar asked. He'd been turned just after a dental procedure. After the dentist had extracted a tooth and a private fee for two hundred pounds, Cuthbert had decided to nip down the alleyway across from the dental surgery as he felt a little woozy. A few minutes later he was even woozier as Santori Letwine had smelled the blood congealing around the wound and extracted the rest of the blood from his body.

Cuthbert had luck on his side that day however, because Santori was already in deep shit for leaving dead bodies around for other Letwine vampires to clear up, so on that day he decided to turn Cuthbert instead and make himself a new ally.

In contrast, Santori himself did *not* have luck on his side as Edmond Letwine, the elder of the clan, declared him too loose a cannon and had him staked, giving Cuthbert all of Santori's assigned tasks in the clan.

It had led to an inflated cheeked vampire, with an inflated opinion of himself.

"You can have the whisky and pay your tab," I informed him. He'd been annoying me all night and while most of the time I ignored drunk vampires who felt it was okay to flirt with me, taking it as part of the job, tonight I was feeling in a mood. Did this puffa fish imposter think I would really be interested in him? Me, Virginia

Letwine? I could only think his inebriation had worked in reverse of how it did for humans, his 'beer goggles' elevating his self-esteem but affecting his eyesight, so he thought I was at his level.

"Oh, come on, baby. Don't be like that. I heard you like money and want a rich man. I'm rich in the pants department if you get my drift, and I'm sure we can work out a way to earn some money. Bet there's a vampire or two here who would pay to spend time with my girl. I could manage you and in return you could give me a percentage of the takings... and the goods."

Everything went red as fury burned through my veins. I broke off a piece of the bar's wooden counter, leapt over it, and knocked Cuthbert to the floor landing astride his thighs. "Oh, Cuthbert, I'm on top of you, just as you were imagining," I teased. "Now let me see to your dick."

I plunged the stake right through his groin. Whether I could have perforated his tiny dick or either of his balls I couldn't know. I just knew it hurt him. Hurt him a damn lot. I twisted it and watched the vampire below me turn a shade of green. Looked like I could sit on Cuthbert and feel highly satisfied after all.

"I'd rather fuck a poor man than fuck anyone as ugly as you," I whispered, leaning over him. The rest of the patrons of the bar were stood back watching us with interest.

"It's all about appearances with you, isn't it?" my brother said from beside me.

"He's ugly inside and out and he asked if he could be my pimp," I said.

"Yes, well looking at him, I would guess he has no doubt now changed his mind. So could you take out the stake because us men have morning wood, not evening wood."

I pulled it out which meant that any wound would close quickly, and Cuthbert would be an angry vampire within seconds. Anticipating this, Lawrie grabbed him by the neck and pushed him up against the wall, the bloody stake now in his hand.

"You'll take a walk now, sober up, and forget all about this, otherwise I'll place this stake through your heart next time I hear you've been propositioning my sister. Now get out before I change my mind and finish you now."

"Thanks, Lawrie," I said. "He just really icks me out and when he said that—"

A voice came from behind me.

"You should have left the bar and come and found me. I'm the elder of this clan and I would have meted out the necessary punishments," Edmond Letwine said in a low, authoritative tone. While I kept standing up straight, inside I withered when faced with our fierce leader.

"I'm sorry, Edmond," I apologised. "It won't happen again."

"No, it won't, because I'm putting Rune behind the bar in your place. He and Acker can manage things."

I couldn't help it. My hands went to my hips, and I folded my arms across my chest. "So the men in this bar can't behave themselves, but I get punished? I lose my job because they think with their dicks after a drink instead of their brains?"

Edmond sighed, looking at me like you might a child after answering their 'Why' questions all day. "No, Ginny. It's because you've been very short-tempered of late. You need to find a job that makes you feel more restful and relaxed. Something that soothes your soul."

I stared at him. "Has Mya been teaching you meditation again?"

"That is not your concern," he answered. "However, when you next bump into her you might like to ask her for some useful podcasts in managing aggression."

"Cuthbert wanted to be my *pimp*." My voice rose with each uttered word.

"And I would have dealt with his impropriety, Virginia."

Full name alert, I thought. I needed to be careful. I sucked in my lips so I couldn't say anything else. Made myself listen and look attentive.

"Now, however, you've taken matters into your own hands, literally by twisting a stake in his penis, and that means his punishment is already served and I cannot sanction anything further against him. Indeed, what you've done is give him leverage to come to me about *you*."

"If I am to be punished, then let me know because I'll go and finish him off," I snarled. If I was going down, I was taking Fuckbert with me. All thoughts of calm were lost as my fangs descended and I knew my eyes would be blazing red.

"No punishments, other than you're fired," Edmond said. "And you're to keep away from Cuthbert. Either find that nice job we spoke about, or take a sabbatical, but either way you need to learn to chillax. Is that understood, Virginia, because I have other much more pressing things to deal with."

"Yes, Sir."

"Excellent. Good evening, Lawrie. I shall expect you to oversee your sister's rehabilitation," he added, and then he vanished, having no doubt whizzed off to his 'pressing matters', which knowing Edmond was his ironing. He was obsessed with a 'traveller's crease' in all his trousers.

I turned to Lawrie. "You don't have to babysit me. I'll behave."

Lawrie tilted his head towards me. "You have been sullener and more irritable of late. What's going on with you?" he asked.

I went behind the bar, took a bottle of vodka and indicated towards the door. Acker could do the rest of the shift on his own and have my middle finger as payment for the bottle of Absolut in my hand. I was done with The Vampire's In(n).

We left the dark bar and entered the soft summer night. There was a gentle breeze as we strolled across the grounds towards the Letwine mansion.

"I'm fed up with everyone," I confessed. "You're all too goddamn happy. I can't cope with it. It makes me want to throw up in my mouth or shove a stake through my own heart."

"What?" Lawrie's mouth dropped open. "So basically, what you're saying is that you are in dire need of a good shag?"

"That too," I huffed. "But I'm an evil vampire, Lawrie, and you were too, and now look at you. You work in a café selling pink glittery cupcakes and kiss your wife every five seconds while declaring your love." I pulled a grimace.

"That's because I'm in love. As Climie Fisher said, '*Love Changes (Everything)*'."

I cast my eyes down to his groin area. "Where's another stake when you need one?"

"Look. Go be miserable in your room for the night. Make a Cuthbert voodoo doll or whatever you need to do. Watch *The Craft* on repeat. But tomorrow morning, come to the café. Spend some time with the girls. You always feel better when you've seen Dela."

Dela was my friend, but she was also madly in love. Her advice now came covered in a smothering of bliss. However, she still was a good friend, and I did like hanging around the bookstore.

"Okay. I'll come around in the morning," I agreed.

"Excellent, I'll see you then. It will all work out okay, Ginny. You'll see. If I can end up with Callie, then miracles do truly happen."

That made me smile.

"A smile? Oh my goodness, be careful there. You'd better immerse yourself in revenge witchcraft before you lose your bitchcraft."

He'd whizzed away before he got to see my raised middle finger, which was getting plenty of action tonight, even if neither I nor Cuthbert was.

As a vampire we needed little sleep, so after a power hour, and catching up on some TV programmes I'd recorded, the next morning I set off for Books and Buns, my sister-in-law's café and bookstore. Travel was a piece of piss as a vampire. I thought of my destination and whizzed straight there.

Callie looked pleased to see me and I soon found there was another reason for it apart from her hubby having ordered me there.

"Ginny, any chance you can give me a hand with the shop this morning?" she said. So much for the red velvet cupcake and pink lemonade I'd been hoping for, but there was a queue forming and no sign of either Dela or Aria.

"Sure," I said. "I'll run the bookstore. Where is everyone?"

"Dela's no doubt in bed, and Aria is sick. She's been vomiting all morning apparently."

I froze. Vampires didn't vomit. In the back of my mind were Merrin's words from last year. Then a customer asked a question and I pushed it all to the back of my mind.

Jason entered the store. He was Dela's boyfriend's best friend, but I remembered him more from being an onlooker when the great undead and unwashed had talked to me like crap. God knows what he was doing being a friend to that... *thing*. One day I would make Merrin suffer, because I'd not forgotten that day when he'd talked to me with such disdain. How dare he act superior to me. Me! I was a Letwine vampire who lived in a mansion in luxury, and he was a zombie who I believed lived in a reclamation yard which I doubted had washroom facilities given the state of him.

Jason's phone rang and I watched as his expression changed to one of panic and he shouted out, "Oh shit."

"What's the matter, Jason?" Callie asked, rushing to his side.

"Ali at the yard has just called. A load of the junk Merrin had stored has just collapsed and Merrin is buried under it all. He can't die from it as he's already dead, but Merrin is extremely claustrophobic. We have to rescue him as quickly as possible. I need Nick and his expertise. Maybe he can use his digger to help?" he suggested.

"There's no need," I said, stepping forward. "Tell me where exactly this place is and I shall go there immediately. I can easily rescue him using my superior vampire strength."

"Er, if you're sure..."

"I'm beyond sure. It would be my pleasure to help him," I declared.

And as Jason reeled off his address and I got ready to whizz over there, I smirked. It would indeed be my pleasure when I removed the crap covering Merrin and he saw just who had rescued him.

He'd be appalled.

And that made my dead heart very happy indeed.

It looked like Lawrie's idea of me coming to work here today had been an excellent one. I could hang with my friends in the shop, plus torment the life out of Merrin for my entertainment. Well, he was dead, but you knew what I meant.

'Let's go then," I said, and I grabbed hold of Jason and whizzed us both to the yard.

CHAPTER TWO

Merrin

My yard was once again being swamped by Gnarly's excess furniture. I was going to have to bring this up at the next council meeting because it seemed the residents of our small village weren't sticking to the 'reduce, re-use, recycle' mantra as much as they once had been. They felt donating their pieces to me for repurposing meant they could buy whatever they wanted and feel they'd done their bit by not throwing it away for the bin men for landfill.

No, it was my land becoming full. Every so often I'd get a large project like when I'd been asked to provide the furniture for Dela Francis' new home, and I'd think I could get a handle on my stock, but then another resident would give their place a makeover and another van full of their unwanted furniture would arrive.

Don't get me wrong, I loved to work on these pieces: restoring, re-purposing, etc, but each piece took time and so more came in than went back out. Even taking on another guy, Alistair, as an apprentice and then showing him how to set up his own business hadn't made much more of a dent in moving stock.

I loved seeing the beauty in things, yet all I could see when I looked out of the window of my small one-bedroomed cottage were the piles of unwanted rubbish; when, with a little gardening expertise, I could have a nice plot outside my house that looked over views of the woodland.

Something most definitely had to change. But in the meantime, I had to get a bureau out from under a few other piled up things as that was what I was working on today. Fenella who worked at the laundry wanted to start writing a Christmas book apparently. Since she lived with Santa, I guessed she had the inside track, but it was June and as the heat of the morning picked up, it was hard for me to think about the festive season.

I thought fondly of last Christmas though. Dela's home had been finished and her boyfriend Nick, a friend of mine, had invited me along for dinner as part of the surprise reveal. Given I'd always been very fond of my own company, I found, rather surprisingly to me, that I'd liked being around the other guests, eating good food and enjoying a beer. It had created a feeling of emptiness within me since. I felt unsettled and had this gut feeling that something big was coming: a change, but also… danger. I hated these 'gut feelings' or 'knowings' because I was generally correct and so I'd spent the last week or so with a feeling of foreboding accompanying me all day and night.

I watched as Alistair's van came up the driveway, the gravel crunching under his tyres, and I went outside to greet him.

"Morning, Merrin," he said, with a wave as he excited his vehicle.

"Morning, Alistair. You come to pick up another piece?"

"Yeah." Alistair smiled. He was older than me, forty to my thirty, but we got along just fine. He and his wife, Terri, had recently had a baby and while Terri went back to work, Alistair was a stay-at-home dad, doing his furniture business during the evenings and in the rare snatches of peace he got in between. And he said he didn't get many of those with a newborn.

"Can you help me get this bureau out while you're here?" I asked. "Only I want to get started on it this morning."

"Sure." He looked over at the piled-up furniture. "Please don't tell me it's in that lot," he said, pointing to the largest stack over in the disused cowshed where my gaze kept landing.

I shrugged.

"Shit. We've got to do something about this place, Merrin. It's a death trap."

"I know. I'm going to raise it at the next council meeting. The villagers of Gnarly must do better."

"Good. Glad to hear it. I'll make sure I'm there to back you up."

"Appreciated."

"Okay then, let's get this bureau out and while we take the other pieces down, I'll see if I can find my own next project."

"Cheers, Alistair. I'm glad you showed up today."

I was even more pleased he was there after what happened next.

Metalwork items and other such things were outside the front of my house, covered in waterproof tarpaulin where needed, but the rest stood inside the disused cowshed. That was where we walked over to now, and we began to move bits of the stacked furniture.

"Let's put the pieces out here separately and then when we've moved your bureau and whatever I choose to one side, we can stack the rest in a more thought-out manner," Alistair suggested.

"Sounds like a plan," I agreed.

I heard Alistair as he walked away, saying he was going to get the ladder so we could get to the top, but I reached over to the pile where there was a small table at the side. I could be moving that.

It all happened in slow motion. As if playing unwanted furniture Jenga, as I took the piece out, I knocked the piece next to it. There was a wobble, and I took a deep breath that it would stop.

The next thing I knew was the pile began sliding towards me, forming a brand-new pile as it shifted sideways with me now underneath it all.

"Oh my fucking god, Merrin, are you okay?" Alistair's panicked voice came from outside of the now rearranged pile of goods.

"I'm not injured. I'm a zombie, remember? Already dead. However." I started to scrunch up my eyes and put my hands in my hair. "I am claustrophobic."

I realised then that I was at the bottom of a pile of wooden goods and couldn't get out. Trapped. It was like being in the grave again. The items my wooden coffin, and me having to punch my way out. I tried to calm myself, chanting, "It's not the same. You're fine. You're fine." But the memories began to assail me again and the darkness closed in.

I screamed. "Alistair, help meeeeee."

I heard Alistair's voice asking for help, though it was muted due to the furniture lying over me. How long would they take to get here though? They might as well also send a psychiatric doctor along with the rescue team because I'd need them by then.

So imagine my surprise when not two minutes later I heard Alistair shouting to me that I'd be out shortly, and then I could hear things moving. Not one minute later I was uncovered, and I caught sight of my rescuer... Virginia Letwine.

Oh God no. Anyone but her. *She'd* rescued me? The spoiled brat vampire. How had she ended up here?

"Well, good morning, Merrin. I'll let your friends check you over, because I certainly won't be going near enough to you to do so, and then I'll wait for your thanks." She stood to the side while Alistair and Jason came closer.

"Cover me back up with all the furniture," I yelled. "Having to thank her is worse than the claustrophobia."

I heard her snigger.

"Are you okay, mate?" Jason said, as Alistair helped me to my feet.

"Define okay," I snapped. "Physically I'm fine. I don't bruise or get badly hurt as I'm dead already. However, my mental health has been severely compromised by being in the enclosed space and facing the fact I've been rescued by *her*."

"What is your problem with Ginny?" Jason whispered. "And stop being so snappy with me when I'm the reason you got rescued so quickly. Ginny was in the café when Alistair called, and her vamp strength meant you were out in super quick time."

"There's no point in whispering," Ginny said. "Super strength hearing also, remember?"

"Right, well, I don't know what has gone on between you guys and why you have this hate thing going on. I can't work out whether it's dislike or if you want to jump the other one's bones hard. Is it hate or intense sexual chemistry?"

"Hate," we both said in unison.

"But why?"

"She's made it clear that the only men of any worth to her are rich ones, which she will use to gain shiny, pretty things. She uses people and has no regard for their welfare. I loathe her kind," I informed Jason.

"He's high and mighty and all holier than thou, when he doesn't know me at all. He's just judged me from the small amount of time he has seen me. His attitude stinks as much as he does, and that is a *lot*," Ginny countered.

"I don't smell. I wash myself at least once a day given I work with chemicals," I protested.

"Well, the look of you makes me imagine a smell when I see you. All old and fusty and like boiled cabbage."

"Okay then, glad I got that cleared up," Jason said. "Hate it is. That's what you're both saying anyway. Personally, I—"

"Want to be drained?" Ginny asked Jason.

"Oh, I realise I have somewhere to be, so I'm going to leave now," Jason said, and he began walking off the premises. Alistair chose a piece of furniture and left shortly afterwards. That left me, and Ginny, who was still standing staring at me.

"You're not going to leave until I say thank you, are you?" I asked resignedly.

"Nope." She rubbed her hands together and then chuckled unpleasantly.

Realising the sooner I got it over with, the sooner she'd leave, I quickly said, "Thanks, Ginny," before walking towards the bureau which I noticed was now at the bottom of a stacked pile of four pieces of furniture. As she'd rescued me, she must have stacked these back up. There was no way I could touch the stack. Not today. I needed time to process what had happened to me when I was alone again.

Ginny appeared at the side of the pile. "Oh, I think you can say thank you to me a lot more sincerely than that."

"No, actually, I don't think I can," I said with total honesty, wondering if I was prepared to sacrifice a piece of the furniture to make stakes. It was getting closer to a yes with every word she said.

She reached out to touch the pile.

"What are you doing?" I shrieked.

She stopped, holding her hands against her ears.

"VAMPIRE HEARING, REMEMBER?" she shouted.

"You don't have to shout. I'm not the one with my hands over my ears."

She took them down. "What on earth was that noise you made?"

"I'm a zombie. It's a zombie cry."

"It's hideous."

"You're hideous."

Her eyes narrowed. "No, I am not. I am amazing actually, and I saved you today and I deserve a thank you for it."

She wasn't going to go away unless I made an attempt at a genuine apology, so it was best I got on with it. It couldn't be worse than being under the pile of rubble, and hopefully I'd be able to avoid seeing her again for a very long time.

"Thank you very much for coming over here so quickly and removing the furniture from me. I'm claustrophobic and so your vampire speed and strength meant I was only under there for a short amount of time. I am therefore truly grateful and thank you from the bottom of my heart for all you have done today."

"God, if you weren't already dead that would have killed you, right?" Ginny laughed and just for a moment she seemed quite normal. "You owe me now, Merbin. That's what I'm going to call you now because you make me think of rubbish."

"And I will call you Ninny for you are a complete nincompoop."

"That the best you've got?" She laughed and whizzed away, after first taking the furniture down quickly. She'd seen my weakness then when I'd been looking at it. It made me want to scream once more.

"For now. But just you wait," I said out loud. "I'll even things up in time."

CHAPTER THREE

Ginny

"Sorry about that. I'm back here to help now," I told Callie as I re-appeared in the shop.

"Hey, Ginny. I'm here too now. I'll go back to the café side if you come cover the bookshop," Dela said.

"Will do." The café was bustling, and business looked good. I wasn't surprised. A lot of Gnarly loved reading. Coupling that with buns and hot beverages meant they couldn't stay away. It amused me given I'd rather watch TV and didn't need to eat. And then Callie brought me over a special red-velvet cupcake and a pink lemonade. The secret ingredient in both was o-neg and as I bit on a piece of the bun, at that moment I would have sworn preference over food in my mouth to cock any day of the week. Not that a male had been near my mouth in months.

"So what happened over at Merrin's?" Callie asked, telling people at the counter she'd be back in a minute.

I gleefully told them my tale of rescuing Merrin and making him apologise. Callie then returned to the counter while Dela stayed to chat.

"I don't understand why you don't like him. He's a nice guy. Poor bloke having claustrophobia and being trapped under the furniture like that." Dela's forehead creased. "I might pop by after work with a goody bag from the café for him."

I rolled my eyes. "You haven't been subject to his uncalled-for rudeness. He helped you furnish your house. Of course you can't understand why I don't like him. But what if he'd said you were spoiled and only interested in a rich man?"

Dela sucked her lips in.

"Come on, out with what you want to say?" I huffed.

"It's just that, it's true. You tell everyone you want a rich guy, and you actively seek them out at the Inn," Dela answered.

"*Sought* out at the bar, past tense. It won't be happening again."

"Oh, have you changed your mind?"

"No, I've been fired."

Dela's jaw dropped. "You got *fired*? When? How?"

"Last night. Stupid vampire offered to be my pimp, so I staked him through his cock. Edmond fired me and told me I needed to go find something that would calm me down. Staking Cuthbert through the heart next would have made me feel fabulous, but that's not what he meant. Mya has my leader on all new age woo-woo crap and so he wants me to chant or some shit."

"That's brilliant," Callie said after dropping two teacakes off at a neighbouring table. Dela and I turned to her, my face no doubt wearing the same 'Wtf?' expression as Dela's.

"You like all the woo-woo stuff too?" Dela asked her sister.

"Oh not that. I meant Ginny having been fired. It's just that while you were out, I heard from Aria and she's not going to be back for a while. So, Ginny, would you like to manage the bookstore for the next few months?" Callie asked.

"She's pregnant, isn't she?" I asked in return.

"It's not my news to announce."

"Fuck, he was right," I managed to get out through gritted teeth.

Resting my elbows on the table, I put my head in my hands. Dela squeezed my shoulder. She'd been there that day. When Merrin was working here getting the shelving and other furniture ready for the revamped café and he'd said that I'd be working here in June when the other fell 'with child'.

"It's not a bad thing that he was right, is it? I mean, you're going to be working here which is much nicer than dealing with inappropriate drunks, and Aria is having a baby. That's something to be celebrated, isn't it?" Dela said.

I sighed and looked up. "I know, but it means he was *right*, and that means he's going to *gloat*."

"Merrin hardly ever comes here. He's too busy on his land. You'll be fine. Please, let's celebrate the fact you're working here." Dela squeezed my hand.

I tore off a piece of cupcake and enjoyed the taste of blood in my mouth. I couldn't even drain Merrin if I wanted to because zombies didn't have any blood. Anyway, I didn't want to picture any part of him in my mouth. Ugh. I pushed away the rest of the cupcake, having completely put myself off it now. My eyes went over to all the books and the cute little corner which would be mine to rule. My little piece of paradise, even if the shelving and counters had all been put in by smelly Merbin.

"When do you want me to start?" I asked Callie, who was now bustling past clearing tables and looking at Dela wearing a 'Can you fucking work now?' expression.

"You were helping me today anyway, so now?" she raised her eyes expectantly. "And I mean right now, because I'm running around like a headless chicken while you two are sat clucking like mother hens."

"Okay. Yes, I would very much like the job," I said, and Dela squealed.

"Fantastic. Right, ladies, get to work," Callie ordered.

"Do you have any cleaning products?" I asked her.

Callie's mouth downturned. "My shop is spotless."

I nodded. "Spotless yes, Merbin's fingers-touched-less, no. I want to make sure I've cleaned out every possible trace of him."

Callie looked skyward.

"Are you praying?" I asked her.

"You're becoming maniacally obsessed with Merrin," Dela said. "It's weird. Go concentrate on selling books and become obsessed with that instead."

I realised then that my behaviour could look odd to those who didn't know me well.

"I'm not crazy. I'm a vampire. We stalk our prey. It's in my very nature to become obsessed with that I wish to torment."

"Are you saying Merrin is a future victim? That you might *kill* him?" Dela enquired, her voice a few octaves higher than her usual tone.

"God, no. He's so useless he doesn't even have blood. However, the playing with pets is almost as much fun as the killing of them, so he can be a little project for me to mess with. I'll make his life as miserable as possible until he begs me to leave him be."

"Remind me to never piss you off." Dela laughed. "Although, you know, there's a fine line..."

"Between best friends and my fangs going rogue?" I batted my lashes a few times while giving her a fake grin.

She mimed zipping across her lips. "Come on, let's get back to work," Dela said. "Before my sister has a meltdown."

Nodding, I stood and made my way over to the bookshop side of the shop and walked behind the counter. The till was similar to the one I used at the pub, and I already knew that the books were all priced up, with easily removable stickers on the back cover. Just like a satisfied woman in the bedroom, no one wanted a sticky residue left behind on them. Everything else I needed, like the recycled paper and card bags to put purchases in, plus the re-usable cotton totes with book quotes on, were at the rear of my counter.

In no time at all I was selling books and I discovered that not only did I enjoy the feeling of selling, but also hearing people chat about their favourite books. I suddenly began to understand Aria's obsession with the written word. I ended up buying myself one of the books recommended by another customer and looked forward to going back to the mansion and reading.

After I'd been to see my friend that is, to celebrate her news—once I'd wheedled it out of her.

The Letwine mansion was vast and the vampires all had suites of varying sizes depending on how many of them shared. Some of them were like frat houses and Edmond wisely split the males living that way and put them in a wing at one end, and any lone females at the other. With couples or larger mixed or settled groups in the middle in bigger suites, it was the best way of dividing up the upper floor. We had bedrooms even though we slept little. They were more for fornication. I considered changing my bedlinen to a sand colour given my bed action was as parched as a desert.

Closing the door behind me, I made my way to Aria and Bernard's suite. Only when I got there, I found there was a queue. Huh, looked like the news was already out. A vampire called Imelda was at the head of the queue, getting people to stay in line. I strolled up to the front.

"Waiting time is approximately four hours and you get ten minutes," Imelda said. "I can give you a ticket and you can come back if you prefer?"

"Are you fucking kidding me? I have to wait to see my own friend?"

"Not kidding. Do you have any idea how rare this is? Once news gets out further than the mansion, there'll be more vampire clans wanting to pass on their regards other than the Letwine vampires. Aria will be treated as a god or a lucky charm. People will wish to touch her, to see if they may be afforded the same luck."

"I'd like to see them try to touch her," I mumbled under my breath.

Right on cue, the door opened, and a vampire named Romilly sailed through it landing on her arse at the other side of the hall.

She stood up and shook herself down.

"I did warn you," Imelda told her.

"I only tried to reach for a thread of cotton she had hanging off her cardigan. Crazy lunatic almost staked me with her elbow," Romilly complained.

While Imelda was distracted chatting to Romilly, I snuck into the room. I heard a "Hey," behind me, but it was too late. I closed the door and made my way to the living room to see my friend.

"If one more person tries to touch me, Bernard, so help me God, I will drain them."

I sauntered through the door and saw Aria visibly relax. "Thank fuck, someone normal. Did you have to queue?"

I scoffed. "I love you, but I queue for no one. I did what all British hate, vampire or not, I queue-jumped; so if I'm never seen again, there will be at least twenty-three suspects, all of whom are currently outside bitching about me to Imelda."

Bernard (pronounced according to him as Bair-nnaarrd) was my brother's best friend and via that connection I'd become good friends with his wife. Also, she was one of the few female vampires I had time for. I found most extremely dull. Most vampire dudes, being as pathetic as they were, tended to turn their 'perfect woman', which half the time was a brain-dead, big-boobed, Barbie doll lookalike. Turning super-sized a lot of things, but boobs and brain cells weren't among them.

"Would you like an o-neg?" Bernard asked.

"Yes please, I'd love one," I answered, more for the fact I wanted him out of the room, than for the fact I was thirsty.

As soon as he was out of vampire earshot, I turned to my friend.

"So it's true? You're pregnant?" I leaned over and gave her a massive hug and then sat down next to her on the sofa. "Tell me all. Well, except for how it got there. I can work that out for myself."

"I felt so sick." Aria stroked her belly. "It was so bad, and I had these strange pains in my stomach. Bernard became concerned and called the doctor, who was stunned when he worked out what the cause was. Unfortunately, not so stunned that he couldn't keep his mouth shut. So much for patient confidentiality. He ran to tell Edmond, and said it rather too loudly, and we know what our kinds hearing is like. Hence the queues outside with people wanting to pass on their best regards. I mean, I'm maybe a month pregnant they reckon, and I'll be pregnant for another six. I'm due December 25th, which means I don't need to buy Bernard a Christmas gift this year, I'm going to launch his present right out of my vagina."

"Thanks for that visual," I told her. "Hey, listen, you know that weirdo who made the furniture at the bookshop, the one who was mean to me?"

"Merrin?"

"Yeah. Well, he's a lot strange and reckons he has these 'knowings' and he said you'd get pregnant in June and that I'd work at the shop. The twat was right."

Aria's eyes went wide. "And you didn't warn me?"

I lifted both my hands, palms up. "I thought he was being

ridiculous, and I didn't want you getting your hopes up. There hasn't been a vampire birth for fifteen years."

"Okay, I get that. It's been quite a shock though. I just hope I'm not going to be hounded day and night for the rest of my days. I can't stand most of them, Ginny." She lowered her voice. "I wish we could move to Gnarly, away from them all."

"What?!" I exclaimed. "Leave Chelsea?"

"Sssh." Aria put a finger to her lips. "I don't want anyone out there hearing. But listen, your brother lives there now, and not only does Bernard miss him, but I have him bugging me more because he's bored. It's how I've ended up pregnant in the first place. Wouldn't it be fabulous if me and Bernard, and you of course, could go live there away from all these idiots? Gnarly is so much more interesting than this Dullsville."

"But you have to apply to reside in Gnarly and you need to find a house. I mean, Dela got that rare spot in the woods to do a new build, but only because there was no chance of anything being grown on it due to the fungus there."

"There must be some room somewhere." Aria sighed in frustration.

That was when I thought of exactly where there was room. Where a certain annoying male had far too much land that he wasted opportunity on by having it piled high with trash.

"What? You have that look on your face. The one you get when you set your eye on a new rich guy. That intense focus."

I tapped my finger against my lips. "I've thought of a possibility, but it needs further research. I don't know who owns the land or how I could get permission for us to build there. Leave it with me for a while. But yes, it would be incredible if we could move to the fell."

Aria reached over and squeezed me. "Oh, this is so exciting. What a day. Finding out I'm pregnant and maybe getting a new home in a lovely little village."

"Well, I don't know if my idea will work yet."

"Oh, let a woman dream. I can think about it while I suffer through the rest of these visitors."

I laughed and then Bernard came back with my drink. We talked more about their surprise and delight about the baby, and my new job, and then I left them to the rest of their evening, receiving visitors.

Back in my own room, I changed into some comfy loungewear and settled back on my chaise with my new book, but I found myself distracted, thinking of potentially living in Gnarly.

I needed to find out if Merrin owned that land and if he did, how to get half of it off him so we could build a house out there for Aria and Bernard, and another for me. And a huge brick wall that separated us from Smelly Merry.

CHAPTER FOUR

Merrin

Jason called me later that afternoon. "Oh, you answered. Thought you might be balls deep by now."

"Balls deep into tidying up the mess over here?" I suggested, even though I knew exactly what he was getting at.

"What is it with you and her? It's weird. I've never come across anything like it and believe me I've had my share of women who don't like me... more than my share in fact."

I knew why I hated Ginny. It was about what she represented. Treating men like a way of gaining wealth and status. I'd been there, done that, in my past, and it had led to such tragedy that I detested anyone who thought it was a way to get on in life. People had feelings, and I had more than most. Risen from the grave, I'd found myself 'sensitive', and at times when my calling was at its loudest—spirits chatting in my ears or sending me images and pictures—I had to retire to my plot of land and hunker down until I got it all under control.

But today, my place of safety had become a place of danger, and *that woman* had been on my land.

"She just irks me, that's all. All that pursuing men for their money. Anyway, was that the only reason you were calling?"

"No, I wondered if you fancied coming out for a beer and a burger? It's a nice night and so the bistro has the tables out in the boulevard. Thought you might fancy a drink after your adventures today."

"Sounds good. I'll meet you there in what, half an hour?" I suggested. Being here was just making me focus on the mess and the fact it felt polluted by Ginny having wandered around. The place needed an exorcism: both to banish a certain female vampire from ever coming here again, and the masses of recycling.

She got you out of there super-fast, my mind chided. *That was a good thing, even if she did it to be smug.*

Now I knew why I disliked her, but why did she hate me so much? She said I made her think of the 'great unwashed'. Hmmm. I decided I'd go find an old, abandoned mirror and take a good look at myself. Not that I gave a crap what she thought, but I did what some others thought. I didn't want to look a mess while out with my friend.

"Make it an hour," I told Jason, and I went in search of my reflection.

From an objective point of view, I didn't exactly rock the look of a hot, sex god. After wiping the dusty full-length mirror with a cloth, I'd stood in front of it and turned this way and that, taking an overall look at myself.

My hair was long and straggly. My body looked waif-like due to the fact I picked up my clothes from *Seconds the Best* and deliberately chose baggy because I thought it hid my slim shape, Instead, it accentuated it. I'd grown a beard and it made my face look elongated and therefore even thinner.

Truth was, I'd never given a toss about my appearance, because I felt beauty was skin deep. But now, as I stared at myself, I felt like I had a point to prove to the vacuous new bookstore assistant. I'd improve my appearance and then if she treated me differently, I'd call her out on it in front of everyone. Show them just how judgemental she was and fixed on looks. She was also fixed on wealth, but we'd ignore that part for now.

Either I'd get Ginny to have a huge personality transplant, or I'd drive her back to the Letwine mansion. But there was no way she was staying in Gnarly as was, poisoning the place with her petty personality.

Not on my watch.

No one else had ever judged me here or insulted me. I was accepted as I was. As a zombie. Gnarly was made of different supernaturals, and our true forms were all different shapes and sizes. Hell, my friend Jason was a dragon! I suppose if Ginny saw his true self, she'd want him to apply a shit ton of Crème de la Mer on his scales because they were too dry and scaly for her eyes to look upon.

And while I tidied myself up to prove a point to her, I'd also tidy my place up so that I might actually get myself the home I craved. It was time to remind the villagers of Gnarly to make better choices other than to overwhelm my land. I needed space, mentally and physically.

I walked away from the mirror, grabbed my wallet, and set off to the bistro. Right now, I was going to enjoy a pint and a burger with my friend. A man who liked me exactly for who I was.

"Man, I need to get laid," Jason said as he drank down his third pint.

"There's a film about you, isn't there? *The 40-year-old Virgin*."

"Piss off, I'm only twenty-nine."

He didn't say he wasn't a virgin because after a prank last summer in a hotel room, Jason had admitted to being exactly that. And despite his best intentions, nothing had changed since.

"It's not like I don't get hit on. Women are always coming up to me, but then I take them on a date, and it all goes wrong."

It was true. While ever we were out together, females tended to look at him rather than me. Any women I'd met were usually goth chicks from if Jason and I headed to London for the night. And there hadn't been many for me either. Just one-night stands that had taken the edge off. No repeats because I liked being a loner, and not having to explain my weirdness to people.

"Jase?"

"Yeah?"

"How come you hang out with me? Like, given I'm a bit weird?"

He spluttered his beer. "A bit weird? Try majorly freaking weird."

"Gee, thanks."

He answered in his typical, completely open and honest Jason way. "You're fun when people get to know you. When you let down your guard. And if you're being stranger than usual, I know there's a reason behind it because I've known you for ages. I mean, you're aware I can be snappy and bad-tempered due to my inner dragon. If I'm being like that you call me on it, tell me to go off and calm down. It's what mates do."

"Cool. That makes sense. Thanks."

"Plus, the fact you look such a state means more babes look at me than you."

It was my turn to splutter my beer.

"I'm joking, Merrin. You have that whole emo thing going on. Some chicks dig that. As we know by the fact you aren't in living in Neverland."

"What's Peter Pan got to do with this this?"

"Funny. Okay, Neverdoneitland. I was trying not to say it so plainly while out in public. You never know who's listening."

"That's so true." Mya walked past, grabbing a chair from a neighbouring table and sitting down next to us. "So you've not done it... ever?"

"Mya!" Her boyfriend, Death, fixed her with a glare.

"Oh go and get me a pina colada and leave me a moment," said the Queen of Wayward Souls.

"It's okay." Jason waved Death off.

"Well, I won't be long. Queues tend to disappear quickly when I'm around." Death smirked and walked off.

"Have you heard of manifesting?" Mya asked Jason.

He shook his head. "Nope." He gave me a quick look of 'help', but I sat back to nurse the rest of my pint and to enjoy his discomfort.

"Basically, you have to keep a positive energy around you while acting as if you already have what you want. Then you'll attract what you want."

"Come again?"

"Say I want some more Louboutins. To attract them I keep positive and then I'll find a pair appears."

Death had returned with Mya's drink and he placed it on the table. "I don't think the fact you're sometimes extra nice to me when you want a new pair of shoes is quite manifesting, darling."

"I can always have a strop," she said, following it up with a fake smile.

"Do take a look online and see if there are any others you'd like, my sweet. Especially ones with a nice heel."

"He likes me to walk on his back in them. It turns him on," she said.

Death put his death mask on to cover up his embarrassment and then he disappeared.

"I'll be in the bad books now for talking about our sex life again, so I'd better go make amends. And by make amends I mean shag him. I'm sorry you've not got any yet, Jason. Once you start, you'll realise what you've been missing."

Jason groaned and I wasn't sure if it was through pain or embarrassment.

Mya zoomed off in that way vampires did, where one minute they were there and the next not. They were sneaky buggers due to their super-hearing, super-speed, and super-strength. Suddenly, my mind was back on Ginny and how quickly she'd moved my furniture. It had made me feel emasculated as she'd gloated about rescuing me.

"What am I going to do?" Jason pleaded, as Chantelle, a waitress from the bistro came to collect our glasses. She was a witch, although at times her magic went wrong.

"Can you perform a spell on Jason so he can get laid, Chantelle?" I asked her, half-joking. The bubbly blonde giggled.

"I can't make someone sleep with him, but I can do something to make him show his best self?"

"Yeah, that'll do."

"Hey, I'm right here!" Jason protested.

"Do you want to attract more women?" I asked.

"Yes."

'Well then."

He sighed. "Okay, Chan. Whatever you can do to assist."

She faffed around, magically clearing the space around us and then she closed her eyes and faced him.

To try too hard, can repel.
So, Goddess, I ask you to please heed this spell.
To attract for this man, his perfect mate.
The one who would be sent by fate.
No matter the action, let true love win through.
Despite frustration your one shall come to you.

"All done," she said. "That should do the trick. Good luck, Jason." She smiled and then she high fived me on her way past.

"Oh bugger," she said, coming back two minutes later. "I didn't close the spell."

"Is that a problem?" Jason asked. "Have you ruined my love life instead of saved it?"

I was tempted to query how you could ruin something non-existent, but instead turned to Chantelle, concerned she'd messed up yet another spell.

"I just need to close it now, that's all. The worst that could happen is it spread to you," she said to me matter-of-factly. "I'd drawn a protective circle around the table."

She closed down the spell while my mind whirred.

"All done now," she confirmed.

"Are you saying the spell could have been cast on me also?" I double checked.

"It's unlikely because I was focused on Jason, but if it did, it will just encourage the future love of your life to appear if you have one. It's gonna happen anyway. This is just a small kick up the bum for fate."

I felt a bit jittery. Was I ready for that? To meet a woman who might like me for me?

Oh fuck it, Merrin. It was probably the four pints I'd now drunk dulling my brain cells' thinking capabilities, but Chantelle went on her way, and I decided to leave the unlikely, but possible spell in place.

At that point Milly and Tilly, the twins wandered over to us.

"Can we sit with you? Only there are no other tables. I just need to grab one other chair," Tilly said.

"Allow me," Jason said gallantly. He'd been very subservient to them ever since he'd tried to trick them into a threesome last year. That had resulted in mine and Nick's prank which had led to Jason's admission of intact virginity. The twins had forgiven him. They didn't have it in them to be nasty and Jason wasn't a sleaze, just misguided.

As they sat down with us, Jason looked over at me with a nod towards them. A nod that clearly asked, 'Do you think these two might be our true loves?'

I hadn't the foggiest, so I just shrugged and let the evening go where it may.

After another couple of hours, I'd learned one thing. My true love wasn't here. Both Milly and Tilly were lovely, but I wasn't attracted to either of them.

They'd been telling us about how Chantelle had worked with her mentor Alicia to perform a spell that meant they could now talk independently of one another.

"So, we will hopefully be able to live separate lives, but while remaining sisters and the best of friends," Milly explained.

"That sounds like excellent news," I replied.

"So what's happening with you, Merrin?" Tilly asked. "You seem okay, but I heard you were in an accident earlier today?"

"Oh, it was nothing really." I dismissed it. "Actually though, I want to come see the two of you tomorrow to discuss second-hand furniture as I need a plan of what to do with everything I have. Might need some contacts from you."

"Of course. Pop in anytime. We'll be in from ten." Tilly giggled.

"We'll need to sleep off our hangovers," Milly explained.

A table became free, and the twins excused themselves to go sit alone.

"Do you think either of those is my one true love?" Jason asked.

"I think you should either wait for fate to reveal her hand or try manifesting." I pretended to go into a trance.

"Want another pint?" Jason asked.

"Fuck me, this manifesting shit really does work, because that's exactly what I just had in my mind." I winked.

Jason bopped the top of my head as he walked past and towards the bistro.

CHAPTER FIVE

Merrin

Going out for a drink with my friend last night had been just what I'd needed. It had blown off the cobwebs so to speak, and this morning it was time to metaphorically blow off a few more. I had a quick shower and set off into Gnarly feeling full of purpose and vigour. First stop: *Seconds the Best*.

The bell tinkled as I walked in and a blonde and a brunette did a stereophonic groan while clutching their heads.

"That bad?" I asked.

Tilly, the brunette, nodded slowly. "I'm trying not to move."

Milly's hand was over her mouth. "And I'm trying not to be sick."

"Have you had some painkillers and water?" I asked them.

"Yes," Tilly said, this time not moving her head. "I could really use a coffee, but I'm—"

"Trying not to move." I finished off her sentence for her.

"It's usually Milly finishes my sentences." She tried to laugh, but then groaned again.

"I'll be back with coffee. For now, shall we close the shop back up?" I suggested.

"You're a superstar," Tilly said. She looked at Milly. "I'm not sure Milly can manage one but get two anyway. I can always drink hers as well. Take some money from the till."

"It's on me," I told them, and with that I walked out of the store, swinging the sign back to 'closed' on my way out, hearing another groan at the sound of the tinkling bell.

I had the perfect excuse now to go into Buns and Books. Entering the shop, I joined the queue and took a look at the gorgeous baking done by Callie who had been brought up as a tooth fairy. The sweet, sugary smells were a delight to my senses. I'd not woken hungover, but I had woken up hungry, and the quick slice of toast I'd eaten had done nothing to fill me up. Contrary to the myths about my kind, we did not feast on human flesh, but rather, the same food we'd eaten when human.

"Hey there, Merrin. What can I get you?" Callie said as I reached the front of the queue.

"Can I get two extra-strong coffees for the twins please to start?"

"Oh dear. That's not like them. What have they been up to?"

"A night on the town last night. Well, at the bistro. I just went to talk to them about some business and they can barely move."

Callie laughed. "It's good to see them getting out more and learning about life as two twenty-somethings, rather than staying cooped up in the shop and at home." She went and made their coffees and put them in a take-out bag with milk and sugar. "Tell them they're on the house."

"That's kind but it's okay, I said I'd treat them," I told her.

"Well, one good turn deserves another, Merrin, and so if you're buying their coffees, I'll buy yours. What are you having?"

By the time I'd finished I had three coffees, three muffins, and three toasties, and only had to pay for the twins' order.

And the best thing was, even though I knew *she'd* be there, in the bookstore side, I never acknowledged her existence. Never looked her way. Gave Ginny no chance whatsoever to spoil the good mood I'd woken up in.

"Have a lovely day," I said to Callie, feeling satisfied with my morning so far, then I left the coffee shop and went back to the twins.

"You look a little better," I acknowledged Milly's pallor was less green.

"Let's just say I've made some room for coffee... but please, no food, not yet." She groaned. Her sister, however, leapt on the toastie like a dog facing a plate of freshly cooked sausages with no human in sight.

After enjoying the refreshments, it was down to business.

"After my accident, I've realised that the amount of furniture coming to my yard is just too much. We need to think of something else, because while I can recycle and repurpose things, even with Alistair taking some, I can't clear it fast enough."

The twins looked glum as they stared around their shop which was also full to bursting. "Everywhere is getting the same. People are forgetting to re-use stuff. They need a reminder," Tilly said.

"Hey!" Milly exclaimed. "Why don't you run some workshops?"

"What do you mean?" I asked, although an idea was already beginning to bloom in my mind.

"Get the people of Gnarly to book a workshop place for a price that covers the cost of materials and your time, and then they choose a piece of furniture and make it their own. After the workshop they take it with them or have it sent through the portal delivery system. You get to show off your talents with teaching them, the furniture gets re-purposed. It's a win-win."

"Why did I not think of that before?" I said out loud, while wondering why indeed I'd not thought of that before. It would also bring people near to my studio, where they could browse my craft pieces, rather than me only selling online, and might generate more income for me.

"So, to get this started, what would you need? Flyers with your telephone number and email on so people can contact you to book a place? Your materials? The place would need to be safe though." Milly pointed out. "Can't have your art students getting buried under furniture."

"Yeah, I'm going to tidy the place up. Haven't quite worked out how yet, but I can always pray for a miracle."

"If you could afford it, you should book the Letwine vampire builders to come modernise that cowshed. Look at how quickly they sorted Books and Buns," Milly suggested. "Though I'm guessing if you could have done it, you would have by now."

"No, actually, it's just been me being, well, zombie-like. Being slow and among decay. I'm realising after my claustrophobic breakdown experience that I can return to my zombie nature once I can chill out around a safe environment. That's why I need your help to make sure I get this stuff done.

"We're more than happy to help," they said in stereo, and then they laughed.

"It's weird when we do that now because it doesn't happen very often anymore," Milly explained.

Tilly got a pad and pen. "Okay, so you can also book Callie to provide refreshments and have breaks during the day. I'm guessing it would take a while. Let's set up a rough schedule of what a 'Design Day with Merrin' would be like.

We spent the next hour plotting out the workshop while consuming the rest of Callie's goods.

"That's perfect," I said honestly as I stared at the sheet of A4 paper in my hand. All I had to do now was to get my land set up and the workshops started. "I wonder if you could also help me with something else...?"

After leaving the shop, I not only had the workshop plan, but a couple of bags of clothes in my hands. Next on my agenda was an appointment to see Charity at *A Cut Above*. Charity had moved to Gnarly a month ago after being accepted by the council and had taken over what used to be a DVD hire store. Gnarly's residents had gone to London for their hair maintenance prior to this, so it was all very new and exciting for the residents to have their own salon.

When the twins had explained to her about my 'makeover', Charity had not only squeezed me in, but agreed to cut my hair in her kitchen and not in the salon.

As I approached the hairdressers, I went around the back as she'd directed.

"Come in," Charity called. She was a slim and very pretty redhead. Her hair was scarlet and her eyes an emerald green.

"Mermaid," she said. "But call me Ariel and I'll feed you to the sharks."

I laughed and she laughed back.

"Sorry if I've caused inconvenience by not going in the salon."

"No, I get it. It's a huge change and can be overwhelming. Best we do it away from the eyes of the others, given that some of Gnarly love gossip more than they love their partners. It's for you to show off your new look, not for them to go telling everyone beforehand."

My heart thudded in my chest then. I'd never thought that I'd be gossip fodder for Gnarly just by getting a haircut. Plus, I'd be wearing clothes that fit. Surely this wasn't anything to get excited about?

Gnarly gets excited if someone clears their constipation, I thought. Being a small village, everyone was always up in your business the first chance they got. People would wonder why the sudden change in the local reclusive weirdo.

Well, I'd tell them the truth. My near-death-if-I-wasn't-already-dead experience had pressed the reset button on my undead life.

That's not the truth. You're doing it in some 'fuck you' gesture to Ginny, my inner thoughts chided. Thank goodness I had wards from anyone reading my thoughts. Especially the bloody vampire herself.

"Okay, take a seat and let's do this," Charity said. "My next appointment is in thirty minutes, so we've plenty of time. Meanwhile, I've got a break from listening to my brother moaning about the terrible date he had last night."

"Oh dear. The curse of Gnarly has lifted but it doesn't mean our dating lives are any smoother, does it?"

"Not at all. So, what are we doing here?"

"Wh-what?" *Did she mean us? Was she propositioning me?*

Charity pointed at my head. "What style do you want?"

"Oh. Erm, I'll take your advice, but I was thinking..."

"Short? And let's trim that beard too. Get you a bit of a Christian Bale look going on."

"Yes," I agreed. I had no idea what I was going to end up looking like. I'd not been all emo-style only due to being a zombie. My parents had been hippies who'd lived off the land, having watched too many episodes of *The Good Life* together when they'd first met. I'd never had short hair. *Ever*.

Now in a salon you had a mirror to face. One that meant as you slowly transformed you saw it happen. But here in Charity's kitchen I did not. So all I had seen were large pieces of hair fall to the floor. I'd felt the draft on my neck where there'd been none before, and the cold metal of the scissors against my nape. Then the buzz of the razor as it shaved in layers.

Finally finished, with my beard trimmed too, Charity brushed the excess hair off my shoulders and removed my gown.

"Excuse my language, Merrin, but holy fucking hell. No one is going to recognise you. Your own mother wouldn't. Listen, I'm going to get the mirror. While I do, why not put on one of your new outfits?" While we'd been chatting as she'd cut my hair, I'd told her about my new clothes and general new image. She left the room.

As I stood there, part of me wanted to run back to my house. To the place where I just meandered around alone and did my own thing, because I had a feeling that I'd just started something akin to the beat of a butterfly's wing: created a ripple that would affect my life much beyond having no need any more for hair elastics. But I rummaged through the bags as yes, it was time to completely let go of the old me and welcome the new one.

Charity returned carrying a full-length mirror, with the mirror part facing her.

"Jesus. Brace yourself," she said. She had the mirror covered with an old curtain and placed it in front of me.

"I feel like I'm on a TV show." I laughed.

But that laugh turned to utter silence when she removed the curtain and I saw my reflection. Short brown hair styled with a little product and off my face, and a smart beard. No longer could I hide behind my hair. I was wearing jeans that fit my actual shape and a pale blue t-shirt with a camel-coloured short-sleeved jacket. While I'd never be anything but slim, I didn't look emaciated. I looked healthy, fit almost. I was just a bit pale.

"Can I do something?" Charity said, pointing to my face.

I nodded because I was too stunned to speak.

She got a tube from her pocket and after removing the lid, she pushed a little into the palm of her hand. She got me to lower my face and dotted it on my complexion and into my neck, then rubbed it in.

"Now look."

Gone were the milk-bottle tones of my skin. A healthy glow matched my complexion to my newly shorn hair and beard.

"Here." She gave it to me. "You might want to look into an all over fake-tan."

"Thank you, Charity. I—"

"You're overwhelmed. It's not the first time I've done a complete makeover and this has happened. But it doesn't happen very often, and it's been my absolute pleasure to do it. Are you happy? Just nod your head, so I don't worry you think you've made the biggest mistake ever and I've got it all wrong."

I nodded.

"You just take your time and get used to your new look while I get my kitchen swept up. Do you want a hot drink or anything?"

"No, thank you. Gosh, I look so different. I'm feeling a bit nervous of going back 'out there'."

She gave me a sympathetic smile. "People are definitely going to stare, Merrin, so prepare yourself. You look entirely different and it's going to have Gnarly gossiping. I can imagine them all now. 'Did you see Merrin? Do you reckon the furniture banged him hard on the head? Done him a favour though, hasn't it?'" Charity impersonated one of the gossipiest old ladies, Barb, perfectly. It was something I was good at doing, impersonating other people's voices, but I didn't tell her that. It did make me get brave though.

"Listen, do you want to come out for a drink sometime? You know, to get to know Gnarly a bit better?"

"Like on a date or just as an introduction to the village?"

"Well... a date, or you could ask your brother too and it could just be a general drink."

"I'd like that, Merrin, and I'll not ask my brother."

Did she mean she would go out with me on a date then? As I stood feeling even more displaced than before, she grabbed a small business card.

"My mobile number is on there. How about you get used to your new appearance and then if you still want to grab that drink with me, you give me a call?"

I nodded and then after paying her for my haircut, I left.

CHAPTER SIX

Ginny

I was at the shop bright and early the next day, and while I didn't get any nutrition from drinking coffee and eating pastries, it was a bonus that every day would start with them.

The smells in the shop were incredible. It was a time where having my vampire super-smelling abilities was a bonus. Baked goods, coffee, hot chocolate, and my new favourite thing... the smell of books. I'd told Lawrie I was annoyed at the fact he was lovesick and worked amongst pink, but now I was beginning to understand. The shop was how you'd imagine heaven to be; somewhere Lawrie and I had been denied by the events of our deaths.

I'd enjoyed lazing around last night and reading. Knowing that unless something horrendous befell me, I would live for eternity, had got me all 'butterflies fluttering in my stomach' excited as I thought about how many books there were in the world for me to read. I didn't have to suffer what customers were telling me: how they wanted to read one more chapter before going to sleep, but their eyes closed and despite their best efforts, the next day they couldn't remember the last few pages. No, I only needed the smallest amount of sleep, just an hour, and then I could carry on. I needed to buy a few more books today. I'd have no wages left at this rate.

Many vampires were rich because they'd lived a long time and had invested in property or businesses back in the day. They'd had time to learn several different career paths, or they'd enthralled and cheated wealthy humans.

I was relatively new in terms of vampire years, having been turned in the seventies, and I had yet to acquire any skills that would set me off on a path to riches.

Pulling myself back into the present moment, I watched as Merrin walked in. My guard up, I waited for him to fix me with a look of distaste, or to walk over to insult me. But he didn't. He didn't look over to where I was *at all*. He got served, said bye to Callie, and then left the store.

The ungrateful motherfucker.

Had I not saved him from a pile of rubble yesterday? From the torment of having to wait a claustrophobic's eternity to be rescued? I'd saved him a therapy bill and yet he didn't even have the common decency to insult me.

And that was the moment I realised I had issues. Because I liked the fact I got into sparring wars with Merrin.

I loved to hate him.

He provided an outlet to all my frustrations, and the fact he didn't seem to care that I insulted him and gave back as good as he got meant I'd actually found something to do that didn't become boring in five seconds flat.

My new daily activities had become: work in the store, annoy Merrin, read books, and now today he'd not given me the satisfaction of tearing him down.

That wouldn't do at all.

"Virginia. How goes it? I hope you're not slipping your number out along with the purchases to anyone who seems to have a spare few pounds." Lawrie had entered the store and after kissing his wife had come over to me.

"I'm behaving, because..." I lowered my voice. "I really like this job, Lawrie. It's so much nicer than the stupid Vampire's In(n). No one leering at me, or being rude, or spilling drinks. Customers here know that if they get food or drink on the books they have to purchase them. It's an entirely different atmosphere."

Lawrie stood for a moment, looked me up and down, and then felt at my forehead, despite the fact vampires did not have human ailments that caused temperatures.

"Have you been bewitched? Only, a couple of days ago, you said you hated everyone being happy and now... you look dangerously close to being exactly that yourself. You'll be falling in love next."

"Huh. I think not. Falling for a rich man's wallet, yes. Falling in love, no."

Lawrie looked down at me with a frown. "You really need to get over this, Ginny. It was a long time ago. You don't need tons of money."

Lawrie hinting at my past made my eyes hurt, so I knew they'd just flashed red. I fought to keep my temper and my teeth under control. My incisors were threatening to come down.

"If he wasn't already dead and dusted, I'd kill him..." I spat out.

Lawrie walked around the back of my counter and folded me into his arms. "But he is, and at least we are free of our sire. Who knows what life would have been like if William had not been dealt with by the breedents?"

I nodded into his chest. Then I pushed him away. "You've got so soft since you got married, I barely recognise you."

"Callie said you helped Merrin yesterday..."

I pulled a face.

"She did point out that you did it as a sign of power and hostility, so at least I knew you'd not suddenly had a complete personality transplant."

"I detest that individual. My actions were entirely self-satisfying."

Lawrie smirked at me. God, at times he could be insufferable. "What?"

"I'm just thinking about how Callie and I loved to hate each other and look at us now." With that he shot out of my range and appeared back at his wife's side before I could launch the corner of a book at his eye.

While I carried on serving customers, I started to think about what Aria and I had talked about last night. About moving to Gnarly. It would be amazing, but at the moment it was nothing more than a dream for me. I couldn't afford it. That didn't stop me trying to find a way to make claim to some land though. Aria and Bernard could get their home built and I could get my plans approved for the future, or Aria and Bernard could build both and I could rent from them.

Always the poor one who has to beg, I thought, and my mind whirled back to a time long before.

"What's for tea?" my brother Duncan asked as he walked in from school. It was only four pm, but fourteen-year-old boys had appetites as big as my mum's debts—huge.

I gave him a bread and jam sandwich.

"Oh, not this again. I had it for lunch," he complained. I didn't tell him that it was my lunch he'd just eaten, that I'd gone without in order that he could eat.

"It's all we have. Sorry."

*Duncan huffed but feasted on the sandwich. Wiping the back of his hand across his mouth he said, "Okay, I'm still **starving**, so what else is there?"*

The truth? There was nothing else. Not one damn thing left in the house. Our mum had fallen apart when our father had left her for another woman and she'd slid into a mess of drink and drugs. When she wasn't unconscious, she was stealing to buy more of both. She'd forgotten we existed, or rather she'd told me that as an eighteen-year-old, I could now stop sponging and provide for the household.

I was a student, learning sciences, and hoping one day to become a vet. I loved animals. Mum's debts had meant me having to give up our six-year-old cocker spaniel, Marla, for adoption as I could no longer afford to feed her. It had broken my heart, so much so that I didn't think it would ever repair. It hurt far more than the pangs of hunger that was for sure. Now it looked like I was going to have to give up my studies too and get a job. I already worked on a weekend and a few evenings, but that didn't go far into buying food for us. I needed a full-time job to do when Duncan was at school, so that I could be around for him when he was home. Not that he did much more than lounge in his room listening to music, gaming, or hanging with his mates.

But we couldn't carry on like this. What was next? Not being able to make rent? Losing our home? I'd taken a wild guess at how our mum was managing to pay for it so far, and it filled me with horror. I somehow needed to get help for mum too, before I came home to find her dead.

"You do your homework and I'll go do a food shop," I instructed Duncan. Grabbing my coat, I told him I'd be back soon, and I set off for the corner shop. I'd rummage in the bins around the back and hope for the best.

I was almost there, and in a daydream wondering about how I could change our fortunes. The street was busy, and people bustled about, mums calling in to do their shopping after collecting their kids from school. Ours had used to be one of those mums.

"Sorry, sorry," a man said as he smacked into me. I turned and saw him scold a young child for distracting him from looking where he was going. Seeing a small black rectangle on the floor, I bent down to pick it up. The man had dropped his wallet as we'd collided. I was about to call him back when I halted. Instead, I quickly looked around to see if anyone was watching me and when I saw they weren't, I darted into a shop doorway. Rifling through the wallet, I found it had six pounds in it. My heart leaped with excitement. Tonight we could eat. Guilt quickly passed through me and away, as I decided to take it as a sign of fate that this had happened. That way it was easier to not acknowledge my theft.

I headed into the shop where I bought bread, sandwich meats, potatoes and vegetables, and some spam. I even treated Duncan to some crisps and chocolate and a small bottle of pop.

That night, watching his face light up as he crammed the food in his mouth, and seeing him look so content when he'd finished, I vowed that we'd be hungry no longer.

Instead of getting a job, I'd 'bump into' more people on the street. That way I could continue my studies yet keep our bellies full and a roof over our heads.

"Do you have any books on home decorating?" A female voice brought me away from the past, and I looked at the redhead in front of me.

"Only a couple at present, but I can order anything else into store," I told her. "Let me show you what we have." Glad from the reprieve from my thoughts, I smiled at the woman.

I pulled the two books from the shelf. "Feel free to grab a coffee and peruse, but know that spills mean purchases," I informed her, holding out the books.

She took them from me and quickly flicked through. "I'll take both please, and then I'll do exactly that. Only, I've not much time before my next appointment, so it's a quick toastie and back to it I go. Then when I've finished, I need to try to make a start on the apartment because it's in dire need."

I nodded. "Okay, let's get you sorted then, so you can enjoy your lunch."

"I'm Charity, the new hairdresser in town," she said. "Let me know if you need a re-style."

"Ginny. Vampire. Stuck with what I've got," I explained.

Charity nodded. "I'm available for updos for special occasions, blow-dries, etc. Doesn't have to be a complete makeover." Her cheeks turned pink. "Sorry, I'm not meaning to come across like I'm touting hard for business. I'm just a bit hyper. I did an amazing restyle for a customer, and it's left me buzzing."

"Before I got this job, I wouldn't have understood that," I replied honestly. "But I love working here and I'm buzzing that I just sold two books. Are you doing a restyle on your place too?"

She nodded. "It needs it. Although my younger brother can be a pain in the arse and will probably pooh-pooh all my ideas."

Immediately I thought of Duncan again, and swallowed hard, trying to push him back out of my mind.

"Feed him first. That usually works," I said.

"Good idea, I'll try that," she replied. I swiped her credit card, bagged up her books and she gave me a little wave goodbye. "Good to meet you, Ginny," she said.

She seemed a really nice person. Genuine. Someone I would have liked to have as a friend. But I couldn't hear her talk about her brother. It would hurt too much. I busied myself ordering two different home decorating books for the store until the moment of pain had been forgotten, buried deep down once more.

CHAPTER SEVEN

Merrin

I'd spent much of the evening gazing at my reflection in the mirror. Not because I was vain, but because I couldn't actually believe that the person looking back at me was *me*. I looked *that* different.

I woke up with renewed vigour, ready to make a start on my plot of land. I made myself some breakfast, some strong coffee to set me up for the morning, and then getting changed into some old jeans and a t-shirt, I took myself out to the cowshed.

Somehow, I had to make a space here for people to work in. My studio didn't have enough room for people to work on large items of furniture. Maybe Milly was right, and I needed to get the Letwine vampires out here? They could make me a large practical workshop. I could extend the studio. I needed to get in touch with their architect, get some plans drawn up and then submit them to the council. That meant I either needed to talk to Mya, Lawrie, or dare I say it, Ginny, to get in touch with the Letwine architect for me. I wasn't sure which was worst. The sassy vampire who stuck her nose in and usually caused disaster; the sarcastic vampire who had only ever really been interested in himself other than his sister, and now his wife; or that sister who was a pain in the arse. Putting it out of my mind for now, I was just about to do some preparation work on Fenella's bureau when I realised she might want to work on it herself as part of my workshop.

I began to feel irritated. Just a general feeling like you got if you'd not had enough sleep and every little thing that didn't go right started to feel like a major nuisance. Clearly, I needed to go into Gnarly. I'd ring ahead to see if I could meet Fenella and then I'd consider who to ask to put me in touch with the architect.

But firstly, I needed to get changed into something a little smarter and make sure I looked tidy, because it was the first time people would see the new 'me'.

"I don't know how you got into Gnarly or what you're selling, but I suggest you clear off, before I get my man on you and he's a big, strong brute who will throw you off my land," Fenella shouted through the letterbox.

"Santa is more likely to give me a cuddle, Fen, and you know it," I shouted back through.

There was silence for a moment and then the door flew open.

Fenella peered at me closely, up and down, like she was an X-ray machine at an airport.

"Merrin? Is that you?"

"It is. I've had a bit of a restyle. Can I come in then or do you need my fingerprints?"

She stood back to let me in. "Merrin, I'm flummoxed. You look so different. I didn't recognise you."

"Yeah, I guessed that when you threatened me with your rugged boyfriend, Father Christmas." I laughed.

"He's just started going back to the gym actually," she whispered conspiratorially. "He's put a few pounds on since we started dating. With Christmas in six months' time, he can't afford to let his health slide."

I was sure Santa was getting some stamina training with Fenella, but I wasn't about to say that to my friend's mum.

"Come and sit down and I'll get you a drink and a slice of cake. Is coffee and a slice of carrot cake, okay?"

"Sounds fantastic, Fen. Thank you."

She bustled around the kitchen clattering mugs and saucers and boiling the kettle, and before long we were sat at her kitchen table with hot beverages and the most gorgeous smelling cake.

"Right. Tell me more about this workshop and how I can help."

I showed Fenella the plans the twins had helped me draw up. Fenella had always been the main organiser of events in Gnarly Fell and so her input would be priceless.

"So if you have time could you help me? You can have your bureau free of charge."

"I would love to help you and no payment is necessary. If it's okay with you, can I supervise, and you do my bureau? You could show people the techniques. Only I'm great at arranging but I'm not great at anything practical beyond baking. I have an eye for what looks good, but I would ruin the piece. I want to pay you for your work, Merrin. You work hard."

"You should get something for your assistance," I argued.

"I will. I'll get to spend my day with other villagers enjoying myself. I'm in my element making sure everyone is fed and watered and so you leave that to me."

That was good. I didn't need the cupcake café to help with refreshments then. Fen had it all handled.

"So what timescale were you thinking?"

I told Fenella about how I needed to tidy up my land.

"I either need to get the vampires on it quickly, or I make do for now, seeing as plans need drawing up and submitting for approval."

"We're forecast to have great weather for the rest of the month, so why don't we set up the first workshop for Sunday?"

"This Sunday?" My mouth dropped open. It was Wednesday now. Could I get things ready to have a first workshop in four days?

"Yes. What's there to do other than get some flyers up and word of mouth and get prepared?" Fen was full of enthusiasm. "The sooner you start, the sooner you get your place cleared up. People can work in the cowshed. Just ask that vampire woman who rescued you from the furniture avalanche if she can help you again. She'd get it moved in no time. Maybe she could bring the architect with her too?"

"You heard about my accident then?"

Fen tipped her head to one side and fixed me with a smirk.

"Merrin, this is Gnarly. We all know about your accident. Plus, my son is one of the biggest gossips of them all."

"Jason told you all about it then?"

"He did. He also mentioned something interesting about your rescuer. I gather you don't get along?" Fen arched a brow.

I felt my nostrils flare. "That's an understatement. So you can see my difficulty in asking for her help again."

"Nonsense, Merrin. We all have to get along. She works here in the fell now, so you must do your best to make amends. You don't have to like her, or become her new best friend, but you must ask her to the workshop. Oh and ask Charity and her brother too, with them being our latest arrivals."

I smiled as she said that. Fenella's eyes narrowed in on me. "Oooh, of course. I'm guessing Charity cut your hair. You like her then?"

"She seems a lovely person."

"Hmm, definitely get her to the workshop. And you must make Jason go. Maybe he might meet someone there. What about this Ginny girl?"

I snorted.

"Not unless he has a few million hidden under his mattress." I told her about Ginny's materialistic ways.

"Hmm, I shall keep an eye on that one then. Callie speaks highly of her though, and she seemed nice enough to me when I popped into the shop yesterday."

"Well, I can only go on what side of her she's shown me, and it's not been pretty."

With that Fen changed the conversation onto a hearty plotting of what needed to be done. She opened her laptop and designed a gorgeous flyer with ease, clearly practiced in such things, and then she handed one to me. It said the date, cost, time, and what they'd need to bring with them, with food and refreshments provided.

"I'll go take the rest of these around the shops and the community centre. They've got your email on so look out for replies, so we know how many to expect. We'll set a limit at twelve, plus us two."

"Thanks, Fen. Are you sure you don't want me to go hand out the flyers?"

"You just take that one to Books and Buns," she said. "And go make nice with the vampire woman because we need her help."

My face must have given away my feelings on the subject because Fenella placed a hand on my arm.

"If there's one thing I've learned from my time here in Gnarly, Merrin, it's that everyone has a story, and I'm sure Ginny is no different. If she feels superior while she's helping you, let her. Inside, you know you're the one winning, not having to enlist professionals to help you move the furniture."

I nodded, and it got me thinking. Why was Ginny like that? So mercenary and cruel. Was it because she was an evil vampire, or was it because of something else? My past had shaped me. Maybe Ginny's had shaped her.

I made a decision that I would go ask for her help and be polite. I mean hadn't my parents brought me up that way?

Just because she reminded me of the bad things in my past, didn't mean I had to drag it into my future.

I hugged Fen, said goodbye, and made my way to Books and Buns, flyer in hand, and resolve in my soul.

I kept saying hello to people and they kept ignoring me. I found it entirely peculiar until I walked into the café and Dela squinted her eyes at me. "You look familiar," she said. "Are you related to someone from the fell?"

"It's me, Merrin," I said, my voice lowered, and I watched as her eyes went wide. Her hand went over her mouth. "Oh my god, you look amazing, and so, so different." I noted her eyes flip to the other side of the store, to the bookshop.

I held out my flyer. "I was wondering if you could put this in the window for me?" Dela looked it over. "Oh, this looks like fun. Count me in. I want some storage for my guest room, and oh, put my mum down for a place too. She can make something for her cabin."

Dela and Callie's mum, Sheridan, had moved to Gnarly in the new year. The council had allowed a small log cabin to be built close to Dela's new home on the same piece of land that the trees didn't grow on any longer, due to a previous fungal infestation that had thankfully been thwarted in its tracks before it took out any more trees.

"Great. That's two already. We're thinking maybe a dozen people altogether."

"Sounds good. I'll ask Callie later, and Chantelle. I don't suppose Ginny's invited...?"

"Actually, I need to go talk to her about something. Try to make some kind of a truce."

"Really? Oh, this I need to see. Hold on while I get Lawrie out here so I can come and tidy the tables nearby."

"Don't even try to hide your amusement at my predicament, Dela. It's fine. I'll just die while I have to try to play nice with the evil vampire because I need her help," I said with a good dose of heavy sarcasm.

Dela shook her head. "That's not why I'm coming over to nosy, Merrin."

"No?" I felt my brow crease.

"Merrin, you're unrecognisable, and, excuse my language, but you look hot as fuck. I want to be looking at her face when she realises who you are."

"Oh!" I exclaimed.

I looked 'hot as fuck?'

This makeover was going to take some getting used to. It looked like Merrin Bruckman couldn't hide away anymore if he wanted to.

Taking a deep breath, I made my way over to the bookstore side, but then I chickened out and went to pick up a book instead. I found myself staring at a copy of 'Investing in Success', a book for successful businessmen.

I felt a presence come to my side. Hah! The stuck-up vamp bitch thought I was a potential rich victim. I'd show her.

I whizzed around.

To find I was being sniffed.

Ginny stood away from me, hands on her hips. She was clearly concentrating, her face scrunched, eyes closed.

Finally, she opened her eyes and looked at me. "I didn't think it could be possible. Thought it must be a sibling. There's a different note there. You changed your shower gel?"

"Are you smelling me?"

"I can smell everyone without having to be that close to them," Ginny retorted. "Superior sense of smell, remember? But you usually smell of fusty cowshed. Today you smell of citrus and sandalwood, and coconut hair products. I came closer to double check and see if it really was you, and you were, in fact, capable of bathing, or if you were a relation."

"Jesus, Ginny," Dela huffed out. "I made my way over here to see your reaction to Merrin's new look and you knew it was him because you could smell him?"

"Well, duh," Ginny replied. "Vampire."

Dela moved back to the cupcake counter, failing to hide her disappointment as she shook her head.

"So what do you want?" Ginny said in a surly tone. "Because I know it's not that book. That's for successful minted businessmen, not losers."

It took all of my inner strength to not put my hands around her neck. That, and knowing that she could bat me off like a midge.

"I need your help please, Ginny," I said.

That did it. Her face took on an overall appearance of shock, exactly what Dela had hoped to see when Ginny had noted my new look. No, that wasn't what had knocked Ginny off her pedestal.

It was her enemy suddenly being nice.

On the outside, I kept my polite expression, but inwardly I smirked with complete and utter satisfaction as I remembered what my mum used to say to me: 'Kill your enemies with kindness, Merrin. It hurts them more'.

Oh, I was about to become the kindest, nicest person ever.

CHAPTER EIGHT

Ginny

I was glad vampires had a superior sense of smell. That, and the fact that Merrin had stayed at the counter for a time while he asked Dela to place him a flyer in the window. He'd forgotten my super-hearing too. Though I couldn't make out his conversation, I could make out it was him. It gave me time to prepare, because as soon as I'd heard his voice and tried to work out how Merrin's vocal chords were coming out of the smart man at the counter, and then realising Merrin *was* the smart man at the counter; well, I'd needed a moment to deal with my shock.

As he'd walked over, I'd pretended to be busy with the till, and then I'd looked up to find Merrin had picked a book up, Dela nearby. What was going on? As Dela looked over to me, with a smirk on her face, I realised. She thought I was going to be fooled by his new appearance.

No, not fooled. I was taken aback though as Merrin turned to face me.

He looked good. Really good. There was no denying it. The unwashed, skinny, tall zombie had been visited by some fairy godmother and turned into a prince. I wasn't blind. Despite the fact I hated him, he now looked and smelled good on the outside. It didn't make the inside any better though. Or so I thought until he...

Asked me for my help. Politely.

I needed a lie down. Gnarly had always been a bizarre place

with strange happenings. Callie and Dela had told me a lot of tales, but this... Merrin mark two. I needed a moment to process.

I went with the word that was stuck in my throat.

"Pardon?"

"I wanted to ask for your help with a project. Erm, if it's not convenient here, could you tell me a time and place that is?"

"What project?" I needed to know if this was all an elaborate trick designed to make me look foolish.

"I'm running an upcycling workshop at my place on Sunday. It's to help clear some of the furniture away and to encourage re-purposing and re-using. Only, I need to get the cowshed sorted quickly, and well, after the other day..." He paused. "I thought I'd ask you."

My first thought was to tell him to go fuck himself, but then I remembered Aria and my plan to put houses on his land. I had to tread carefully though. He'd get suspicious if I wasn't a pain in his backside.

"Why would I help you again? You're a jerk."

I saw Merrin swallow. He might be acting nice, but his movements gave him away. He was wishing he had a stake right now.

"Don't think of it as helping me. Think of it as helping Gnarly. After all, the people here are being welcoming to you."

I made him wait a little longer before agreeing. "Fine. I'll come over to your place after work. I'll be there around six."

With that I walked off and went back to my counter and refused to look at him again. I heard him walk away and say goodbye to Dela.

It was then I noticed there was a twenty-pound note on the table next to the bookshelf. I wandered over and saw he'd taken the book. Huh, looked like Merrin had ideas above his station. It'd take more than a few upcycles to make him a decent amount of money. Selling his land, now that was a more realistic option for him.

The moment the place had a lull in business, Dela came over to my side. "So, what did you think? Still hate him?"

I sighed and rolled my eyes. "If someone shaved a skunk, would it not still stink?"

"What did he want to talk to you about? He said he wanted to make some kind of truce."

I scoffed. "He doesn't want a truce. He just wants use of my super-strength. The puny weakling needs help moving his furniture and so he came slithering in to ask me to help him."

I actually felt a bit mean as I said this as the guy had asked me politely.

"I'm guessing you told him where to go then. Shame. I'm looking forward to the workshop."

"No, I said I'd help," I replied.

Dela stared at me with focus. "What?"

"I said I'd help."

"Did he offer you money?"

I guffawed. "Of course, the man formerly known as a hobo offered me money. Don't be silly. He just basically begged for my help, so I said yes. It's an opportunity to watch him squirm and also feel weak and inferior at the side of me."

Dela leant on the table near me.

"Is that really your aim? Do you dislike him that much?" She paused. "It's what he said to you that day, isn't it? How he shamed you for wanting a man with money. That really did hit a major nerve."

I looked at the floor.

"Why does his opinion matter so much, Ginny? You do you. And if that's marry a man for money, not love, then go for it. Don't let grumpy Merrin's judgement swamp your shoulders. And certainly don't let it eat you up so much that all you can think about is hurting him back. Just be indifferent."

My friend sounded like she was speaking from experience, and I guessed I knew the root cause of this.

"Are you thinking about your dad?"

Dela nodded. "My father doesn't want to get to know Callie or myself because he wants to keep the Royal Court trouble free and not bring shame upon his wife. And I totally understand that; I do. The cost would be huge, and the queen has already helped us enough. But at first, I hated him. What father doesn't want to know his daughters? Now, though, I have a good relationship with my mother, a loving husband of my own, and I've realised that I'm not missing a father who I've never had. I was making up a dream person, someone I imagined would be overawed to see me. I was craving acceptance and Nick pointed out the truth; all I needed to do was to accept myself."

I thought about what Nick had told her.

You just need to accept yourself. I murmured the affirmation in my mind.

"Merrin's words hurt because something in them must have rung true. You need to look deep into yourself at why, and then accept who you are or make changes if needed." Dela took a breath. "Jesus, I'm spending too much time around Mya. I sound like a self-help guru. Sorry, Ginny. I didn't mean to come over and start a lecture."

"No, Dela, you're absolutely right," I replied. "The things Merrin said cut deep and I need to look into why that is."

I needed to take a good hard look at myself and decide what I wanted, and what I needed.

And I might have to ask Mya for some guidance.

But for now, I needed to finish work and then make my way over to the farm.

I whizzed to the perimeter of the land where rickety fence panels surrounded what must be over an acre of land. It was more or less level, and wildflowers and shrubs grew in between the rotted and broken panels. At the other side was Gnarly woodland, with the gnarled branched trees that gave the fell its name. I walked up the driveway, a mixture of sand, clay, and stones, and assessed the plot as I went. There was scrap and furniture everywhere, some covered in waterproof tarpaulin, some exposed to the weather. I saw old metal gates, chimney pots, piles of broken up wood. It was just one huge mess.

As I reached the top of the land, the cowshed came close to view, along with Merrin's home and his studio. If the land was cleared there would be plenty of room for Merrin and he could easily allow two more homes to be built near him. Aria and Bernard would make it worth his while. He could split the land and the other houses be placed near the bottom. Aria would love looking out over the woodland. I wondered if any supes lived out there. When I called Mya, I'd ask her.

As I walked past the cowshed, I realised that Merrin had not told me where to meet him. Walking towards his front door, it opened and he walked outside, giving me a brief wave in acknowledgement.

As we met up there was a huge awkwardness as we looked at the other, neither of us knowing what to say. We didn't do hello; we did why don't you fuck right off.

I cast my eyes over Merrin again. The truth was he really did scrub up well. He looked handsome. But appearances meant nothing to me. They were deceptive. I'd learned to trust no one. If you kept yourself acerbic and distant, you stayed away from danger. If you let no one in, they couldn't hurt you. Yes, it was better I served a large slice of what Merrin expected: Surliness, sarcasm, and sass.

"What's with the makeover of yourself and this shit tip?" I went for the jugular, but only rhetorically for a change.

"It's just time." He shrugged. "I couldn't carry on like this. Hiding away from life." As he spoke, he looked a little taken aback. "Shit," he said. "That's it. I've avoided life for years, thinking I was safer here, on my own land, and then when the furniture landed on me, it showed me that there's danger everywhere. That's at the root of all this. Refusing to hide away anymore because what's the point? If shit is going to hit the fan, it can happen anywhere."

"Erm, right," I said, more than a little discomforted by Merrin's honest admission. "So where do you need me to help?"

"The cowshed first. That needs clearing ready for the workshop. I know it's going to take time to get my land back from the salvage, the excess furniture, and from where Mother Nature has attempted to take it back, but for the first time in a long time I feel like I have aims. It's like I've suddenly woken up from a coma or something."

I felt weird for a moment and then I realised what it was. Concern. It had been a while since I'd felt that emotion. "Maybe something weird is going on with you and you should see a doctor? Like, aren't you supposed to walk around everywhere extra slow and wailing?" I asked him, as he was being super strange and not at all Merbin.

"And do you spook at the sight of garlic and need to avoid sunlight?" he snapped. Phew, the Merrin I knew was still there. Arsehole.

"No, though at least in the dark your face would be less conspicuous. And garlic, being pungent, would mask the smell of your body."

"At least if I wailed it would drown out the sound of your incessant bitching," he retorted.

And then the strangest thing happened. As each of us stared at the other, waiting for the next barbed insult, I began to laugh, and then Merrin joined in.

"As much as insulting you is the ultimate entertainment, I actually did come here to help you, so let's go see what needs doing," I said.

"Shall we call a temporary truce?" Merrin suggested. "It will get the task done quicker if we aren't bickering."

"Agreed." I held out my hand and he took mine in his and we shook. But as we did something weird happened. A tingle went right from my hand, and it seemed to fizz through my body.

We sprang apart. "Electric shock," Merrin said, as if what had transpired just then had been static electricity.

But as my lady parts woke from a deep slumber, I wasn't sure that's what it had been at all.

CHAPTER NINE

Merrin

What the hell had just happened? One minute we were laughing, the next she'd shaken my hand and some kind of zing had fired up my zang, if you caught my drift.

Seeing Ginny looking as uncomfortable as I did and guessing the strange electricity had shot through her too, I blamed static and started for the cowshed.

The last time we'd been here, Ginny had been picking furniture off me. This time we were on a more equal footing where I wasn't having an emotional claustrophobic breakdown and was thinking about my business instead.

"So, ideally, I need to go through these items and get them safely organised. I thought I'd take out the furniture that would make good, simple makeover pieces and put them over there," I said, pointing to one corner that was packed tight, "ready for Sunday. But as you can see, first I have to make some space in general."

"How about I do what they do on the cluttered house programmes, Merrin? I'll move absolutely everything outside and then you can tell me what to do with the furniture one thing at a time."

"Sounds good," I said. "Erm, why did you agree to help me again, only this all feels very weird."

"I can call you Merbin if it makes you feel any better?" she drawled.

"No thanks."

She placed her arms across her chest, making me notice she had small boobs. A nice amount to fit in a hand. I actually put my fist in my mouth, appalled at my thoughts.

We hate her. I reminded my libido. What had that shock thing done to me?

"Have you put a thrall on me? I have wards in place, but just checking?"

"Oh good lord, are you freaking out, Merbin because I'm not being a psycho?" She rolled her eyes hard. "Listen up. I like Gnarly Fell. It's much better than the Letwine mansion and I'd like to move here one day if I can. If I spend time getting involved with the community it will look good when I apply to live here. So that's why I'm helping. Nothing to do with you. It benefits Gnarly and mostly it benefits me, and we all know how much I love myself, right? You happy now?'

I nodded. "Yes, now I see that it's to further your own interests that's much more believable and therefore settles the discomfort that was rolling inside of me. You being genuinely nice didn't ring true."

She huffed. Stomped over to the corner that had been earmarked for the workshop furniture and with speed began moving everything outside.

I wondered if I'd gone too far. It wasn't like I knew the woman well. But I did know a poor unfortunate soul who'd once been out on a date with her: a fellow artist who lived in London. I'd sat with him one night when all he'd talked about was the vampire woman who'd led him a merry dance of chasing after her, only for him to be suckered in and find out it was clear she wanted his money and not love. Once Lawrie had come to the village and his sister visited, it soon became clear she was the Virginia my friend Rupert had talked about. Since then, his work had become dark and morose and he didn't come out anymore, preferring to stay in some kind of tormented fugue state. No woman should have the power to do that to a man. To ruin him. It reminded me of my own losses because of the power of a woman. Something I'd vowed would never happen again.

And this was the truth about why I'd been so dismissive of Ginny. By leading my friend into his dark ruin, she reminded me of what I myself had faced, and I didn't want a reminder. It was why I wanted her gone.

But now. Now she was working in Gnarly and talking about living here.

That meant I either had to get used to her and what she represented, or... I had to drive her out of here.

Before today, I'd have happily got behind the wheel, but as I watched Ginny looking pissed off in an upset way, rather than an 'I want to break all your bones' way, I wondered if it was possible that I'd misjudged her.

So give her a chance, Merrin, I heard my inner conscience tell me. Go ahead with the truce and see what she reveals. *Then if she's as selfish as you first thought, rid Gnarly of her presence by turning the villagers against her.*

It was a plan of sorts, and so I strode outside with purpose, determined to form some kind of a tentative friendship with the woman.

"I'm sorry. Genuinely. And look, you've not had to force the apology out of me this time," I said, as I moved closer to the salty vampire. I had to appreciate the fact that she was neither out of breath (helps if you didn't breathe), nor had broken a sweat. She was stretching out her limbs, which revealed a slight sliver of skin between the bottom of her t-shirt and the top of her jeans.

"I don't fucking care. Stick your opinions up your arse where shit belongs." She narrowed her gaze.

I stepped closer to her. "Whether you care or not, and I think you do because it's clearly demonstrated in your manner, I do heartily and genuinely apologise."

"Have you heard yourself, Merbin?" She impersonated my tone. "'Gincompoop, it's clearly demonstraaaattted in your mannnerrrrr'. You are such a condescending twat." She stomped her foot on the ground. "How do you manage to be so uppity when you've spent so much time under the ground?"

"I don't mean to be." I decided to be honest. "Look, I heard some things about you, that made me form an opinion of you without my knowing you personally. And you weren't exactly kind yourself, judging me on my appearance and how I live. Please, please, please, can we make a truce and actually try to get to know the other a little, because if you do intend to live here then it won't be good for the village if we hate each other."

I watched as her eyes flitted towards the bottom of the field and the woodland. "That's shifter territory," I said.

"Huh?" She gave me a blank look.

"The woods. The part that backs onto my land is shifter territory, although at the moment there aren't many shifters in Gnarly. Mainly Jason and then Mitzi from the general store. You'd not be allowed to live there."

"Oh, right. Thanks for the heads up," she replied.

"We're full at the moment. At present, other than Charity who applied to take over an empty business premises, Gnarly's residents have increased by the new relationships formed since the curse lifted. If a place becomes available, it's possible they'd consider your application. But because you can travel quickly due to your vamp speed and have a place in Chelsea, they wouldn't see it as a priority," I told her honestly.

"So unless I take over a business premise..."

"Of which there currently aren't any empty ones," I finished.

"Or I marry a resident?" she enquired.

I swallowed. My mouth and throat suddenly as dry as clothes left to bake too long on a washing line.

"Your face." She laughed. "Don't worry. I'm not going to marry Jason just so I can live in the woods. You already know I like the finer things in life. I currently have a very comfortable, well-furnished apartment. I'm also immortal, so I can happily put my name on a waiting list and for the years that pass to seem like no time at all to me. So, calm down before you make flyers warning all the men of Gnarly that I'm on a mission for a husband."

I remained speechless, because my mind *had* gone to her marrying my friend, and I'd worried that she'd do the same to bubbly Jason that she'd done to Rupert. I'd need to keep a close eye on Virginia Letwine because you couldn't trust the words of an evil vampire.

"Okay, what's next?" She pointed to the furniture.

"Next, can you help me with a few repairs to the cowshed? I meant to ask you to get me the details of the Letwine architect as I'd like to make a few changes to the place. That will have to wait for another day now."

"Okay."

Once we got back into the cowshed, Ginny proved herself very useful as she helped me to patch up some leaking parts of the roof. The fact she could fly up there made me quite jealous I'd not been turned, as opposed to the fate I'd ended up with.

While she did that, I swept the ground and tidied the floor space, imagining where to put things for the best use of the building.

"I think the roof is actually watertight now, Merrin," Ginny said, coming to stand by my side. I noted the fact she'd not called me Merbin. It was a definite improvement. "I don't mind staying longer and helping get the rest of it a bit more secure. I can get those fixed." She nodded towards the old cowshed doors that lay on the ground outside covered with clear tarpaulin. "I just need a short break," she explained. "And a feed."

"At least I know I'm safe there," I joked.

"Yeah, that seems so weird to me, that you don't have any blood at all. Hey, I think that's why your smell struck me so much." Her eyes went wide. "It's because with other people their blood sings to my nose, whereas with you, it doesn't. It's not that you stink. It's that you actually don't smell... of blood."

"Thanks. I think," I replied.

"I brought my own dinner," she said, before moving to pick up the bag she'd brought with her and rummaging inside until she brought out a small bottle filled with bright red contents. I didn't want to invite her into my home, where people usually had dinner, because that hadn't been tidied up yet, but the studio was excused of being messy by explanation of 'work in progress', so I went with that option. "There are chairs in the studio if you want to drink in there?"

"Okay." She followed me towards the art studio.

I stopped just before the door and turned to her. "Before we go inside. I'm very sensitive about my artistic work, so please don't insult it."

"Don't worry, I'd rather insult you than inanimate objects." Ginny smirked and I rolled my eyes at her.

Approaching the door, I got the key from my pocket and unlocked it. Then I beckoned for Ginny to step inside. "I allow you into my building. Go straight ahead. At the other side of the studio, there's a kitchen with a small table and chairs."

"Thank you for your permission," Ginny said before setting off as directed as I locked the door behind me. It was habit more than anything. I had wards up that protected my buildings from harm or theft.

I saw Ginny push open the kitchen door and then she let out an almighty piercing scream as she stepped inside. The door closed behind her, and I ran towards it, pushing it open and wondering what the hell was inside.

The scene before me knocked me off-kilter. Ginny was crouched in a corner, staring into space, rocking.

"Ginny, what happened?" I asked her, nervous to get too near to her in case she attacked me. I could see no sign of anything else having been in the room and couldn't understand what was happening.

"No. No. No. No. No. No," she said over and over. I saw then that something had triggered her. She was lost to past memories, and all I could do was keep trying to bring her back to the present moment.

"William, noooooo. I beg you." She wailed again, making a sound that I recognised. One of a broken heart. Wherever Ginny's mind was, it was from a time when she'd loved hard.

CHAPTER TEN

Ginny

Life was good. I went into central London on a Saturday and lifted a few wallets and purses. Shoppers got distracted: with talking to friends, in love with potential new handbags, on the phone. It made it so easy.

There was food in the house and I was able to study, and also be around for Duncan. Miracles hadn't happened: Mum still spent most of her time drunk, but I hoped that soon I'd get her to see she needed help. Then we could be a family again.

Tonight, I had a date. I'd met him in the supermarket when we'd both reached for the last loaf of white bread. He'd told me I could have the loaf, if he could have a date.

Though he must have been twice my age, I said yes. He was so handsome, and charming, and... irresistible. We arranged to meet at The Red Lion, the pub around five minutes away from my house.

Duncan had eaten and gone up to his room and Mum was in hers, so I went and got ready. I'd not had a date in what seemed like forever and I enjoyed putting on make-up and doing my hair. Tonight I could be a carefree eighteen-year-old for the first time in a long, long time.

There were a few familiar faces in the Red Lion and I was greeted with some waves, hellos, and a couple of polite, 'How's your mum?' comments. Lindon insisted on buying the drinks while I found us a table. He took a seat opposite me now, placing down the white wine I'd ordered and his own pint.

Sitting back in his chair, he stretched his long limbs out and sighed. "It feels good to get to sit and relax. I've had a busy day today. How about you? What do you do again, Miss Virginia Bates? Remind me."

I told him about how I hoped to be a vet one day, and how I looked after my mum and brother. Conversation flowed so easily, and I found myself telling him things that were very personal, almost as if I had no control over the words coming out of my mouth.

"I'm so sorry," I said after telling him all about my mother's addictions. "I shouldn't be burdening you with this on a first date. It should be fun and carefree."

Lindon waved away my concerns. "We have a connection. Surely you feel it too? I wasn't sure I believed about love at first sight until I almost got into a fight over a loaf in the Spar, but..." He stared into my eyes and my heart skipped a beat. "I think I believe it now."

I knew what he meant because there was definitely a connection between us both. I felt hypnotised by him, like my world now began and ended with him. Something special had happened and I believed I had now met the love of my life. Even better, it sounded like he had more than enough money to take care of us all. He told me he lived in a large mansion in Chelsea and he worked within the financial services.

By the end of the evening, I was convinced I'd met my future husband.

"Would you allow me to escort you home?" he said, in that old-fashioned, polite manner he had about him. I liked it. I liked that he was older, and not stupid and immature like the guys my age I'd dated before.

"I'd love that," I said.

"How did you get here?" I asked him as he began accompanying me on my way home.

"I got a taxi, and I'll call one to take me home from yours. I didn't know how much I'd drink and I don't drink and drive."

He placed his hand in mine. It was a little cold, so I wrapped my warm one around his to provide him some comfort.

It was a May day and the weather was calm. It was neither warm nor cold, just a day of averages. Nothing special set it out as a day that would be talked about as we chatted and walked down the streets towards my home. Blossom hung from the trees and gathered around our feet, and I commented that I wished the pretty blossom stayed longer.

"Yes, it is a shame that such beauty doesn't last long, before it becomes dried, dirty, and stepped on. I'm glad you share my view that it would be better if such pretty blossom was able to be kept as it was for an eternity."

There he went again with his strange way of talking. It was charming and I squeezed his hand. We looked at each other and shared a smile.

"This is me," I told him, gesturing towards my front door. I'd planned on a chaste goodnight kiss on the doorstep and arrangements for a further date, but Lindon walked me up to the door, leaned down and said, "Invite me in." And I did.

As he followed me through my front door, I wasn't sure why I had, because I'd not wanted him to potentially see my drunk mother. I just had to hope everyone was in bed.

"Is that you, Ginny?" came from the living room. My mum was up. Shit. I hoped she wasn't drunk.

"Yes, Mum. I'll be through soon," I said, hoping Lindon would understand that I needed to end our date now, and for him to leave.

But as I turned to face him and looked up into his eyes, I let out a silent scream. Silent because Lindon's hand was firmly across my mouth. His eyes burned red as he looked down at me. And then he smiled, revealing fangs.

I tried to shake my head frantically but could hardly move while in his grip. Letting go of me, he strode purposefully towards the living room and towards my mum.

"No. Please... get out... leave."

His amusement shone in his eyes. "Oh, Virginia. It's too late. You already invited me in. You can't take it back now, that would be rude."

I had no alternative but to dash after him.

In the living room, my mum sat on the sofa sewing a pair of Duncan's school trousers. She was sober. Duncan himself was beside her and watching the TV while stuffing crisps in his mouth.

"Good evening. I thought I'd just pop by and introduce myself. I'm William Letwine," Lindon said. *William? Who was this man really? No, not a man... vampire. An ice-cold sensation ran through my veins. I needed to get him out. What was it killed vampires? A stake to the heart, right? I began to look around.*

"Oh, Ginny," the vampire said. "Do you not know I can read your mind? I thought we had the beginnings of a beautiful love affair, but now you want to kill me." He tutted. "Do you know why I really chose you?" *He cast a derisive gaze down me from head to toe. It made my skin feel like a thousand spiders ran underneath the epidermis.* "Because you are a very adept pickpocket."

My mum's breath caught. Duncan's eyes shot to mine. I gave him an imperceptible nod, as to not do or say anything.

"Pickpocket? Is that what you've been having to do to pay our bills?" My mum began to cry. "Oh, Ginny. I'm so sorry. I actually went to the doctor today and I'm starting treatment. We're going to have a fresh start." She looked at William. "Now, would you like a drink?" *she said, as if he hadn't just announced to the room that I was thinking of killing him. As if he wasn't standing there with his fangs descended and red eyes. Why weren't either of them seeing this?*

But before I could acknowledge to myself that the vampire was hypnotising them in some way, William bellowed with amusement.

"I'd love a drink. Thanks for asking," *he said, and he flew at my mother and bit into her jugular.*

As I launched myself at him, to try to get him off her, he threw me off with ease and such force that I landed on the smoked glass, hexagonal-shaped dining table at the other end of the room. It smashed into pieces under my body, and I laid on the floor in great pain, feeling blood flow from a cut in my arm and another on my leg. William grinned at me, from a mouth dripping in blood as he threw my mother's lifeless body on the floor and grabbed my screaming younger brother.

I wanted to scream.

I wanted to launch at William.

I wanted to save my brother who shouted, "Ginnnnnnnyyyy."

The brother I had always cared for and protected. Now, I'd been compelled into muteness, unable to move, as in front of me, the vampire tore into Duncan's neck and his wrists before throwing his dead corpse on top of my mother's.

William stalked towards me, even though his prey was caught in a vampire's web, invisible strands holding me in place, powerless.

"And now it's your turn, Virginia... Letwine," he said, and while I prayed for death, to join my mother and my brother, William instead turned me into his daughter, to thieve for him, and help make him rich beyond his own capabilities.

And I didn't get free until William's world, and a stake, caught up with him.

"Ginny? Ginny? Virginia?"

In the distance I could hear words. Someone calling? But I was lost. Lost to a room where a smoked glass coffee table had become my prison.

"Uptight, money-grabbing, pompous bitch."

The words became louder in my ear.

"Gold-digging, judgemental, pain in the arse."

My vision began returning to the present. There was someone here with me. I could make out a blurred, indistinct shape. I sniffed the air but could smell no blood.

There was no blood here. I wasn't in my home, in the past, where the blood assaulted my senses once I was turned. Here, no blood, safe.

"Gincompoop, you sanctimonious, high and mighty, coffin-dodger chasing mercenary."

"Coffin-dodger chasing?" I questioned as Merrin came into view and I remembered where I was.

"I was actually running out of insults. Welcome back," Merrin said.

"What's a coffin-dodger?" I asked, grateful of a distraction while I centred myself and became fully present.

"I meant a rich man with one foot in the grave, like old, wrinkly and more-or-less at Death's door, and you go after him because he has money."

I smiled. "I don't need to be that desperate. Not when I can compel human men to do as I wish."

"What happened, Ginny?" Merrin's lips pursed, his voice lower, gentle.

And then I remembered. Remembered the table that sat in the centre of Merrin's kitchen. Hexagonal, smoked glass, circa the 1970's.

"I'm sorry, Merrin," I said, and rising to my feet, I pushed him aside, lifted up the table and ran at speed outside with it. Once out on the land, I picked it up and slammed it into the ground over and over and over. Shards flew everywhere and the metal buckled, until there was no further reminder of my past other than broken fragments that carried hints of a previous existence but were now beyond recognition.

Merrin appeared from behind me. He stood looking desperate to assist me, yet helpless faced with a powerful vampire. I knew that feeling well. I dropped to my knees and began sobbing. Before I knew it, his arms were wrapped around me. "It's okay, Ginny. It's okay. Whatever it is. I can help."

"I'm sorry. I will clean up the mess," I told him.

"You've already cleared up far more mess than you've made. Don't worry about this. I can clear up broken glass."

"Okay. Well, I'm still sorry if you liked that table."

"Nope, had no particular feelings for it. Alistair put it in the kitchen when he started calling in more regularly. Tried to organise me a little. Before there'd been a wine barrel. Preferred that myself." Merrin moved in front of me and lifted up my chin.

"My house is a mess, but I want to invite you inside, until you feel better, okay? You don't have to explain your actions, but I don't want you to go home until I know you're all right. Well, as all right as you get given you're a supercilious bitch."

"I suppose I could hold my nose in order to recover in your home," I snapped back.

"That's better," he said, and then Merrin helped me to my feet, and I allowed him to link his arm through mine and lead me towards his home.

CHAPTER ELEVEN

Merrin

I was glad the electric shock thing hadn't happened again as I'd linked my arm through Ginny's. The strangest of situations was happening though as Ginny—super-vamped-up-everything Ginny—just seemed deflated and vulnerable. Her snark had no real bite about it.

Pushing my front door open, I wished I'd had the foresight to open some windows as the odour of warm, stale air clearly hit Ginny's nostrils and she flinched. She said nothing though. Just stood while I opened the windows and moved some clutter off the sofa so that she could take a seat.

"If you'd rather we went back outside, that's okay," I told her.

Ginny's eyes cast around the space. "No. This is good. All this crap everywhere is distracting me, and the overwhelming smell of fustiness is bringing me back to recent times, like when I met you at the bookstore."

"I am intending to tidy up."

"Why?"

"Sorry?"

"Why? Why have you had the makeover, why are you tidying up your space? You said it's because you realise you need to live your undead life, but only do it if it makes you happy, Merrin. If you'd rather sit and be stinky with piles of crap around you, go for it. You do you."

"What's going on, Ginny?"

She placed her head in her hands. Then she took a deep breath, and she told me about what happened to her family.

To say I was stunned was an understatement.

Shocked. Speechless. Sorrowful. Devastated. Many emotions crossed my mind during the time she took to tell me her story. But mainly there was bewilderment. Why confess to me of all people?

There was one thing for sure though: I'd got Ginny all wrong. She'd fought for money to keep her family, then been forced to steal for a vampire, and finally, had sought what she thought was the security of it.

"You see if I have enough money, then just maybe I'll feel secure again, and free."

She threw her head back against the sofa's headrest. "I can't believe I've just revealed all this to my frenemy."

"A what now?" I didn't have the foggiest as to what she was talking about.

"A frenemy. A friend who's an enemy. Not that we're friends. We made a truce. A peacekeeping negotiation. I don't know what the term for that is."

"Well, how about we become friends now, huh?" I suggested. "Then it's simple what to call each other. You no longer think I smell, and I'm no longer judging you for being a gold-digger now I understand the basis of it."

I held my hand out for her to shake, but she shook her head.

"No? You don't want to be my friend?"

"I'm not shaking your hand again. I got that weird electric shock last time. I'll just say the words. Friends. Also, if you tell anyone what I've revealed to you this evening, I'll come dig a deep hole and place you at the bottom, then fill it back in. Just thought I'd make that clear before we become best buddies."

As soon as I pictured it, me at the bottom of a giant grave, I began to shake, and try as I might, I couldn't stop myself.

"Fuck, Merrin, what have I said? I'm so sorry. Oh fuck, what do I do now? Listen, I won't bury you in a deep hole, I'll, I'll- slap you across the face."

But I was still lost, deep inside myself until...

Thwack.

I felt at my cheek. "Y-you hit me?"

"Have you stopped shaking? Yes. So actually, you should thank me."

My cheek was smarting now, so I held it carefully in my palm. "Is this what frenemies do? Do they pretend to be your friend and then smack you one?"

But Ginny was pacing. She seemed to have gone from depressed to manic. Could a vampire be bipolar?

"I can't just sit on your sofa, Merrin. I need to do something. Let me get the drink I didn't manage to have earlier. I brought a spare bottle. Can you remove the one I left in the studio later?" Ginny went into her bag and pulled out another bottle.

"Yes, of course."

"When I've had this let's clean your house, and then after that, I'll tidy a bit more of your yard before I go home."

I watched Ginny consume her drink within seconds. Her cheeks pinked up, as did the end of her nose, making her look pretty damn cute. Until she did a large belch.

"Sorry. I'm not supposed to drink it that fast, but I'm late for my feed because of what happened."

"Don't worry about it. I'm friends with Jason, I've heard and smelled a lot worse," I said, trying to crack a joke to distract her.

But she was still pacing, rolling her shoulders backwards and forwards and then she did a few star jumps. "Merrin, I feel antsy, and... full of frustration, some rage... just, generally unsatisfied. I need to do something to get it out of my system. So... let's go to your bedroom," she said.

My jaw dropped open.

"Hang on, that's not frenemies, that's friends-with-benefits."

She stood still, her eyes on mine, pupils dilated. "Well, I actually meant we could start cleaning there. You should always work from the top down. But, hmm, have you ever had hate sex?" she asked me, her eyes now dancing with unbridled lust.

"Probably not in the way you mean, but I bet a few times they've hated it," I mumbled under my breath.

"Vampire...."

"...hearing," I sighed. "Come on," I held out a hand for her to take.

Ginny licked across her fangs. "Okay, but which are we doing? Cleaning or hate sex?"

"Ginny, I'm getting you a mop and a bucket, and anything else you need to get this... need quenched, because I'm not being used for sex."

The mop and bucket were out of my hand in an instant, and I sat tucked into a corner on a chair as a vampire whizzed around the place in what appeared to be a blur. It was so fast I had to stop trying to look. Within an hour the place was sorted and orderly and Ginny was lying on the sofa, moaning as if she'd had twenty consecutive orgasms.

"God, that felt soooo good," she almost mewled. "Thank you."

"Shouldn't I be thanking you?" I asked.

She moved her hair out of her eyes and looked over at me. "Thank you for letting me clean and for not having taken me up on my other suggestion. I'm afraid I got a blood lust from the delay in feeding and then drinking so fast."

"You're welcome, and I'm very grateful that in order to quench your lust you attacked my home, rather than my body. I'm not sure I'd have survived."

"How do you work that out when you're already dead? It's your brains that have to be destroyed, isn't it? Your body is infallible."

"You'd have fucked my brains out. I'd have been very much dead," I quipped.

There was a stunned silence and then Ginny burst out into noisy laughter. Before long she was holding her stomach, while red tears ran down her cheeks.

When she finally stopped, she sat up and turned to me.

"This has been one strange evening. The evening I made a new friend and found out he's actually pretty damn funny."

"I have my moments." I shrugged nonchalantly.

"Let's go sort out a few more things in the yard and then I'll call it a night," Ginny suggested. "Hey, I might even come along and design a piece myself for my apartment."

"You'll need to tell me because I only have limited places."

"Okay, put me down for a place and my friend, Aria, too. She can make something for the nursery."

I stood and faced her with my hands on my hips.

"What?" she said.

"I told you so. I told you she'd be pregnant, and you'd be working in the shop."

"Oh God, you're so smug." She shook her head. "Bet you didn't see us becoming friends though."

"No one could have predicted that, not Nostradamus himself," I said.

We focused on getting the cowshed as organised as could be for Sunday and had the furniture that was ripe for upcycling spread out against another wall. We'd been thorough going through the pieces I had and there was now a pile outside earmarked for firewood. Ginny, of course, refused to break any wood up in case she staked herself. It was a fair point.

"How is Aria getting along?" I asked Ginny. "It can't be easy, trying to get used to being newly pregnant when it's such a rare thing."

"I saw her briefly last night and it's already taking its toll. The vampires at the mansion flocked to visit, wanting her 'good luck' to rub off on them. It's not going to get any better either. I wish there was something I could do to help her. She needs to rest and to be able to give her baby the best start in life, not be having her belly rubbed by people she's never met before."

"I've heard that happens to human females too," I replied.

"Yes, but that's the occasional few. Aria's going to end up with friction burns."

"I can help," I said.

Her gaze probed mine. "Oh yeah?"

"Follow me," I instructed, and I headed out into the middle of my field. It took me a couple of attempts to find the right piece of tarpaulin but eventually I unearthed a statue of a pregnant woman.

"This was a garden ornament that Mya found up at the mansion covered in vines. She said the only woman allowed to be around Death was her, other than the wayward souls. I reckon with a little bit of work I can have this looking like a replica of your friend. She can put it out in the garden of the Letwine mansion and all who want to can rub its belly. With a protection spell around it so that it can't be damaged or stolen, you'll be sorted."

"Merrin, that's an amazing idea. She'll love it," Ginny said, and she flung her arms around me and kissed my cheek.

I threw her off and she stumbled a little before righting herself.

"Sorry. Wasn't expecting that," I said.

"Me neither. I didn't have my vampy senses on, or you wouldn't have been able to move me. Merrin, I do believe I just had a genuine moment of gratitude."

"Well done," I congratulated her, but I was distracted.

Because the moment her lips had met my cheek that electric shock had happened again. Was it only happening to me though? Ginny hadn't mentioned it that time.

"I'll make a start on this tonight then," I said, pointing to the statue. "Then Aria can pick it up on Sunday when she comes to class."

"You really have come up with a great idea there, Merrin. My friend might actually get to enjoy her pregnancy."

I widened my stance and stood with my arms folded. My expression smug.

"What's with your face?" Ginny asked.

"I'm waiting for a thank you," I said.

"I already thanked you."

I shook my head. "No, you didn't. You said it was a great idea, an amazing idea, but you didn't say thank you."

Her eyes narrowed. "You're really enjoying this, aren't you?"

"Yup. Make sure it's a genuine and clearly spoken thanks. I will after all have done your friend a huge favour."

Oh how the tables had turned this evening, and not just the one Ginny had upended and broken.

"Huh, well, some... no... *most* men would have taken my kiss as a thank you, but of course, you're a weirdo, so—"

"Think you'd better start again. You can't call me a weirdo in the same sentence as you thank me."

I could tell Ginny wanted to lower her fangs and raise her middle finger, but instead she walked closer to me.

"Merrin, thank you so very much for upcycling this statue for my friend. It will make a genuine difference to her life and for that I am extremely grateful."

"See, didn't kill you, did it?"

"Only because I'm already dead or I'm sure it would have done," she said, and then she was gone.

Leaving me realising I'd enjoyed her company.

CHAPTER TWELVE

Ginny

As I returned to the Letwine mansion and entered my apartment, I dropped all my belongings to the floor and sat on my sofa. Leaning forward, I pulled my bag towards me, took out my mobile and sent Aria a quick text.

Ginny: How have things been today?

It didn't take long for a reply to come through.

Aria: Visitors all day and Bernard fussing. If I didn't feel so sick and was trying not to move, there would be a lot less Letwine vampires now. How's your day been?

Ginny: Strange. Good day at the café, but then Merrin wanted my help at his place, moving furniture and so I went there. He has a solution to your visitor's problem.

The phone rang moments after I'd sent my message.

"When you have such exciting gossip, you do not text. My day has been crap. As my best friend, your role is to keep me entertained and this... news you spent time with the zombie you hate, is gossip. Spill. I want all the details. Every single one."

"There's not much to spill. He wanted my help to tidy up as he's going to run some upcycling furniture workshops."

"And he couldn't ask his strapping male friends for assistance?"

"There was a need for speed. I took it as a chance to have a good look at his farmland. There's definitely room for a couple of houses there, if he was willing to sell some land."

"Excellent, and what was this about a solution to getting rid of the lingering Letwines?"

I told her about the statue and how I'd put our name down for the upcycling.

"You are the best friend in the whole damn universe. Not only have you found potential land for a new home, and a solution to getting rid of all the suckers wanting to molest my belly on a daily basis, but we're having a girly day. I can escape Bernard. Thank God."

"I'm right here," I heard him say. "You're just so rude."

"What about your constant nausea?" I asked her.

"We'll just share a piece of furniture and I'll sit still and watch while you upcycle. I'll bring a bucket, just in case."

"Sounds good. I'll let you know the times etc when I have more information. In the meantime, do the vampire equivalent of taking a deep breath with the Letwine clan. Only a few more days and then they can worship the statue instead of you."

"I'd not thought of that. They are, aren't they, worshipping me? Do you think there's any merit in a product line? Lucky charms, t-shirts, that kind of thing?"

"End the call, wife, it's time for you to listen to a romantic fairy tale on audio instead of making one up in your head," Bernard told her.

There was a heavy sigh. "I've got to go."

"Goodnight, bestie, love you," I said.

"P-pardon?"

"I said..." I stopped, stunned.

"Love you?"

"Erm... fuck." This was new.

"Aria, end the call. This is not a 'you hang up, no you hang up' situation."

"Bernard, *shut up*."

"Charming."

"Did you just say the L-word, Ginny?"

"I- I did. Bestie, I love you." As I said it, tears ran down my cheeks. I wiped them with the back of my hand, pink streaks across my skin. "What's happening to me?" I asked Aria.

"You're having a breakthrough, sweetie. I don't know why it's happening now. Did something happen tonight?" Aria asked gently.

"I- I confided in Merrin about my past." Aria knew it, her and Bernard, and other Letwine vampires such as my brother, but I'd never told anyone outside the clan. "I saw a table, like the one we had at home, and I had a complete meltdown. I felt I had to explain myself."

"Virginia Letwine, I love you too, honey. Me and Bernard both, and our little bloodsucker. It sounds like it's been quite an evening. Go rest up, and I look forward to seeing you Sunday. You know where I am in the meantime if you need me."

I ended the call and sat back on my sofa.

I craved quiet. Just an hour of no time to think. So I closed my eyes and let sleep take me for a short while.

"Have you ever had hate sex?"

"No, because I never hated anyone before," Merrin snarled, coming closer to me. There wasn't an inch of space between us now.

"I've hated plenty of people, but I usually just drain them. It sucks that I can't do that to you. I can only destroy your brain, so what was it you said about me fucking your brains out?"

"I can think of worse ways to go," Merrin said, staring down at me.

"At least you don't stink now," I informed him, noting that actually he had really nice eyes and if he stopped narrowing them at me, I could probably sink into their depths.

Merrin began unbuckling his trousers.

"What are you doing?"

"The only thing I can think of right now to stop you from talking."

He freed his cock. It was long like him, but it wasn't thin...

"Get on your knees," he ordered me.

. . .

I woke up with my mouth open wide. It saved me the trouble of opening it in shock. Thank God, I had woken up before I had given Merbin a dream blow job and God knows what else.

Then I faced facts. One, that I could have ended up sleeping with Merrin earlier because I had actually propositioned him, and two, it wouldn't now be the worst thing in the world.

Was I that vacuous? He'd smartened up his appearance and now I found him attractive? Or was it that I'd realised he was a half-decent person? Maybe it was the trauma. Like how a patient fell for their doctor. He'd listened to my admission of my past and so now I was having some kind of transference issue.

"Ginny, you are a complete mess right now," I told myself. And to make matters worse, I picked up a romance novel and refused to acknowledge the times when Merrin's face made an appearance when I read about the main male character.

"Morning, Ginny," Callie said happily in greeting as I walked into Buns and Books.

"What've you heard?" I quickly looked around me, relaxing when I saw we were alone.

My brother came out from the back of the shop.

"She's just happy because she's had orgasms for breakfast, but what do you think we've heard?" Lawrie's face wore the inquisitive, yet cat-catch-a-mouse expression us vamps got when we had a potential new focus.

"Nothing," I said, finding Lawrie suddenly in front of me.

He sniffed me. "You smell of something familiar…"

"Soap? Shampoo? You smell of desperation."

"Merrin. You smell of Merrin. It's on your handbag. You've been to his place."

I dragged my handbag away from Lawrie's nose and chucked it behind my counter. "Lawrie, I'm busy. I helped Merrin move furniture yesterday ready for his upcycling day on Sunday, that's why my bag smells of his fusty home."

Lawrie's nose came a little too close to my body and so I drop kicked him. He landed on his feet back in front of the counter.

"Someone is far too defensive." He smirked.

"Someone got too near to their sister. We're not in *Flowers in the Attic*."

"Ew. Though we aren't actually related. Not really. But still, ew."

I watched as Lawrie looked at Callie. "Sorry, wife, for getting a bit too close to Ginny. I don't like her like that. I do see her as an annoying little sister. I was just trying to see if she'd been dallying with Merrin."

Callie stood there with her hands on her hips. Oops, looked like my brother was in trouble.

"*You've* read Flowers in the Attic?" she asked.

Lawrie shrugged. "I have a lot of spare time while you are asleep. I've read most things in this store."

She turned to me, "And *you've* read it?"

"Saw them talk about it on Facebook."

"Well, I never." She turned back to her husband. "You don't have to explain your weird vampire ways, Lawrie. There will never be anything as weird as the fact I fell in love with you after hating your guts."

And there it was. The answer to finding out how hate could turn to love was right in front of me. Callie and Lawrie. Not that I was considering being in love with Merbin. Just the fact I didn't hate him as much anymore.

Lawrie became distracted by canoodling with his missus, and I went to get my bookstore organised. I decided I'd make a little display on crafts: sewing, painting, etc. I'd put some in the window and reposition Merrin's flyer into the centre of the display. It might get Gnarly's residents in an arty mood and spending in the store.

And it might get my mind off everything that had happened yesterday.

The café got busy and that kept Lawrie out of my hair as he helped his wife serve the customers. Working on my display kept me busy, and in the afternoon I had to replace a few books as customers came and purchased them.

One of them was Charity who'd bought a book on making your own wall art.

"How's the decorating going?" I asked her.

"Not too bad. I'm thinking of finishing touches now. I have a lot of driftwood and many shells and so thought I might decorate a mirror or something."

"Are you going to Merrin's on Sunday?" I asked her, thinking she could upcycle one of his pieces.

"I'm not sure. I want to go, but… well… it's a little awkward…" her voice trailed off.

"Oh?" I leaned in closer, not that I needed to be nearer to hear her lowered voice, but because it was a non-verbal response people found reassuring when confessing things they were questioning whether to confess or not.

"He sort of asked me out."

"He did?!" I'd raised my voice and several café customers looked over.

"Sorry. It's just… Merrin."

"What does that mean?" she asked.

"Erm, well, he's kind of shy," I lied.

"Ah. I guessed as much," Charity said. "Only he asked if I wanted to go for a drink with him, but then he said I could bring my brother, so I wasn't sure if it was just a 'welcome to the neighbourhood' kind of invitation. He seemed a bit unsure and so I gave him my business card and asked him to call me if he wanted to take me out… alone, and well, he's not called. But if he's just shy…"

"I think you should go to the event on Sunday," I said firmly. "Then you can get a feel on whether he is attracted to you or not. Worst case scenario you leave with a nice piece of furniture, best case you leave with a date."

"You're right," Charity said, giving me a wide smile. "Thanks, Ginny. I'll do that. Will you be going?"

"Yes, I'm taking my friend Aria and we're sharing a project."

"I'll see you there then. It'll be nice to have a wing-woman."

"Sure. I'll see you then," I told her, finishing ringing up her purchase and watching as she walked out of the store, giving her a final wave.

So there it was. Merrin liked Charity and had asked her on a date...maybe. I could get over my weird transference issue now and look for a date of my own. As I swiped through Tinder between a lull in customers, I realised that them being rich wasn't a good enough reason to date them anymore. It seemed I was actually thinking of looking for love, now I realised I was capable of feeling it again.

Sure it's not because of Merrin? came to the forefront of my mind.

CHAPTER THIRTEEN

Ginny

I walked out of the shop armed with a book on stencilling. I'd thought that whatever piece of furniture Aria and I worked on, I could make it pretty by drawing bunnies on it or something. Or would that make the baby hungry? I had no knowledge of how to deal with a baby vampire. None of us did. It would definitely be a learning curve.

Mya shot out from around the corner, making me jump, and my book fell on the ground.

"Jesus, Mya," I snapped. "You'd better not have damaged the cover."

"At least I don't want to damage a hairdresser," she snarked.

"What?"

"Me, you, bistro," she said, and once I'd picked up my purchase off the floor, Mya put her arm through mine and set off at a determined pace.

The doorbell jingled and Chantelle stepped forward. "Table for two?"

"Yes please, Chan, and two glasses of red..." Mya coughed, "...wine."

"Of course. Let's get you seated, and I'll get right on that."

With us now seated and Chantelle off sorting our drinks, I finally got a chance to ask Mya, "What the hell is this all about?"

Mya flicked her dark hair and smiled like a cartoon villain.

"My app. That is my Book of the Dead app, has been pinging today. Three times Charity Feeley came up as going to be drained by Virginia Letwine, and three times it disappeared as fast as it was there."

"I wasn't really going to drain her." I pouted. "It sucks that your app tells you my darkest thoughts. Can't a girl have any secrets? They were only tiny little thoughts of sucking her dry. Then I remembered she's a nice woman and changed my mind."

"Of course you can have secrets. As long as you share them with me. So what's the new girl in town done to offend you?"

"She's not done anything. She's lovely."

Mya mimed biting into a jugular.

I tried distraction. "I was going to ask to see you actually, Mya, so you've saved me the trouble. I'm having a difficult time at the moment processing some thoughts and feelings, and I'd wondered if any of your weird woo woo might be able to help me."

"I can't help you if I don't know what's going on, so can you give me bullet points? I have Death's sexual needs, and wayward souls to take care of. I don't have all day."

She wasn't going to give up, so I gave her the shortened version of recent events.

"Hate Merrin. Don't hate Merrin. Opened up about how my family were gutted by William Letwine to Merrin. Told my bestie, Aria, I loved her. Found out Merrin asked out Charity."

Chantelle arrived at the table with our drinks. "Sorry, did I just hear you say Merrin asked out Charity?"

I put a finger to my lips. "She's not sure whether it was a date or new neighbour thing. Please don't mention it. She's going to see if he seems interested on Sunday at the upcycling event."

"Ooh, I'm going to that. Okay, I won't tell a soul. Do you know, I did a spell on Jason the other night for him to attract his ideal woman and it went awry and might have spread to Merrin. I wonder if Charity is his one? Anyway, enjoy your drinks, and let me know if you need anything else." She walked away as if she hadn't just admitted to a) eavesdropping, and b) casting a spell that had gone wrong and maybe matchmade Merrin and Charity.

"What's this thing on Sunday because everyone seems to be

going to it?" Mya's interest was peaked until I told her she'd have to actually do something.

"Oh God no. That sounds dreary as fuck. I might come hang around though, just in case you decide to drain Charity again. Yes, that's a good idea, I shall come keep you company."

That was two people I was now bringing who weren't going to do anything to help. In fact, quite possibly they'd do the exact opposite. Especially since Aria was Death's ex, a fact usually glossed over to keep Mya's temper from boiling over. I thought I'd better tell her.

"I'll be with Aria. I'm designing something for the baby."

"Ah, yes, the rare pregnancy. I'm so very happy for her and Bernard," Mya declared, and I realised she was. I guessed this confirmed Aria was no longer a threat.

"Death has eyes for no one but you," I said.

"All of his body parts are for me," she declared. "All of them."

"That's... great. So, to get back to our earlier conversation, I'm not intending to drain Charity Feeley. If I keep having an untoward thought, just ignore it."

"I think we'd better do some work around your feelings. Have you heard of journaling? I think it could really help you. It's not a diary, but every day, you let your mind flow out across the page and write out all your thoughts and feelings. It helps get out the things you're keeping trapped deep inside you. Frees the blockages. It's like a colonic irrigation really. The shit comes out and its uncomfortable, but then you're clear and feel less compacted."

I could just see Mya as a holistic guru now, with her stadium tour entitled 'Shit for the Soul'.

But I guessed that in some way, she was right. Getting my feelings down on paper might help.

"I'll give it a whirl. What have I got to lose?" I told her. "Thanks, Mya."

She shrugged.

"So, are you happy here in the fell?" I asked her. "If we're sharing secrets."

"Yes, I truly am," she said. "But my vampire death was different to most."

She moved her hand across the table and laid it across mine. "I was happy enough in life, with my job at the bookstore, but I had no family around me, no real friends. I was lonely. Yet, when your brother was going to drain me, I didn't want to die. Because there's always hope. Hope for better days. And of course, there were books. I'd have happily read all day and all night then."

"I'm getting like that now," I admitted, and she smiled.

She moved her hand back to her glass and took a sip. "Then Death appeared and I'm not going to sugar coat the human experience of being faced with Death and the horrendous pain that comes with the change because you already know it. But I was given a choice. I could have had nothingness on your Field of the Drained. Instead, I chose to be queen and live in Gnarly, and as it turned out, here I have a lovely boyfriend, a lovely home, many friends, and turrets full of books. It's not like your turning, Ginny, where you lost people you loved and became the very thing that destroyed your family in the first place."

"Did you look them up on your app?" I asked. "Is that how you know who I lost?"

"No. I'm a vampire touched by Death. You can't block me from your thoughts if I choose to read them. I've seen it all, Ginny. What you went through was horrendous. There's no wonder you shut down. But admitting you care for your friend. It's the first step on your journey of healing. You can't change the past, but you can enjoy the future, Ginny."

"Mya, thank you. Your words mean a lot."

"It's just a shame you said you loved that woman first. Does everyone love that woman first?" She winked.

I laughed. "Death never loved Aria."

"I know, but my joke wouldn't have worked otherwise, and it brought a smile to your face, didn't it?"

"It did."

"Come on then. Drink up now. Then go home and write out all your feelings. Burn it afterwards if you don't want to leave evidence of it behind. It can be quite cathartic to burn it, especially if you have access to Hell in your basement like I do."

"Your life really changed drastically, didn't it?"

"It did… but then I also started living a dramatic life with a happy ever after, so really, I'm living the dream, just like I used to read about."

Only Mya could be given the job as queen in purgatory, with Heaven in the loft, and Hell in the basement and equate it to a love story.

Her phone beeped.

"Oh, there's a D to sort. Gotta go."

"A D? Oh, you mean a death."

"No, silly. If it was a death I'd say death. I say D because I don't want to say there's a dick to sort at my house out loud."

Heads turned to us.

"See, now everyone knows my business. Oh, by the way. I learned something yesterday. If you pretend to shake a saltshaker on your tongue you can actually taste salt. How weird is that?"

"Really?"

"Yeah, try it. It's amazing."

I pretended that I had a saltshaker in my hand, held it above my tongue and shook it. Nothing happened. No taste of salt. I looked up and Mya wasn't there. but the rest of the bistro patrons were watching me agog and I realised I looked like I was wanking a dick into my mouth.

I'd have killed her if she wasn't already dead.

Back home, I fed, and then sat at my dining table with a pen and a notebook. I tapped the pen against the edge of the table repeatedly.

How to start?

My name is Virginia Bates. I was re-named Virginia Letwine after my murder, but it's not who I am. I am Virginia Bates and I feel responsible for the death of my family.

There, I said it.

My stealing led to William coming into my home and the murder of my mother and brother.

No.

My mum's drinking problem led to my stealing.

No.

I didn't have to steal. That was my choice. The wrong choice. I could have given up my studies. I could have taken an honest paying job.

Yes, I could.

But no, it's NOT my fault.

William Letwine was a cold-blooded killer. He could have threatened my family and I would have done all of his bidding. Instead, he murdered them, for his own entertainment and feeding.

*It was **not** my fault.*

Tears dripped onto the page, spreading to resemble rose petals as I faced the fact that what happened was not my fault. We'd been the victim of an opportunist: a bad man, and an even worse vampire.

I felt lighter somehow, and so I carried on writing.

It is not a bad thing to carry on living (undead). To want happiness. Whether I am sad or happy does not bring back my family. They are lost, but I can find myself.

What do I want? What do I really want?

I want what Aria has. A happy life but one with sparks flying... passion, that's what I crave. I would like to adopt one day. To take in a boy, not as a replacement of my brother, but in honour of him. Or a girl. Someone who has had a traumatic time and needs my help.

I gasped at what I had put on the page. I wanted to be a mother? Maybe it was my friend becoming pregnant that had started this process, these feelings inside me spilling out. But it seemed it was no longer the security of money I craved, but the security of love and family.

Walking over to my fireplace, I tore the paper into shreds, and I set it alight. It took a few goes for the paper to be turned to ash, and then I realised something.

I'd forgotten the apartment had a smoke alarm and sprinklers. The alarm went off and the sprinklers came on, dampening my skin. But they couldn't dampen my mood.

CHAPTER FOURTEEN

Merrin

With everything already set for Sunday, I decided that I'd work on the statue for Aria. The sooner she had it, the sooner she was free of the other vampires making her life a misery.

I brushed it, before cleaning it with a mild detergent and then rinsing it down. It was a hot sunny day and shouldn't take long to dry, after which time I'd carry it to the studio to finish off the rest of the restoration.

Looking around the place, I smiled as I took in the more orderly organisation of furniture, and the pieces earmarked to be upcycled and to leave after Sunday. If I did this regularly, it would definitely re-educate Gnarly on the ethos of re-using and would get me doing more of what I loved. Making things.

I made myself a coffee in my tidy home. It seemed twice as large now everything was away. Even though I wasn't sure where everything was now, as Ginny had put things where she no doubt kept them in her own place, it wasn't taking me too long to work it out, given my place was only small. Yes, it now felt like the kind of home that I could invite someone to, and no longer feel self-conscious.

It wasn't long before the statue was dried and so I moved it into my main studio and began work. I used epoxy putty to make the statue whole again and to sculpt bits that made it look more like Aria. Next, I filled in any hairline cracks, and then finally, I went over the other bits with a little natural yoghurt which would encourage moss growth once it was in the garden. I'd touch up the new areas when it was dried. By tomorrow it would be ready and so I'd decided I would drop it off at the Letwine mansion. I would call ahead and make sure Aria was in. Maybe I could check in on Ginny while I was there? Make sure she was okay after her admissions of last night.

Or maybe I was doing all this because I wanted to see her again?

Jesus, I was fucked in the head. I decided to go back to my house, get something to eat and check my emails to see if any more workshop places had been applied for.

Sure enough, when I clicked into my mail, I had another couple of applications. Miranda from Pizza the Action had applied for a place, and so had Charity. Every single person who had applied was female. I was glad I'd told Jason he had to be there.

I looked at my list of attendees:

Fen (helping) – didn't count

Jason (forced into attending by me) – total 1

Dela, Callie, and Sheridan – grand total 4

Ginny (with Aria who was spectating) – grand total 5

Chantelle from bistro, Mitzi from Saverstore, Milly and Tilly, and Miranda from pizza place – Grand total 10

Charity – 11.

I had one space free and decided to get another mate on board. I rang Nick.

"Hello? Everything okay, Merrin?"

"Yeah, all good thanks. I just wondered if I could get you along to my event on Sunday as there's a lack of male participants. I only have Jason."

"You need male participants at your workshop because Jason doesn't count as one?"

"I didn't say—"

"What? I have a huge fucking cock I'll have you know. Apologies actually for the expletive there, Connor, and it's true it's huge but it doesn't actually... you know what. I'll be quiet," I heard Jason mutter in the background, through Nick's laughter.

"Just messing with you, Jase. Merrin's trying to get me to go as well because it's all women. I can't think why..."

"What are you talking about?" I said. I'd only called to try to get him along, not to have some extended confusing conversation.

"Do you think it might be all women because they've noticed that underneath the Neil from the Young Ones look there's actually a hottie?" Nick asked.

"Don't be silly. Most of the people coming are loved up."

"Loved up, not visually challenged. You have my permission to get Dela fired up on Sunday, mate, like you do a ceramic in the kiln. It's all good because it's me she'll come home to for the final touches."

I was beginning to feel more like the usual me: awkward and uncomfortable.

"Leave the poor guy alone," I heard Connor's voice, who was the head chef at Smokin' Hot. "Just answer his bloody question."

"You'll have to count me out, Merrin. You're a good mate who I'd do almost anything for, but I say almost because you'll be with my girlfriend, her sister, and her mother, and no thank you. They don't come up for air when they're all together, and Sheridan keeps hinting about how Callie is married and she missed that wedding, and how she hopes she won't miss Dela's."

"And you don't want to propose?" I asked.

"Me and Dela already know what's happening in that regard. One day she'll wear my ring, but right now we just officially moved in together. It's only been six months. I'd like to save up so I can give her the wedding of her dreams. While she's out Sunday, I can take on some extra work and put the additional wages away in my savings account."

"Fair enough."

"Tell him I'll come. I'll get my deputy to cover the kitchen for the lunch shift," Connor said. "I'm available for all single women, and what the hell, married ones too if they're willing."

The sound of a phone clattering to the counter almost perforated my eardrum and I heard, "I'm joking, you muppet. You've got to be able to take it not just dish it, you know? I've lost a button on my shirt now."

I heard someone mumbling but couldn't make out their voice.

"Sorry about that," Nick said having picked the phone back up.

"Did you just face off with Connor over his comment? As if Dela would look at him, when she's madly in love with you."

"No, it wasn't me, it was Lawrie. Dumbo, with his large ears heard what Connor had said from outside. Anyway, you've another potential attendee now as he says Callie is not going without him."

"So why is that potential? Isn't that a definite?"

"I think Callie might have something to say about him being all caveman and not trusting her."

This was all starting to hurt my head.

"Tell Connor I'll see him on Sunday, and congrats to you on moving in with Dela, although to be honest you've kind of lived there ever since she moved in."

"Yeah, but it's official now. I'm growing up, which is more than can be said for Jason, who right now is begging Lawrie to take him for a ride around the fell."

I lowered my voice, although why I didn't know given that Jase was no longer near the phone.

"Something that's always puzzled me. I thought dragons could fly? I've seen him change, but never fly. I just thought of that."

"Dunno. Maybe it's connected to his other performance-related issues?" Nick laughed.

"Okay, with that comment and thought put in my head, I'm going to end the call now," I told him.

We said goodbye and I did just that.

I stretched and smiled. My first workshop was full, and any further applicants would be offered a place on the next.

I made myself another drink, and thought of what they'd said, that some women might be coming just because they now thought I was attractive. Was that why Charity had applied? I'd been shilly-shallying about getting brave enough to ask her out, and then Ginny had sent me into a dither. Now I wasn't sure what I wanted to do. Maybe staying single and growing my hair back long was the way to go? Life seemed a lot less complicated then.

And it was a lot less fun, I thought.

I'd see them both Sunday and I might see Ginny tomorrow. It would give me some time to work out if I *liked* them, liked them, and if I could be bothered with all the baggage that came with dating: getting jealous, and people putting pressure on you to get married or have kids. Jesus, I just wanted some nice conversation over dinner and then maybe a shag to end the evening, or at least a really good kiss goodbye.

My mind felt overloaded with everything and so I went and sat on a hand-made bench that looked out over the field. Slowly sipping my drink, I concentrated on emptying my thoughts, and making space in my brain.

And then it all whooshed in. In my vision I saw a plume of black smoke and heard crying. A voice said, 'We mourn the passing of Josiah'. Another voice said, 'We must find the heir'. I saw more flames but as my own sight returned and the 'knowing' faded away, I was perplexed. Because I had no idea about any of what I'd just seen. Not one clue as to the people involved. All I could do was wait until more was revealed to me. In the meantime, I would feel like I was wearing a layer of invisible dirt, giving me the ick with no one else aware of it.

The following day, I woke early, hit the shower and dressed in a smart red t-shirt, and the pair of jeans I felt showed off my bum best. Not that I was trying to impress anyone. I simply wished to deliver this statue and do a good deed for the day.

I'd called the Letwine mansion and they'd put me through to Aria's suite. She'd been delighted when I'd told her the statue was ready early and I could bring it today. After saying she needed to talk to Edmond and call me back, we eventually arranged that I would bring it at two pm and it would immediately be placed in a corner of the Letwine gardens.

I placed the carefully wrapped statue in the back of the van and set off for Chelsea.

Aria greeted me at the entrance and hopping into the passenger side, directed me to park the car at the furthest edge of the driveway.

"We agreed we would put the statue over there, just outside the rear entrance of the grounds. Then no one will be spoiling our lawns as they trample to molest the fake me." Aria sighed.

"Oh, congratulations," I said, suddenly reminded of what had brought this situation about in the first place. "Maybe you'll actually get to enjoy being pregnant now?"

"I hope so. I know how lucky Bernard and I are to be in this position. But the pregnancy is making me feel ill and worrying that someone might harm our baby in order to try to get pregnant themselves... it's an additional worry." Aria visibly swallowed and then gave me a nervous smile.

I placed my arm on hers and as I did another knowing came over me. Aria, with a babe in her arms, and then I caught sight of Bernard in my vision too.

"Aria, all will be well. More than well. And the babies will both be absolutely fine," I told her.

She stared at me, her eyes wide. "B-babies? Pl-plural?" Her voice trembled and tears came to her eyes. It was a little off-putting that they were crimson, and as she threw her arms around me to hug me, I realised that a red t-shirt had definitely been the right choice.

"Ah, now the reason for her pregnancy is revealed. She has been unfaithful with a zombie," a spite-filled, female voice declared loudly, and Aria stepped back. We found ourselves surrounded by around twenty female vampires.

"I can see why though. He is fine, is he not?" said one of the others. "Maybe this is the way forward for us all? We change to more modern times, like those who use other people's donations in the human world. We could use zombie sperm?"

"I'd like it fresh from the source," said yet another and the vampire women began closing in on me.

It was only slightly less frightening than being trapped underground. I looked helplessly at Aria as the women closed ranks on us.

CHAPTER FIFTEEN

Ginny

After my sleep, I'd felt much more settled, and almost... excited even. Like I was ready for a fresh chapter in my life. I'd had both good and bad times while at the Letwine Mansion and the thought of being able to have my own place in Gnarly, and to start again, gave me hope. I realised that as a vampire some of the older ones might have had this fresh start over and over with their eternal life. Time was so different when it was of no consequence. Things like humans waiting for a certain amount of time before getting married or putting out meant nothing when a sharp piece of wood could take you out at a moment's notice.

What humans didn't realise was that life carried its own potential sharp pieces of wood and they lived denying this to themselves, not seizing the moments, when they should live every day like their last. I'd sacrificed so much for my mother and brother and although I'd do it all over again, the fact was it hadn't benefited any of us in the end.

But it was coming up on being fifty years since my turning and it was time to make peace with what had happened. I'd put myself through further torture mentally for long enough, and now it was time to try for happiness in my vampire life. Oh, I'd had some good times, mainly because of people like Aria, but I'd never allowed myself to be blissfully happy. Felt that it would be wrong after what had befallen my family.

Later that morning my phone rang. Aria. I immediately panicked.

"Is the baby all right?"

"Everything's fine. I just wanted to let you know that Merrin is calling around today. He finished my statue early and thought I'd benefit from having it here as soon as possible."

"So why are you telling me? What do I care if Merrin is coming? What are you trying to insinuate?" My words rushed out in a major protestation while in my head I was wondering what to wear.

"Calm down. You arranged this, didn't you? So I'm just letting you know that it's coming today. You don't have to see him, though you're seeing him tomorrow anyway, so I don't know what you're being weird about." She paused. "Oh. I do know what you're being weird about. Someone's caught feelings."

"I have not!"

"Such defensiveness. Are you sure you've told me *everything* about when you were at Merrin's?"

"I'm hanging up now."

"He'll be here at two pm, and the unveiling of the statue will be at three pm. What you choose to do with that information is up to you."

"I'll be there for the unveiling because it's you."

She laughed and ended the call.

And damn it, I went to check my hair and get changed, but only because I wanted to support my friend you understand. No other reason. Oh that and this transference thing. Considering my mental issue, I called the resident psychiatrist at the mansion and made an appointment for Monday morning.

"Virginia! How goes it?" boomed Edmond from behind me, making me jump a foot in the air. I spun around.

"I'm okay, thank you," I replied politely, while being not at all okay because if I had a beating heart it would have been thumping in my chest with nerves. What was happening to me?

"How is the new job going?"

"Really well," I said truthfully, smiling widely as I thought of the bookstore. "I love the place and also I've a new found enjoyment of reading."

"Mya said she'd seen you and spoken with you about journaling. I do find that helpful myself, I have to say."

The thought of the main vampire elder who could be the deadliest vampire known to man journaling, almost had me burst into a fit of giggles, but I didn't allow them outward. Edmond could read my mind anyway if he so wished, but he usually didn't bother. He said after all these years he found most vampire minds dull.

"I did some last night and I do believe it really helped."

"Good, good. I have to say, Ginny, that your disposition seems altogether brighter and you appear more settled than I've seen you in a long time. Keep up the good work."

"Thank you."

"Are you off to meet Aria?"

"Yes, she said the statue is being erected and so I thought I'd see if she needed any help or advice on positioning."

"That's where I'm headed myself so we can walk there together."

I nodded, but once we were through the entrance of the mansion and we saw the crowd and heard them, we flew with speed down to the ruckus.

As I got there, I realised it wasn't the statue that the vampire women wanted erect and in position. It was Merrin.

"GET AWAY FROM HIM," I yelled like a possessed spirit, my eyes burning like fire, and my fangs descending. I flew into the circle and tossed every single vampire besides Aria out of the way. They landed in a huge pile, but all I did was turn towards them and hiss, before Edmond took over. There was going to be serious ructions from our elder. I dropped to my knees so that I could get myself calmed down.

"Ginny, thank God," Aria said.

I held up a hand. "Gimme a sec?" I asked, and I listened to Edmond whose voice bellowed around the grounds.

"Our distinguished guest brings us a statue that we can worship because of Aria's blessed situation and I find you encircling him like he is bait? You." He pointed to one of them. "Explain yourself."

"It was Kelly's fault. She said Aria was pregnant to the zombie and so then we all wanted him."

I wouldn't want to be Kelly right now, knowing how Edmond's eyes would have fixed on her at that moment.

"Aria is pregnant to her husband, Bernard, and any more such fabrications from yourself will lead to your trial in the vampire court. Do you understand? Such rumours fuel dangerous reactions. What would have happened today had I not arrived with Virginia? Would you have taken this man without his consent? Every one of you shall attend vampire lessons run by the breedents and shall revise the do's and don'ts of our clan. We do not attack generous visitors. Not without my permission in extenuating circumstances anyway. Now scram before I stake every damn one of you."

They flew off at speed, and Edmond came back to us.

"Your protection of the zombie was something to be admired, Virginia."

"I was worried for my friend," I said. My eyes caught Merrin's and I thought I saw his own dull.

Then I caught Aria's and she put a hand on her hip and shook her head from side to side.

Edmond frowned at Merrin in concern. "Are you okay, Merrin? I would understand if you'd like to leave. Please know that what you have done for us has us in your debt within reason. If at any point you need my help, I will give you my direct number."

"I'm sure that won't be necessary, but thank you," Merrin told him. "It's my absolute pleasure to be able to help Aria have a safe pregnancy, and I *know* she will do now."

My head shot back to Aria, who mouthed, "Later," at me. It seemed Merrin had had one of his weird fortune-telling moments, but if it meant he knew my friend would safely deliver her baby, I was ecstatic.

Edmond helped Merrin to take the statue out of the van and then we watched as he carefully unwrapped it. I'd seen how it had looked before and I gasped when I saw the changes that had made it look like Aria.

"That's perfection," I stated.

"Oh, Merrin, you are beyond talented," Aria said.

Bernard arrived at that point, making a quip about whether he could keep the statue version of his wife as it would be quiet, and put Aria in the garden. Aria filled him in on all the happenings so far and then excused the two of them for a moment, saying she'd be back. Edmond excused himself to go in search of the vampires needed to erect the statue, which left me with Merrin.

And an awkward silence.

"So..." I said.

"So..." he replied.

My phone beeped, interrupting the silence.

I stared at the text in surprise.

Rupert: I wondered if you'd like to have dinner again sometime?

"Is everything okay?" Merrin asked me.

"I'm just a bit bewildered. This guy has asked me if I want to have dinner with him and we had one of the worst dates ever. I don't understand."

"Wh-what was so awful about it?" Merrin enquired.

"Shall we sit?" I gestured to a stone bench.

He nodded and we walked over and dropped down onto it.

"He was an artist, and I'll be honest, I thought he was rich and that's why I'd agreed to date him. I know you understand where all that comes from now, but still, I do feel bad about that. He was really dejected when he realised I wasn't that interested in him as a person."

"So what are you going to do?" Merrin asked me, not maintaining eye contact.

I waited until he did look at me. "What's your advice? What would you do? I mean I didn't give him a fair chance at a date. Didn't appreciate that a starving artist could be a decent date." Oh my god, I no longer believed I was talking about Rupert. If Merrin liked me, now was the time for him to speak.

"Only you can decide whether or not to date him, Ginny. It's none of my business. Just don't use anyone again, it's not kind."

"Yeah, I know. I heard you asked Charity out?" I blurted.

Merrin cleared his throat. "Oh, er, yeah."

"That's good."

"It is?"

"Yeah, she seems really nice. Although she told me she wasn't sure if you were asking her out on a date, or as a welcome to the fell thing."

"Yeah, I botched it a little. Chickened out. I had meant to ask her on a date."

"So..." I said.

"So..." Merrin replied.

"We both might have dates then?" I finished.

"Yeah, seems so," he replied.

There was another awkward pause and then Aria and Bernard returned beaming.

"I can tell you now," she said coming towards me. "Merrin let me know that we're expecting twins. I've booked to have a scan, but given he knew I'd be pregnant before I did, we believe him."

Thoughts of my awkward conversation with Merrin were forgotten as I hugged my friend and gave my congratulations to her and Bernard once more.

"Merrin, I cannot thank you enough," Bernard said. "Given the news of the multiple pregnancy, this idiocy from the other vampires would have worsened considerably. Now, because of you, they will instead gather around the statue. If you ever wish for me to drain someone, just let me know and I shall be at your service."

I thought I heard a whisper of the word 'Rupert', but as I turned to find Merrin now busy telling the vampire men who'd arrived with Edmond on how to carefully handle the statue, I decided it must have been my imagination.

And wishful thinking, that annoying inner voice added.

CHAPTER SIXTEEN

Merrin

Rupert had asked Ginny out again? After everything he'd said to me about how she'd ruined his life. How dark and dismal all had become. I wanted to call him to ask what the fuck he was playing at, but it wasn't my business who Ginny dated.

No, because I'd already asked out Charity, who was waiting for me to name the date and time. One-night stands had been much easier. Dating fucked up your head before you even went out on the date itself.

After watching the unveiling of the statue, I was pleased to see that they'd had it blessed by one of the ancient vampires, a breedent, and she had declared it only had to be gazed upon for luck. Radaya also reminded everyone that all vampire births were still a rare thing and no amount of 'lucky charms' would make a pregnancy happen. She was very brutal in her delivery of the facts, and I reckoned that after a month, no one would bother with the statue any longer and everything would return to normal. As normal as vampire life was, that is.

"Thanks once again." Edmond shook my hand. "I'll escort you safely out of the premises after what happened earlier."

"Oh, yes, okay." I said goodbye to the others and with one last look at Ginny to whom I said, "See you tomorrow," Edmond escorted me to my van and I was on my way home.

I woke to a beautiful day. Neither too hot nor too cool. Goldilocks would have declared it just right for the workshop. Fenella and Jason arrived and we placed all the refreshments in my kitchen for Fen to bring out during the class. Jason and I moved his choice of furniture, a bedframe, into position on the yard.

"My mum's moving in with Stan now that Nick has officially moved out," Jase explained. I'd really like to be able to find a new place of my own but helping in the laundrette doesn't pay much and so for now, mum's letting me stay in the house. She's giving me a little time to sort myself out. Says it'll be good for me, the independence. So I'm going to redecorate the main room, and do this bedframe up, get a mattress for it and then hopefully I—"

"Can sleep in the most blissful comfort," I said, widening my eyes and trying an imperceptible nod of the head, trying to warn him off finishing his sentence.

"No, I can make a shag pad." Jase looked at me like I was stupid, until the penny dropped.

"My mum's behind me, isn't she?"

"She is," Fenella said, "but you sow as many oats as you need to in order to find the one for you, son. I mean look at me—"

Jason put a hand over his ears, "Lalalalalalala."

Fen rolled her eyes. "I was only going to tell him I'd re-found love at my age, not anything inappropriate," she said to me. "I really shouldn't have spoiled him; he's grown up clueless. I do hope there's someone out there who'll actually put up with him."

She slapped him upside the head.

"Ow, that hurt."

"Stop being such a baby and get helping your friend. The others will be here soon. I'm going to fix myself a drink, you want anything?"

We both said no and Fen headed off back to my house.

"Please tell me you've not designed a bedframe that's red or has handcuffs on it?" I asked my friend.

"Of course not," he said, then he went in his pocket and I heard him scrunch up a piece of paper.

"I don't know much about women myself, Jason, but we shall get you dating and… mating," I said.

"I'm only part-shifter, so I don't know if I will mate for life," he mused. "It's doubtful given I don't fly or even blow out fire. I can change to a dragon, but then I just change back. I'm entirely bloody useless," he said.

I patted him on the back. "I don't have much other than my friends and my art. No significant others. You have your very loving mum. You'll get there and so will I. We have to believe. Look how many of Gnarly are now loved up. Our time will come, okay? Deal?" I held up a hand to high five and Jason met it.

"Deal. So how would you suggest I upcycle my bedframe?" he asked.

All attendees had arrived and chosen a piece of furniture. Jason had been helping me move the pieces until Ginny arrived, at which point she and Mya took over. Mya was an unexpected attendee, who then got cross at Ginny for not telling me she was coming.

"If I do this again let's just say I'm your assistant okay, so that I don't have two hangers on, neither of whom intend to help with the upcycling at all," Ginny said to me as we moved her choice, a blanket box, to her place in the yard. Of course there was no 'we' about it. I was standing back watching while Ginny re-jigged furniture around.

"Fine with me. Why are they here anyway?" I asked.

"They're both nosy and didn't want to miss out. But I'll give it thirty minutes tops before Mya finds an excuse to leave unless something exciting happens. Aria will boss me around, because I'm making this box for the nursery, so she'll stay until the end. Also, she's enjoying a break from Bernard's fussing. She's given him the job of emptying out the guest room in their suite and painting the room cream." She paused. "Do you know what they're having?"

I shook my head. "No. I saw two babies, but both were in cream rompers."

"That's good because she's hoping to keep that a surprise for their births."

Ginny's expression dulled and she looked a little upset. I closed the space between us and placed a hand on her arm. "Are you okay? You seem a little down." I noted there was no frisson between us this time when I touched her.

She shrugged. "It's all the changes, I guess. Aria's not going to want me bothering her when she has two babies to take care of, is she?"

"You don't know that. She might need you more than ever."

"No. She'll need her husband more than ever, and I don't want to get in the way of that. Their little family. Such a precious thing. I'm glad I have the job at the bookstore now because that's become important to me. Is it selfish to hope that she doesn't want to return, so I can stay?"

An image came into my mind, and I moved to lean against the wall.

"Merrin, are you okay?" Ginny's face was close to mine as she peered at me. The tables had quickly turned and now *she* was worrying about *me*.

"Fine, and able to tell you that you will indeed work at the shop for a long time to come."

My head was scrambled and not just from receiving such a vivid image.

"How do you know?" she asked.

"Because I just had a knowing and you were wearing a wedding ring as you served a customer," I replied.

Ginny froze. "A w-wedding ring? Are you sure?"

"Positive. I saw you hand over a book to Charity, and it was clearly there."

"So, did you see who I was married to?"

"I'm afraid not."

She placed her hands on my arms. "If I touch you, can you try to do your weird mojo. I want to know who the groom is."

I struggled but managed to get her to loosen her grip. "It doesn't work like that. I only get brief glimpses of things. It might be months before I get anything else."

"That is so annoying," she said.

"Hey, you're married. Hopefully happily, *and* you work at the store. Most people would be ecstatic to learn that."

"I'm not most people. Like, I was going to tell this Rupert guy no, but now I feel I have to go on the date because it could be him, right? He could be my future husband." She pulled her phone out of her bag and called him right there and then.

"Rupert? It's Virginia. Hello. Yes, what about tonight? I can meet you at *Fauna* at nine. Okay, bye."

Before my brain had chance to catch up to my body, I'd grabbed her chin and tilted her face up to mine. Now sparks were back, flying up my spine, and I saw her tremble under my touch. "Ginny, don't rush this. Don't predict your future husband is Rupert. Please go on this date with your eyes wide open because it might *not* be him."

Our gazes held a little too long, and then I went for it. I leaned closer.

"Is there a problem, only we're all waiting to start?" Charity's voice had me dropping my hand.

"It's my fault. I couldn't decide on what piece of furniture I wanted," Ginny said quickly, putting distance between us. "I don't want to get it wrong, but I currently seem to be caught between two different pieces because Merrin's confusing me about which are actually available to consider." As she looked at me, Ginny's hidden message was clear.

"That's because until a moment ago I didn't really know how much I liked one piece of furniture myself. I've also had two pieces to choose from, and don't want to make the wrong choice."

"Merrin, you're trying to get rid of furniture. That's what this whole day is about, so you need to let Ginny decide. Let her try one piece and if she doesn't like it, then let her try the other," Charity advised.

"Sounds like a wise decision," Ginny answered.

"There we go, problem solved," Charity announced. "So come on, because I can't wait to get started on my new wardrobe. Although Jase has been hiding in it and making me jump while we've been waiting. He's such a riot."

"Okay, we're on our way," I told her. When she'd gone, I turned to Ginny.

"There we go then. You go on your date," I said. But I couldn't hide how pissed off I was that she'd arranged a date with Rupert. I stalked off and spent the rest of the session immersed in the reason I'd set the event up in the first place. Helping everyone to upcycle.

The day was a huge success and one thing I'd noticed was that Charity and Jason were getting on like a house on fire. So much so that as I said goodbye to her, she asked me if it was okay if she went on a date with him.

"Yes, that's absolutely fine. I'd only suggested us going out as a 'welcome to the village' kind of thing," I lied.

"I thought so," she said. "Otherwise I figured you'd have called me by now. That's great then. Thanks for today, Merrin. It's been incredible. I've had such a good time doing up the furniture and hanging around with everyone. And I'm leaving with a new wardrobe and a date too. Who'd have thought it?"

We'd decided all the furniture once dry would be sent via the portal in my studio straight to the client's home, so there was no need to arrange vans or delivery. Only the Letwine mansion was without a portal and Ginny was strong enough to be able to whizz back there carrying her piece.

The best news was everyone who'd attended today had signed up to do another project in two weeks' time. I made a mental note to collect extra shiny things for Mitzi to stick on her upcycles.

Fenella and Jason were the last to leave. Jason gave me a high five for a great day and went off to start the car. Fen hung back.

"You're not too disappointed that Jason and Charity seemed to hit it off, are you?" she enquired. He didn't know you'd kind of asked her out."

"I made it clear to Charity that I asked her as a friend," I said.

"I think that was wise, given your heart is clearly with another."

I stilled.

"For two people who hated each other, it sure does look a lot like love to my eyes. But then again, my eyes are old. Though since Stan came into my life, I feel years younger." She gazed into the distance for a while, before refocusing and looking back at me. "The trouble with Joe turned me off love for a long time. Silly really how much we let the past get in the way of the future."

"Ginny's on a date with another man tonight, so I think the jury's out on her feelings for me," I said in a surly and jealous tone.

"Then you've no one to blame but yourself. Why didn't you tell her to cancel the date and take her out, you dufus?"

I looked at my feet.

"Stan liked me for years. I liked him for years. Wasted time. Don't make the same mistakes we did, Merrin, okay?"

"Come on, Mum," yelled Jason. "I'm going out."

Fenella patted my arm. "I'm always here for you, Merrin. You might think you have no family, but my home is always open to you."

She walked away and as she almost went out of earshot, I shouted, "Fen, thank you."

She turned back, smiled, and made her way over to Jason.

Left alone, I stared out over the now bared piece of land where the workshop had taken place. I'd spent so long on my own and yet today had been so much fun. I could do a lot more if I put my mind to it. Maybe do some jewellery classes using recycled glass etc. I made a note to definitely attend the next council meeting, and have it put on the agenda to make a few changes to the space, and to talk with Milly and Tilly about how we might work together more cohesively.

For a guy who only a week ago went out occasionally with his friends, but largely lived a reclusive existence, I was now enjoying company and there was romantic potential.

If the woman didn't fall in love with another guy tonight that was.

But I wasn't the kind of man who went all Neanderthal and demanded a person was mine.

I was a man who needed to know I was wanted... for me. For my grumpiness, my need to sometimes be alone, my fears about dark spaces.

Tonight, I would sit in my house in the quiet and let my thoughts wander so that I could fully explore how I felt about Virginia Letwine.

And I'd see what tomorrow brought.

CHAPTER SEVENTEEN

Ginny

"So what did you think about Merrin's land then?" I asked Aria, as we appeared back in the grounds of the mansion having whizzed there, although I now felt incredibly guilty about the fact I'd ever had the idea to move onto his patch. For anyone who really 'saw' Merrin, it was clear that he needed his space, literally and figuratively. And now I'd royally pissed him off, if his ignoring of me for the rest of the workshop was any indication. I'd just watched and listened to his instructions of the techniques he'd used on Fen's bureau and applied them to the blanket box, ending up with a shabby chic effect in cream that Aria said would look perfect in the nursery, although I seriously doubted anything made of wood would make it into the babies' room. I'd refrained from painting bunnies on it and so she could put it anywhere.

"I've decided I actually prefer the mansion," Aria replied. "Now that it appears things are calming down on the fang-girl front." She paused. "That's what I'm calling them because they're fangirls, but they have fangs. It was Mya's idea. Anyway, I wouldn't feel safe out here without Edmond close by. I know you threw them off, but when I saw his command of the fang-girls, it made me remember why Bernard and I lived there in the first place. The security of our leader. Plus, he's told us we can expand into the suite next door, now there are going to be two babies. Dominique and Alfred are moving on and going to Canada apparently. They're bored of Chelsea."

Aria and Mya had spent most of the time during the workshop chatting away like old friends. I wouldn't have believed it, had I not seen it with my own eyes. They had a mutual love of books and Mya was 'so happy' about Aria's pregnancy.

"Are you cross?" she asked me.

"No, I'm really not. I'm going to ask for a place on the waiting list for Gnarly, because I do want to be there. I want to be near Lawrie and Dela and the bookstore."

"Is that all you want to be near?"

"I'm not having this conversation with you. I'm saving it for my psychiatrist tomorrow," I told her.

Aria cackled with laughter.

"You can't help who you fall in love with. I ended up with a fool who believes he's French because he was turned there."

"I'm not in love with Merrin. It's transference."

"It's what?"

"Transference. When he chatted with me after I had my 'episode', well, that's when I started to catch feelings for him. Clearly, it's a therapist/patient type situation. Anyhow, tonight I'm out on a date with a guy called Rupert, who could be my one, because Merrin saw me in one of his knowings and I was wearing a wedding ring."

"Shut the front door! A wedding ring! Rupert? Isn't that the artist who declared you'd ruined his life as you'd ruined his ability to paint anything joyful?"

"Erm... yeah..."

"And you're going on a date with him. Why?"

"In case he's my future husband."

"God, you are stupid. Which do you think is more likely to be your potential future husband? The guy you went on a shit date with and who was rude to you about it, or the guy you admit you might have caught feelings for?"

I let out a long, drawn-out sigh, which was all for dramatic effect since I didn't need to breathe.

I picked up my phone. "Hey, Rupert. I can't make it tonight after all."

"But, but... I need to see you," he protested.

"I'm sorry but I changed my mind. Things didn't work out last time. I don't know what I was thinking saying yes. It would be a mistake. You said yourself that I made you miserable."

"Yes, yes. Exactly. And I created the most desperately black, morose art and it sold for so much money. And then I met someone else, and I was happy, and my art went back to normal. Now the critics are slagging off my work and wondering where my 'edge' went."

I huffed. "So you didn't actually want to date me? You wanted to use me?"

"Yes, like you used me."

I thought about what he was saying. He was right. I couldn't be annoyed with him, because I'd set out to use him. Why shouldn't he use me right back?

"Fair enough. I will come and meet you tonight," I said, as Aria looked at me in horror after hearing all the conversation easily. You couldn't really do privacy with a vamp. "But know I shall take you to the depths of your fears and it's a one-time only deal."

"Okay, fine."

I took his address as there was no need for an actual date now. It wouldn't take me long to use compulsion on him to give him inspiration and then take myself forever from his mind.

"I owed him," I told Aria, at which time we reached the entrance of the mansion and parted company.

The deed was done. I'd made Rupert recall everything that had made him morose the first time around but informed his mind he only felt this way when painting. I didn't want his new girlfriend suddenly dealing with a misery guts. Then I'd taken myself out of his mind, so that he'd never contact me again.

After a night spent pacing the apartment and eventually managing to distract myself with a good book, I arrived at Dr Milton's office at eleven am sharp. I booked in at the reception and then waited until I was buzzed through.

"Good morning, Virginia," Dr Milton said. "I have to say I was pleasantly surprised when I saw your name. Have you come to address your anger issues?"

"No, I fucking have not, you rude cretin," I snapped.

Dr Milton sighed and took a seat.

I slouched further into my seat. This wasn't a great start. "My apologies for my little outburst. I'm just very delicate about people calling me on my temper when it mostly arises when other people are being stupid."

He raised a brow. "Wow. A sort of apology. That is progress."

"I'd like to apologise again for insinuating you might have been being stupid. I didn't mean you. I meant that I last lost my temper in the bar because Cuthbert approached me and said he'd be my pimp. Yet, *I lost my job*, and my guess is he's still drinking at the bar as if he never did a thing wrong."

"You mean you didn't hear?"

"Hear what?"

"Cuthbert arrived home one evening this week in a state. He'd been drained to the point of weakness and then dropped off at a dominatrix's house who'd been given a large amount of money and told he loved anal play, the bigger the better."

I snorted. "Really?"

"Yes. He's fine now physically, as of course he just needed a feed, but mentally... I don't think he's going to be offering to pimp for anyone for a long while," Dr Milton said.

"Do we know who did it? I can't be the only woman he was sleazing around on. Only I feel I need to high five them."

"I'm afraid I can't divulge the name of the person due to patient confidentiality, you understand. But, to *think* of *anyone* who would be *capable* of carrying out such a heinous act on a clan *brother*."

I smirked as I decoded his sentence. My brother had got revenge for me, the superstar.

"I appreciate your position in not being able to disclose the information. It's probably against some *law*... right?

"Indeed. I'm glad you understand that it's the *law*," he said.

My brother was my hero.

"So, what is it I can actually do for you then, Virginia, if it's not to deal with your temper? Have a think about booking in for that though."

I glared at him.

"No pressure."

"Dr Milton, please call me Ginny. And basically, I'm having issues of transference. You know where a patient falls for their doctor?"

"Oh, gosh. Well, erm, I-I'm flattered, b-but..."

"Not you, you dipshit."

"Phew," Dr Milton said with relief. "I actually welcomed that insult."

I explained about how I'd hated Merrin. How I'd then ended up going into my background of when I was turned, and how since then I had found myself thinking of Merrin in a romantic way.

"So you see, I clearly have issues," I declared.

Dr Milton clamped his lips together.

"Are you desperately trying not to say something sarcastic?"

"Mmm-hmmm."

I rolled my eyes. "Okay, I may have a little..." I separated two of my fingers by a centimetre's width. "... issue with my temper occasionally, but I must ask you to concentrate on the reason I came to see you today. My transference issue."

"Okay. I'm going to say some things to you, and I want you to come back with a one-word answer for each one. The first thing that comes into your mind. That's how we're going to get to the bottom of this. Don't question why. I just need you to go with the process. Okay?"

"You're the doc."

"Ready?"

"Yup."

"Aria," he said.

"Bestie," I replied.

"Blood."

"Food."

"Books."

"Escapism."

"Very good," he said. "Gnarly?"

"Homely." I placed a hand over my mouth. I really did see it as a place I could settle. I knew what was coming. He was going to say

Merrin and I genuinely didn't know what my first thought would be.

"Stop over-thinking this, Ginny."

I dropped my hand back onto my knee. "Okay."

"Cuthbert."

"Arsehole." I sniggered. "I meant in his attitude, but with what I just heard, it's an even better name for him."

Dr Milton smiled.

"Charity."

"Bitch." Again, my hand came to my mouth. "Oh my god. She's not a bitch. She's really nice, but..."

"But...?"

"One word answer?" I queried.

"It's entirely up to you this time."

"Competition," I voiced. "Merrin likes her. He's going to ask her on a date."

"But how does that matter if this is just transference, and you don't really have feelings for him?"

"Err."

"Back to our one-word answers. Fish."

"Chips."

"Ball."

"Chain."

"Black."

"White."

"Merrin."

"Mine." I threw my handbag across the room. "I fucking hate this game. Look what you made me do," I yelled. "You've made me confess that I like Merrin, the bloody zombie I told everyone I hated. You're so bloody... gaaaahhhh."

"Good at my job?" Dr Milton said, following it up with a smirk. He began typing into his computer. "Issue investigated. Patient does not have issues of transference, she just *likes a boy*," he said in a piss-taking voice.

"I'm out of here." I picked up my bag and dashed for the door.

"Oh, Ginny?"

"What? What do you want now? My blood?"

"Your phone fell out. It's still in the corner."

I stomped over to pick it up.

"Do feel free to book in about those anger issues anytime," he added.

I gave him my middle finger as a reply as I exited his office.

CHAPTER EIGHTEEN

Ginny

I remained in a mood while I got ready for work, having arranged to go in after lunch. What a mess. I'd fallen for the person I said I hated, which was going to make me look like an idiot, and my crush not only thought I'd gone out with another man last night, but he was going out with another woman.

At work I said hello as cheerily as I could manage, (ie through gritted teeth) to Callie and Dela and stayed behind my desk, not putting any books out on display as I was scared I might slam them onto the bookshelves, and that just wouldn't do.

"What's going on?" Dela said, having walked over to my side of the shop during a lull.

"Nothing."

"Then why are you scaring the customers away with your face?"

"It would appear I am in love," I announced, to which Dela almost swallowed her own tongue.

"This is what you look like when you're in love? Are you sure there's not something else, like a bee stinging your butthole?"

"This, Dela, is the look you wear when you realise that the person you declared a total loser is the object of your affections," I announced.

Callie walked over.

"I suppose you want to know why I look like this as well?" I sighed. "I'm sorry for the lack of bookstore customers due to my lovesuck expression."

"Don't you mean lovesick?" Dela queried.

"No, I mean love...suck. It sucks. I don't want to like Merrin. I want to go back to when I thought he was an unwashed moron."

"Why?"

"Because it's just so stupid. That's why."

"I'd not come over to ask you," Callie said, "because I've worn that exact look on my own face, remember? I hated Lawrie. Hated him with a passion. Until I realised that he wasn't the person I thought he was, and that's what's happened with you, that's all. We told you he was a nice guy and now you've found out for yourself."

"But I feel ridiculous after all the fuss I made about him being so horrible."

"Every one of us has felt stupid at some point. I failed to believe Nick was the son of Father Christmas. I thought Santa was Satan," Dela said.

We all laughed.

"So what are you going to do, now you've realised your feelings for him?" Callie asked.

I shrugged. "I don't know yet."

At that point Lawrie appeared and I speeded over to where he was and flung my arms around him.

"Thank you. Thank you. Thank you," I said, snuggling my face into his neck.

"What is happening?" Lawrie said, while standing like a statue. "Callie, please help me. I'm out of my depth here. My sister has thanked me and is snuggling me. Could you get Dr Milton on the phone. Meanwhile no sudden movements."

"Your sister has discovered her feelings, just like you did. She's in love."

Lawrie pushed me out to arm's length.

"With whom?" he asked, his fangs descending.

"Can I just finish my 'thank you', before you get all brooding big brother on my behalf? I worked out that you saw to Cuthbert and delivered him a fitting punishment. In fact, actually, an extra-large one. I'm extremely grateful." I swallowed. "The thing is, Lawrie, that as you know, I lost my little brother when I was sired and it's affected me, a lot. But we are related by blood in a way too because we were both sired by William and so his blood went into us during our changes. You are my big brother and I love you. I need you to know that. Thank you for looking out for me."

Lawrie smiled, showing his teeth had returned to normal, and he enveloped me in a hug. "You're my very best sister ever, and I love you too, and that's not only because I had no other sisters. Welcome to your new feelings. You can now be less bad tempered too, so it's a win for us all."

The door opened and Charity walked through. I hissed under my breath. Lawrie looked at me, the only one capable of hearing it, and he said, "Interesting. Seems I spoke a little hastily."

"Hi all. Sorry, is the café closed?" Charity said, looking around and seeing there were no customers, which was a rare occurrence.

"No. Just the sign of an extremely hot day. The ice-cream van in the park will have most of our customers now," Callie explained.

"There's an ice cream van comes to the park? How did I not know this?"

"Didn't Merrin tell you?" I huffed.

She looked at me weirdly.

Callie continued her explanation. "It only appears on hot summer days, and no matter how many times anyone buys an ice cream or ice lolly, none of us can ever remember who served us, or what the van was called. It's just another of Gnarly's strange ways."

"Oh, I might have to check it out when I've been in the book-store," she said.

"Why not, you check everything else out," I mumbled, getting a dig in the ribs from Lawrie.

Deciding I needed to be civil to Charity as it was my job to do so, I headed back over to the book section.

"Anything in particular you're looking for today?" I asked, noticing how perky she was. Even perkier than usual.

"No decorating type books for me today. I'm in the mood for a feel-good romance read. Only I went on a date last night and it went really well."

My stomach plummeted. I was too late. Charity was Merrin's 'one', and I was going to marry another man.

"Oooh," Dela half-squealed, coming over to my side. "Did I hear you say you had a date?"

"Nosy much?" I barked out. "Leave the woman alone."

"No, it's fine, honestly," Charity said, beaming. "I did. It went really, really well. I was so surprised because it felt like I'd known him forever, right from the start. Don't say anything, but I think this could be the start of something special."

"I just need to borrow my sister for a moment. Dela, can you serve Charity?" Lawrie asked, and the next thing I knew we were in the park in front of the ice cream van.

"What are you doing?" I harrumphed as he asked for two cider lollies.

"Cooling you down. What was going on back there? I could see you digging your nails into your palm."

I looked, but of course if I had done, any cuts would have healed over.

"Charity was going on about her date."

"So. What's that got to do with you?"

"It's Merrin. She's laid claim to Merrin." I huffed. "I thought he was my future husband but he's not. He's her 'one'."

"No, he's not. She went out with Jason last night," Lawrie stated.

"J-Jason?"

"Yes, J-Jason," Lawrie mocked.

"Not Merrin?"

"Why the fuck would I say Jason if I meant Merrin? Callie told me that Charity and Jason completely hit it off at the workshop and then arranged to go out. Did you not notice? You were there and you have *vampire hearing*?"

"No, I was pre-occupied with the fact that Merrin was pissed at me and ignoring me because I was going on a date with Rupert."

"I'm not going to even ask. You hurt my brain. No, I am. Who the fuck is Rupert?"

I told him and with a large sigh, Lawrie sank down onto a bench at the park, tapping the seat next to him until I joined him.

"You need to go to see Merrin and tell him how you feel, Ginny. Stop tormenting yourself and get it done. Otherwise Merrin *will* go ask out someone else. I mean he doesn't know that *you* didn't go on *your* date, does he?"

"No."

"You've started to tell everyone about your newfound feelings, and he's the next on your list. Go get your happy ever after." Leaning over, he kissed the top of my head and then we ate our ice lollies.

"I'm so glad that vampires can go out in the daytime. Can you imagine if the myth was true, and we only came out at night? There'd be no ice creams in the park, no seeing such amazing colours."

"True. And I've seen some pretty damn incredible colours today," Lawrie said.

"Oh yeah? What? Where?" I sat up straight and looked around.

"Your true ones," Lawrie said.

I laughed.

After returning to the café, I realised that I could not for the life of me remember who'd served us an ice-cream or what the van had looked like. How very strange.

I spent the rest of the afternoon in a good, though nervous mood, wondering about how I would broach seeing Merrin.

In the end, I decided I would go to see Aria after work and ask her advice.

Walking around the bookstore, I gathered up three romance books that I held in high regard and on my way home, I called in at *A Cut Above*. Or rather, I stood outside.

"Hey," Charity said, looking at me with a question in her eyes.

"Can you invite me in?"

"Oh gosh, yes. Sure, come in. I'm just cleaning up. I'm afraid I'm closed though."

I held up the three books I'd chosen. "I got you these. Pressie for the fact I was a little off with you earlier. I'm so sorry. I've been going through a few issues."

"Oh wow. You didn't need to do that."

"No, I did. I'm happy you had a good date, Charity. Sorry if I seemed a bit weird."

She snorted. "Oh, Ginny, it's Gnarly. We all *are* weird."

I tilted my head while I thought about what she'd said. "Yeah, I guess we all are." I smiled at her. "Anyway, enjoy your reads. There's a really good one there about a woman who falls in love with a dragon." I winked and tapped on the Katie McAlister book in the pile.

"Oooh, I'm going to get straight on that," she said.

"The book?" I raised a brow.

Then I laughed as Charity blushed.

"Aria, Ginny's here," Bernard yelled from the doorway.

Aria came through. "Why do we sometimes still do human things like yelling, when we can hear?"

"Because we retain some of our humanity, although it lessens over time," Bernard replied. "Then we become more of the vampire, which is why I am now so French, mon amie."

Aria rolled her eyes. "Mon dieu," she replied. "You are full of merde at times, Bernard." She beckoned me into the babies' room. "Look, it's a room for babies," she said excitedly. I gave her a squidge.

"You're having babies, Aria. Two babies. And they will be in those plastic cribs. Oh how cute that they're shaped like coffins."

"I know, right? It's all bespoke. Bernard is in his element. He says I am growing the babies, and he is providing. He's being all manly and protective. If I wasn't already pregnant, I think he'd make me pregnant."

We laughed.

"Anyway, enough about us. Get me up to speed with what Dr Milton said."

"He tricked me into saying I like Merrin."

Her brow creased.

"I don't understand. He tricked you? So, he made you say it, but you aren't?"

I stuck my tongue on the front of my teeth as if trying to block myself from speaking.

"He did this one-word thing and I said Merrin was mine, and then I realised I liked him, maybe even felt love for him. I don't know, it's all so confusing. And then I was bitchy with Charity because I thought she'd gone out with him, and it was Jason, and Lawrie bought me an ice lolly, and I bought Charity some books and here I am."

"Oh, my bestie. Your emotions have you in a complete tangle. So, what's next? How will you tell Merrin?"

"I have no idea. In fact, I can't do it," I declared. "I can't tell him because I'm all in a kerfuffle. I'm going to go to my suite and lie down. I might even book a few months in a coffin to have a brain break and just avoid the whole dilemma. I'll ask to be released just before the babies are due."

"Go to your room and read while I have a think," Aria said. "And do *not* book a space in the Coffin Cave."

I knew I was being avoidant, and I knew that while I delayed telling Merrin how I felt he could ask someone else out, but as I sat on my sofa in my suite I realised that I was frightened of rejection, because my undead heart had been shattered into a thousand pieces fifty years ago, and I wasn't sure it was sturdy enough to risk using it again.

CHAPTER NINETEEN

Merrin

My phone rang. An unknown number. Something within me urged me to answer it anyway.

"Hello?"

"Merrin?"

"Yes, speaking."

"Good, good. It's Edmond Letwine, Merrin. Are you free to talk?"

"Certainly. I'm just home. What can I do for you?" I asked, wondering if someone had damaged the statue already.

"Actually, it's more what I can do for you. Do you remember I said I owed you a debt? Well, I'm here to pay it."

"Oh?" I was intrigued.

"Aria spoke to me a few minutes ago, knowing about the debt, and she asked me to pass on some information to you. When I do so, if satisfactory, you need to say this settles the debt. Okay?"

"Sure."

"Virginia Letwine believes herself to be in love with you."

"What?"

"It's true. She's seen a doctor and that was the conclusion. However, she's now in her room contemplating a trip to the coffins. That's where vampires go when they're tired of life or need a brain break. She's very scared that she might be rejected and so is procrastinating in her suite. Oh, I almost forgot. She didn't go out with that artist man. He was just using her because he wanted to paint drab art and make more money."

I paused to take this all in.

Ginny hadn't gone on a date with Rupert.

Ginny thought she might be in love with me?

"The debt is settled," I declared. "Now I just need to come over to the mansion. Are you able to offer me some protection from the rest of the clan?"

"Aria herself will be with you..."

"Right now," she said through my open window. "Come on, loverboy, let's go get your woman."

I wobbled on my feet outside of what I presumed was Ginny's front door.

"You okay?" Aria asked, looking concerned.

"Yeah, my first whizz. Just need a sec," I said. "Erm, will Ginny be able to hear us out here?"

"No, you'll be pleased to hear that all suites are soundproofed, otherwise we'd never get a minute's peace." She smirked. "Also, it means that whatever happens in Ginny's suite, stays in Ginny's suite, so feel free to bare anything you like: maybe your soul for instance?" Another smirk. "Right, I'm off. Good luck," she said and off she whizzed.

I rang the bell.

And waited.

Then I rang it again.

And waited some more.

So then I held my finger on it.

The door flew open. "For fuck's sake, can I not... Merrin?"

"Surprise," I said. "Erm, can I come in?"

She smiled. "How very strange. It's normally me asking that question. Yes, of course, come through."

I stepped inside and I looked around Ginny's suite. It was all very elegant.

"Don't compare it to your place. This is just superficial. I know now that it's feeling at home that counts mainly, though I'd never want to give up thick pile carpets, Egyptian cotton sheets, and cashmere bed socks. Come through to the living room?"

I nodded and walked through.

Now I was here I didn't know what to do. I couldn't just blurt out, 'Oh by the way, Edmond told me you might be falling in love with me', could I?

"Edmond said you might be falling in love with me," I blurted out. Oh, it seemed that was the way my brain and mouth had decided to go. FML.

"What?"

"Err..."

"Oh my god. Edmond actually told you that? I'm so embarrassed," Ginny declared, her face even paler than normal.

"Is it true?" I asked.

"Yes," she said.

"Oh," I replied.

"It's okay if you don't feel the same way. I know a good vacation place where I can go, for you know, a few centuries until my embarrassment dies down. Oh actually, you're also immortal, that's a bugger."

"I do feel the same way," I interrupted her rambling.

"Oh," she said.

We both just sat there. Then Ginny put her hand on mine. Cool to the touch it might have been, but I felt other places in me warm up as the familiar sparks flew. Her gaze met mine.

"I want to be entirely honest, Merrin. When I first came to see you, to help at your place... I was checking your land out, and I was going to see if you'd let Aria and I build houses there. I saw it as a potential way to get into Gnarly."

"What?" I said, moving away from her hand while I thought back to the night where I'd believed everything had changed. "So all the time I was being sympathetic after you went catatonic, were you being genuine, or were you just spinning me a line to try to... Oh God, I'm just another victim, aren't I? You were using me like you used all the others."

"No, I fucking was not," she spat out. "Well, I was, but then I wasn't. Did you just hear what I said? I don't care about you being poor. I think I love you. Get it in your thick skull, you dumbarse."

"Well, if that isn't the most romantic declaration ever. But what did I expect from Virginia Letwine, the tantrum queen."

"I do not tantrum," Ginny said, stamping her feet.

"That's quite enough," Aria said, coming into the room from the hallway.

"Where did you come from?" Ginny asked.

"The guest room. I figured I'd make sure all was going well and then I'd leave you to it, but my hunch to hang around was correct, because the pair of you need your heads banging together. So, until you make nice, make up, and make love..." She grabbed Ginny, and Bernard appeared and grabbed me. "You'll stay in here," she said. There was a short whizz, a door opened and then we were thrown into a dark room. A lock clicked.

"Oh fuck. Aria, noooooooo," Ginny screeched. 'Fuck."

"Wh-where are we?" I asked. "P-please put the light on."

"No. Stay in the dark, Merrin, until I can get us out of here."

"I can't stay in the dark. Are we in a small space? Tell me it's a large space." I could feel the walls closing in and I was losing it. "I beg you. I need the light on."

"Okay, Merrin. Don't freak out, please. I'm here," Ginny said and she flicked a switch, bringing me face to face with a small room packed to the hilt with around fifty coffins. Some closed, some open.

I freaked out.

"Merrin, there's talk of the wild being around the fields," my mother said.

I stilled.

"Have the animals been attacked again?"

"Yes. Mrs McGuiness has lost all two hundred sheep. Every one of them left like the soul itself had been lifted from it. Eyes wide but not in a passed on way, she told me, but more in a terrified to death way. So I need you to help keep an eye on the flock. You're eighteen

now. A man. So you can take a turn with me and your father. We must protect the animals until the threat has passed."

"Sure, Mum," I said. "I'm an adult now."

I was proud to have been asked. It was time to show my worth as a farmer. I'd take over the land eventually from my parents, so I was ready to step up.

That night I lie in wait in the field, hidden in the grass, both nervous and excited because if I caught the wild animal I'd be a hero to all.

But that wasn't what happened.

Instead, I was caught myself. So busy watching the sheep, I'd not thought to keep an eye on my own surroundings. Plus, the zombie made no sound as she placed the cold hand of death around my neck.

"Son," she said.

"I-I'm not your son," I protested.

"You are now," she declared.

"No," I gritted out. "My mother is called Gracelyn and she is irreplaceable. Whatever you wish to do to me, know you will never be my mother, not even close."

"How much?" she asked.

"I don't understand."

"How much for you to be my son? You said your mother is irreplaceable, but my experience has shown me that when offered a financial compensation high enough, minds change. I mean, if not for yourself, what could your mother do with one hundred thousand pounds?"

"She'd do nothing, because you are wrong. My family is not impressed by wealth of a monetary value, only wealth of a family value, of love and contentment."

"Then your punishment shall be that they will no longer be family or contented," she snarled, and she stuck her hand straight through my chest, clutching it around my heart.

I didn't understand because there wasn't blood. She hadn't physically ripped into my chest but had used energy of some kind to force her spirit within me and drain mine out.

I watched as my skin greyed out, and I felt the life drifting out from my body, and then I saw him. A man in a dark cloak standing nearby. Death. Mentally, I tried to thrash and protest against what was happening, but my body had no strength to do so.

The last thing I remembered was that a shot rang out. The zombie woman's brains splattered across me. I heard my dad's voice, "Merrin, hold on."

Death kneeled beside me, while my parents held my body in their arms and prayed. "Are you taking me?" I thought, unable to speak.

"I'm so sorry, Merrin." I heard him say in my mind. "I will be back for you. But I can't help you yet. It's beyond my control."

"Why? You're Death. Don't you take me?" I asked again through our mind connection.

"Yes, but you aren't dead yet. You're in the between. The woman who attacked you was a zombie. Stay strong," he said and then he was gone.

My parents mourned me and buried me, but I was in a deep paralysis, not dead. The doctor didn't know about zombies, none of us did, so he'd detected no breath or heartbeat and called time of death. They spoke of the woman as a madwoman, escaped from a secure unit, and me as the unlucky victim. I heard everything, but couldn't speak, or move.

I was in the ground for years. Just me and mental torture.

Until one day, my eyes opened, and my body moved, and I went frantic as I scratched at everything around me until I got out of that earth. When I burst through, Death was waiting.

"It's time," he said. "I have a house sorted for you. It's in a place called Gnarly Fell."

It would turn out that he lived nearby. Death taught me to live a new existence. I kept to myself for a long time, until gradually I began to get to know the others in the village. They didn't mind if I kept to myself for a long period. They understood. Most had their own traumas and stories to tell. I began sculpting and dabbling with art. It let me release some of my inner torment. I liked to create beautiful things. Because I wasn't one. My limbs were now long and gangly, my face thin, my hair long and straggly, my cheeks hollow. I did not look like the eighteen-year-old that was buried alive. Years had passed it seemed. Death had told me I was twenty-three back then. It was seven years ago, but it felt like yesterday still at times.

Five years underground and months to push my way out. A living nightmare.

And I was back here now. I could feel it. Somehow, I'd been placed back in the coffin, needed to find my way back to the surface. I begged and pleaded, and then something strange happened.

Cold lips on my own and the words, "I love you, Merrin. Please come back."

CHAPTER TWENTY

Ginny

Aria had been so determined for us to sort out our differences, she'd completely forgotten about Merrin's fears.

As he laid down on his back whimpering as if he was once again trapped in a small box, his thoughts were so loud, that enchanted or not, I could hear them clearly. As Merrin's history played out, tears poured down my cheeks. Tears for his past, tears for his fears, tears for my treatment of him. I now understood only too well, why, when he learned of my reputation for seeking a rich man, he had despised me.

We'd been so wrong about each other and now as I looked at him, I wondered if he was mentally lost. If I'd ever be able to get him back.

And that was when I decided. Whether they managed to break through, or he never knew of my words, it was time for me to be honest.

I leaned over and put my mouth to his in a soft kiss. "*I love you, Merrin. Please come back.*"

It took a minute. A minute that seemed like the longest in existence. Then he opened his eyes.

Lifting my head up, I said. "Merrin, are you back? Are you okay?"

He answered me by pulling my head back down and kissing me like I was his last chance of survival.

I might have had vampire strength, but a horny Merrin managed to hold his own. We kissed, long and hard, and then, when I realised he was keeping his eyes tightly shut, I pulled back.

"Merrin?"

"Uh-huh?" he said, his eyes still not open. "Please tell me you've not changed your mind."

"Do we need to take this back to my room? Only I can see from the fact your eyelids look glued that part of your mind is on the room and not me."

"Only a teeny bit."

"Oh, Merrin. Do you not know me at all? I'm greedy, remember? I want it all." I stroked his cock through his trousers, and he groaned. "Have you heard of exposure therapy?"

"Is that a polite term for flashing?"

"No." I laughed. "It's when you confront the thing that scares you."

"How do you know this?" he asked.

"I got interested in psychology once William was dusted. Wanted to attempt to understand my feelings a little. Not that it did anything much other give me the excuse that my anger issues were justified."

"So how do we do this exposure thing? It's worth a try, right?"

"I think so. Now in therapy it's done slowly, but I reckon I could give you a non-psychologically trained, completely unprofessional lesson."

"Oh yeah? How?"

"Trust me," I told him. "Open your eyes."

He looked around and I held onto his hand as he gazed at all the coffins. "Are there people in the ones with lids?" he asked.

"Yes, Letwine vampires who want a break, a rest. This is where they lie."

"Can they hear us?"

"No. Not unless they are close to their re-awakening, and none are at present."

"So if I really wanted to test out that exposure therapy, none would know what we were doing?" he said.

"Merrin Bruckman, what exactly do you have in mind?" I asked him.

And that was how we ended up putting a lid on an empty coffin, and my lying upon it while Merrin pushed inside me; completely immersed in me and not the box underneath. And even when I went on top and we broke the coffin lid and fell in, Merrin managed to hold it together, while we moved onto the floor and chased our orgasms. Finally, laid in each other's arms, he said, "That was amazing, but I'll always be afraid of coffins."

I reached over and kissed him. "And I'll always be afraid of hexagonal, smoked glass coffee tables. But the difference this time, Merrin, is we'll have each other. Which reminds me." I looked at him smugly. "I rescued you from 'hungry for your body' vampire women. I think I need to hear you say thank you."

"Get us out of this room and I'll get on my knees in gratitude," he said.

I broke the door off the room.

EPILOGUE

Merrin

The next upcycling workshop was in session. Since the last I'd been in contact with Gnarly's planning committee and it was agreed that I could renovate the cowshed to make a storage area and extend the studio so that I could hold workshops even in the winter months. I'd also provisionally got permission to extend my cottage if I felt I wanted to in the future.

Ginny and I were head over heels in love and lust and she spent increasing time over at my cottage, saying she preferred me and Gnarly to her suite at the mansion. However, the pile of books she seemed to be amassing was growing and if things worked out, I'd like to make her a library room.

I'd also had one of my visions where I'd seen a scared little boy of around eight hold Ginny's hand and got the feeling that he was important. Ginny had told me of her wish to one day foster or adopt and it looked like it would be the case. But I wouldn't tell her. Some things I needed to keep to myself, because I always wondered if one day, I might get a vision wrong. I mean the weird one I'd had about the black smoke and the heir had never been explained.

"Merrin, you've zoned out again. You were showing us your splattering technique," said Charity.

"I think that's why he's zoning out, hey, Ginny? You've had him showing you his splattering technique all night," Jase joked, earning himself a "Jason," from both Fenella *and* Charity.

Fen and Charity looked at each other and laughed.

"I've bloody two of em at it now," Jason said, grinning.

A vision slammed into me painfully. I gripped my head.

Played out like a short movie, I watched as the edge of my field came into vision. The land below—the shifter land—had woodland and also a series of boulders set in a circle, and I watched as one moved, revealing a dark entrance. My sight travelled down underneath, to where a secret cave revealed itself. There was a meeting. Twelve men sat around a table.

"He is not trained as a dragon. This is ridiculous," one man said, slamming his hand down against the table top. "We should let Griffin succeed. He's spent years as deputy."

"It is not the way. Not if there's family and you know it."

"He's a half-breed."

"He shall be given a trial. If he fails, then the council will reform and rediscuss. This is my final say on the matter. *Understood?*" bellowed a brute of a man who was sitting in the largest chair, but I didn't think it was because of his size, but because of his importance.

"Very well," said yet another. "Josiah's heir shall be awarded the trial. Everyone say aye." All did, even the one who'd protested.

"So now we just need to inform him. Get me the address of Jason Gradon," the larger man demanded of another.

I snapped out of the vision. Finding Ginny and Fenella right at my side. "Merrin, Merrin, are you okay?"

"Fenella," I said. "Who is Josiah?"

Fenella closed her eyes for a moment and then with a steely look she said, "Jason's uncle. His father's brother."

"He's dead and they're coming," I warned her.

THE END

Read on for Jason and Charity's story in HOT AS SUCK...

HOT AS
SUCK

CHAPTER ONE

Jason

I'd had the best two weeks of my damn life. My mum had moved in with her boyfriend and had left me with a home of my own, and I'd met Charity, a beautiful mermaid who worked as a hairdresser in Gnarly. She'd recently moved to the fell and I'd met her at one of my friend Merrin's upcycling workshops.

It was early days, but I was quietly optimistic that my V-card would soon be a thing of the past. Yes, that's right. I was almost thirty and still a virgin. For reasons I couldn't fully understand, but worried were due to my personality, I was still to get to *that* base.

Now here I was again at Merrin's second upcycling workshop. The first time I'd made a bed frame for the bed I'd at that time hoped to bring a girl back to, not realising I'd meet someone while designing it. Thank goodness I'd screwed up my sketches for a red headboard that handcuffs fitted to!

This time I was next to my *girlfriend*. Oh lord, I couldn't believe I was actually saying that. I had a *girlfriend*, a *proper* one. Not that I meant I previously had a fake one, like a blow-up one. Not that I'm judging anyone who does. I mean you could for instance practice kissing on one when you're a teenager and then find your mum has dressed it up and put it in the village square on Halloween, thinking the mouth hole was someone screaming in fright. When put right about it, I'd had a large whack around the ears while my mum had thanked every deity there was that I'd only kissed it and prayed for me to be given common sense.

She wasn't particularly religious and that's why she said I never seemed to be delivered of any sense. That or she blamed my father.

"Jason, what furniture are you picking this time?" Charity asked me. I turned to her, immediately struck by just how beautiful she was. With that scarlet-red hair, pale skin with freckled nose and cheeks, her emerald-green eyes with long lashes, and the soft-pink lips that were currently smiling at me. At *me*. And we'd been on three dates now. It was nothing short of a miracle.

"I'm honestly not sure," I said. "Have you got any ideas?"

"Well..." She paused, looking a little apprehensive. "I was thinking maybe we could both do a small set of drawers..." She pointed to an identical set, narrow with three drawers in each. "...and then if you stay at mine or I stay at yours the other has somewhere to keep some stuff." She blushed, and before I could think, I closed the gap between us and almost knocked her over as I planted a kiss on her lips. Steadying her and apologising for my lack of balance, I declared her idea perfect.

Everything was going so well.

My friend Merrin was also in love. He'd fallen hard for a vampire called Ginny and it was amusing me watching him as he kept grinning at his girlfriend. It had only been the week before last that we'd sat outside the bistro and had Chantelle, the witch who worked there, work a spell that would bring forth our true loves. Now Chantelle's magic could go wrong on occasion, but this time it seemed she'd done us both proud.

Merrin just needed an attention spell now, so he'd stop forgetting to train us in upcycling while he got lost in love and lust.

"Merrin, you've zoned out again. You were showing us your splattering technique," said Charity.

"I think that's why he's zoning out, hey, Ginny? You've had him showing you his splattering technique all night," I joked, earning me a "Jason," from both my mum *and* Charity.

Mum and Charity looked at each other and laughed. I loved how they were getting along, given they had me in common.

"I've bloody two of em at it now," I said, grinning, and feeling unbelievably smug.

HOT AS SUCK

But then my friend clutched his head, and I knew he was having a vision.

"Shit, we need to help him," I shouted, though Ginny was already at his side. My mother was also on her way forward. She might have been my mum, but she'd become the mother of most of Gnarly since my father had disappeared after burning the house down when I was little.

"Merrin, Merrin, are you okay?" Mum asked. Charity and I hung back, not wanting to overcrowd him.

Merrin was guided to a seat.

"Fenella," he said. "Who is Josiah?"

Fenella closed her eyes for a moment and then with a steely look she said, "Jason's uncle. His father's brother."

"He's dead and they're coming," he warned her.

I stared at my mum as her face paled and she dropped to her knees. Immediately, I dashed forward and put my arms around her.

"Mum, are you okay?"

She shook her head and turned to me, and I noted the tears trickling down her cheeks. It took me back to a time many, many years ago.

"I need you to tell me what you saw, Merrin," she instructed before swallowing hard.

"Look, you go to Merrin's house, and I'll close the workshop. We'll reschedule for next Sunday," said Ginny. She turned her attention on me. "Merrin will be okay now, but you and your mum need to hear what he's seen. Charity, will you help me to sort out rebooking everyone?"

"Of course," she said. I felt her hand on my arm. "Is that okay with you, or would you rather I came with you?"

"I think I'd better just be with my mum for now."

She nodded and walked away.

Just minutes ago, I'd been so happy that my life had taken a turn for the better, that I was happy and had hope for the future, and now it seemed the past had decided to blast through it all. I'd seen the disappointment on Charity's face, just for a split-second, that I'd turned her away. But the fact was, Charity had been in my life two weeks and my mother had been there twenty-nine years, and my mum needed me now.

Merrin recovered quickly and we walked back to his cottage. As I walked in, I couldn't help but notice how tidy it was. My friend really had changed from the messy individual he'd been before he'd found love.

"Take a seat," he directed us, and for the first time since I'd known him, I was able to trust that I could sit down and not end up with a slice of cold pizza stuck to my arse.

"Would you like a drink?" he asked my mum.

"I could really use a scotch," Mum said.

Now I began to feel really anxious. My mum did not drink liquor at eleven o'clock in a morning.

Merrin headed to his kitchen and came back with a hot coffee with an extra aroma of whiskey. "Thought you'd appreciate it this way," he said.

"Can someone just tell me what the fuck is going on?" My voice was slightly raised, having come to the end of my patience.

"I'll tell you the vision I saw," Merrin said. "Then we'll take it from there, okay?" He was looking at my mum for a response and then he fixed me with a look that firmly said, 'Don't be a twat'.

"Okay," I replied.

"The other week I saw a vision that I didn't understand. I saw a plume of black smoke and heard crying. A voice said, 'We mourn the passing of Josiah' and another voice said, 'We must find the heir'. I didn't know anyone called Josiah and so I just put it to the back of my mind. I knew the visions would continue and reveal who the message was for in their own time. I had no inkling it was connected with either of you. There was no hint of dragon to it. Then today, the vision I just had played out like a short movie. I watched as the edge of my field came into vision. One of the circle boulders on the shifter land moved, revealing a dark entrance. My sight travelled down underneath, to where a secret cave revealed itself. There was a meeting. Twelve men sat around a table. One spoke and he was angry. He said *he* is not trained as a dragon and that Griffin should succeed given he is the deputy."

"Who is *he*?" I asked, only to be shushed by my mother.

Merrin continued. "There was further arguing about family succeeding and about the new heir being a half-breed."

The penny slowly began to drop.

"Y-you m-mean—"

Merrin continued, interrupting me.

"—they said he shall be given a trial. That if he fails, then the council will reform and rediscuss. They agreed, all of them, even the one who first protested, and then... he asked for the address of Jason Gradon," Merrin finished.

My mother knocked back her coffee. "Can I have another please, Merrin? And this time make it without the coffee."

"Of course," Merrin said, and he rose and went back to the kitchen leaving my mother and I alone.

"You said you never knew my father's family, Mum," I challenged. Truth was, I didn't know what to say. What did this all mean? Dead uncles, trial. I mean, what sort of trial? I could change into a dragon, but I couldn't make fire, or fly, or anything else dragon-like. I was going to die at the trial.

I began pacing. "I just get a girlfriend and I'm going to die. I'll be flambéed by this one who called me a half-breed. They're coming for me right now, Mum. I'm going to die a virgin," I declared at the top of my lungs, just as Charity appeared at the other side of the open window with Ginny. "Mum, actually, kill me now," I begged, feeling my cheeks burning like I'd entered Hades.

"Erm, Charity and I are going to head into the village. Can you let Merrin know and ask him to call me later?" Ginny said to Mum, while Charity and I just stared at each other. It wasn't how I'd thought I'd broach the subject of my never having had sex. I'd not actually come to a decision about how to confess to that yet, swinging between winging it and pretending I'd not had a lot of experience, getting drunk and blurting out the truth, or being a grown up about it and having a sensible discussion. Let's face it, the third option had been the most sensible and the least likely.

Shouting it out of the window to my girlfriend hadn't crossed my mind as a possibility. Today was really not going my way.

In the end, Charity just gave me a small wave and followed Ginny. I watched her walking away and wondered, was that a wave of see you later, or a wave of 'Goodbye, because I've realised I'm dating a loser'?

Merrin came back with the drink. I pinched it from him and cleared it in one mouthful. Then as I coughed and spluttered, I thanked my useless body for not actually being able to breathe fire or I might just have followed in my father's footsteps and burned the house down.

CHAPTER TWO

Charity

Jason's loud voice echoed in my ears, *'I'm going to die a virgin'*. I'd been so shocked, that after we'd stared at each other for a moment, I'd just given him a small wave and then carried on walking, like I'd not heard him. Which was ridiculous. He'd shouted it so loudly they'd probably heard it back at the boulevard.

I could feel Ginny's eyes burning through me.

"Take me to the bistro for an alcoholic beverage and I may comment on what I just heard," I told her.

She grinned. "You're on. I need to know everything. I wonder what's going on back there? It's a shame I had to help tidy up. I could have eavesdropped with my super-hearing."

I walked up to my small Volvo.

"You know I can whizz us there?" Ginny pointed out.

"I know, but that would still leave my car here, so climb in, we're doing this the human way."

"Like you're human," she commented.

This was true. I was a mermaid, but my skills were with water, and so I just had to suck it up and drive home like a normal person.

I was quiet in the car, lost in jumbled thoughts of wondering what was happening with poor Jason and his mum, but also thinking that the easy-going dating we'd been doing was probably now a thing of the past.

And I needed easy, not complicated. I'd been there, done that, bought the swimsuit.

I pulled up in the street behind my flat above the salon. It was only a short walk to the bistro.

"Sorry about being so quiet," I told Ginny. "Thanks for just letting me be."

"That's okay, I just listened to everything in your head. You never put a guard up." She flashed me a mischievous grin. "We have so much to talk about over a Bloody Mary."

"You do mean the drink, right? You're not about to drain an old lady?" I quipped.

She laughed. "I'm so pleased you didn't date Merrin so that we could be friends and not mortal enemies," Ginny added sweetly, and then she pushed open the door of the bistro, requesting a table for two. I decided that yes, indeed, I was very glad I didn't want her man, while also wondering how I had suddenly become friends with a prickly female vampire. This time I made sure my guards were up so that she couldn't read any more of my thoughts, just in case.

We were seated at a small table near the window, looking out over the boulevard. The gnarled trees were full of vibrant summer leaves, the sun shone, and for a moment, I craved the sea. To feel the quench of the water as it met my flesh, my weightlessness, and the tingle as my legs became one giant fin. It had been months now since I'd walked out onto the beach, not sure if I'd ever return. Turning my back on the life I'd had there. On everyone except my younger brother who had stood by me and come with me to the fell.

"So what do we think is going on with Jason?" Ginny dragged me out of my inner musings. "His uncle is dead, and someone is coming? Who do you reckon the someone is?"

"I've no idea," I replied honestly. "We've only had a couple of dates, but Jason was pretty clear that it's only been him and his mum since his dad burned their house down when he was younger."

"Did his dad die in the blaze?"

"He said his dad disappeared afterward. He's never heard anything else about him. It clearly still affects him because he looked so sad when telling me."

The thing with Jason was that he was a laugh. Easy-going and pleasant natured, he clearly had a good heart, and he was also daft. In a lovely naïve way. He came out with the most ridiculous things, and yet, I adored the fact he was like that. He made me giggle, and God knows, my life had been short of laughter the past couple of years.

Now I wondered if his life was set to change with Merrin's announcement that someone connected to his uncle was coming.

The server came to take our order at that point. I realised I felt hungry. The smell of the meat from the carvery had been wafting tantalisingly under my nose since we'd walked in. "I'll have a coffee please and the beef."

"A roast and a roast," the guy quipped.

I looked up at him in surprise.

"Sorry. I've not been working here long. I'm attempting humour so that if I get your order wrong, you'll forgive me."

"Another newbie in the fell? Who are you related to, because I know no one else is getting in right now," Ginny enquired.

"I'm Connor's younger brother. Been away for a while and now I'm back. Staying with him until I decide what my next move is. The meanie is making me earn my keep." He held out a hand to Ginny. "I'm Kaf."

She took it and shook, and I watched as her eyes narrowed as she stared at him.

"Vampire," he said, breaking the grip and rubbing his hand. "Christ, your fingers are like ice."

"Hmmm, allowed to take the Lord's name in vain, are you?" she said. "Angel."

My eyes widened. Kaf was an angel? So, did that mean Connor was one too? I didn't know why, but I expected them to have halos on their heads to give an indication to the general public, which was stupid because I didn't wave my mermaid tail around, did I?

"I'm allowed to do a lot of things when I'm not on official duties." Kaf wiggled his eyebrows before his eyes firmly met mine.

"Mermaid," I told him. "Pretty new here myself."

"Maybe we could—"

"KAF. SERVICE," Connor bellowed across the restaurant.

"Bloody Mary for me," Ginny shouted at Kaf's retreating back. He turned and gave a nod while mouthing, "Sorry," at her.

"It would appear if Jason's otherwise tied up, there's another man willing to enter the fray," she remarked.

"No, thank you. He looks like a whole heap of trouble, angel or not. If Jason puts a pause on things, I'll keep to my uncomplicated existence." I sighed. I'd been in such a good mood this morning, ready to make the little drawers at the upcycling. "Anyway, things with you and Merrin seem to be going well."

Ginny leaned closer. "The sex is off the charts. If you'd have told me a few weeks ago I'd be in love and having the best sex of my life with the great undead and unwashed, I'd have staked you for your insolence. Just shows you that you can never predict who you'll fall in love with." She proceeded to go off into a daydream until Kaf returned with our drinks. He didn't linger this time. In fact, he slammed the drinks down so fast that my coffee sloshed into the saucer which was my pet hate.

We watched as he then lingered and flirted with a woman at the next table.

Quick as a flash, Ginny lifted the cup, stuck her finger in the saucer and froze the swimming coffee. She then picked up the icy clump of coffee and threw it, so it hit Kaf in the back of the head as he walked away putting a phone number in his pocket.

Acting like nothing unusual had occurred, she then put my cup back on the saucer. "You really do need to keep those mind guards up, but yes, I agree that was fucking awesome."

"I'm annoyed I didn't think of doing that myself. Shall we have some fun with the new guy?" I asked her as I watched him flirting with yet another customer. I knew it was mean. The guy could do what he liked, but I felt like I needed cheering up.

"Oh, Charity, I do believe you're about to become a new best friend. What do you have in mind?" she asked.

I started off slow, but having control over anything with water, every time Kaf lingered to flirt, he found strange things happened to him. He carried a carafe of water to one table and on his way, I got it to trickle just ever so slightly, making sure the water ran onto the front of his groin. "Shit," I heard him say, which caused him to spill even more water onto the floor. I got the small puddle to travel up his trouser leg. Within minutes he looked like he'd pissed himself.

Throughout, Ginny and I smirked at each other like naughty schoolkids.

"*Ladies.*" I turned my head to see Connor standing at the side of us. "Would you by any chance have anything to do with my younger brother's current mishaps?"

"Sorry," I answered, feeling a hint of redness hit my cheeks.

"Don't apologise," Connor said. "I'm just letting you know your meals and drinks are on the house. Look how conscientious he's being carrying things now. You've knocked his confidence, and believe me, that was sorely needed. Anyway, how come you're here? I thought you were at Merrin's today? I had to miss this one as there was no one to cover."

"Merrin had a vision. We made sure he was okay and then left him to have a sleep," Ginny lied. "We decided to have some girly time instead."

"Then let me get you something else. Another Bloody Mary, Ginny? And what would you like, Charity?"

You know when you're just having so much fun that you don't notice you're drunk out of your mind? It wasn't until we'd had a few more drinks on the house and I re-entered daylight that I had to grab onto the nearest lamppost to prevent myself from face-planting the pavement.

"Virginia Letwine, you are a bad influence," I yelled, sliding down to sit on the ground.

Her phone beeped and my eyes registered at least two versions of her looking at it.

"They've left and Merrin is now home alone, so I'm going to drop you home and then make my way to Merrin's for an afternoon T—and by that, I mean an afternoon tryst."

That reminded me that the man I'd been dating was a virgin. *Really? He'd never done it. Not at all. Never ever. Zero. Zip.*

"Just means you get to teach him, honey. No bad habits. You can have him do it exactly as you'd like," Ginny said. My mind guards had clearly disintegrated alongside my soberness. "Now let go of the lamppost. I've things to do... like my boyfriend."

"Whoa!" I screeched as Ginny grabbed me and dropped me back off outside the rear of the salon.

"Are you going to be okay?" she asked.

"I'm fine. Totally peachy," I replied while swaying and contemplating the potential regurgitation of all I'd consumed that afternoon. "And my little brother can make me a nice fresh cup of coffee to help me see properly again," I said. I took three attempts to ring the doorbell, gave up and knocked on the door.

Nothing.

"You can go," I told Ginny.

"Not until you're safely inside," she said.

I backed up my path, got some gravel and began throwing it at the upstairs window. Then my foot gave way, and with a resounding topple, I crashed backwards through a small evergreen bush. It held me in its branches like a fly in a spiderweb.

I watched from my vantage point as Ginny flew up to the window and banged on it hard. I heard a shriek, before she shouted, "Get some clothes on and let your sister in."

I held up a hand and she pulled me out of the bush. "I do not want to know what he was doing," I informed her.

"He wasn't doing anything. I just meant for him to change out of his night attire."

"You're not used to teenagers then?" I said, as Billy opened the door, hair mussed and with his lounge t-shirt and shorts still on.

"Why didn't you use your key?" he said. "And why have you got leaves in your hair?"

"See you soon, Charity. Thanks for a nice lunch." Ginny gave me a quick hug, the sheer shock of the coldness of her body sobering me up for a moment.

"Bye," I replied, but it was to fresh air.

"Are you drunk?" Billy eyed me suspiciously.

"Not at all," I told my brother adamantly while attempting to walk a straight line the few steps to the open doorway. Unfortunately, one of the leaves shifted into my vision, making me think I was being attacked by something, and as I moved to escape any would-be attacker, I staggered backwards several steps and fell onto the lawn.

"I thought you were supposed to be the adult around here?" My brother huffed, as he tried to pull me back upright.

And there was the problem. I was sick of having to be the sensible one all the time. That's why I enjoyed Jason's company so much. He was fun.

My brother helped me to my bed and left me to go make a coffee. I began wondering about what Jason was doing and then the next thing I knew my eyes were closing.

CHAPTER THREE

Jason

"I think it's time we went home, Mum," I said. "These dragons are coming imminently, and I think we need a chat first to get ourselves prepared."

Mum looked decidedly uncomfortable, her face contorting like she needed a fart but was scared it might follow through.

"Yes, you're right," she finally said. "Come on then, let's go back to yours."

And that's when I remembered that my mum had moved out, leaving me all alone in the family home, where I was now potentially in danger of being captured by dangerous dragons.

"What am I going to do, Mum?" I wailed.

She grabbed hold of my arm. "You're going to listen to me first. Then we'll meet with your father's side and discuss what happens from here. But, Jason, you must not go into a blind panic. This is not the time for you to go hide in your bedroom."

Merrin snorted.

I snapped my head around in his direction. "It's only a very short time since you had a panic attack because furniture landed on you, and you had to be rescued by a *girl*."

"It's only a short time ago that you felt my dick because you thought I was one of the twins and you might finally lose your V-card."

"If you don't both shut up, I'm going to describe in great detail what Santa actually has in his sack," my mother declared. We both firmly closed our mouths and with a quick goodbye we left and returned home.

Even though we had far bigger issues to deal with, my mum still took a look around at the pots piled high in the sink, the dirty socks on the floor, and sighed loudly.

"Not now, Mum. Now is not the time to tell me off for being lazy. So there are a few things around. It's no big deal."

She shrugged. "You're an almost thirty-year-old man, Jason, who now lives alone. If you don't want to tidy up, don't. As long as I can take a seat on a clean sofa, I'm good."

Luckily the sofa was spotless as I tended not to use the living room at all, going mainly from my bedroom to the kitchen and vice versa. It hadn't quite sunk in yet that I had use of all of these rooms. I might make the living room a large games room.

Mum sat down, refusing a drink as she'd 'had enough at Merrin's', even though I knew it was really because of my housekeeping skills and she was clearly afraid of catching some deadly disease from a mug.

For a moment there was silence as we knew this was unchartered territory. That the past was now catching up with us, and Mum needed to tell me anything she could think of that could help.

"Okay, Mum," I said. "Tell me everything you think I need to know."

After a large exhale of breath, she began:

"When I fell in love with your father, it caused a lot of trouble with his clan," she said. "Many frowned upon relationships with humans or other supernaturals, preferring that the clan chose another dragon, not only to stay purebred but also for politics. To marry into another powerful clan and have an heir was felt the best outcome. Joseph left, and then when his father passed away it was his younger brother Josiah who claimed the throne."

"Joseph and Josiah? So both brothers were Joe?" I noted.

"Dragon names are not shortened. They will address you as Jason, and for goodness' sake, don't give any of them a nickname."

"Why? What's the problem?"

"They do not use pet names because they are adamant that they are not pets."

"Oh, right, so it's insecurity that they might not be seen as a big manly dragon?"

Mum nodded. "Now you get it. It's very much manly dragon showing how virile he is while little woman dragon sits at home growing babies. At least that's how it was, but twenty-five years have passed since I last had anything to do with them, so it could have changed. Though I very much doubt it," she added.

I thought about the fact that Merrin had said twelve men had sat around a table discussing the situation and decided I very much doubted it as well.

"Did you have to make me an only child?" I complained.

Mum ignored me and carried on.

"Your father made his decision and made a home with me. We moved to the fell and had you. He turned his back on the dragon side of himself for a long time, and for the first few years we were so very happy. But then once we'd had you, his inner arsehole dragon reared its ugly head. Life in Gnarly wasn't enough for him. He kept reminding me that he was the rightful heir, that you would now be the next in line in succession. It caused many, many arguments, including the one where your father burned down our house. Accidentally, then deliberately. At first, his temper had got the better of him and he'd turned part dragon. Flames had shot out and he'd set fire to the curtains. Curtains I'd made from scratch. The very first thing I'd done in our new marital home. I know it's just material, really, but they represented to me the love that had gone into our home. The home he now wanted us to leave. He was pacing and demanding we went back to the clan. That he would fight his brother for rule. I didn't recognise him. It's only afterward that I realised that your father was pretending to be someone he wasn't for love. Pushing away his natural inner dragon. But that in the end love wasn't enough."

Mum stared into the distance for a moment, lost in thought. Her eyes glistened as she held back tears and as her voice had sounded thick with emotion, I let her have the break she clearly needed.

"I'm going to go wash a few dishes, Mum. Give you a minute."

She nodded.

As I got up and walked into the kitchen, I noted I needed this mini break in recalling the past just as much as my mum did. Feelings of confusion and guilt swam in my stomach, making all the liquid I'd consumed gurgle there, and I felt the scorch of the scotch in my throat as it rose from my oesophagus. I'd gone through life with blinkers on. I knew I'd asked my mum about my father in the past, but I'd settled for whatever she'd told me, because I was content; spoiled really. I didn't like to see people upset. It was why I played the joker, and so I'd always seen my mum's uncomfortableness and not pressed further.

Today was different. Today I was giving her a moment—giving us both a moment—but I would return to the living room, and we would be discussing the past, the truth, no matter how much it hurt. But for now, I'd get these dishes soaking and try to clean up the kitchen a little.

Around ten minutes later, I returned to the living room. Mum looked up at me with brighter eyes.

"You ready to continue?" I asked her, wanting to be sure she was okay.

"I was ready about a minute later, but no way was I interrupting your sudden burst of domesticity," she joked.

We smiled at each other, and it was a smile not only of the joke, but of the fact that no matter what was said today, we knew we would be okay, me and Mum.

"I didn't recognise the man who stormed around our house that day cursing. He blamed me for bewitching him, said many unforgivable things that made it seem like our years together had not been the idyll I had seen them as. His dragon had taken over and it was terrifying. And then he bellowed and set fire to more of our home. You were in your cot asleep. I'd never for a moment thought that your father would do anything that could put your life in danger, or I'd have got you and left there earlier; left him with his fury. I managed to avoid the flames, run upstairs and grab you from your cot. As I came back down and stood next to your dad, trying to get through to him, he turned to me and told me that he was burning everything. That then there would be nothing tying us to the fell. We'd have everything when he was king. That's what he thought. That happiness to me would be living in a cave with people who didn't like me because I wasn't a dragon. I stood and watched as our house became nothing but ashes. Mine and your father's relationship went the same way."

"What happened to him?" It was the question she'd only ever answered by telling me he'd disappeared.

"I sought refuge in the village hall where so many kind Gnarly residents looked after us both. I told them everything and one of them contacted the clan on my behalf. I spoke to Josiah, the first and only time I ever spoke to anyone from your father's side. I told him his brother planned a coup. That he'd lost his mind and burned down our house. Put you in danger. Josiah said he'd deal with him and that's all I know. I never saw your father again. When I said he disappeared, I told the truth."

"But my uncle was behind it?"

Mum shrugged. "I presume so, but all I was interested in from that point forward was your care and wellbeing. Gnarly rebuilt our home, reassured us we were safe, and—" She dropped her chin to her chest, unable to meet my gaze.

"And what, Mum?"

Her chin trembled as she looked back up at me. "And I got a witch to dampen your full dragon nature."

I gasped and reared back, standing and pacing around the room.

"That's why I can't breathe fire? Because there's a spell on me?"

She nodded. "I couldn't risk losing you to your inner dragon like I did your father, and I was scared that while you were younger you might accidentally harm us, set fire to something. I'm mortal and know very little about that side of you. I'd always planned to tell you one day, but... you were happy. We were happy here. It's selfish, but I decided to leave things as they were."

My mind was imploding. "You had my dragon nature suppressed and even when I became an adult, you chose not to tell me, not give me the option to decide for myself what I'd wish to do?"

She slumped forward and tears crashed down her cheeks as she sobbed hard. This was it, all the weight my mum had carried on her shoulders, all the feelings and truth she'd suppressed were messily spilling out like tipped over buckets of fish guts.

I wanted to be angry. I wanted to punch and kick and scream and shout about the fact I'd not been allowed to be my true self. But as my mum had sat and told me about my dad's wild and unrestrained behaviour, I couldn't say that it was a bad thing she'd protected me. I closed the space between us and wrapped my arms around her.

Tears soaked through the material over my shoulders, and she kept mumbling that she was sorry. I held her by her shoulders and looked at her directly. "You have nothing to be sorry for. You did it all because of how much you love me. To protect me. You were just being a mum." She nodded and then began sobbing all over again.

'Let me get a loo roll," I said. "I don't have tissues. I'm not that domesticated."

She did a little snort and a snot bubble appeared at her nose. She went into her pocket, extracting a tissue she already had.

Just as she was blowing her nose noisily, there was a loud knock on the door.

I looked out of the window, and the eyes of a huge brute of a man met mine. His gaze cold and calculating.

"He's here," I told my mum. "The dragon."

CHAPTER FOUR

Jason

I directed my mum upstairs to go wash her face in the bathroom. "Do you want to be down here to see what the guy has to say?"

"Yes, if you don't mind waiting."

"I don't mind, and they can wait for as long as necessary. No one asked them to turn up uninvited."

As Mum went upstairs, the door knocked again.

I wandered over and opened it, finding myself eye to eye with the guy. It was then I realised that although I'd called him a brute, I was just as tall and almost as wide as he was. Guess I was just used to myself and didn't give much thought to the fact I was bigger and bulkier than my friends. We all had our own species quirks and that's how I'd always thought of it. Whereas today, standing in front of this dragon dude, I stood straighter and made the most of my physique.

"Can I help you?" I asked the guy. He didn't know a psychic zombie had given us a head's up.

"I need to speak to a Jason Gradon as a matter of urgency. Would that be you?" His voice rumbled like distant thunder.

"It would. And what's this regarding? Because I don't mean to sound awkward, but I don't let strangers in my home, especially not when I suspect they're a dragon. Only the last dragon my mother and I knew burned our house down and put us in danger."

The guy nodded. "I understand. I'm here in connection with your father's clan. I have news of your uncle and with that, some other news to impart about your clan. I can assure you I come in peace and a dragon's word is to be relied upon. However, if you'd rather meet with me on more neutral territory, that's okay too. It would need to be now though, if possible. Seeing as I'm already here in Gnarly."

I didn't bother saying that the mouth of the cave he'd departed from was in Gnarly too because again, we weren't supposed to know that.

My mum's footsteps sounded at the top of the stairs.

"Let him in, Jason. It'll be fine."

The guy's eyes flicked over to my mum, and I saw him give her the once-over. My own narrowed in on him so that when he looked back at me, he startled a little. To me, my mum was in her fifties, and one step off grey hair and bingo nights. Already, thanks to her boyfriend Stan, I kept being reminded she was still *active*, if you got what I meant. I didn't need a dragon eyeing her up. She'd been there, done that, scorched the t-shirt.

Mum went past me and towards the living room and I held back and indicated for this guy to follow. But as he stepped through the door, I got in his way and held my hand out. "Jason Gradon. And you are?"

"Griffin Wheeler. I'll tell you the rest if you'd let me get a seat. Only it's a little warm out here, even for a dragon. Could I trouble you for a water by any chance?"

"If this is a trick and you do anything to my mum, I'll tear you limb from limb," I ground out, even though at times I struggled to tear across a grab bag of Minstrels.

"I will wait here for you, so as not to make your mum feel uncomfortable," he said, and with that I went to the kitchen and got three bottles of water from the fridge.

When I returned, we walked into the living room. I took the seat next to my mum, and Griffin sat in the chair opposite. I passed everyone a drink. Me and mum watched as Griffin unscrewed the top and took a large swig. I watched his huge Adam's apple bob up and down.

"I'm sorry to have turned up unannounced like this, but right now, there are things we need to address among the Rulefort dragon clan." He turned to Mum. "Your husband's brother, Josiah, has passed away after a short illness. His desire was that Jason take the crown after him." Griffin looked between us. "You don't have to do this, Jason. You can continue your life as it is now and appoint someone to rule in your place. But the council spoke and were in agreement that in the first instance you should be invited to see and visit the Rulefort land, and also to help arrange the funeral of your uncle."

"This is a lot to take in," I told him.

"I know, and personally, as deputy for the last twenty-five years, I feel it would make a lot more sense if I stepped up. However, I'm a fair man and I'm not going to lay claim on a clan that's not mine through birthright. I am however going to tell you that no one would think less of you if you handed it all over to me. I've proved my worth and trustworthiness to Rulefort."

"And when am I supposed to decide on all this?"

"Come visit and let's get the funeral done. Then we'd like you to accept to do a series of trials to see if you have the abilities needed to rule a dragon clan. If all that works out, then in a week or so you can decide whether to reign over Rulefort or stay here in Gnarly."

"Would I be able to go between the two?"

"I think it would be difficult, but I never say never about anything. Just know that there are other dragon clans who would try to encroach on Rulefort land should you not be there to keep an eye on it. But as a powerful Rulefort dragon I'm sure you'd soon put them in their place. And that brings me to my next question, personal as it may be. As a half-breed did you inherit all of your powers, or are they diminished?"

My mum and I both remained steadfastly silent as we looked at each other.

Griffin noted the uncomfortable exchange of our glances.

"I don't want to seem rude, but this is an all-cards-on-the-table question. If you don't have any dragon abilities, you will last three seconds before someone challenges you for Rulefort. Me included."

Give the guy his due, he seemed pretty direct about his intentions. My first impressions were that he was a straight talker and a get-the-job-done kind of guy. I had no doubt that if he felt I wasn't up to the job, he'd want the crown. Merrin had indicated as much.

"We don't know what powers I possess," I told him truthfully. "My mother had them suppressed by magic after my father disappeared."

Griffin's mouth dropped open. "You don't know?" he clarified.

I nodded.

"You've never used your dragon abilities?"

"I didn't think I had any, other than I know I can shift."

"Co-incidentally, I told him this morning about how I had his inner dragon stopped after what his father did to our home," Mum added.

"You can guess therefore that this is all a little much right now? I don't know how much of a dragon I am, and now I'm facing challenges to see if I can rule a kingdom. I'm envisaging *Indiana Jones* or *The Hunger Games* style survival trials."

"Endurance will be one of the things tested, Jason. You're not going to be challenged to a game of Snap."

I shivered inwardly and wished once again I could time travel back to yesterday and then stay there.

"I will leave you to think on everything I've said." Griffin went into his pocket and pulled out a business card. It said he was an accountant. "You can't write clan deputy, and I do handle the finances," he said, having guessed my query. "Call me if you think of anything you want to know. At any time."

"That's very kind of you," I said.

He looked at me strangely. "Jason, right now you are the heir of the Rulefort dragon clan. Every one of the clan is at your service."

I wanted to shout, 'Fucking hell', but managed to refrain from doing so outwardly. I might be a dragon heir, but my mum would have still clipped me around the ears.

"Actually, there is something I want to ask," I stated, and Griffin sat back down. "Do you know what happened to my father?"

He looked at Mum. "You don't know?"

She shook her head. "I called Josiah and asked he deal with Joseph, and I said I didn't want to know. That way was easier. I just got on with my life. I'm not saying I never wondered. It's never really left my mind. But I decided it would be easier to wonder than to know."

"I understand." He paused for a moment. "Joseph lost his mind completely. He was imprisoned in the cave jail by his younger brother, and the council ruled he was not fit, would never be fit, to rule the dragons. He has remained in the jail since in his human form. He's never spoken and never used his dragon abilities again."

"He's alive? Is he nearby?" I said, quite unnecessarily, but I couldn't help myself. I'd always figured he'd have been killed or come to some harm another way, or he'd have moved far away.

"Our caves are vast, extending out over much of London and he is held in a jail under Gladstone Park in Cricklewood."

"So if I want to, I can see him?"

"Yes, of course. Whenever you like."

"How does he spend his time if he doesn't speak?" Mum asked.

"He reads, and he exercises... obsessively," Griffin said. "He's an extremely strong dragon, despite his years."

"And so he's still potentially volatile. Basically, a ticking time bomb?"

Griffin raised his hands. "Who knows? All I know is that since his capture and imprisonment he has caused no trouble. He walked willingly into that cell, and he's never made any demands beyond those for reading material."

"Thank you for letting us know and thank you for coming here today to explain the current situation and how we go from here," I told him, before standing up. It was time for him to leave and for me to think about everything that had happened today.

Griffin nodded. "We shall speak more tomorrow," he said. "You understand that some matters, such as your uncle's funeral cannot wait?"

I nodded. "I will call you at some point tomorrow."

With that, I escorted Griffin out of the house. Closing the door, I slumped against it. All I wanted to do was to see Charity, but I knew I couldn't burden her with all this right now. It wasn't fair. Not until I was clearer on what my future held.

If the dragons didn't like a dragon marrying a human, I wondered what their position was on a mermaid? Not that I was thinking of marriage. God, no. We'd only had three dates. Unless she believed in no sex before marriage, in which case I was so desperate I couldn't rule out dragging her to Gretna Green.

It looked like new experiences were on the horizon. But where I'd thought I'd be setting fire to the sheets, instead, my dragon powers would be getting a trial run.

If I had any...

I returned to my mum, who'd stayed on the sofa.

"What a day," I remarked.

"You could say that. I'm sorry, Jason. I should have told you everything a long time ago."

"We're not doing this, Mum. No apologies. It doesn't serve any purpose. We need to explore my powers, and I need to go see the caves."

"Whatever you decide to do, you have my backing, son," she said. "Whether that's getting to know your father or taking on rule of Rulefort. I'm not going to pretend I'm not concerned. Especially about your father's seeming muteness. It always goes quiet before a storm, and he wasn't allowed his kingdom."

"I don't think I can do this, Mum." I put my hand through my hair. "I'm not known for my intelligence. I'm known for being a bit of a prat. It's hardly the right qualities of a king, is it?"

"Caring, generous, a sense of humour when times are tough, fit and strong, and you believe you aren't capable? The only thing you have ever lacked is confidence in yourself, Jason Gradon, and maybe one way or another it's time you believed in yourself."

"Is our surname really Gradon?" I asked her. "I mean it's an anagram of dragon."

She shook her head. "I changed it when your father left, but there's no reason why you can't now take on your rightful name. You weren't christened, but as your father's son, you earned the right to be Jason Rulefort."

"I'll stick with Gradon for now. I'm making no drastic decisions."

And that's when our gazes met, and we knew that I was already changing. Because me and thinking things through hadn't exactly been a pairing before.

CHAPTER FIVE

Charity

I'd spent most of the evening recovering from my earlier indulgences, so by the time the alarm went off at eight, I was pleased to find I felt normal.

Over the next thirty minutes, I got ready while repeatedly telling Billy to get up for college. It was like communicating with the dead, receiving just snatches of conversation and moans in return.

Eventually, my bleary-eyed younger brother appeared in the kitchen.

"Want a coffee?"

He pulled a face at me, went in the fridge and brought out a can of Monster.

"What have I told you about those kinds of drinks?"

He side-eyed me. "You're in no position this morning to advise me on what to drink, Miss *I think I'm going to die*."

"Oh shut up."

He grinned and then swiped my slices of toast off my plate, stuffing them straight in his mouth and walking back out of the room. Five minutes later, I heard the door close, leaving me on my own. I decided I'd have my next coffee in the salon and go sit down there and await my first customer.

Looking in my appointment book, I had thirty minutes before

my first appointment of the day, or so I thought. Then a vampire queen knocked on the door at exactly nine o'clock.

"Good morning, Charity," she said breezily as she waltzed in. "Which chair would you like me in?"

"You don't have an appointment," I pointed out.

She waved a hand around the shop. "You don't have any customers. I'll pay double for a wash and blow dry."

Given that she was a vampire whose hair didn't grow, there was only one reason Mya Malone had come to my salon today. Oh, shit, there could be two.

"I'm not going to die, am I? You're not here to accompany me off the mortal plain?"

She left me hanging for the longest minute of my life, the cow.

"No, sweetie, I'm here for all the gossip on Jason. You see Ginny is still in bed with Merrin and she wasn't very impressed when I knocked on the bedroom window. Then I couldn't get a response from Jason's, and I found he wasn't in, and so I thought you'd know what was happening now you're dating, so here I am."

Mya was the Queen of the Wayward, the unsettled souls that weren't clearly destined for Heaven or Hell. Mya had to work with them and decide in which direction they went on to—up or down. I'd met her at the first upcycling event, and she was a case of once met, never forgotten.

I escorted her over to the sink and got her to sit back in a chair. "I don't know anything," I said truthfully. "I've not spoken to Jason since I left Merrin's yesterday. He's not even sent me a text."

"Ouch. And what are you thinking about that?"

I shrugged. "I don't know what's happened. He could be really busy with something. You've said yourself he's not there."

Or he doesn't care about you.

Or he's in danger.

"Fuck, what if he's in danger?" I panicked.

"Why didn't I think of that?" Mya said, clapping her hands.

My face scrunched in a grimace. "There's no need to look so happy about the fact my boyfriend could be in danger."

She pulled a face back. "No, silly. I just thought that his mum will know what's happening. Back in a tick." With that she whizzed off, leaving me standing behind a spinning empty chair.

HOT AS SUCK

I went and got myself another coffee. I had a feeling I was going to need a lot of it today. While I put the pod in the machine, my thoughts ruminated over the fact Jason hadn't sent me a text. But then again, I'd not sent him one either, had I? Taking my drink back to my workstation, I picked up my mobile phone and sent a quick text.

Charity: Hoping that everything is okay. When you get a minute, let me know.

I kept the phone in my hand, thinking there might be a reply, but my phone stayed silent. There wasn't much time for me to brood though as Mya whizzed back in. I jumped and my phone sailed through the air. Luckily the swift Miss Malone caught it and passed it back to me.

"I have an appointment at half past, so if you really want a wash and blow dry, you need to get your arse in the chair," I told her.

She sat down and I started running the water. "Is that the right temperature for you?"

"As hot as you can stand it, please," she requested. "I'm always cold. I can close my eyes and enjoy the heat on my scalp."

I turned it up to the maximum my own hands could stand. Mya sighed happily as I began to soak her locks.

"I have the latest from Fenella. She said she planned on telling you this morning if only I'd have given her a chance to actually get out of bed and get to the launderette. Honestly, these people should be grateful that I broke the curse that prevented them from falling in love, not get annoyed that they have to break off from their shenanigans for a minute or two because I need information."

I rubbed shampoo into her hair and began massaging her scalp.

"Okay, so Jason's uncle died. He was the king of the Rulefort dragon clan. Now Jason can inherit the crown and a deep underground cave dwelling that goes on for miles. That's if he wants to. He's not sure at this point. This morning, the deputy called for him and they went to spend the day in the caves, introducing him to the clan. If he wants to rule, he has to undertake a series of trials. Oh also, he's not been able to be a dragon as Fen had his inner dragon magicked away, and so he's got to embrace that too. He'd asked her to pop in to see you and explain that he was sorry he didn't message last night but his brain was scrambled, and today he overlaid. He's not sure what phone reception he has in the caves or whether he might be too busy, but he'll get in touch as soon as he can."

"Fenella just told you all this?" I rinsed off the shampoo, feeling she'd got a lot of information in a small space of time.

"She said, and I quote, 'We both know you can read my mind, so do that and bugger off, I'm busy'."

"At least I know what's been happening now, so thank you," I said, pouring conditioner into my hand.

"That's not all. Jason's dad is in the caves in a jail. He burned their house down and disappeared. That's where he's been all the time, in a jail. Not talking or being a dragon. Just reading and exercising. I wonder if he's like a ripped silver fox?"

"Doubt it or one of the dragons would have eaten him," I quipped.

Mya giggled. "I like you. I'm sorry you've been through such shit. Hopefully, here you'll get your happy ever after. Gnarly is a place of community. It's what held everyone together through the hardships of the curse. They couldn't fall madly in love, so they loved each other in other ways, in being there for one another."

I accidentally dropped the shower head and water sprayed in my own face.

"Goddammit." I turned the tap off. "We'll let the conditioner sit for a moment while I just dry myself off." I grabbed a nearby towel.

"Sorry. Death says I shouldn't keep letting people know I can read all their thoughts. I can't help it though. I'm super-powerful and super-nosy."

"That's okay. But no one other than my brother knows why I left Bridlington and I'd rather it stayed that way for now. Even Jason doesn't know the specifics."

"I think the fact you've opened yourself back up to love is really brave," she said. "It can't have been easy, your *best friend* and your husband."

I closed my eyes for a moment and pressed my lips firmly together as a vision of them together came into my vision. "No, it wasn't easy. It was painful." *But not as painful as the fact I lost my family apart from Billy,* I thought.

"No, that really sucks," Mya said. I'd forgotten once more that she could read my mind.

I put the water back on and washed the conditioner out of Mya's hair, and talked about the weather, letting her know that for now, that conversation was done. I'd come to Gnarly for a fresh start and this morning my head was already swimming with thoughts of whatever Jason was encountering with his newfound clan. I didn't need it swimming with thoughts from back in the sea.

Thankfully, silence reigned due to the noise from the hairdryer, giving me time to gather myself together a little.

"Okay, so straightened or some curls?" I asked her.

"You decide," she said.

I plugged in the tongs. "I've never seen your hair in waves. I think it would look amazing. Anyway, tell me what's going on in your own life. It must be non-stop, dating Death and dealing with the wayward."

"It's been a busy week, not least of which because something really strange happened a few days ago," she said. "And strange happens all the time, but this was extra strange. Death said it had never happened before and he blamed me even though it most definitely wasn't my fault."

"Erm, I'm not sure I need to hear this," I said.

She paused for a moment and the curling tongs beeped that they were ready at the same time as Mya understood what I was saying.

"Oh, not that. Death never has a problem getting it up. No, I went to send a spirit up to Heaven, and it went up there fine, but then an angel came back down. Landed right in the room at my feet. Tried to get them to take him back up there, but they said he couldn't go back right now. He'd got a lesson to learn and a job to do."

I began curling her hair.

"I think Heaven's taking a bit of a liberty. I sort out wayward souls, not wayward angels. I have enough to do already. But they said I owed them because of when I first started and I sent too many up at once and they were so busy it threatened how heavenly Heaven was as there was disgruntlement with the queue when everyone up there should be all, 'Oh wow, Heaven'. The chuffheads should just have been glad I decided they could go up there at all, but that's humans for you. Always finding something to moan about," she carried on.

"This angel," I said, finally putting two and two together. "Is he called Kaf by any chance?"

"Yup. Kafziel, also sometimes known as Cassiel. He's an archangel apparently. Not that I'm up on what the angel hierarchies are all about. Death says the archangels tend to things of great importance for mankind. Apparently, getting me to the top of the waiting list for designer goods is not part of this. I checked, obvs."

"So is Connor an angel too?"

"No. At least I don't think so. I don't know Connor that well, and I didn't spend long with Kaf because he just rejoiced at being free and said he was off to stay with his brother. After they wouldn't take him back upstairs, I went off in a panic to find Death and spent the next two hours trying to convince him I'd not accidentally reversed the soul machine and ejected an angel from Heaven. Death finally believed me, spoke to them upstairs, and they said the same thing, that Kaf had things to learn and things to do."

"Interesting," I said.

"Yes, well, I need to keep an eye on him until we work out why he's here and what lesson he needs to learn," she said. Her eyes met mine in the mirror as she blatantly sucked all the thoughts from my head.

"Interesting," she said back. "Making customers wet and getting wet himself."

CHAPTER SIX

Jason

I was surprised I'd slept as well as I had, but I presumed my brain had just decided to completely switch off from having to think about it all. That and help from the beers I'd consumed while I deliberated over everything. I'd woken at a quarter to nine with my heart palpitating over having to meet dragons and take part in trials, now coupled with the fact I'd only got fifteen minutes before I needed to set off. By nine am, Griffin had arrived to take me to the caves as I'd decided the quicker I got there, the quicker I stopped worrying about 'What-ifs'. I'd called my mum on the way, letting her know that I was okay and off to visit the caves. After reassuring her I was fine to go alone and wasn't about to start any trials today, I then asked her to let Charity know the situation. I knew my mum would worry, but right now I was only information gathering. No one was forcing me to become a dragon king. This was just about me meeting the others and getting a feel for the place.

Now I stood here at the entrance of the caves watching the large boulders move to let me in. I started thinking about the fact they would also move back in place to keep me in, and the palpitations started again.

"When are we going to get the magic spell taken off me so I can harness my dragon powers?" I questioned Griffin. "I mean, doesn't this make me vulnerable today? Other dragons might take me out so they can be king."

"Dragons have to challenge you, they can't just 'take you out', and today is all about introductions. You'll have no need of any powers, and in any case, we'll be exploring that at a later date in a safe room in the caves, where you can't harm yourself or others." Griffin patted me on the back. "It's going to be a busy day, Jason, just let yourself take it all in, and if you need a breather, let me know and we can come back up here for a bit."

I nodded. "Thanks." Then Griffin began moving towards the open mouth of the cave and I told myself, 'You got this' and followed him.

We walked for a good five minutes down some steps and along a gradual incline until large metal double doors appeared. Of course, there would be plenty of security to get inside, though having to move large boulders wouldn't be the easiest of activities.

My questions must have been written on my face because Griffin turned to me. "We have to protect ourselves from the weather as well as any unwelcome guests. We're underground. We need to be protected in case of flood. This is a weather door."

"Got you," I acknowledged.

Griffin radioed in to ask for the door to be opened, before pointing at a small doorbell tucked in a crevice. "There's also a camera and intercom operating for visitors, so you can just buzz and wait."

With a loud creak, the doors began to open, revealing a large crowd. I started to feel like I was a boxer about to enter the ring as they all looked at me and began chanting and shouting.

"That's the new king?"

"Fuck, he's fit. He can rule my pussy."

"Get out, half-breed mutant. You're not welcome."

"That's him? I'm gonna challenge him. Pussy looks shit-scared."

"Stand back," Griffin roared, and suddenly there was silence, and everyone stood still. And there was my first taste of the power of a leader. The deputy had spoken, and all were now mute.

Wow.

"Go back to your dwellings and your business. There will be plenty of opportunity to meet our guest, and that's what he is right now. Not the future leader, but a guest. Today, Jason is here to get to know Rulefort better and to be introduced slowly to our clan.

Anyone found inciting trouble can spend the night in a jail cell. Am I clear?" Griffin's eyes went between the two who'd been less than kind with their comments. They both nodded and then looked at the floor. I was dying to shout, 'Hah', but didn't think that should be my first words to everyone. I realised then that I hadn't said a word to anyone yet. I was potentially the future king; I should say something.

I raised a hand. "Good morning, all. I look forward to meeting you and getting to know you better."

A few bowed and curtsied. I forgot myself, turned to Griffin, and went, "Man, you must get endless pussy." I only whispered it, but Griffin's eyes flashed yellow, his lips curled, and he fought to resist a snarl, so I immediately shut up.

The crowds parted as we walked through deeper into the caves. The place was vast and reminded me of the inside of an airport with shops, cafes, and places to sit. From there the place just exploded with different entrances that Griffin said led to dwellings and more infrastructure. He led me to a large room, this time with wooden double doors, deeply engraved with what appeared to be the Rulefort crest. When he pushed them open it revealed a large room, in the centre of which was an enormous rectangular wooden table with elaborately carved legs, around which were a dozen or so elegantly carved chairs.

"This is where the council sit. They will be here shortly to meet you. In the meantime, why don't you look around the room. Would you like a drink while you wait?"

"Yes please. What do you drink here? Mead?"

Griffin bellowed with laughter. "The furniture is old but we're not in some King Arthur re-enactment, Jason. We drink what everyone else drinks."

"I'll have a cup of tea then please. Lots of milk and two sugars."

"Coming up." He walked over to what looked like panelling, pressed it and it opened to reveal a small kitchen. He turned and pointed to another one. "Gents loo is behind that one for future reference."

That was good because the jury was out on whether or not I might shit myself before I met the other council members.

There were paintings of the previous rulers on the walls. I

finally found the one with my uncle on. He'd had dark brown hair and eyes, and a long beard. He looked like he belonged in a 1% motorcycle club. It was a shame I'd never get to meet him. There was also a large, framed piece with the rules of the Rulefort Clan contained inside. I quickly moved on. I was sure they'd give me a copy for homework.

Pulling up a chair, I plonked myself down and leaned over, resting my elbows on the table and my head in my hands. I was in a dragon's lair. Not only that, but possibly, *MY*. DRAGONS. LAIR.

For a moment, I allowed my mind to picture me with a crown on my head, lighting a fire in the hearth with my own flaming breath, and then moving over Charity's body to light a fire in her hearth. I didn't know which felt more unbelievable: ruling a dragon kingdom or being rid of my virginity.

Charity. What must she be thinking? I hoped she wasn't pissed off at me not contacting her yesterday. I'd felt paralysed by all the news. I'd not wanted to talk about it with anyone. But as I put myself in her shoes, ignored, I realised I might have fucked up.

Griffin walked out of the kitchen at the same time as the doors sailed open and a large group of sturdy men swaggered in. One of them took one look at me and roared.

"What the fuck are you doing sat in the king's chair? *Get out, NOW.*"

Closing my eyes, I resigned myself to the fact that I might be a virgin, but I still kept fucking up in other ways.

"Viper," Griffin snapped. "He doesn't know. He just sat down. He's a little overwhelmed."

I'm sure Griffin meant to help but that didn't plead my case very well.

"Overwhelmed *before* the trials? He's only just got here. I tell you, Griffin, either you need to step up or we need to put this out for tender. My son would stand forward to rule."

It was time to go big or go home. I stood up, flexed myself like I would have pre-Charity in a nightclub on a Friday night, and I yelled. "I'll put you out for tender if you don't quieten down.

Chicken tenders are lush. I wonder what Gnarly would think to dragon ones?"

Griffin's mouth curled up at the corners in a smirk. Viper shut up, but not before his eyes flashed with dragon yellow. I carried on, having stood back from the table. "It's been a lot to take in, and so unfortunately, I decided to take in a large amount of ale last night. I needed to sit down and pulled out the nearest chair. I didn't know it was for a ruling king. Now, maybe everyone could grab a seat, let me know where I *can* sit, and let's get some introductions done."

"Sounds like a plan, Jason," Griffin said, and I could tell he was enjoying himself. He gave me a wink when the others weren't looking.

People took a seat, and I noticed that Viper sat in the king's chair. So that was why the arsehole was annoyed at where I'd sat. For some reason *he* sat there. Looked like he also felt his son should be ruler. I needed to keep a close eye on him.

"As current Chair of the council, Viper keeps the ruling seat 'warm'," Griffin told me, pulling up a basic fold-out wooden chair for me. Fabulous. Talk about roll out the red carpet. Mine would be faded and threadbare. I sat down next to Griffin at the very opposite end of the table to Viper, meaning he could fix his beady eyes on me.

"Chair calls the council to order," Viper said. "Drago will take notes. Present today are council members: Viper, Drago, Griffin, Chance, Kenna, Sol, Blaze, Azar, Brenton, Nithe, Tyson, and ARson."

He pronounced the last one A... R... son. My eyes darted to Griffin who didn't look at me, but who did dig a finger into my thigh under the table. Someone had called their kid arson? I'd have called him arse for short if I'd thought I could get away with it.

"In attendance today is Jason Gradon."

"It's Jason Rulefort, actually," I said, because no matter how much stronger than me Viper might be, if I was going down it was having annoyed him immensely.

"Jason Rulefort, I beg your pardon. We were just going on the last name we had for you," Viper said.

"No need for grovelling apologies," I continued, when in actual fact he'd said it through gritted teeth. "Gradon was correct, up until yesterday. I didn't know my actual surname, or many other things for that matter. But I think while I'm down here, people should be aware of my birth-given surname. Now, is Jason okay or should I call myself J... A... son?" I winked at AR-son and received another dig in my thigh from Griffin. This time all five fingers and it *hurt*.

My mother always said my mouth would get me in trouble one day. I'd better shut up for now.

"Let's get to the matter at hand," Viper said cold as ice, which must be quite a feat for a creature of fire. "Griffin, over to you."

"Thank you, Chair. Jason is here today to look around the cave and meet the council. It's possible he will bump into other clan members while he is here, but I intend to keep that to a minimum. For the next couple of days, I hope to acclimatise Jason to the caves and to imbue him with dragon knowledge, so that before he makes a decision about whether or not to begin the trials, he is confident of everything being a Rulefort dragon entails."

"And at which point do you foresee the start of the trials?"

"Saturday."

My stomach lurched. Just five days away? Couldn't I just hang here and try the crown on?

Griffin continued. "Today is Monday. Tomorrow, Jason will remain home with some scholarly texts. Wednesday, he will return to help plan his uncle's funeral. Thursday will be the funeral. Friday, we shall prepare for the trials, and Saturday they will start if this suits the rest of the council."

"All in favour say 'aye'," Viper said. One by one they went around the table and repeated it. I kept my mouth shut for once, knowing I didn't have a current say in any of this. I had five days to learn to be a dragon. I was screwed, but again not in a sexy way.

"Should Jason Rulefort fail the trials, then the morning following his defeat, we will pin notice inviting potential leaders," Viper added, and I swear he smirked at me as he said the word defeat. "If there's nothing further, we shall adjourn and meet here again at ten am, Wednesday, to plan the funeral of Josiah Rulefort." He looked around. "Anything else?" Eventually his eyes settled on me.

"Can I be excused to use the bathroom," I said, as reality hit, and my stomach gurgled.

CHAPTER SEVEN

Charity

I'd enjoyed my day in the salon. Everyone in Gnarly was so friendly and chatty and I loved seeing the sheer joy on their faces when I transformed their hair. I already felt more settled here than I ever had in the North Sea. I might have been born there, but I had no real attachment to it. I loved water, but preferred being in it alone. My dream was to have my own private pool, rather than having to share the sea with everything and everyone else.

Just as I was clearing up at around four pm, my phone beeped indicating a text.

Jason: Sorry for the silence. Are you free tonight for dinner at the bistro?

Part of me wanted to play hard to get and to ignore him for a bit, but I also wanted to know everything that had happened, and so I quickly typed back.

Charity: Yes. Eight pm okay?
Jason: Great. See you there xo

I didn't reply back, but I smiled at the kiss and hug symbol at the end.

Feeling in a buoyant mood after a good day in the salon, and now with a date in the evening, I closed up and walked to the saverstore to get some goodies in for Billy's dinner seeing as I was deserting him for the evening again. I filled my basket with fizzy pop, chocolate, crisps, a couple of microwave burgers and a pizza.

Billy usually ate his dinner and then a couple of hours later ate the equivalent of another.

With a straining lift, I hefted the basket onto the counter.

"Oh dear," Mitzi, the owner of the store said. "I heard on the grapevine that you were dating Jason but that he'd left to rule a dragon kingdom and marry a fire-eater. Judging by the contents of this basket, you are eating your feelings. You've missed the offer on ice-cream though, three cartons for the price of two. Shall I get you some more?"

I smiled. "Yes, you can, but it's not for me, it's for my brother. I've a date with Jason tonight. He's not ruling any kingdoms or marrying fire-eaters. At least, not yet. I'm hoping for an update on all his news tonight."

"I should have known Hettie wouldn't have got the right facts. I think she has more potatoes in her ears than in her chip shop," Mitzi huffed. She lowered her voice. "Anyway, can you have a word with Jason on my behalf? Should he come into possession of any shiny new possessions, I would be interested in first refusal." Being a magpie shifter, Mitzi was addicted to anything shiny, including mirrors. She was often so entranced with her own appearance that the shop ended up with a large queue. She went off to get me the ice cream and then rang everything up and placed it into bags.

"I'd better get these back to Billy and let him know I'm off out again." I lifted the two bags and groaned once more.

"Charity, we have a portal, remember?" Mitzi reminded me. I had in fact forgotten that portals connected the shops and homes of the fell, meaning that by the time I got home, the shopping would already be there. It didn't work for people though, so I needed to walk back.

"Don't forget about any shiny relics," Mitzi said, and she gave me an idea. Getting my purse out I took out my wedding ring from the zipped back pocket. "I have no use for this. Can you do something with it?"

Mitzi's eyes lit up. "Are you sure?"

"Yes. I've been walking around with it in my purse, not knowing what to do with it. Can't exactly burn it, and I thought the money might come in, until I had it valued. My ex told me it was platinum, but it's silver. I shouldn't have been surprised to find that out really."

"Your kindness is much appreciated. It shall go in my collection. I smelt items and make other beautiful shiny things for my home. And, as a solo magpie, you let me know if you want me to do anything to this ex. One is for sorrow," she said. "I promise I can make him entirely miserable."

"He's not worth it, but thanks for the offer," I said, and I left the shop feeling a lot lighter, and not just of money and shopping.

By the time I got home, Billy was already tucking into the goodies I'd bought for him.

"You going out then?"

"Yes, with Jason. Will you be okay on your own?"

He gave me a look. "Like I hang out with you anyway." He then put his hands up in surrender. "Nope. I can see that look coming over your face, the 'thanks for coming with me to Gnarly' look. I'm going to my room to eat and to play on the Xbox. Try not to come home wasted tonight, hey? Only it's a school night." He dashed upstairs before I could call him a cheeky twat.

After putting the shopping he'd not taken upstairs with him away, I grabbed a glass of water and then made my way to my bedroom in order to get ready for the evening.

When we'd been on our previous three dates I'd wondered when Jason might hint for me to put out. Now I realised his reticence had come from his secret. As I'd overheard his confession and he knew I'd overheard, would that make things weird? And if we did get down to business, was I going to have to teach him? I was overthinking and decided to just play the date by ear. He might even tell me that with his new dragon duties he couldn't see me anymore, so there was little use in trying to guess the future.

At that point my phone rang, and the name 'Ginny' flashed across the screen.

"Hello?"

"Merrin just had another vision. This time about you."

My stomach lurched and nausea threatened. Was my past now going to catch up with me?

"He says the doors are in your future."

"Doors?"

"That's what he said. "Oh and fire. Doors and fire."

"What?" I started pacing around my bedroom.

Suddenly, a man's voice came on the line. "Charity, it's Merrin. Do not panic. The fire is not a real one. All will make sense after this evening. That's all I can say about this right now." He chuckled and ended the call.

I was more confused than ever, but I knew one thing for sure: a glass of wine was definitely in my future.

"You look beautiful," Jason said, grinning at me from just outside the entrance of the bistro.

I beamed back and for a few minutes it was like there was only the two of us in the whole universe. My eyes swept down his body, taking in the tightness of his shirt, the part translucence of the white revealing hints of those fine pecs and biceps, and then his black chinos stretched over his thighs. I bet his butt looked like a peach.

His own eyes had swept over me, taking in the pale-yellow strappy sundress I wore emblazoned with a cherry print. Ruching at the top kept it tight against my chest, but then it flowed out from the waist, teasingly wafting in the breeze like it might do a Marilyn Monroe at any moment.

Jason moved closer, leaned over and kissed my cheek. It was gentlemanly and yet it launched a fire down below.

Then he was moving towards the doorway and holding it open for me to enter.

"Hey," greeted Chantelle, a witch who worked at the bistro. "I got you a good seat in the corner." She beckoned for us to follow her over to a small booth at the back. It was partially screened by fake plants and so was more private and romantic.

The smell of the food made my stomach gurgle, and I felt my cheeks heat.

"I need to fill this woman up," Jason said to Charity and then I watched as his own face went beet red.

"At least buy me a drink first," I quipped. He laughed, though still looked bashful as we took our seats in the booth and ordered drinks. I decided on a bottle of wine and Jason asked for two pints.

We both gave the excuse that then we wouldn't have to wait for further drinks given the bistro was busy, but it was obvious we were both nervous.

When I'd come to Gnarly, I'd had no intention whatsoever of falling for another man. Dates and sex, yes. Love, hell no. But something about Jason just drew me in. I felt at home around him. I didn't want to scare him off, or set myself up for a fall, but I enjoyed being in his company. How he looked at me made me feel like a princess.

Was that it? Was I just so desperate to be seen after the rejection I'd experienced that I was throwing myself in at speed? I didn't think so, but I had to consider the possibility.

Once we had our drinks and had perused the menu and ordered, I sat back and relaxed a little.

"Okay, Jason, so lots has been happening with you. Tell me everything. I mean, one minute we're about to paint furniture and the next Merrin's got a vision about you."

Jason told me everything that had happened since he'd gone into Merrin's house, right up until he'd returned home and texted me to come out to dinner. Again, I was reminded about how open and honest he was. He was Jason, take him or leave him.

"Wow. So how do you feel about it all?" I asked him while he drank some of his beer. Our food had been delivered by then and so we were chatting around mouthfuls of food and drink.

"To be honest with you, I feel like I'm in a dream and going to wake up at any moment. It's gone from me knowing nothing about my father other than he'd burned our house down and his bridges with our family, to now I might rule a clan of dragons, own a massive underground sprawling cave, and I have these challenges to do. And the biggest challenge of all is whether I'll have any dragon powers whatsoever. Something we don't know yet."

"And they're going to remove the spell from your powers and test them?"

"Yes. At which point if I don't perform, I'll be walking away with my tail between my legs. My dragon tail that is."

Immediately I thought of his dick, hanging there limply. At that point my bladder let me know I really needed to pee. Glancing at the wine bottle, I noted I'd almost drunk three quarters of it already.

"Excuse me while I just visit the ladies," I said. "And if they ask about desserts, I'd definitely like to see the menu."

He nodded, but he looked uncomfortable, and I wondered if he was worrying about the elephant in the room. *Its trunk in particular,* I thought.

"How goes it with you and Jason?" Chantelle said as I passed her.

"Good thanks," I replied, a silly grin erupting despite my attempts to try to be cool about everything me and Jason.

"Oh yay. Only I did a spell for him to meet his perfect mate, you know? You two look so fantastic together."

"Thanks. It's very early days though. This is only our fourth date."

Chantelle looked off into the distance for a moment. "Yeah. It can seem like you've met the one and then it all goes to shit, and you realise you were fooled by an arsehole," she replied.

I flinched a little, surprised by the venom in her words.

"Sorry, ignore me. I didn't mean to be a downer."

"Oh dear. Your own dating life not going well then?" I was plaiting my legs now, but felt I had to ask.

"Nope. Diabolical. But I'm sure at some point my prince will come. Anyway, you'd better hurry back, Jason's looking a bit weird."

I turned to see that he was taking deep breaths and mumbling to himself. He looked... nervous. This had to be about the other subject we'd failed to discuss. It was getting ever closer to the end of our fourth date.

I excused myself to go pee, and to think. On my way back out, I beckoned over Chantelle. "Do you think you could do a little spell on Jason, just to make him less nervous? Only—"

She interrupted. "He's a virgin and you're wanting to deflower him?" She winked.

Once more my cheeks burned. "Something like that."

"I'll sprinkle some confidence dust on his dessert. It's chocolate sprinkles, but I'll bewitch them."

"Thank you." I made my way back to our table and shortly afterwards Chantelle came and took our dessert orders.

By this stage Jason looked like he might hyperventilate, and so I leaned closer. "Jase?"

"Yeah?"

"If it's okay with you I'm going to come back to yours tonight. I can't stay over, but I thought we could make out. No pressure."

"Oh there's pressure. I can feel it down below. I've been horny for you all night, Charity," he confessed. "All I've been thinking is that your dress is adorable, but it would look better off you."

"Really?" I grinned.

He nodded. "Shall we leave the desserts, get the bill and get out of here?"

I had a split-second to decide whether or not Jase could use the extra help. I watched as he swallowed nervously.

"No, I really want my tiramisu," I blurted out.

"Oh, erm, okay. I might leave my trifle though. My appetite seems to have switched onto something else," he teased.

"You can't upset the bistro staff, you must eat up," I replied curtly. I needed him to have the confidence sprinkles. I was sure it would help him.

He looked at me strangely, and then shrugged. When his dessert came, he ate it down in three fast mouthfuls. I sat there; my own mouth having dropped open.

"Now the staff will be pleased at just how much I loved their dessert. Can we go now?" he pleaded.

I nodded, looking forward to what was to come.

Hopefully, both of us.

CHAPTER EIGHT

Jason

I'd been trapped in an underground cave and faced ferocious dragons and yet nothing had me as nervous as right now. I wanted to get back to mine and get it over with, and I meant that in the best way. To do my best as I'd imagined it many a time and then to keep going until Charity was satisfied and decided I was the best lover she'd ever had.

When Charity had insisted on a dessert, I felt it was an indication that she was also nervous. Like ripping off a plaster, it was time to get on with this: fast, maybe temporarily discomfiting, but then it would be done with. Not the most romantic of thoughts, but I could only become a better lover by practice. *Practice made perfect* they said, and I wanted to be the perfect lover.

As I ate my dessert quickly, I began to worry again. Charity had been married. Had probably had lots of sex. What if I was hopeless in bed? If I was, I would go back to the caves and either pick a fight with Viper, so he burned me to ash, or I'd wait for my uncle's funeral and throw myself on the pyre.

Anyway, I needed to remember what she'd said. No pressure. Just home to mine to make out.

Thank God I'd tidied up once we'd arranged our date, *just in case.*

I insisted on paying the bill, despite Charity's protests about wanting to be equal. In fact, I wasn't sure what happened, but suddenly, I just felt fine. No longer nervous. It was as if my brain and body decided that this was the evening we'd been waiting for, and I should just enjoy it.

I noticed as we waited for the receipt that Charity kept glancing at me and fidgeting with her napkin.

"Are you sure I can't pay towards this?" she asked again.

"I'm providing all the satisfaction tonight, wench," I said, feeling frisky and in the best mood ever. "Firstly, I've satisfied your hunger for food and then I'm going to—"

"Thanks, Chantelle!" Charity ripped the receipt from her hand and then grabbed my hand. "See you soon." She basically dragged me out of the bistro.

"Someone's keen to get me home," I stated, waggling my brows at her, and then I picked her up, put her over my shoulder and began walking down the street.

"Jason. *Jase*. I've just had a load of food and drink. I'll barf if I stay this way up," Charity protested. I placed her back down on the ground and re-picked her up in my arms, so she was across me.

"Better?"

"People are staring. I'd rather walk."

"Sorry, but I've got you in my arms and that's where you belong," I said, staring down at her. "You're so fucking fine, Charity. Fine and mine," I sighed.

I was sure I heard her mumble, 'What have I done?'

"What did you say?"

"Erm, I said that's better for my tum. You know, being this way up."

As I reached the entrance of my house, I placed her back down on the ground, and went in my pocket to extract my key. However, my trousers had gone extra tight with my hard on, and I couldn't get the key out.

Fuck it. I popped my button and yanked them down. Unfortunately, my pants also came down and my erection sprang free.

"Jesus, holy mother of God," Charity exclaimed, her eyes wide and transfixed on my member.

"Erm, could you get my keys out of my pocket? I'm having trouble," I asked her. She knelt and reached around, scrambling in my pocket for the errant key.

"Excuse me, Jason Gradon, but we don't do that kind of thing outside our houses," said an elderly voice as I looked around and met the gaze of Barb who was clearly on her way back from bingo with Delores, who stood beside her.

"It's not how it looks," I said. "I'm just having trouble getting my key and Charity is helping me find it."

"Oh so that's who's down there," said Delores. "What key's she looking for? The front door one, or the keys to paradise?" She cackled. "Jason, if I were a few years younger I'd come *look for the key* myself. Only it wouldn't fit my lock now. Four kids and old age do that to you. The only thing getting in my knickers now is a TENA lady."

"Found it," announced Charity, standing back up. She faced the two elderly women, waving the key dramatically. "Jason's had a bit too much to drink and so I'd better get him inside."

"Inside what though?" Delores quipped.

Charity took a deep breath. "Night, ladies," she said, and she opened the door and walked inside, leaving me on the street with my knob out in front of two old women.

"Good luck." Delores put her thumbs up. "We're rooting for you."

I pulled up my pants and trousers and walked into my house. I should have felt embarrassed. I'd just flashed two of Gnarly's oldest residents. But I didn't. It must be the beer I'd consumed. Maybe it was a stronger brew because I just felt... sexy. And inside this house was a woman who liked me. Was here to make out with me.

I slammed the door behind me and stripped out of all my clothes. And then I heard Charity's voice shout, "I'm in the bathroom," and I ran upstairs.

"I'm in the bedroom," I announced as I heard her footfall pass the door.

She pushed the door open, and her eyes seemed to come out on stalks as she caught sight of me propped up on the bed. I'd arranged myself, hands behind my head, my erection front and centre. And then somewhere from deep inside me came song. I began to sing the chorus of The Doors, *Light My Fire*. I hadn't even been aware I'd known the words.

I beckoned Charity over with a curl of my finger. She was... giggling? Why was she giggling? Climbing off the bed, I brought her close to me and shushed her by closing my lips down on hers firmly. My hands fixed in her hair and our mouths devoured the other's. When I broke off the kiss to catch my breath, she whispered, "Strip me," and I obliged.

Her body was mesmerising. Just the right amount of boobs for my large hands. I cupped them, feeling their weight and then closed my mouth around one nipple and then the other. I'd not managed to get my end away before today, but I'd done other things. Picking her up and thinking I might come right there and then if her little moans continued, I laid her on the bed and dived between her thighs. Forget tonight's trifle, this was the most delicious taste I'd had on my tongue all night.

Charity's breathing became more ragged and she lifted her hips more. She was close.

"Jason, I need you," she begged.

I had no nerves. It was time. This must be fate, because I thought I'd be so nervous I'd be unable to perform, yet everything was perfect.

Moving off the bed, I grabbed a condom from the drawer, and then I moved back over Charity and nudged my dick at her entrance. If I died right now, I'd be happy.

"I'm gonna light your fire," I said, and I pushed inside her.

It was *everything*. Her pussy was warm and wet, and I moved slowly in and out as I noted what sensations my dick got from this that it had never experienced in my hand, not even with the use of baby oil. I could have seated my dick in her pussy for life, I thought, before Charity tilted her hips and started milking my dick by tightening her core around me.

Fuck me. Literally.

I responded to her movements, plundering in and out of her, increasing my speed until I felt beads of sweat on my brow. Then a familiar tightening sensation came over me. I placed my finger between us and flicked Charity's clit. She exploded around me with a, "Godddddd, yes," and I followed her over, emptying my load. But as I did, it was like I emptied out my confidence along with my man milk.

Not sure what had happened but feeling like I'd been radio-controlled from the restaurant to the bedroom, memories assailed me of showing my dick to Barb and Delores, singing, lying on the bed with my dick out, and then losing my virginity.

"Jason?" Charity looked at me. "Are you okay?"

Putting it down to alcohol, and then my release, I reflected on where I currently was. Deep in Charity's pussy and having lost my virginity at last. My anxiety faded away.

"I feel fucking amazing," I said. "You?"

"I feel fucking amazing too," she replied. "Shall we rest and then do it again?"

I kissed her forehead. "Yes, but if it's okay with you, the beers worn off, so it won't be accompanied by singing," I told her.

"You definitely lit my fire." She giggled again, but it was so cute, and I was so damn happy. I pulled out of her and folded her into my embrace. We fell asleep for a little while before I made up for lost time.

My virginity was definitely lost.

Yet I felt found.

"Shit, I fell asleep. I should be home with Billy," Charity's panicked voice startled me awake.

"What time is it?" I mumbled.

"Six." She jumped off the bed and began pulling on her clothes. "I'm his guardian. It's irresponsible of me to leave him alone like that. I'd told him I'd be home."

I pulled her into my arms and kissed her. "I'm sure he's fine. Why not ring him?"

She laughed. "It's six am. He's dead one way or another. I just hope it's with sleep."

"Listen, I'll come with you," I said. "I'd like to meet Billy properly, and I'm not ready to not be around you yet. We'll check he's okay, get him off to school, and then call for breakfast at *Books and Buns* before we both go to work."

"You're working today? I thought your mum might give you a pass this week with all the dragon stuff."

"I want a day of normality. I find the hum of the machines in the laundrette relaxing. Griffin has given me some stuff to study, and I'll be able to look at it there."

"Fair enough. Okay, get dressed quickly then."

"You're begging me to put my clothes on? Not how I thought this morning would go." I winked.

"Oh, and how did you think this morning would go?"

I gave her a chin lift. "Thought you might have woke me up with your mouth around my cock."

"What have I started?" She laughed.

As Charity pushed open the back door, there were puddles of water all over the floor.

"What the heck has he been doing?" she said, wandering further through. I followed her up the stairs which were also wet and squelchy. She pushed open a bedroom door, and I waited outside while she went in.

"Everything okay?" I asked as she came back out.

"He's fast asleep and his room's not wet..." her voice trailed off as she looked at the floor near another door. There was a piece of seaweed on the floor.

"Oh no," she said, pushing her door open and walking inside. It was my first look at Charity's bedroom. She'd decorated it in soft greens and cream, but I doubted she'd left it last night with dirty, sodden footprints on the carpet. There was a note on her bed.

Either you contact me, or I'll return here. And next time, I'll take Billy back with me.

She sighed and slumped down onto the edge of the bed.

"Who's it from? Your ex? He can't take Billy away, can he?"

She shook her head.

"No, it's not from my ex. It's from my mother."

"Oh. Why do you think she wants to see you? Is it to try to get you to return home?"

Because she could fuck off.

Charity's face crumpled and tears began to flow from her eyes. I rushed over to her, and sat beside her, folding her into my embrace, and feeling the wetness on her face soak into my shirt.

"Hey, it's okay. Whatever you need, I'll help," I said, desperate to reassure her that she could count on me.

A few minutes later she gathered herself and sat back a little, though her posture was stiff. "It's not that simple. I don't want to see her, but she can take Billy back with her if he wants to go and I can't do a damn thing about it, so she has me over a barrel."

"She probably just misses you."

She scoffed. "You know how I told you my husband went off with my best friend?"

"Yes."

"It was my mother. My mother was my best friend. Always had been. Until I found her in bed with my husband. And then I lost two of the great loves of my life in one fell swoop. And now she's threatening to take Billy. Billy is all I have." Covering her face with her hands, her stiff posture collapsed as she slumped.

My jaw dropped, and then I rose to my full height, fisted my hands, and said with determination, "She will not take Billy. We won't let her. But, Charity, Billy's not all you have. You now live in Gnarly. You have this entire village who will support you.... and you have me."

As she closed the space between us and curled into my chest again, I vowed to become the best dragon I could be and to rule the clan. Because then if I needed to, I would destroy her mother and ex-husband.

CHAPTER NINE

Charity

The past...

"You're always working," Rutger complained. "I barely see you."

"Don't be silly," I replied. "I only work nine until seven, Monday to Saturday. There are loads of hours left where we spend time together."

"But I miss you." He pouted. "Can't you take a sick day today?"

"And have angry customers complaining that their hair's a mess? I don't think so. Now, there's plenty of housework to do if you get bored."

"I won't get **that** bored."

I shook my head. This was the thing that annoyed me. Rutger didn't work. He came from money. He thought I shouldn't work either. That I should just spend my days with him. But I loved my job and I'd been a successful hairdresser way before I met him. It was my identity, part of my own DNA. I wanted to work, needed to do it to keep me occupied. I'd told him again and again that if he kept the house tidy, we'd have time to spend together, but he couldn't even be arsed to organise a maid. He left the place like a shit tip and loafed around.

He'd not shown this side of himself when we'd first met two years ago. He'd come for a haircut and proceeded to sweep me off my feet.

So charming. I'd been impressed by all the flowers, chocolates, and lavish displays of romance. Having quartets perform outside my window. Love letters posted through the letterbox. He'd always kept himself in shape and active, and he was always full-on in his attention on me.

His proposal had been just as fancy. Taking me to my favourite wreck—an old fishing boat. He'd had lights strung around it and had paid to have it cleaned up and repaired enough for us to eat a meal there. A meal provided by a head chef for just the two of us. In my private opinion, he had spoiled the wreck, but I'd excused it as he'd done it through love, not malice.

I'd accepted his proposal. Been carried along by family and friends into the spectacular that was my wedding and then afterwards the honeymoon period had soon come to a halt. With no longer any need to woo me as he now had me, he just complained about my working on a daily basis and asked when we were going to start a family. He needed an heir and a spare.

But I already felt like I had a child. It was another reason I wanted to keep working and another reason I was in no hurry to give birth. Then I'd be forced to stop working because I'd have a child and a home to run, while Rutger carried on doing what he goddamn felt like. Mainly playing golf or hanging around the mayoral office with my mother.

My father had died a few years ago. He and my mother had split up when we were younger, but we'd all still lived together. They'd just said they were better off as friends. Neither had moved on with other people. Now Mum just had Billy, my younger brother, for company. She got on well with Rutger as he was interested in her role as lady mayoress of the sea. My cynicism put it down to him having aspirations to become the major himself in time. I had no doubt they were in receipt of his most charming persona there.

I loved my husband. I just didn't particularly like the version of him he'd become. However, I hoped he'd eventually come around to a compromise where we could start a family, but I could still work, at least part-time.

Every day, I wondered whether I'd have ever found out what was going on behind my back if it wasn't for the simple fact of having two customers cancel and deciding to make an effort after all.

I'd decided to cook Rutger and I a romantic dinner and follow it up with an early night. He'd asked me to take a sickie earlier and now Fate had stepped in so that we could have the time together he'd asked for after all.

I swam home after popping to the shops for food and wine. Now under the sea you just got used to there being water as if it wasn't there. Sounds strange but that's how it was. Water just worked with us. If we needed to swim, we swam. If we needed to clean, it helped us clean. If we wanted to sit in our houses as if it wasn't there, it became inactive.

I quietly let myself into the house because quite often I got home and Rutger was having a nap. This time he didn't appear to be home, so I went into the kitchen and began unpacking food. And then I heard our bed banging above me.

Had he brought another woman home? Was he doing DIY? Was he up there having an epileptic fit or a heart attack? I left everything, raced upstairs, and threw open the door. But what I saw took a long while to sink into my consciousness. My mother and Rutger in bed together, kissing, and clearly lost in each other.

I screamed when it hit me. A tortured scream of disbelief, of knowing life would never be the same again. Then I ran.

And despite Rutger and my mother trying to talk to me, instead I spoke with Billy, told him the truth of what I'd discovered. That our mother had been sleeping with my husband, and I told him I was leaving. He said he was coming with me. He hated the North Sea and could pop back to visit our mother if he ever wanted to.

I didn't know where to go, just as far away from Bridlington as I could. Somehow, I ended up in Gnarly Fell where I saw there was a business space free for a salon. As we spent more time together, Billy confided he'd never got on with our mother. That his life had been miserable since our dad had died and that he'd stayed there and not said a word because he hadn't wanted to upset me. I vowed I would make sure my brother had the happy life he deserved, and that hopefully, one day, I would too.

And now my mother was threatening to ruin it all.

Jason and I were in my flat's kitchen now as I recounted exactly what had led me to moving to Gnarly Fell three months ago, beyond the scant 'my husband had got together with my best friend' excuse I'd pedalled out.

"I'm so sorry that happened to you. You didn't deserve it," he said, squeezing my hand.

I took a cleansing breath. "The thing is, I don't think Rutger and my marriage would have lasted much longer anyway. It's not even the fact he's now with my mother, which obviously is taking some time for me to get my head around. It's the fact they went ahead and forgot that I existed. They lied to me while Rutger cheated, and my mother broke a moral code. No matter if they love each other, they should have loved me enough to not go behind my back."

And though I'm sure I would have still taken time to accept the situation, I wouldn't have the mental scarring from the shock of seeing what a wife and daughter should never see.

"Well, I'm glad your life went to absolute shit, so you had to move to the fell and pop my cherry," Jason said.

I couldn't help but laugh. And that's what I liked about Jason. He just had this way about him. Supportive, but made you laugh in the face of adversity, and also, was not afraid to laugh at himself.

"And you even wore a commemorative outfit." He pointed to the sundress with its cherry pattern.

"Oh my god, I wore cherries and took yours. That's very Freudian, I'm sure."

We heard evidence of someone moving around, a door opening, and footsteps from the landing getting closer.

"That you, Billy?"

Yeah. You decent in there, Sis?"

"Of course. It's the bloody kitchen!"

"Means nothing. There are walls, a worktop, and chairs." He came in. "I don't remember giving you permission to bring a boy home." He arched a brow.

Jason stood and held out a hand. "Hey, Billy. I'm Jase."

"I'm Billy, as you know. This one's protector, so state your intentions."

"Billy!"

Jason put his fingers up as if he was in the Scouts. "I promise to treat your sister with respect at all times and take her out on a lot more dates with your permission." He paused. "I'm aware of the past and won't be putting any pressure on your sister for anything."

"And you vow not to shag our mum?"

"*Billy*, for goodness' sake."

"What? If you'd asked Rutger that you could have saved yourself a lot of bother."

Jason guffawed. "Charity, your face. Billy, I promise to only shag your sister, okay?"

"*Jason!*"

Billy began laughing and took Jason's hand, shaking it. "Permission to date and shag my sister granted. Just not in earshot of me. Also, I have an Xbox if you ever feel like a game or feel like buying me any games."

"Billy!" Billy said, mimicking me before I had a chance to open my own mouth. "Right, let me grab a breakfast bar and an orange juice and then I'm off to college."

He went in the cupboard and fridge and then left with a salute in our direction.

"I like him," Jason said.

"I think he liked you too. Now, shall we go to Buns and Books or have breakfast here? I guess it depends on what you want. I have coffee and toast and the breakfast bars."

"We have the place to ourselves. I want you for breakfast," he said. "Now, where's your bedroom again?"

I took a shower and then made myself a coffee and grabbed a breakfast bar to consume while I opened up the salon. Jason had kissed me repeatedly in the doorway, so much so that I was sure my lips must be twice their normal size, but my customers didn't seem to notice any change in me.

The day passed in a blur, between customer chatter and me getting lost in my own daydreams of what had happened. I was surprised I'd managed to cut hair in a straight line, but it was all second nature to me, my hands and the scissors just had a connection with my brain to create magic on people's heads.

At lunchtime, Jason had sent me a text.

Jason: I need to read up on more dragon stuff tonight, but I still need to eat...

Charity: Do you mean food?

Jason: I did, but now you've said that...

I grinned.

Charity: I'll come over and bring a takeaway from the bistro. We can go over the dragon stuff and then you can light my fire again, before I go home and supervise Billy.

Jason: I still can't believe I sang. See you around half seven?

Charity: See you then.

While I had my phone in my hand, I texted Ginny.

Charity: Tell Merrin thank you.

Ginny: For what?

Charity: For his prediction.

There was a delay.

Ginny: I've told him, and he laughed. Spill! He won't tell me. Says it's personal. Gah, I can't read his mind.

Charity: I'll come to the café for lunch tomorrow and tell you all!!

Ginny: The wait is going to kill me!

Charity: You're already dead.

Ginny: Oh yeah, hahahahahahaha.

I called in at the bistro and Chantelle was working. "Hey, I've come to collect my takeaway order."

"Why didn't you have it delivered by portal?" she queried.

"Because I couldn't come in and say thank you if I did that." I winked at her.

"Eeek, did the confidence dust do its thing?" she whispered, leaning in.

"It really, really did." I couldn't help the large grin spreading across my face.

"I'm so pleased. It's nice to keep getting spells right lately," she said. Chantelle had been known for making some blunders in the past.

"I owe you, so if you ever need a wingwoman, just let me know," I said.

"Huh, I'm off dating for now. The men I meet are just arseholes," she spat out.

Our eyes were assaulted then as every male in the café became exactly that. She quickly changed them back.

"Oops," she said, but not before most of us females in the bistro had dry heaved and been psychologically scarred for life.

CHAPTER TEN

Jason

I'd had a lovely evening with Charity. We'd enjoyed the food she'd brought, and she'd helped me look over the dragon texts until I'd asked myself why I was reading about dragon lore when I could be exploring Charity's body instead. Then I'd carried her upstairs, my reading material discarded on the floor. I'd planned to have another look once Charity had gone home, but by then I was physically exhausted, so instead I went back to bed, only this time to actually sleep.

At eight am Wednesday morning, I knocked on the door of Merrin's cottage. He pulled the door open and beckoned me in while grinning at me.

"What?" I felt at my face.

"I had a 'knowing' but luckily without too much 'seeing' about you singing to Charity," he told me as I followed him inside.

"So you know about my lost innocence?" I double checked.

"If I didn't with my vision, the swagger you've greeted me with would have given it away." He held up his hand for a high five. "Good on ya, mate."

"At least now if I die, I'm not dying a virgin," I declared. "Have you had any knowings about my time with the dragons?"

"Nope, not a thing," he replied.

"So no idea if I survive?"

"Nope."

"That's just typical. You get to see me singing in bed, but not anything that might help me live while I spend time with dragons."

"Believe me, I'd have much rather had a vision about you being killed off, than one when you're wooing and oohing."

"Thanks, I think."

"Anyway, what brings you here this morning? Is it just to check on my visions and to gloat about your prowess?"

"Of course, and also to say if I am killed off make sure everyone knows I wasn't a virgin."

"Duly noted." He laughed. "Cuppa?"

"Yes please. How are things going with you and Ginny?"

"Very well. There's a lot to be said about having a fiery other half. She brings those sparks to the bedroom." His eyes twinkled.

"Look at us two talking about our women," I noted. "We ought to go see Chantelle some time and thank her and see if we can return the favour."

Merrin snorted.

"What?"

"I don't think we've progressed that far that we can help other people with their love lives. It's still very early days with our own."

"Yeah, you're right. We'll just get her a bottle of wine, hey?"

"One of each. I'll pay half."

"I'll sort it. If I get out of the caves alive."

I sat down while Merrin made us both a drink and then he came to sit with me. It took me back to when I'd last been sat here, learning about the dragons.

"Are you going there again today?"

"Yes, today I'm sitting and helping them make plans about my uncle's funeral. Griffin, the deputy, sent me some information on what usually happens, so I have some idea of what's expected, but I'll just let the council decide. They've been there a lot longer than I have."

"Just make sure they don't think you're a pushover though."

My body decided it wanted to stretch at that point and I reached out my arms and legs and unkinked myself.

"I want to learn that side of myself, the dragon, but I don't want a shit ton of responsibilities that I can't handle and to have to live with people I don't know. I like Gnarly. It's my home." I got Merrin up to date on the week ahead.

"It's going to be a busy week but try not to let the pressure get to you, mate. One step at a time. Get to know what you can about being a dragon, and don't be forced into any decisions. If you can be king, then surely, you can make your choice about when you're ready?"

"I don't think dragons work that way. I think it's act or be challenged."

He gave me a slight nod in acknowledgement. "I'll let you know if I get any knowings about you. It's too late for today, but maybe you could get Chantelle to put a spell on you for protection?"

"Yeah, maybe."

"You also need a witch to remove the spell your mother put on you. It's a shame Alicia moved on." Alicia had been Chantelle's mentor but after her ex-husband came back as an evil entity possessing bodies, she'd decided to move again for a fresh start. Her parents had also sold up and gone with her and their grandchildren.

We carried on chatting until it was time for me to make a move down to the cave entrance at the other side of the bottom of Merrin's field.

The boulder moved apart and so I knew whoever worked the cameras had seen me. Sure enough, as I reached the double weather doors, they opened, and before I knew it, I was entering the cave again. Only this time, Griffin didn't come to meet me. I made my way to the boardroom while the eyes of all the dragons present followed my every move. It was like when you saw movies where the eyes moved in paintings. Completely unnerving. However, I just reminded myself I'd got laid several times over and allowed that swagger to carry me through the door and up to the table where the fold-up chair had been positioned by Griffin once more.

All but Viper were looking at the floor. I took my seat and then met Viper's eyes. He looked at his watch and sighed. I looked at mine. It was five minutes before the meeting started, phew. When I looked back at him, he just looked away with indifference. I tried to catch Griffin's attention by mentally saying 'Look up at me', but his gaze remained on the floor.

At ten, all became clear when Viper said, "Now we have spent fifteen minutes in quiet contemplation of our time with our ex-king, we can move onto the meeting. Jason, I didn't invite you to the remembrance meditation seeing as you never met Josiah. You'd have had nothing to think about."

I could have done with fifteen minutes now to think about all the different ways I could punch Viper in the nose. However, I wasn't letting him get to me. Not outwardly anyway.

"A wise thought, dear Chair. However, I would have spent the time in silence and in gratitude for the service he provided to the clan if I had been made aware. I do believe it says in dragon lore that any dragon heirs should be privy to all information about the clan after the death of the king, even before they are crowned, does it not?"

Griffin quietly snorted, but in a room of silence he may as well have shouted, 'Buuurrrrn'.

But this game, akin to that of a Wimbledon final, went to Viper as he served his ace. "I'm glad you think so. I shall fill you in on all matters currently pertaining to the clan after this meeting. I hope you have no plans for the rest of your day or evening?"

Fuck.

"No, nothing that can't wait," I replied, realising I'd been a dickhead. The dick in my pants would get no action now later.

"Okay, now to the order of today's business. The funeral and commitment ceremony of Josiah Ashton Rulefort. As always, there will be the open coffin displayed in the vaults from five pm this evening until ten am tomorrow morning, so that clan members can come pay their respects."

An open coffin? Would I be expected to go? I didn't remember anything about that in what I'd read.

"I'll now pass you over to Brenton who will furnish you with the rest of the details in his capacity as events organiser."

Our heads turned to Brenton, a slightly rotund, grey-haired fellow. He cleared his throat. "Council, and Mr Rulefort." He nodded in my direction. "At ten am while the last of the mourners pay their respects, eight of us will then carry the closed coffin outside. Griffin, you will accompany Mr Rulefort outside to where the pyre will have been stacked. Azar, Blake, and Kenna shall also wait there.

After the funeral procession and gathering of mourners, we will then have a speech from Griffin, before the fire is lit. Afterward, dragons will stay behind to wait for the ashes to cool so they can be collected and brought back to the council room where they will be stored.

"Notice of the upcoming trials for Mr Jason Rulefort will then be pinned to the tree next to the pyre, and ballot papers given for clan to vote on which three trials he shall experience. Clan will also be asked who wishes to spectate on each trial, and a draw will take place at ten pm tomorrow night where we shall announce the trials and who has won tickets to which event."

"People get to watch me?" I asked.

"Of course. They shall want to see you are worthy of the position of king," Nithe said, and I decided I'd meditate on punching him too.

"The feast shall begin after the fire. Willow has that in hand."

"Who's Willow?" I asked. "The cook?"

Viper scowled at me. "She's your uncle's wife. Your aunt. But of course you wouldn't know that as it's not in the papers you read yesterday. Which shows you still have much to learn."

I didn't mind how much I had to learn, as long as I didn't find out they did a barbecue using the funeral pyre.

"Is it possible I could meet her before the ceremony?" I asked.

Viper smiled wickedly. "I would have said yes, if it were not for the fact you clearly reminded me you needed to be abreast of all clan information, so actually we shall move to the library now so I can begin. We shall be quite some time."

Viper drew the meeting to a close and said he would give me thirty minutes to talk with Griffin and re-arrange any plans I had. I sent a text to Charity saying I was likely to get home very late and wouldn't be able to see her.

She quickly responded saying that she should spend the evening around Billy anyway.

It served to remind me that we both had large responsibilities, and I wondered how much these were going to interfere with our blossoming romance. That, and the fact her mother was threatening to interfere with her life.

And just like that, I remembered my promise to myself to learn how to become the best dragon I could, so that if Charity needed me or my clan, we would be there for her.

"You finished?" Griffin said, nodding his head to my phone.

"Yeah." I placed it back in my pocket. "Can you give me a heads up to where the library is?"

"I'll give you a heads up on a few things. Firstly, don't resent Viper. His family have been around a long time, and he very much likes to keep the history of the clan alive. You can learn a lot from him. He doesn't have to have your respect because as heir you can do what you like to a certain extent, but he deserves it. Yes, he's got you going to the library as a punishment for your mouth, but ultimately, it's a good thing."

"I'm going to be the best student he ever had," I said. "Learning about my dragon side is important to me."

"Glad to hear it. Tomorrow morning, be here at six am, and I'll take you to meet your aunt," he said. With that he patted me on the shoulder and walked away.

"You've not told me how to get to the library," I shouted at his retreating back.

He turned around. "Saturday you'll be doing trials far more challenging than finding out which room has books in. One clue. It's very near to the boardroom for obvious reasons." He gave me his back again.

I walked towards the boardroom and passed a large door with a sign with books on that said LIBRARY. It was the room before the boardroom, and I had walked past it a number of times already. My observation skills needed to improve a whole lot if I was to survive the weekend, that was for sure. But for now, I'd improve my knowledge.

I knocked on the door and waited for Viper to ask me to come in.

"Enter."

I pushed open the door and found Viper sat at a table with multiple documents piled around him. Jesus, I really was going to be here all day and night. I'd probably be going to the funeral straight from here at this rate.

"Could you put the 'do not disturb' on the door please? I've booked the room out so we can work without others around us."

I did as he asked.

"Thank you for the giving of your time in order to furnish me with this information," I said.

Viper studied my face intensely.

"The first serious statement that seems to have been issued from your mouth," he snarked.

I lifted a hand to my chest. "I'm aware I can be flippant. It's my go-to defence mechanism. But with your help in teaching me about the ways of dragons, maybe I can discover a better alternative?"

"Very well," he said, reaching for a book entitled *Rulefort: The Beginnings*. He looked back at me. "It is not that I wish you to fail so my son can reign, Jason. It is that as a half-breed with no knowledge of your heritage, you put the clan in danger. Should I see you are worthy of the title of king, I will support you."

"Thank you. I appreciate that," I replied, wondering if the impossible seemed to be happening. That Viper and I might become friends.

"Of course, I doubt that will happen and I fully expect us to be crowning King Thor in the not-so-distant future," he said, before opening the book to the first page. "Okay, let's start at the beginning."

I needed to remember to keep my mum updated on everything, as at six pm my phone pinged and a panicked message of 'Are you okay?' appeared on the screen.

"It's my mum. Is it okay if I quickly call her, only she's worrying?" I asked. He nodded and so I was able to reassure her that I was still alive, before we got back to the books.

The refreshments kept coming but so did the words. By the time I left at midnight, my mind was swimming with everything he'd told me, and I was back to wondering if I could do this at all, or whether I should just let Thor take over. I mean, God, even his bloody name sounded magnificent.

You have until the trials begin to decide, I reminded myself. For now, I'd go home, text Charity, and then try to get some sleep before I returned back to the cave.

CHAPTER ELEVEN

Charity

I woke bright and early. After a refreshing shower, I made a cooked breakfast for Billy, (who wolfed it down), and a continental one for myself. I loved a crispy pain au chocolat. I did a half day on a Wednesday and so after work I was going to the café bookstore to hang with Ginny for lunch.

My carpets were still damp and smelled of the sea despite me getting a carpet cleaner, which didn't help with me trying to forget that my mother's threats were hanging over me. I needed to talk to someone about things, and that couldn't be Jason, not while he had so much of his own family shit going on. Mya might be outspoken, but she knew my situation and I decided that I'd ask her advice. So, work, go to the café, and then call up to the Home of Wayward Souls. That was my plan for the day.

Work once again passed quickly, helped by the fact I loved my job. Before I knew it, I was pushing open the door of Books and Buns. The shop was owned by a fae called Callie and the café side was run by Callie and her sister Dela, along with the occasional help from Callie's vampire husband Lawrie... who happened to be Ginny's brother by sire.

When I got inside, I saw that Callie was busy serving at the counter, Dela was delivering to tables, and Ginny was waving me over. Deciding I'd order lunch after saying hi, when maybe the queue had lessened, I walked over to the bookstore part where Ginny worked.

"Mind blocks suck, lady!" she admonished me.

I grinned back wickedly. "No way are you just reading everything from my head. I want to be able to tantalise you with all the juicy details. That's what friends do. I bet you peek inside Christmas presents," I said.

"Of course I do. Then if it's shit, I can pretend I like it, otherwise this face shows the truth." She pointed to herself and made a grimace like only Ginny could. The kind of face she used to pull at her now-boyfriend. "I am getting better though. I no longer read the last page of a book or read it at super-vampire speed. I've learned to savour a good book like I do Merrin's co—"

"Cooking?" I finished for her. "Let's say cooking."

She shook her head in disgust. "This gossip is not going to be up to standard if you can't even say the word co... cooking. Are you going to continue to speak in food analogies? Did you taste his sausage? Did you swallow any gravy? Did he put his sausage into the oven?"

"I was going to have a sausage sandwich for lunch and now you've put me off."

She came closer. "Why? Was it not... appetising? Large, and satisfying?"

I rolled my eyes. "Look, I'll grab some lunch and sit down, and you can come over if you're not busy with a customer and I'll tell you all about it in non-food language before I develop an eating disorder."

"I have one of those," Ginny said.

My pinched expression softened. "Oh, Ginny, I didn't mean to make light of a serious condition."

Her brow creased. "I meant I can't stop eating Merrin's co—"

"Cooking."

"Go. Go get some lunch and don't come back over here until you're ready to utter salacious words about your naughty night."

I'd just reached the counter when Ginny yelled over. "Callie, no sausages for Charity. She's had enough at Jason's if you get my drift."

I felt my cheeks burn.

Callie smiled up at me. "We love Jason here so good for you."
Dela came over to the counter. "He's a close friend of my fiancé's, we'll have to go on a double date sometime."

"She's my friend, hands off," Ginny yelled.

"Testy vampire alert. Doesn't want to share her toys," Dela batted back.

I found it all a little overwhelming, but also great. I was making new friends all the time, and Ginny, though domineering, was making claim as a future bestie. I grabbed a ham salad sandwich and a pink old-fashioned lemonade and went back over to the bookstore side where I pulled up a chair at the table nearest to Ginny.

"I can have more than one friend, you know?" I said to Ginny, laughing softly afterwards.

"I know, but I don't have many, and my other friend, Aria, is pregnant with twins and no fun whatsoever. She just talks about babies all the time when I'm trying to talk about Merrin."

I nodded my head in sympathy. "It's difficult when people's lives change, but I'm sure you'll adjust. When they're born, you'll have two gorgeous babies to cuddle, and perhaps one day you and Merrin might even have a baby?"

"I asked him if he thought we'd be able to conceive despite our species differences and he drank four whiskies in four minutes," she said.

"You've only been together for two weeks!" I exclaimed, my voice shrill.

She shrugged her shoulders. "I was just curious. His overreaction was completely unwarranted. Any man should be grateful to consider the opportunity to house their seed in this fine body and that's what I told him. Anyway, you are my new friend, and we are both just courting new men. We have lots in common, not least of which is getting lots of co—"

"Cock."

"Thank fuck for that." She walked out from behind the counter and put a CLOSED FOR LUNCH sign on it. Then she sat opposite me and said, "Tell me all."

Ginny had been, 'Thrilled for both me and my pussy' and had laughed when I'd explained about Merrin's prediction. When I left the café, I felt great: lighter of heart, and content with being both full of food, and considering my budding romance and friendships.

Now it was time to see if Mya was around. I fancied having a closer nosy at the mansion anyway that sat at the top of a hill just outside of the village gates, so I set off walking.

It was a bloody big hill. I rested partway up and then I screamed at the top of my lungs as I was grabbed and carried up in the air like I was a sparrowhawk's prey.

Dropped on the grass outside the mansion, I saw my 'bird' was Mya herself. As I oriented myself, I also saw that Death was dead-heading roses.

"Thought you'd love to see them rotting," I queried.

"There is beauty to be found sometimes in death, but not in my rose bushes," he turned and said before returning to his task.

"There's beauty in the little death you cause within my own bush when I grow it out," Mya threw back.

"If only your mouth was as sweet as your pussy, darling," Death retorted.

"I gather you were coming to see me?" Mya asked as I sat there still recovering from being moved at high speed without a heads-up, never mind having to listen to the two of them banter with each other. "I spotted you from the window. Let me know next time. That hill is there to prevent people from ending up amongst the wayward. Death has been privy to many an attempt in the past as they've appeared in The Book of the Dead about to collapse and breathe their last."

"I may have had to have a few rests. I'm usually incredibly fit, but having been away from home, I haven't been doing my usual amount of swimming."

After we received another 'Death stare' Mya beckoned me inside. "He comes out here to get time away from me," she explained as I walked through the large front door and into an old-fashioned mansion. It was all black paintwork, and the flooring was a black and white check pattern.

The place was fastidiously clean but seemed to have been

largely frozen in time, which highly surprised me seeing as Mya was seldom seen without her designer clothes and Louboutins.

"I don't know what I expected, but I thought you'd have modernised," I told her.

"Me too, but then Gnarly taught me about recycling and trying not to be wasteful, so I largely just cleaned up, although I had some things updated, like the shower for instance. But being a vampire, I can clean at speed. I have little use for most appliances. We have the laundry service, and my food is delivered in bottles which we return for re-use and so get a discount. It used to be plastic packets for the blood, but they've changed now to be more environmentally friendly. It all leaves more money for my shoe collection." She beamed with pleasure. "I found an unused turret and have started a library of designer shoes."

We'd reached a living room that had thick dusky-pink carpets. I left my shoes outside the door and felt the pile under my feet.

"Would you like a drink? I have a coffee machine in the kitchen," Mya asked.

"That would be lovely, thank you," I replied.

"Okay, well take a seat and I'll be right back."

While Mya went to get my drink, I took in the room around me. There were black velvet curtains and nets at the windows, and lamps with frilly shades on mahogany furniture. It was very unexpected, although suited the gothic style house.

"I didn't see you as a frilly net curtains kind of woman," I said as Mya came back in.

"I'm not, but this house has a personality of its own. Like it has a soul, you know? I know that sounds crazy, but then I've seen more than my fair share of that since I was turned. If I think of upgrading, I get an inner feeling of ick. When I leave it be I feel an inner peace, a homeliness."

"That's good. That it feels like home."

"More than anywhere I ever lived when I was alive. So, anyway, what brings you up here?" Mya asked, while taking a sip of her blood.

I took a deep breath. "I hope you don't mind, but I need to talk about things and think of what to do, and you're the only one apart from Billy and Jason who knows the whole story. That is, if you've read my mind. I've let my guard down."

"Of course I've read your mind."

"Then why did you ask why I was here?"

She placed down her bottle and began gesturing with her hands. "Minds are not linear. They are a whirl of thoughts, both real and not real, and it can be difficult to know things for sure. Plus, it would be incredibly rude not to let people talk. As I tell Big D when he repeatedly asks me to shut up for a minute, the only place for silence is in a library or one of those retreat things with Monks. Now, tell me in your own words what's on your mind."

I stared off into the distance as I went into my memories. "The days after I found out what happened were extremely unpleasant. I didn't realise how much Rutger had moaned to everyone about my working hours and 'neglect' of him. My mother is also held in deep regard as she's the Sea Mayoress of Bridlington. So, rather than people being sympathetic of the betrayal, many said I'd had it coming. Others said true love wins out and mine and Rutger's obviously wasn't. I can't argue with that. It's true I didn't love him. I thought I did, but I was in love with the idea of love, and with an idealised version of Rutger which just wasn't real."

"So instead of getting sympathy as the victim, you were portrayed more as the villain?"

I nodded. "If it wasn't bad enough to be betrayed by your husband and mother, I found that I was betrayed by most I knew under the sea." I gave a half-hearted shrug. "It made leaving easier. I would have stayed for Billy. Would have endured anything until I knew he was over eighteen and could lead his own life, but luckily, he wanted out too. I went to the law offices and put in for my marriage to be dissolved. Rutger didn't contest it, didn't turn up for the interview, and so forty-eight hours later we were divorced.

"Wow, things happen quickly under the sea."

"Thank goodness. I was quickly done with him as a husband. But now my mother wants to see me…"

"But it's difficult as your mind is full of contradictions, because she was your best friend, yet Billy says they didn't get on. She was a great mother, but then betrayed you with your husband. Now you're fearing she wants Billy home. That about sum it up?"

HOT AS SUCK

I nodded. "Billy is eighteen in August, so my mother can drag him home now, but it would only be for a couple of months. However, what if Billy changed his mind and decided to stay there? Then I'd have lost *everything*." My voice cracked on my last word.

Mya leaned over and patted my hand. "If there's one thing I learned from my human life, it's that something can come from nothing. I had no family around. Nothing really except the love of my job. But I always kept hope, that from rock bottom things could get better. Then obviously Lawrie tried to kill me, and Death basically blackmailed me into being his assistant and I thought things had descended to a whole other level of deep shit. But it didn't. It turned out to be the best thing that ever happened to me. So, my advice is go see your mother. See what she has to say. Get *your* questions answered, and then say you need time. Don't be forced into any decisions, but make sure they're based on all of the facts. I didn't have a choice in my future, not really, when the alternative was to live on the Field of the Drained, a whole nothingness. You do have choices, and you're dating Jason, so you already know things can change for the better." She grabbed her head. "Oh, good lord, woman, how many dramatic scenarios can you create? Please put your shields back up. I don't need to see Jason's lily-white arse as you imagine him with a potential dragon mate."

I clung to her arm. "But it could happen, right? If they make him king, they'll want him to have a queen, and they'll want her to be a full dragon. What if I lose him too? We only just got together. He probably won't think twice about ditching me for a dragon woman. I mean they can bonk in both forms, can't they? Have animal sex. Doing it doggy is the nearest I can do to compete."

At that moment, there was a knock at the door before it swung open and a male appeared. He grinned at me, showing a slew of rotten teeth. The guy looked dishevelled and had a wooden leg.

"Miss Malone, I brought yee tha mail," he announced, walking in and presenting her with an envelope. However, all the while his eyes were on me, giving me a good onceover. "And who is this delightful creature?" he asked, sniffing the air. "I'm getting hints of seaweed, saltwater. As a sailor I know a seawoman when I meet one." He reached out a hand to me. "Spence, at your service, Miss...?"

"Miss-*take* if you flirt with her much longer," said another voice, and a woman walked in.

Mya sighed. "Charity, this is Spence and Jenny. Spence is a ghost pirate and Jenny is the witch who cursed Gnarly, but who now lives here. They're guardians of the place. Charity is dating Jason from the village." She handed the letter back to Spence. "Writing me a letter that says, 'Give me a minute, it's a long time since I saw a nice fit woman' is not my mail."

I was expecting Jenny to kick off again at this but instead *she* looked me up and down. "Ohhh yeeeaah, Spence, I do get what you're saying. She has great boobs. I'm just imagining feeling them with my hands."

"We've got to go, good seeing ya," Spence said. On his way out from practically dragging Jenny out of the room, we heard him say. "Ya saucy wench, ya gonna describe for me exactly what ya'd do with her?"

"They don't get out much. What can I say?" Mya explained.

"It's okay. I'd better be getting on. I don't suppose you fancy a trip into the sea with me tomorrow?"

There was a shimmer in front of my eyes, like the walls rippled and then Kaf appeared. "I'll go with you," he said. "I can travel under the water no problem as an angel."

"Have you been listening the whole time?" I huffed out, folding my arms across my chest.

"Most of it. I felt I had to. I'd just been up in the attic asking for a clue as to why I was supposed to be here, and they didn't reply. Then I sensed your presence here, and I'm wondering if it's connected to you, so what time tomorrow?"

I thought about things for a moment. In lieu of Jason, who would need permission to come under the sea, I guess it couldn't hurt to take Kaf.

But it was Jason's father's funeral tomorrow, so he might need me.

"Give me your number and I'll text you in the morning," I said.

"Sure. It's 111111," he said.

After that, Kaf left, and I gave my thanks to Mya and went home. Knowing I needed to talk to Billy about everything and see if he also wanted to go 'home'.

I'd been hoping that I might get to talk to Jason if only for a little while, but later he texted to say he had to stay late at the cave and then would be back there early the next morning.

It looked more and more like Jason and I had just met at the entirely wrong time, and I slept badly, wondering if love ever did run smooth because all I ever seemed to feel were jagged cuts and aching wounds.

CHAPTER TWELVE

Charity

When Billy returned home from college, he found me waiting in the kitchen for him. His eyes perused the table.

"A can of Monster and a six-pack of beef crisps. Must be some huge favour or bad news."

"I'm going to speak to mum tomorrow night and wondered if you were coming? I'd like you to come," I corrected. "We need to talk about what we want and make sure she knows it. That there's no point in her turning up here demanding."

Billy shrugged off his backpack to the floor, pulled up a seat, and pulled the ring pull off the can, taking a large swig. He followed it with a small burp, though he did place his hand over his mouth. "Excuse me." He tore open the outer crisps packet, grabbed a bag from within, tore that open and stuffed a handful in his mouth. "I'll come with you," he said, small splinters of crisps dropping from his mouth. *Boys.*

I let him eat his crisps, because for one, he looked ravenous, and for another, I didn't want to watch him talking while eating. He got through two bags and most of the can before he sat back looking ready to finally chat.

"So what's the plan of action?"

"There's an angel, Kaf, who has been sent here for a purpose, but he's yet to find out what it is. He overheard me talking to Mya and said he'll come with us. That it's possible this is what he's back on earth to do. At seven pm tomorrow, we'll set off for under the sea. I'm not letting Mum know ahead of time. I want to be at the advantage when we get there. Then I intend to make sure she knows once and for all that I now live in Gnarly. The question is, what are your intentions? And if it's that you don't know, that's fine. I just want us to be firm."

"For now, I'm staying in Gnarly and finishing college. Then as I see it, the whole world is my oyster. I don't know where I'll end up, but what I do know is that I will be deciding for myself. Mum needs to know that she's made her choices and we can make ours."

I smiled with relief. "Great."

Billy kicked at the leg of the table and looked awkward for a moment. He scrunched his face up a bit. "Look, I'm happy here, with you. I like that you've started dating and that you're allowing yourself to move on a bit, and it's helping you to not be so overprotective. I'm appreciating you being a little less intense now you have a distraction."

I leaned over and ruffled his hair.

"Get off, you lemon." He squirmed out of my reach.

"You're always going to be my little brother, but I am aware that you'll soon be eighteen. I'll make sure I give you space and I'm sure if I don't, you'll let me know." I raised a brow.

"Cool. Right, I'm off for a game or two on the Xbox. Let me know when dinner's ready." With that he swept up the packet containing the remaining crisp bags and left the kitchen.

Leaving me drumming my fingernails against the table wondering whether I'd hear from Jason.

It was around twelve thirty when my phone beeped with a text, the screen lighting the room a little. I was in bed but hadn't managed to drop off to sleep yet as I'd kept running possible scenarios about meeting my mother through my mind. Reaching over, I grabbed my phone off the table.

Jason: Hope I haven't woken you. Ended up being

coached in dragon history and have only just got home. And I'm due back at 6am for the funeral. Plus, I'm meeting my aunt. Hope all is well your end. I should be free tomorrow evening, if you don't have plans?

So there was no mention of me coming to the funeral. Well, duh. They didn't even like half-breeds, so they weren't going to entertain a mermaid girlfriend. Plus, it was very early days. Although I knew Fenella, we weren't at the 'meet the family' stage were we. I was falling too fast and too deep. I sighed. It was just with Jason everything was so easy and just felt right.

I typed a message back.

Charity: Sorry, tomorrow I'm off out with Billy and it's something I can't change.

The reply text came back quickly:

Jason: No problem. I should be free Friday evening if I survive getting all my dragon powers back. Let's provisionally schedule you coming to mine for a meal?

Charity: Sounds good xo

Jason: Looking forward to it xo

Charity: Hope the funeral goes okay, and meeting your aunt of course.

Jason: Thanks. Hope whatever you're doing with Billy is fun.

Charity: Thanks.

Fun? Huh, probably as much fun as the funeral. I re-read our messages back. It just served to remind me of our complicated lives. Placing my phone on the bedside table, I pulled the covers up over my head, determined to get to sleep so I didn't have to think of anything further.

CHAPTER THIRTEEN

Jason

I'd managed little sleep as my mind ticked over with the information I'd been given about the history, the clan, and the funeral. They'd told me to wear a smart suit and clean underwear and that as they lit the pyre, I would be expected to change into my dragon form. That was fine. That I could manage. The question was, after the spell was taken away, would I be able to do anything else?

I was getting nervous now. Time was getting on and we'd not got around to removing the witch's spell yet, and until they did that, I couldn't risk visiting my father in the jail if I decided I wished to. Visiting a psychopathic dragon without powers would be like coating myself in jam and walking into a wasp's nest. But still, it was all going to be rather last-minute for my liking. Maybe I needed to have a drink of whatever I'd had the night I lost my virginity? That strong blend might just help me at the cave too, although what if I sang about lighting my fire there among a massive group of dragons? They might torch me with their scorching breath.

I made sure that at six am sharp I was there to meet Griffin at the reception area. A queue of the clan stretched around the area, all waiting to pay their respects at the vault, many carrying wildflowers. Some ignored me. Others nodded in my direction. I nodded back.

Griffin beckoned me towards him. "Come, let's go walk deeper into the cave and chat while we make our way to your aunt's dwelling."

I reached his side, and we started a steady walk together.

"I have consulted a warlock who will remove your powers in the safety of the training room tomorrow morning," he told me. "From there we will have the rest of the day to see how you measure up and to make the decision of whether or not you can, or even want to, proceed with the trials."

I swallowed hard, stumbling over my reply. "Gr-great."

"Until then, I suggest you don't think on it and keep your mind on today, for there is much to happen and people will be watching you closely, both supporters and enemies."

"Sounds peachy."

"I can't work out where your head's at with all this, Jason. You're showing all the right enthusiasm in terms of showing up as instructed, learning the history, but there's something else, a reticence. I can't tell if that's because you don't know your capabilities yet, or if you're just not interested in ruling here." He stared at me. His eyes clearly suggesting I confess all.

"I don't know what to do, and that is the truth," I said. "I've known what I am for days in terms of being dragon royalty. In terms of who Jason Gradon is, or should I say was, well, that was largely a layabout with a good sense of humour. A kind heart but a bone-idle arse. So it's a bit of a shift change, pardon the pun, to suddenly be a potential dragon king. My self-esteem tells me I can't do this, that I'm not made for leadership, but my stubborn inner musings argue that without learning everything, how can I make an informed choice."

"And which are you leaning more towards at present?"

"I feel that until I know my true dragon, I can only doubt myself and my capabilities. Tomorrow can't come soon enough really."

"Fair enough. I'm sorry that I didn't sort this earlier."

"Don't be. It would have added an extra layer of complication, when right now I need to concentrate on my uncle's funeral."

We dropped into a comfortable silence until a few minutes later, we emerged at a series of caves within the large cave. Griffin picked up and dropped the huge door knocker on one of them.

"I thought the place would be bigger, given she was queen?"

He gave me an incredulous look. "I thought you'd read what I sent you? Willow is not a queen. She lived separate to Josiah."

I was speechless for a moment. "You've lost me. Also, I didn't receive anything about dragon weddings and queens."

"Shoot. I must have missed it off my list. Jason, when you become king, there is no queen. We don't acknowledge women in this way. They stay in lesser quarters while you will have a royal suite. Not that this matters to you at present given you are single. But if king you shall select a good wife for breeding, then invite whoever you desire and is willing to your cave each night."

I think my eyes had bugged out of my head now.

"Whoever I desire?"

"Absolutely. Most of the dragons would be delighted to offer their bodies to their king's service."

My mind did not wish to think on any of this new information. I could just imagine if I stayed with Charity saying, 'Oh, honey, here are your shitty digs. I'm just off to my luxurious quarters where after dinner I'm having several of the residents service me. Go incubate my dragon spawn while I go assuage my urges'. Luckily, my aunt opened the door then. She looked me up and down before stepping forward and bowing to both Griffin and me. I opened my mouth to tell her not to, but Griffin intercepted my reaction and shook his head at me. "These are the current ways," he said. *Current,* I noted. I could change things if I took rule. This was something to definitely look into. Maybe my rule here could do something good. To give more power to those who deserved it. Women were treated as less, and half-breeds even less than that. The Rulefort dragon clan needed an update, and I could be the man for the job. That was, if Willow would help me. I needed to find out what she knew from being the wife of a king, although after what Griffin had said, I wondered if it would be not much at all.

"Please come in," she said, and I noted she was softly spoken. My aunt was small but stocky. She was wearing a black dress and a belt that was engraved with the Rulefort crest, and wore black boots.

As we followed her inside, I inspected the cave. It was basic but functional and when she asked us to sit, the red sofa was comfortable enough. The interior was plain. Nothing much there in terms of décor or soft furnishings.

"Would you like a drink?" Willow asked, picking up a bottle. Three glasses were already set out on the slate coffee table.

"Yes, thank you," Griffin said. "And also, once more may I offer my condolences for your loss."

"Yes to the drink please, and also sorry for your loss," I said, copying Griffin.

"My loss is your gain," she said, with an edge to her voice. "Has Joseph been told yet?"

"No, he has not. Once we know who the next king is, they can choose what they do with Joseph."

"Do? He needs to stay there. The man is a danger to us all," she snapped. "But of course I am not allowed a voice am I? Heed my words, Jason. If you see your father, do not be fooled if his mute mouth begins to murmur sweet nothings. He is the devil in disguise." She poured all three of us a drink, pouring her own last and taking a deep drink. After I saw that, I took a good drink of my own, hoping it was alcoholic and satisfied she'd not poisoned it if she was drinking it herself.

Silence reigned for a moment until I decided that I was the one who had requested this visit and so I would make the most of whatever time I had here.

"Are you aware of the fact that my mum and I didn't know what happened to my father, and that I didn't know Josiah was king or had nominated me as heir?"

"Yes. Josiah kept an eye on you from a distance. He felt it was his duty. But he respected your mother's decision right up until the point where it came to nominating an heir. Then the future of the Rulefort dragons became more important than you spending your life working in a launderette."

"He watched us?"

"I watched you. On his behalf. Not often. We used trusted magicians to show us what you were doing. I guess all this must have come as quite a shock to you?"

I nodded. "Yes, that's a bit of an understatement."

"I did much supporting work for your uncle: letters, business things. He wasn't keen on the 'boring' side of things. I should be happy to support you in the same way, or if you prefer to do the admin yourself, I will show you the ropes. That is if you pass the trials of course."

"Thank you."

"It's such a shame I'm only getting to know you now and that your uncle couldn't have met you. You are very much like your grandfather."

"Really?"

"Yes. Let me get some old photographs and paintings out to show you. We have time to delve into a brief family history before the funeral starts, don't we?" she asked, checking with Griffin, who nodded. "Great, it will distract me from thoughts of my final goodbye to my dear husband," she said.

I rose and hugged her. She folded into my embrace before pushing back. "I know your uncle would have loved you," she said and then she left the room.

"She seems nice," I noted to Griffin.

"She is, and she was a major though largely unseen support to your uncle. If you have a role for her, such as her continuing with the admin side, she would be very useful to you, and also, it would keep her mind occupied."

"I have so much to think about," I mused.

"As the king there will always be so much to think about." He said this strongly but not with ill intent or rudeness. Just a general reminder that the path ahead may not be an easy one if I chose to rule.

While we waited, a maid came in and asked us if we'd like further refreshments. Then Willow returned holding many paintings and old photographs and a copy of a family tree, which she handed to me first. "I had this updated to add you to it. It shows you your line of descent from the Rulefort clan."

"Thank you. I really appreciate that," I said. Looking at it, I noticed that wives' names were written in a small and more feint script than their husband's bolder tones, and that there were no female offspring.

"Does no Rulefort ever have a daughter?" I queried.

"No," Griffin said. "There have only ever been sons."

But as I looked at my aunt's face and she quickly looked away, I had the strangest sense of unease that Willow was hiding something, something huge, and I was determined I would find out what that was. But for now, as I asked to see one of the paintings, my aunt's posture relaxed once more, and she chatted away happily to me about my family until Griffin told us it was time to get ready for the service.

Standing, I made my way over to my aunt who had also risen to escort us to the door. "Would it be okay if I returned some time to speak with you further?" I asked.

"You are family and welcome anytime," she said. We hugged and Griffin and I bid farewell and left her to make her final preparations before her husband was buried.

"Thank you, Griffin. I feel better for seeing Willow. For getting to know my uncle a little through her. Even if I never rule, at least I will have made that connection."

"Your uncle was a good man, Jason, and he ruled well. That's not to say he didn't fuck up ever. He was no saint. But he kept the clan in order, and you will see at his funeral today how most respected his rule. As you look at the faces of his mourners today, you will gain an inkling into how you want these people to look at you. Think to yourself about how you will need to present yourself to get that expression on their faces. Their trust and respect. That, son, is the biggest lesson you can learn from today. Now come, we must move with haste and get to the site of the pyre. They will be bringing his body soon."

For a brief moment it was like my soul left my body and stood back looking at where I was and what I was doing. How was this Jason Gradon? Yesterday, I'd been guiding people on items that needed to be dry-cleaned only. Now here, I was Jason Rulefort, dragon heir. It was like I'd somehow gone through a monitor and into a computer simulation.

I wondered what was happening back in Gnarly and I felt a deep pang as I thought of my home.

CHAPTER FOURTEEN

Kaf

"Can't help you at the bistro tonight, bro," I said, standing in the living room doorway.

"Oh yeah? Finally discovered the reason you're here isn't just to annoy me?"

"Actually, there *is* a possibility I found out why I'm here," I confirmed. That had Connor sitting up straighter.

"Seriously?"

I sat in the chair near him and told him about Charity and what was going on in her life. "And so I will accompany her to the sea this evening, where hopefully, if I help her sort out her problems, I will be okay with the big guns upstairs once more."

Connor folded his arms across his chest and stared me down. "Are you sure you've told me everything about how you came back here? I mean, you were dead. I wasn't expecting to see you again, as amazing as that is. You sure you weren't flirting up there and being un-angely?"

"Amazing. You think you'd worship the ground I walk on, not only for the fact I'm an angel, but for getting to see me again after I passed on. But no, I'm still getting accused of flirting." *Though I had been.*

"It did kill you."

I stuck my tongue out. "And got me admission to Heaven. So why are they not happy with me now? They knew who I'd been on earth. Now they're saying there's a lesson for me, and I'll help someone. What lessons do I need? I'm awesome."

Connor's brow raised. "Maybe one in being less egotistical? Anyway, do you fancy a brew? I'm going to make myself another."

"Please," I answered. Since I'd returned, I could do angel things and mortal things, and that meant I could enjoy a lovely cuppa, as well as *other things*... I'd yet to satisfy my libido though. I'd been flirting, yes, but since being up in Heaven spending time with all the good people, I seemed to have a bit of a conscience now when it came to just having a one-night stand. Plus, every time I flirted with people in the bistro, I somehow kept spilling liquids down myself. I'd come back to earth clumsy. I guess we did float around a lot upstairs, feeling as mellow as we did, so no doubt I just needed to get used to my earthly body again.

Being back here was weird. I'd been dead for over six years now. Since then, Connor had moved to Gnarly and opened the bistro. It was strange how we'd fallen back into our normal sibling behaviour, despite everything that had happened.

Six years earlier...

"See you later, you sad fucker," I snarked at my older brother as I straightened my jacket. I was dressed to impress, having bagged myself a date with Portia, the daughter of the big boss at the car sales company I worked for.

She was absolutely gorgeous and had said to me repeatedly that she didn't date her father's staff, but I'd used my cheeky charm and sales patter until she'd relented, saying I could have, 'One date only'.

And that date was tonight. The only thing was, I did feel a little pissed off at the fact she wanted me to meet her for an evening picnic at a park because she didn't want anyone who knew her or her father, to see us. I'd been reassured when she'd added, 'Unless of course you get me to break my one-date rule like you have my no-dating-staff one'.

I followed her directions and arrived at the spot at the park. There was a gap in the trees where you could walk through near to a smaller lake. True to her directions, I saw where a tree had been cut down and there she was just inside, sitting on a blanket beside a bottle of opened champagne and a Fortnum and Mason hamper. She smiled at me and flicked at her honey-blonde fringe. Then she patted the blanket next to her, and for the next hour we ate and drank and got to know each other better. I'd not had champagne before, and it made me a little foggy headed. I'd been enjoying her company and soaking in her appeal. The way her pink tongue kept darting out to lick crumbs from her lip. The feel of her hand when she'd tapped my arm or knee when talking. I'd just kept drinking: both drinking her in and drinking the champagne. I'd caught a taxi here and had intended to get one home if I wasn't invited back to hers.

Slumping against a tree trunk, I mumbled, "I'm going to need you to order my taxi home. Think I've had too much to drink."

She smiled and replied, "Don't worry, you're not going home."

Up until this point I'd have been delighted to be invited to Portia's place, but now I was clearly in no fit state to perform.

"I really need my own bed. Sorry, Portia, I've never had champagne before."

"Don't worry, Kaf. I'm gonna take good care of you," she said, and that was when I saw the glint of the carving knife she'd used to slice up the fresh ham joint, and I realised that my wondering why it wasn't pre-prepared in the hamper, given Portia was her Daddy's princess and never lifted a finger, had been a point I should have considered a little more. I tried to get up, but stumbled, and Portia just laughed. She went into my jacket pocket and took out my phone. "I'll need this to misdirect your family and the police," she said. "Just like I have so many times before." That was the last thing I'd heard before pain and a bright white light. But what Portia didn't know was that my brother and I had had personal safety drilled into us by our completely over-the-top and overprotective policewoman mother, who had given us enough horror stories and guilt to make us do what she asked. Not only had I told Connor exactly where I was going and who with, but I had an extra burner phone set with an unsent message that I'd never expected to use in my lifetime and had my location available to be picked up. I'd felt under my t-shirt and pressed send, and then as Portia approached with the knife, I pressed record and hoped it did the trick. Thank goodness for Braille on the phone.

"Kafziel."

I opened my eyes, having shut them when I'd found myself in the all-white interview room with the angel sitting at the desk opposite me. At the back of him was a completely mirrored wall and I wondered if there was a room behind it like Mum had talked about them having in some interview rooms back at the station.

"So, I'm dead?" I asked.

"Yes. I'm sorry, but you are. However, the actions you took tonight meant that Portia will be caught, imprisoned, and will murder no more. Therefore, not only will you enter Heaven, but you shall also return as an angel. We recognise a soul reborn within you and now returned to us. That of Cassiel."

"Erm, thanks but I'll need a moment to process this," I replied, to which the angel sat across from me smiled.

"Take your time," he said.

I realised I wasn't breathing. That would take some getting used to. I stretched out my body, because it felt weird—lighter, floaty—and then I felt the movement on my back. I was catapulted out of my seat and hit the floor in front of the desk before rising up as my wings opened fully. It was then I discovered the reason for the mirrors. Because in those I got to see my angel self in all his glory.

I really did rock the angel look with my white-blonde hair.

And that was where I'd stayed; in Heaven, overlooking the earth, and helping where I was allowed. I'd been called into the 'office' a few times for flirting with some of the incoming, because there was a rule that the ones who'd had true love had to wait for the true love to join them. Liking the harder-to-get women in life hadn't changed after my death and so I'd tried to break the rules and had, in fact, been given a final warning.

Had that stopped me? Not when a reigning Miss World had come in.

And so, I'd found myself on the floor of Mya's attic room, where she'd made enquiries and told me why I was here. She'd given me a room to use there, but I received a text from number 111 (ie Heaven) that my brother had come to open a bistro in the exact same village where I'd been ejected.

Coincidence? I thought not.
Then I laughed to myself as I decided to go see him.

I'd waited until he was about to wake up after a good night's sleep.

"Whooooooooooo. Whooooooooo," I wailed.

Connor stirred and I watched as he opened his eyes.

"Whooooooooooo. Whooooooooo," I said even more tortured. "Hel-llpppp me, Connor."

He sat up faster than a speeding F1 car, and his eyes seemed to bug out of his head. "Kaf?"

"I'm trapped in a portal. You have to help me, brother." I pretended to feel around me as if trapped behind glass.

Connor rubbed his eyes and then leapt out of bed when he saw I was still there. Thankfully, he was wearing pyjamas.

"What the fuck drug have I been given? This can't be real. It can't be."

"Help meeeeeee," I said again. Then as he came closer, I threw my arms around him.

"Honey, I'm home," I yelled, at which point my brother screamed and wet himself.

What we didn't know for definite, but presumed, was that as soon as I'd done my good deed I'd be returned back upstairs. At first, I'd thought I'd just take my time and enjoy being in Gnarly, but as the days had passed Connor and I had talked more and noted that as we didn't know what I was here to do, I might just accidentally do it anyway. We agreed that I'd work at the bistro so we could spend as much time together as possible. Then Mya had come with a message that I was being watched and any attempts to not help people would be met with immediate withdrawal back, not to the angel realm, but to the Home of Wayward Souls, where Mya would give me lessons in thinking of others. The thought of being on the end of Mya's wrath or endless talking of shoes was enough to focus my mind.

Then I'd met the gorgeous Charity.

A mermaid who'd just started dating a dragon shifter called Jason.

I told myself that meeting her tonight and accompanying her to the sea was work related only and in no way anything to do with her being so attractive. She was dating someone, and I was now dead. I had to reform from being the male who always lusted after the hard-to-get women.

I kept repeating this to myself until it came to the time to meet her outside of the bistro.

My delight at seeing her was immediately dulled by then seeing the younger male at her side.

"Hey, Kaf. This is my brother Billy," she said, gesturing to him.

"Thought you'd have wings," he said.

I ejected them to their full glory and basked in Charity's surprise and adulation.

"Whoa! Fucking A," Billy yelled. "And can you fly?"

"Course I can fly," I scoffed. I folded my wings around them and off we went to Bridlington. Aware of Charity's body heat in my embrace, I was glad I'd soon be in the sea so I could cool down and remind myself of why I was here.

CHAPTER FIFTEEN

Jason

"We need to visit the vault before we make our way to the pyre," Griffin said.

Damn, I'd hoped he'd forgotten that. I'd never seen a dead body before that hadn't been re-animated like Merrin's, and I didn't really want to start now. Praying internally that I wouldn't vomit, I nodded and reluctantly followed him. I let out a deep exhale when I saw there was still a huge queue waiting to get into the vault.

"Oh what a shame," I said.

Griffin turned to me. "Huh?"

"The queue."

"Oh yes. Well, they shouldn't have left it so late. The doors will close at ten am regardless of the queue, so the ones at the end may as well go get ready for the service."

"Agreed." I turned to face the other way.

"What are you doing?"

I pointed to the queue. "We don't have time."

Griffin laughed. "As if the heir and the deputy have to queue." He guffawed then. "Oh, Jason, your naivety does crack me up."

We'd see if he was still laughing when I threw up on his feet.

As we walked nearer to the vault doors, I asked, "So what has my uncle been dressed in? Will he be cremated in his crown and robes?"

That earned me another bellow of laughter. "Our king does not wear a crown. His magnificence and attitude indicate his bearing. Clothes." He shook his head. "Honestly."

"He's naked?" I double-checked.

"Yes, Jason. He has no need of clothes in this state."

I almost said I didn't wish to entertain the idea of being the future king anymore just for this reason alone. I knew my deceased uncle wouldn't be aware of what was happening, but everyone coming to see his naked body? I felt embarrassed for him.

"And he's laid facing up, right?"

Griffin stopped and stared at me for a moment, and then his upper lip twitched with further mirth. Without another word he just carried on walking.

Dick.

Oh God. As I thought the word, I realised I was going to see my dead uncle's dick.

We were at the front. It was time for a deep breath and to think of Charity as I saw my dead uncle. No, that wasn't a good idea. What if I saw his naked body, his dick, and thought of Charity and got a noticeable erection? My breath began to come in short gasps. Washing machines. I'd think of washing machines from the laundrette.

And then the doors were pushed open, and I saw... a dragon. A huge, blue and green coloured scaly dragon, on all fours, no dick on show, though a large tail was. It looked like something from a museum.

"You utter fucker," I said to Griffin, who grinned from ear to ear.

"Come on. Let's do this. I can't believe you thought the king of the Rulefort clan would be in human form."

"I'm not sure you've sent me any information to date that has actually been of any practical use," I said through gritted teeth.

"We only have to stand here for a few moments to pay our respects and then we can move on," Griffin told me as we reached the front. The few gathered at the front already either left the room or stepped back to let us through.

I'd stand with my eyes shut, pretend to pay my respects, and then leave.

"Future king, it is my absolute honour to be in your presence." I opened my eyes to find a woman in front of me on her knees. Never did I think I'd find myself in such a situation where I wanted the woman to *get up*. "I would be so grateful if I could hear your own words of respect."

"Yes, yes," I heard as others gathered around. As they packed in closer together it meant they let more of the queue in and soon the room was filled with dragon people. And they were all looking at me. Most had dropped to their knees, which now had me thinking of washing machines again because the power might just give me a hard on after all, while others stood, hands on hips, glaring at me.

"This should be interesting," Griffin said, with rather too much amusement in his tone.

What the hell did I say?

I looked at my uncle's dragon body.

"I am here to pay my respects to my uncle, Josiah Ashton Rulefort. To thank him for his service as leader of the Rulefort clan and for being a good husband to my aunt. I am sorry that I was not able to know him in life and feel humbled seeing his majestic presence albeit after death. I can see he was truly a magnificent ruler." That'd do.

People clapped and applauded. "Yes, yes. Continue..."

Continue? What? Oh well, I'd done okay so far. But... I had nothing left in my mind. I stared at the dragon. *If you're in there, Uncle J, and can communicate, please do so now.*

Nothing.

Alive dragons might blow flames, but dead dragons just sucked. End of.

"They say that blue and green should never be seen," I muttered. "But clearly, Josiah showed that to not be the truth because his scales look perfectly delightful."

People began to look and talk to each other.

"That's the discolouration from death," Griffin whispered. "He was black before."

Fuck.

"He may now be in the first stages of decay, but do not worry, dear dragonfolk, for soon he shall be laid on the pyre, where he will linger in the flames until he becomes ashes." Nervously, I checked the crowd. Things seemed to be going okay again. Phew. "I understand that the ashes are collected to be placed in the boardroom and it's good to know that I will be able to be near him in some way after death. And wow, his initials are JAR. JAR will be in a jar!"

Griffin began to clap and holler loudly. "Hurrah for King Josiah. Let him shine bright in Heaven's light."

"Shine bright in Heaven's light," they repeated, and while they did, he grabbed my arm and dragged me in the direction of the door.

"Hey, you're hurting my arm," I complained.

"Smile at everyone, because it was going to be a toss-up who got thrown on the pyre if you carried on talking," he added, turning to smile at everyone as we walked past.

Rude.

In position with the others at the side of the stacked pyre, Griffin had told me more times than necessary that luckily, he was doing the speech for the service as my uncle's second-in-command.

A trumpet sounded and then the crowd fell silent as the rest of the council appeared carrying a litter with my uncle laid across it. His body had been draped with a ceremonial purple cloth with the dragon's crest on the side in embroidered orange stitching. On the bottom of the litter were some of the flowers that had been left in the vault.

They reached the front of the pyre and then stood to one side. Griffin stepped forward where a lectern had been prepared. He leaned over to the microphone.

"Thank you everyone for joining us today as we lay to rest the body of our dear king, Josiah Ashton Rulefort. Josiah governed us for twenty-five years and helped many of us here today. He was also a loving husband to Willow Jaspar Rulefort," he added, looking into the crowd. I followed his gaze seeing it reach my aunt who was a way further down the line of people gathered around, men before her. The misogyny here was starting to get on my nerves. She should have been up here near her husband.

Griffin spoke at length about all of my uncle's achievements and then he began to draw his speech to a close. I was glad because I'd been standing up so long my legs hurt, and I was in dire need of a pee and a drink.

"As you know, unfortunately Josiah left no heir, but nominated his nephew Jason to inherit rule. The Rulefort clan welcomes you here today, Jason, officially, and tonight shall mark the start of the trial nominations."

Once again, many more cheered, but there were a few boos and mumbles of 'half-breed'. I just thanked people and sank back between Azar and Kenna.

"It is time, dear clan, to say goodbye to Josiah. Blaze, can you please light the pyre."

I snorted. Of all the shifters, they'd chosen the one called Blaze to start the fire?

"Get ready to shift, all."

And then I wasn't amused any more. I'd got to become my dragon, and I'd not changed into it for *years*. What if I couldn't do it? What if I got shafted by my inner shifter?

All around me people began to shuck off their clothes and change and within seconds I'd seen more tits, cocks, pussy, and arse than a nudist colony in peak season. Wishing I'd drunk a lot of alcohol, I stripped off and then noticed—everyone had turned to stare at me. There I was, built enough to not feel inferior on that score, but with my limp dick hanging while everyone, and I meant everyone, looked at me. Not at the now established pyre, but at me.

"What's going on?" I panic-whispered to Azar.

"They're waiting to see what your dragon looks like. If it meets their approval as a possible future king."

"Oh right." I decided it was better to be a dragon than stand with my limp dick on show, so I thought about my inner dragon and...

I felt it. The tremble of my body and then the feeling of my bones strengthening. But it was so much more than it had been before. Like joy flowing through my veins as my body seemed to scream its acceptance of my dragon form. The next thing I knew, I was looking at my dragon body. I was standing at a great height, compared with before, and taller than most others around me. The dragons either side of me had moved to give me space where I'd been pushed against them while changing.

My scales were shiny and *silver*, and dragons around me began to fall to their knees, making the weirdest noise. When I'd changed in Gnarly, I'd been grey, but here amongst the clan, my coat was majestic. I looked at the dragon I just 'knew' was Griffin and I heard him in my mind. *'There are prophecies of silver dragons being of great luck. We have never had one before. There will be those who will argue it's from your human genetics and because you are not a full dragon, but most here will revere you'.*

Holy shit!

The litter carrying my uncle's load was placed on a crane-like contraption and raised into the air and then it tipped so that he was dropped onto the top of the pyre. Soon the smell of charred dragon flesh permeated the air and I decided that I'd need Chantelle to perform a magic spell on me ASAP or I'd never be able to visit the bistro again. Right now, all I could think of was seeing crispy dragon wing on the buffet afterward.

People began to change back into their naked selves and re-dress. Griffin announced the feast would start and reminded people where they needed to go to nominate the trials.

I got dressed and looked forward to having a pee. I wasn't feeling hungry at the moment given the current smell of Uncle J in the air.

"I need the bathroom," I explained as Griffin came forward.

"No you don't."

"I do! I've been standing here ages and I'm bursting."

"I mean that you don't need a *bathroom*. You're in the middle of woodland. Go find a tree!"

"Oh yeah, duh. Then what do I need to do? Hang around and entertain the crowd? Get to know people?"

"No, you'll be sitting around the pyre with the rest of the council until the fire is done and then we shall wait for it to cool and collect the ashes. Did you not listen to this at the council meeting?"

I'd probably zoned out at that point. My mind did jump to thinking about Charity a lot lately. Absence definitely made the heart grow fonder. I might start pining soon.

"Oh yes, of course. I forgot. It's the grief," I lied.

HOT AS SUCK

Griffin sighed heavily. "Go pee," he ordered, and I made my escape.

Finally, alone for a while and behind a tree, I delivered my urine with satisfaction that was close to an orgasm. Knowing it might lead people to thinking I'd taken a dump, but not caring, I lingered close behind another tree, thinking about my dragon.

"Got to admit, Jase, you're a hot dragon," I said to myself. "Not hot like Uncle J is right now though, thank God."

CHAPTER SIXTEEN

Charity

Because of Kaf's angelic abilities, we arrived under the sea at my old home within minutes, yet it felt like we'd not travelled at all. Unlike vampire speed, which disorientated you, angelic travel was subtle, just a small vibration like you could feel a buzz of energy but you couldn't tell you were moving. It wasn't until Kaf re-opened his wings and Billy and I found ourselves returned that I realised we'd moved at all. I told him so.

"Yes, our movement is exactly that, a vibrational change. What is the plan of action now that we've arrived?"

I shrugged. "Knock on the door and…" I winked and pointed at the folded feathers on his back. "Wing it."

He and Billy both groaned loudly behind me as I walked towards the door.

My heart thudded in my chest as I waited for someone to answer. Then a chain was removed, a lock unbolted, and my ex-husband stood in front of me. The change in him was startling. He was unshaven, his hair grown out, and he was dressed in a t-shirt and shorts. My first thought was that he and my mother must have fallen out for him to look so dishevelled, until my mother walked into the hall behind him, saying, "Who is it?" before clocking my appearance.

My mother looked the same amount of dishevelled, her hair up in a messy bun like she didn't care what she looked like, and I acknowledged that what I was seeing were two people, who up until my arrival, had been very relaxed in each other's company. It hurt. I couldn't deny it.

"Charity..." The look of surprise on my mother's face annoyed the shit out of me.

"You sound surprised I'm here and yet you trudged sea water all over my new furnishings and left me a note of blackmail." I could feel my nostrils flaring.

"Please come in," Rutger said, and they both moved back as I entered, followed by Billy and Kaf. I was sighing at now having to be invited into what had been my own home until I became distracted by Rutger's eyes widening.

"Where did you come from?" he asked Billy.

"This dude made me invisible by cloaking me in his wings. Neat trick, huh? So, just think, at any time I could be spying on you," he quipped.

"This is Kaf," I announced. "He's an angel and he's come with me. It's a long story, and I'll explain more later."

We went through the motions of awkwardness as we took a seat and my mother asked if anyone wanted a drink, and then we all sat in silence. I turned and stared at our mum. She was the one who'd ordered us to come here. She could start the conversation.

She lowered her gaze. "Firstly, I'd like to apologise for the message I left. I'd had a lot to drink, became frustrated, visited Gnarly and... well..."

"Broke into my home," I said testily.

She looked up at me, nodding.

"I'm surprised you resisted helping yourself to anything you found there that you liked, given you have form for taking my things." I gave her a narrow-eyed look.

"Charity," Kaf said.

I turned my gaze towards him. "I know. I need to be more adult about things."

"Actually, I was just going to say you haven't properly introduced me."

"Oh."

"I'll do it," Billy said. "So this is Kaf. He's an angel who doesn't know why he's here on earth, but it might be to sort us out. That's why he's accompanied us. He's totally awesome because he can move fast without us knowing and can make me invisible. It's a shame he's here to be good, because otherwise I would use his skills to have a lot of wicked fun." He grinned at Kaf, who grinned back.

"Can still have fun, mate."

I wasn't particularly happy about Billy being so struck on Kaf and I couldn't put my finger on why for a few minutes until he added,

"I like my sister's new friends. Kaf and Jason are both a right laugh."

My mother and Rutger exchanged a look before looking back at me.

"I'm dating again. Not that it's any of your business. He's called Jason, and I like him a lot. Kaf is just a *friend*."

"I'm happy you've met someone," Rutger said.

"Well, let me go pop some champagne now I have your approval." My sarcasm and attitude were fierce, and I needed to get them under control, or nothing would be achieved. I was just thinking this when Kaf placed a hand on my arm, and I suddenly felt calm flooding my body. I gave him a half-smile, then turned to look at Rutger.

"Sorry. It's just all still quite raw."

"I know," he said softly. He looked like he was about to apologise again, but I raised a hand.

"I'm not here for anyone to apologise. I'm here because my mother came to my new home and left a note threatening to take Billy."

"As I said, I was drunk," Mum said. "We were so very close, you and I, and now I've ruined it. I wanted you back, you and Billy."

"You want me back? All you ever do is shout at me!" Billy's voice rose.

Our mother ran a hand through her hair.

"I have so much to make up for. When your dad died, I began to rely on you, Charity. We'd always been so close, and you, Billy, you were the apple of your dad's eye. And you look like him, Son. So much like him. It's not your fault, but seeing you reminded me of my loss, and sometimes when you were around, I felt like I couldn't breathe for the reminder of him. I loved him so much. We might not have been able to make our marriage work, but we couldn't be apart either. He was my best friend."

"I wish I could have fallen in love with anyone else, Charity, but when I met Rutger, I fell hard."

"And what about you?" I asked my ex-husband.

"My parents insisted I give them an heir. That I was to marry well. You were the mayoress' daughter. Beautiful. Kind. I thought I could make it work. But then I fell in love with your mother and began to not care about any of my parental pressures anymore. From the bottom of my heart, Charity, I am so very sorry."

"Not so sorry that you didn't do it," I said.

"So let's say we hadn't," my mother said. "Were you better off in the loveless marriage you were in, or did my actions actually do you a favour in the long run?"

I truly knew the expression of your chin hitting the floor then. My incredulity at her statement beyond words. "Oh my god, do you hear yourself? I'm so happy you slept with my husband, Mum. It saved me facing the fact we were better apart over a few further months."

She sighed. "I can't change the past, Charity, but we are focused on the future now," she replied. "A future that we hope eventually has you and Billy in it."

"Do you intend to make him return?" I asked, tilting my head. My hands were scrunched into fists under the table.

"Not if he doesn't want to," she replied. "However, there is something to be discussed. "We plan on getting married. Soon. In a month's time actually."

I stood up fast. "From a wife to a stepdaughter. What in the Jeremy Kyle is fucking happening here?"

"We're also planning to adopt in time," Rutger added.

"This is just too much," I said. "I'd say congratulations, but I wouldn't mean it because actually I want you both to go fuck yourselves."

"We know this is hard, but we'd like you to be there," Mum added.

Billy stood up. "You know what, Mum? And you, Rutger. It's cool for you that you've fallen madly in love and want to get married and are thinking of kids. But it's only a couple of months since you were caught cheating on your daughter, and your wife. Instead of being caught up in your heady love, acting like the leads in some Disney movie, maybe you could get your heads out of your arses and realise that you've hurt your kids, and your wife and brother-in-law. Instead of thinking of having more, maybe reflect on how you've fucked up with the ones you have."

Billy shook his head. "We're out of here, and I suggest you leave drinking alone for now, Mum, because you aren't welcome in Gnarly. We went there to be rid of you. Maybe one day we'll feel like we want to get in touch, but I think I can honestly speak for the both of us when I say it won't be anytime soon. I hope you have a wonderful wedding and a happy future, because if you've done all this and it goes tits up in two months' time, Rutger, I might just come back here and throat punch you. And Mum, you were a complete shit to me. Me reminding you of Dad is not an excuse for being a twat. You're two selfish, entitled arseholes who are welcome to each other. Come on, Charity and Kaf, we're done here," he finished.

I followed him out of the room, and we left the house. As soon as we were outside, I flung my arms around him. "You were incredible, Billy," I said. "So grown up."

"I might only be seventeen, but I have fucking feelings and they keep trampling all over them. But the day they both upset my sister, they went too far."

Kaf came closer. "Let's take you both home," he said. "It's been a complicated evening, and you have a lot to process."

Once more he wrapped us in his wings, and the next thing I knew we were outside the back door of our flat.

"I'm going in because you no doubt want to talk to Kaf about things behind my back," Billy said, disappearing inside.

When he'd gone, I gave out a long, low sigh. "You're still here."

"Rude much?"

I laughed a little, though I knew it wouldn't have reached my eyes. I was too bone weary with my ragged emotions. "I meant this can't have been why you were here, on earth, because you're still present."

"Not for tonight, no. But maybe I'm still here for you? You and Billy are having a difficult time."

"That's life though, isn't it? The rollercoaster of great times and shit times."

"Indeed. Anyway, I'll let you go make sure Billy is okay. If you need me for anything, let me know."

"Thanks. I really appreciated tonight. And your hand when it touched me... I felt so calm. You really do have the magic touch," I said, stepping forward and giving him a hug.

"Huh. I finally get a chance to come see you, and find you've already replaced me," said a familiar voice, and I leapt out of Kaf's embrace, turning to face Jason.

CHAPTER SEVENTEEN

Jason

They'd eventually let me go home once J.A.R. was in a jar. People had voted on my trials, but I wouldn't know what they were until they started. All I knew was I felt like falling into my girlfriend's arms if she was around. Even just for a few minutes if she was busy. I felt mentally and physically exhausted.

It was then I decided I'd call at hers on my way home. Yes, I smelled of bonfire, but she had a shower if she decided I could stay over. Griffin had said I didn't have to be back until two pm tomorrow. For me to rest up ready for gaining my full dragon powers and working through the testing of them. In less than forty-eight hours, I'd be starting the trials to become king.

At first, I thought I was seeing things when I heard Charity talking to a really good-looking man, an angel of all things, and then she'd stepped into his arms. Looked like while I'd been busy dealing with the dragon side of things, Charity had got her own bit on the side.

"Huh. Am I not *good* enough for you, that you've had to cop off with an angel?" Even in my temper I still managed a joke. I couldn't help myself.

Turning on my heel, I decided I'd call for some beers and then fall into an inebriated sleep as soon as possible. I should have known things were going too well. Romantic love just wasn't my friend.

"Jason," Charity said from behind me. I ignored her and continued to walk, though I slowed my pace so that I could hear her hopefully beg for forgiveness.

"Jason, you stupid fucker. If you don't turn around and hear me out because there's a legitimate explanation, I will soak your temper using the water from the Gnarly fountain," she yelled, sounding mighty pissed off.

I turned around and placed a hand on each hip.

She did the same and we stood facing each other looking like we were about to duel.

"I've been to see my mother tonight. Kaf took me and Billy. He'd just dropped us off and I was thanking him with a hug. It's been an emotional evening. That's all. He's been a support."

I walked off and punched the trunk of the nearest tree, completely forgetting its magical powers, until a gnarled branch whacked me in the stomach winding me. I fell to my knees, trying to remember how to breathe.

Charity came over to help me up, though she was pressing her lips firmly together.

"Go on, have a good laugh," I huffed.

She burst out laughing and I ended up joining her, both of us sat on the pavement.

When we'd finished and gone silent, I confessed the truth. "I'm angry that I've been so busy that I wasn't there for you. That this angel dude accompanied you to see your mother instead of me."

"Kaf's here on earth to help someone and he doesn't know who. He thought it could be me and Billy. That was why he came. No other reason, or I would have just gone with Billy. I didn't actually need a companion. I like you, you dipshit. I thought I'd made that perfectly clear."

I gave her my best puppy-dog eyes. "I'm sorry. Do you forgive me?"

She nudged my arm with her elbow. "Course. I quite like the fact you were jealous. Shows you give a shit. But there's no reason to be, Jason *Rulefort*. I only have eyes for you."

Leaning closer, I kissed her hungrily. When we broke off, her eyes fixed on mine. "You absolutely stink of bonfire, and of... barbecue?"

"Barbecued uncle to be precise."

"Ew," she said, moving away from me. "I'm not coming anywhere near you until you are clean."

I turned to eye up the fountain.

"You can come to mine for a shower."

I raised a brow. "Is that all I'm coming for?"

"We'll see," she said. "Depends if Billy is still up and about, and if you can manage to completely get that stench off yourself."

Billy had been busy being loud on his Xbox with his mates. Charity had overlooked his heated outbursts while game playing so that we could play our own games.

It was now the next morning and we had been talking about our current situations for the last hour.

"You have to work today. As much as I would like you to be there with me, and meet people down at the cave, I can't guarantee their reception would be a good one, and you'd piss off your customers."

"But tomorrow the trials start and what if something happens to you?"

"If the trials mean I have to risk my life, then I'm walking away," I told her. "I will try to prove myself in terms of leadership, of strength, but there's a line. I don't know these people, and some of their ways are outdated and ridiculous. If I am the heir, I'll shout out and make my voice heard. I don't have to risk my life and I won't be doing."

"Oooh, you sound all masterful," Charity said.

"I am all masterful," I winked and proceeded to demonstrate it in the bedroom.

"I'll see you tonight," Charity said, kissing me in the doorway of her downstairs kitchen/utility that was part of her working space. This was where she had transformed Merrin out of sight of other customers. She didn't realise it, but she was transforming me too, just without scissors. I felt happy and content, despite the dragon heir side of things.

Now I'd pop to see Mum at the launderette, before going home to have a nap ahead of my dragon lessons.

"Oh thank God, Jason," Mum said, rushing over and almost knocking me down as she flung her arms around me. "I've been so worried. I know you've kept texting, but I figured that could have been one of the dragons having pinched your phone and that you might have been being held hostage somewhere." She pushed me out to arm's length and looked me up and down. "Is that a bite? Have those dragons been getting physical with you?" she raged.

"Erm, no, Mum." I put my hand on my neck.

Realisation dawned, and then she smacked me across the arm. "I've been worrying about you, and all the time you've just been at Charity's?"

"I've been in the cave mostly, Mum. Go pop the kettle on and I'll get you up to date. They're removing the spell on my powers this afternoon."

"Oh God."

"I'll be in a training cave with Griffin. It'll be fine, Mum."

"I'm closing the launderette. I'm coming with you," she said.

"Don't be silly, I—"

"Jason. I. Am. Coming. With. You."

I sighed.

"I want to see these caves and people for myself. I'm the mother of the next potential king and it's about time I faced these people who would've treated me like dirt. I'll get dressed up and show them I will make an amazing king's mother."

"And if they still treat you like crap?"

"I'll explain how their children won't be getting Christmas presents this year. Because I only have to threaten to withhold a gift from Santa, and he'll be more than happy to do my bidding."

"God, Mother. Do you have to put that picture in my mind?"

"Says the person with a love bite on his neck."

I sighed. "Make me a cuppa, I'll get you up to date, and then I'm going home for a nap, and I'll meet you later."

On her way to the kitchen, she spotted the fire extinguisher on the wall behind her counter and paused near it. "Remind me to take that with me. Just in case. In fact, I have a fire blanket I can take instead and wrap myself in."

"Your faith in me is heart-warming," I said, expecting her to say it was the other dragons she thought might try and roast her in more ways than one. But she didn't. Charming.

The day passed far too quickly, especially after I'd napped for a couple of hours. Having called for Mum on the way, before long we were at the entrance of the cave, and she watched with interest as I did what was needed to get us inside.

Having passed the weather doors, Mum took a deep breath as she walked into the main part of the cave for the very first time. When she'd been with my father, she'd not been invited. She'd heard all about their non-acceptance of her, but none had ever deigned to come meet her. Eyes swept over us from the dragons around the place. I was a little early and so I decided to take Mum to call on my aunt.

"Jason," Willow said as she opened the door. "Was I expecting you? Because if so, I'm so sorry, I forgot."

"No. If you can't see us that's okay. But I brought my mum today and I thought you'd be a great person to introduce her too, being a dragon and a relation."

Willow opened the door wider to see Mum. "Oh my! You must be Fenella? Come in, come in. It's such a pleasure to finally meet you."

We went inside and Willow stepped forward and hugged Mum. I saw my mum's shoulders loosen and realised that she'd been extremely anxious about being here. I'd been right to bring her to see Willow. She could help Mum in terms of getting familiar with the dragon lair and making introductions.

We settled in my aunt's living room where the maid came in and laid out refreshments. Once she'd left, I addressed Willow. "I thought it would be good if you could explain dragons from a female point of view, because, Mum, they are really set in very old and fixed ways when it comes to how they treat women."

Willow blushed.

"What do you mean?" Mum asked.

"Aunt Willow didn't get to live in the castle rooms. She had to live here. They treat women like second-class citizens here. She wasn't allowed to be part of Uncle Josiah's rule, right?" I turned to my aunt. "They like the little woman to sit at home, yeah?"

Willow sighed. "Yes, that's how they like it to be seen. Even though most of us wives work or have worked tirelessly to support our husbands, while they do all the nicer parts of ruling Rulefort."

"What do you mean?" my mum asked.

"I mean that if I hadn't supported my husband, he'd have been a very poor king. I basically set up every policy, handled all his paperwork, and directed him on ninety-nine percent of things. He then floated around the place revered while I had to sit at home accepting the fact that as king, he would be expected to take many lovers. If it weren't for the fact I knew Josiah loved me deeply, and indeed, sent these 'callers' to his most trusted warlock, who spelled the visitors to believe they'd enjoyed the attention of their king, I might have started a rebellion. But he asked me not to, and I was a devoted wife."

"Jason, things have to change," my mum said. "You have the power to make this happen. All you need is the courage."

"Mum, I'm as annoyed by this as you are. But how can I take on all the dragons of Rulefort by myself?"

"You wouldn't be by yourself. You'd have almost all of the women of the clan behind you," Willow said. "We have been awaiting such an opportunity for a long time."

"I don't know," I said. "I need some time to think."

"Maybe this will help you," my aunt stated, as she whistled loudly, and shouted, "Amaryllis."

A few minutes later, the maid walked back through the door.

"It is time. Reveal who you truly are to the future king."

Amaryllis looked directly at me. "I'm your cousin, Jason."

It took me a moment to be able to speak. Then I looked closer at the maid, noting some maternal resemblances. I turned to my aunt. "But you have no children."

"No, Jason," she said. "I had no son. Therefore, in the eyes of the dragons here, I had no heir, no baby of merit."

And I knew then, that gaining my dragon powers was imperative, and the trials the dragons intended to give me were not the greatest battle I faced here.

CHAPTER EIGHTEEN

Jason

My mother gasped. "You've had to hide your daughter among your household as a maid?"

"It's not even 'hidden' really," Willow said. "Everyone is aware of women's pregnancies, and then if it's a girl, people just act like no birth happened at all. The girls are expected once old enough to help the household, until such time as a male dragon decides to choose them as a wife."

"That's disgraceful," I said.

"I'm seventeen," Amaryllis said. "If I'd been eighteen you can bet one of your rivals would have proposed marriage to me in order that they could make a challenge to the throne as the son-in-law of the deceased king."

"Look," I told her. "I fully intend to act on this information, but not only do I need time to get my head around what you've just revealed, but also, this afternoon, I'm gaining my full dragon powers. I don't want to promise you action when I may not be capable of fighting for you."

Willow and Amaryllis exchanged a look.

And then I explained how my powers had been suppressed.

Before long, it was time to make my way to meet Griffin in the now empty vault that yesterday had hosted my uncle's dead dragon body. I'd tried my best to get Mum to stay with Willow, but she was having none of it, insisting on accompanying me and bringing her fire blanket with her. She'd reluctantly left the extinguisher at home due to its weight.

"Hello again, Fenella," Griffin said, his expression stating this was a surprise he'd not expected this afternoon.

"Mum insisted on coming," I explained.

"I've brought a fire blanket just in case," she informed him.

"Very well. Let us go now and see what we have in store for us. Fenella, I will make sure Andy, the warlock who will lift the curse puts a protection spell around you also."

"Also?" I queried.

"Do you think I'm not going to protect myself from a half-breed dragon's unknown skills with fire?"

"Bit harsh," I mumbled as we walked inside the vault.

The room was completely clear now, with all of the flowers removed and no evidence of the mourning that had taken place in the room over the last days.

A knock came to the door a moment after we'd entered and a man walked in, introducing himself as Andy.

"That's a very normal name for a spellcaster," I noted to the thirty-something looking, short brown-haired man, who did look like he'd potentially just come from quoting on a plumbing job. I'd expected the full ceremonial robes, which was stupid given Chantelle never wore anything like that. She'd put her spell on me wearing her bistro apron.

"My name is Andromeda Jupiter Neapolitan Prosperity Freud Jones. As I'm sure you can imagine, I'd much rather introduce myself as Andy Jones, than explain why my parents included their favourite ice-cream in my names." He rolled his eyes.

"Oooh, why did they?" I asked.

"Jason, not now," Griffin ordered.

"My mother craved it through early pregnancy," Andy whispered, and I decided I liked the guy. He was down to earth despite his wizarding skills, and also, had ignored Griffin.

After placing the protection spells on everything that needed protecting, including the lair itself and everyone present, I was asked to sit in the middle of the vault.

"Okay, I'm now going to take off the spell on you," Andy said.

"There should be a song for that too," I said, thinking of the Nina Simone song for putting a spell *on* someone.

"Jason, focus," Griffin shouted.

"Don't you shout at my son," my mum yelled at Griffin.

Griffin tilted his head and gave my mother a condescending look. "Fine. I'll let him loose with his new-found powers, and we'll see what happens, shall we?"

"Point taken, but you're getting nothing this Christmas," Mum snapped.

I thought Griffin might cry. He was about to say something when my own patience broke.

"Be quiet. Andy needs to do the spell and I need to concentrate."

Andy began:

"A dragon's powers are strong and sure,
No longer will they be demure,
Held back until now, please deliver with care,
In the safety of the Rulefort lair.
Let Jason Rulefort now embrace his true dragon self.
While keeping him in perfect health."

"Is that it? I don't feel any different," I asked.

"It might be you have no other dragon powers," Griffin said.

"You mean after all this I might not change?" I snarled, and a ton of flames shot out of my nose, reaching Griffin, but going no further than the layer of protection.

Andy and Griffin high fived each other.

"Works every time," Griffin said. "Antagonise the fiery dragon."

Griffin got me to perform some different tasks to assess my skills. We discovered I was still a silver dragon, but my scales now had a golden sparkle to them. I could reach targets he set with my flames, which could come out of both my nose and my mouth. Shortly afterward, I realised I couldn't smell anything.

"That's a normal side effect. Your nostrils just have to adjust to sharing space with fire. Should come back within the day," Griffin said. I breathed a sigh of relief, which of course came accompanied with a side of flames.

"You'll get there," Andy re-assured me.

"Good, because my trials start tomorrow," I told him.

"Oh dear. I mean, oh right," he replied. "Well, my job here is done. The protection spells will last while ever you are in this room and then you're on your own, mate. All dragons have to embrace their new selves in a real-life environment, just like baby birds jumping out of the nest."

"But some of them die," I stated.

Andy just shrugged, and then left. As he opened the door, a security guard came through.

"This better be important, Abe, because the 'Do not Disturb' was there for a reason."

"And this is why I did not disturb until the warlock left. But, Deputy, there has been an incident you need to know about." He looked at me and then at Griffin.

"Go on," Griffin instructed.

"The prisoner, Joseph Rulefort. From nowhere he stood up, smelled the air, and began pacing his cage, banging the cell doors, and demanding to be released. He said he could scent his son. That he knew the dragon that shared his DNA was here. I managed to get him to agree to sit down if I came to find you, Griffin. He demands to see you and his son."

"Tell him, I shall visit him when I get a moment," Griffin said.

"I want to go now," I announced.

My mum slumped onto a chair in the corner of the room. "I've dreaded this moment."

"It was bound to come though, Mum," I said, walking over to her, sitting beside her and placing her in my embrace. "It's time for me to reunite with my father and see what he wants."

"Oh I know what he wants," Griffin said. "He wants to rule the clan, and he can't do it himself, so he will try to use you."

I couldn't believe my own father could be so heartless, and was sure once we were reconciled, he would apologise for all his wrongdoings. But there was only one way to find out.

"There are protections in place for us in the jail, correct?"

"Of course. Or there would have been several murders and a free evil dragon by now," Griffin said. "Don't let your family ties blinker you to his true nature, Jason."

"I thank you for your advice, but now it's time for me to make up my own mind," I said. "Before now, my mother protected me from my dragon heritage, and now you try to protect me too. It's appreciated, but I am a man, almost thirty years old, and it's now time for me to take the lead myself. I suggest we go see my father, and then we go to the boardroom and discover what trials have been set for me tomorrow."

"We also need to have the ceremony to put your uncle's remains away with the ancestors."

"Very well. We have a lot to do, so let us be on our way to the jail. Mother, you shall wait outside there, or I can arrange for you to be escorted home or to Willow's."

"I'll wait outside," she said.

"For the first time you have spoken like a true king," Griffin said, patting me on the back. "Now dismiss Abe, and we shall be on our way."

I'd never really given transport a thought until Griffin directed us through a doorway and I saw a monorail system there. We climbed aboard the carriage that waited and it set off.

"This is so quiet," I acknowledged.

"Can you imagine any more noise? It's bad enough there are so many people in close proximity. Our dwellings are soundproofed, but still the place gets busy inside. You can also cycle anywhere you like but I much prefer the monorail. It's quick and I don't have to get changed."

I just knew my mum was imagining Griffin in a pair of tight cycling shorts and I cut her a look. "Behave."

She just sniggered. I was a little relieved that something had distracted her from the fact we were about to meet my father shortly, even if only for a brief amount of time. But before long, the clouds came back over her gaze. The last time she'd seen him he'd burned down the family home and placed me in danger. Had broken our family apart completely.

"Next stop," Griffin said, and we readied ourselves. Eventually exiting the monorail and following Griffin to a heavily protected gated entrance. He spoke with the guards, then we were let through.

It was another long walk down a corridor. "Bloody hell, wish I'd remembered to wear my Fitbit today," I whined. "Couldn't Andy have just whizzed us here?"

"Dragons are not lazy," Griffin said. "This distance is nothing and mostly it's been off foot. Anyway, we are here now," he declared. We went past two further doors, both with security guards and coded entrances. Finally, we reached a smaller doorway, which was not only protected by a guard, but also a dragon, a fingerprint and coded entryway, and a door that clearly had magic and/or electric as it hummed/buzzed and green and blue sparks came off it.

We went through being scanned and given permission to visit.

"How come that one stays in dragon form?" I asked.

"So he can kill someone in seconds," was the answer I didn't really want to hear from Griffin.

Eventually, the doors opened, and we walked inside. The room was large and well lit, with the cell at the far end. And there behind metal grills that also sparked with electric and magic was a large man. He was easily four inches taller than me, wider, and his face was heavily lined. Were it not so pale, I'd have thought he'd spent too long in the sun. But the most alarming thing was his physique. He had muscles Arnold Schwarzenegger could have only dreamed of. He made him, Sylvester Stallone, and Dolph Lundgren look like Milky Bar kids.

He smiled at me and it was the most terrifying thing I'd ever seen. If it weren't for the fact she'd remained outside, I'd have shouted for my mum.

"Son," he said. "We're reunited at last."

CHAPTER NINETEEN

Charity

I called into Books and Buns at lunchtime. For one thing, I fancied one of their cheese toasties, and a strawberries and cream cupcake, and for another I wanted Ginny to see if she could get me any books on dragon shifters.

I was surprised to find Mitzi from the store sitting there. From what I'd heard, she didn't mix very often. As I passed, she pushed out the chair opposite her with her feet. I'd not planned on stopping long, as I had a client coming in thirty minutes, but I decided I'd better sit for five. I felt Ginny's curious gaze on us as I took the seat.

"I flew over the shifter ground when it was the funeral," Mitzi said. "I saw your boyfriend shift, and do you know what colour dragon he is?" Her beady eyes landed on my face.

"Erm, no. It hasn't come up in conversation actually."

"He's a silver dragon. Beautiful shiny silver. If he ever loses a scale, please keep it for me and I will pay handsomely for it."

"I hope he never does lose one, but I'll let him know you were asking about them."

"First perusal?"

"I can't speak on Jason's behalf."

She sighed. "I suppose not, but please mention it to him at a favourable time."

She winked, and I realised that she was hoping that in the middle of doing the deed I'd bargain for a silver scale on her behalf.

I was about to put her straight, but the bell of the door dinged as Kaf walked in. Mitzi saw him and her eyes widened as much as they possibly could.

"Who is that? He glows with silver hues."

"That's Kaf. He's an angel. You can't collect him."

She carried on talking but her eyes never left Kaf. "No, it is just an aura, but I can gaze upon it. What a lovely sight."

Of all the things to stare at on Kaf, his aura wouldn't have been what I went for, but Mitzi was a weird one, and so I just nodded my head in agreement.

The man himself got a bun, a coffee, and then came to sit with us. It was looking less likely by the minute that I was going to get to speak to Ginny about dragon books.

"Did you sort things out with Jason the other night?" he asked.

A vampire slid into the one remaining seat. Bloody vamp ears. "What happened with Jason?" Ginny asked.

"Nothing," I said, at the same time as Kaf said,

"He saw us hugging."

"Fully clothed hugging or naked hugging?" Ginny queried.

"A normal, platonic hug of thank you. As soon as I'd explained the situation everything was fine."

"You mean you boned him?" Ginny said.

"His body is incredible in dragon form. I cannot imagine having to settle for his human one in the bedroom," Mitzi announced.

"What would a bird like you know about shagging dragons?" Ginny said.

"Bit derogatory, calling this woman a bird," Kaf said. "I bet you wouldn't let me get away with it as a man."

"She is a bird. A magpie shifter," Ginny explained.

That got Kaf's attention. "Really? I'm an angel. Nice to meet someone else who has wings, though mine are significantly larger I guess than yours."

"Size doesn't matter. It's what you do with them. You are very shiny," Mitzi replied, tilting her head from side to side to look at him more in depth.

"Er, it is hot today. Can't help my skin sweating."

"She's not talking about your skin. She's discussing your aura. Mitzi loves gold, silver, and anything shiny. And you're shiny, which is why she's staring at you as if you hung the moon," I explained.

"So have you been flying around Gnarly a lot lately?" Kaf asked her. "Only, I'm here to do a good deed, and I'm not sure what it is yet. Maybe I could get you another coffee and you could let me know anything you've seen that could give me a clue?"

"I will accept a coffee as that gives me more chance to admire your shiny aura. It is such a shame I cannot procure an aura. Not without killing you for good anyway."

I'd heard enough and I turned to Ginny. "Are you able to get me something like a Dummies Guide to Dragon Shifters? Only Jason starts these trials tomorrow and I'd feel better if I'd done my best to read up on all things dragon. I might be able to help him."

"I'll go look and see what Mya has. All the good mystical books are kept in the turreted libraries at the home of the wayward. Back in a sec." Ginny excused herself and went off to her counter where she began tapping into her keyboard.

"Well, I best be making my way back to the salon," I said.

"Don't forget I still owe you a favour for the ring," Mitzi said. "If you need me just shout Mitzi Magpie three times."

"And if you need me just shout stud muffin three times," Kaf said.

I groaned but Mitzi laughed. It was time to leave them to it.

Approaching the counter, I said to Ginny, "Found anything?"

"Couple of possibilities. I'll check them and send any of use through your portal later. Now what's happening with Jason? Bring me up to speed."

I told her all I knew.

"So tonight, he'll find out what these trials are? If you need me and Merrin just let us know. Not sure what use he'd be, but I can go in and drain a dragon or two if needs be." She tilted her head. "They should have done a film about that. Would have been much more interesting than training one."

"Maybe 'How to Drain Your Dragon' could be the sequel?" I said sarcastically.

"I may just write to them and suggest it. I could star in it too," Ginny said, flicking her blonde hair.

"Do not use your powers of suggestion on Hollywood. No one

needs a kids movie sequel where poor Toothless also becomes Bloodless."

"It's such a waste of a good title," she whined. Hey, if you accuse Jason of something it would be 'How to Blame Your Dragon'. Or if you embarrass him, "How to Shame Your Dragon'."

I stuffed my cupcake in her mouth. I could buy another on my way out.

On my way past Mitzi and Kaf, I watched as an annoyed Connor walked over to them. "Kaf, do you think you could come and do some work? You know, with it being lunchtime and extremely busy."

"I am working. I'm doing angel work," Kaf explained.

"Chatting up Mitzi is angel work, is it?" Connor shook his head in disbelief. "It's about time you stopped flirting and started helping."

Mitzi was looking at Connor. "You are so dull," she said.

Connor folded his arms over himself and scoffed. "Sorry I can't be as entertaining as my brother, but some of us have businesses to run." He stalked off out of the store.

"I meant his aura. It is very dark," she told Kaf, whose face paled.

"What do you mean? Is that bad?"

"Dark auras mean negativity or being stifled. Something along those lines where he just can't be himself. He's unhappy and stuck. He needs to work on himself. It can change."

"But it's not a negative energy as in an evil entity or anything like that?"

"No. Just a man who needs to seek happiness." She turned to me.

"Jason's aura was like a grey storm before he met you. Now it has lifted into a white that shows his pure heart when he is near you. I do believe he is falling in love."

"And what colour is Charity's?" Kaf asked, winking at me teasingly.

"A girl never gives away another girl's secrets," she said, also winking at me.

And it was true. Mitzi hadn't spilled what I'd told her about my marriage, and I knew that no matter how strange she was, we

HOT AS SUCK

had formed a tentative friendship of sorts. Whatever kind of friendship a lone magpie settled to anyway. She'd offered to help me if needed and that meant a lot. And she didn't need to tell me my aura colour. It would be whatever colour falling head over heels was.

Now it was time to get back to work, before settling down to whatever books Ginny sent to me while I waited for my man to come see me.

My man.

I'd found a new home, and a potential new love.

If he survived the weekend...

I went to pick up a couple of pizzas for the evening meal. Billy and I would eat at the usual time and then there would be some to warm up if Jason hadn't eaten.

Walking into *Pizza the Action*, I found Chantelle arguing with the man behind the counter.

"I have told you a hundred million times that pineapple on pizza is an abomination," the man thundered.

"You're an abomination," she yelled back. "I want pineapple on my pizza and if you were bothered about me, you'd put some on."

"And if you were bothered about me, you wouldn't ask me to."

The guy put her ham pizza on the counter. Chantelle said some words and pineapple appeared on it. She quickly snatched the box before he could take it back.

"Hah," she said.

"It does not count that you put it on yourself, baby girl," he drawled.

Baby girl? What the heck was going on with these two?

Chantelle smiled at me as she walked out, before turning around and giving the man her middle finger.

"My apologies about that. What can I get for you, and it is on the house?"

"Oh that's not necessary. I'll have a large margherita and a large meat feast please." I perused the board. "And maybe some garlic bread. My brother is always hungry."

"I will give you that for free then. Once more, my apologies. There is just something about that woman. She drives me crazy."

"All the best women do," I quipped, and he sighed.

"Saint Haines has no time for women who make his head spin," he said. "And once that was literal. Her spells go awry."

I laughed, imagining them together while he took my payment and then went and prepared the pizzas.

"You know what I think?" I said, leaning closer as he put my order on the counter. "I think you're starting to like the idea of pineapple with pizza because of that woman and you just don't want to face up to it."

I picked up the pizza and walked away, hearing him say. "Damn pineapple," under his breath.

"Oh, yeaaaasss. Pizza," Billy said, sniffing the air as I walked upstairs. I passed him the box with the meat feast. "Can I eat it in my bedroom?"

"Just this once," I said. "But the box needs bringing out to the recycle bin straight after."

"Okay, boss."

I smirked. We both knew full well that I'd be nagging for him to put that box in the bin for the next ten days as it grew into a collection with crisp packets, chocolate wrappers and dirty cups.

I opened the cupboard door that contained parcels sent via the portal and sure enough there was a book there. Just one: *The Rulefort Dragons: whisperings from the clan*.

That was my evening sorted until Jason turned up. I'd eat my pizza, and then read.

And hope to find something that would help Jason.

CHAPTER TWENTY

Jason

I made my way closer to the man in the cell, but not so close that he could grab me by the neck or anything. My father he might be, but I'd also been warned of his temper too many times not to proceed with caution. The man had such strong self-control that he'd managed to not utter a word in twenty-five years.

I remembered very little of my father, and though his features bore some familiarity, and sparked my prior knowledge of him, his aging and training had made him something else entirely. He was more weapon than anything.

Griffin had been correct in keeping me from seeing my father until I had my full dragon powers. I'd have been a hen wandering into a fox's enclosure otherwise. He may have been built like a solid wall of muscle, but my dad's face was calculating and wily.

"So what brings my son to Rulefort?" he asked.

I looked around me, and finding a chair, I brought it to where I'd been standing, and then sat. I indicated for him to do the same. He dragged a seat over and lowered himself onto it, but his gaze never left me.

"Your brother passed away," I told him.

His eyes widened and his mouth curved with a snarl. "When? How have I not been informed of this?" His voice rumbled with an unfurled anger.

I turned to Griffin. He could explain. It had been his decision.

"When you were told was of no consequence. You wouldn't be allowed to contact the family or to attend the burial. I therefore decided to seek the heir and give him the choice of whether or not to inform you."

"He was my *brother*," he gritted out, his fist curling tight and his jaw setting.

"Yes. The same brother who threw you in jail and never visited you." Griffin noted.

"My time here is limited," I interrupted. "So shall I carry on, or do you want to continue complaining instead?"

My father laughed derisively. "You sound just like your mother. But then you would, given she got to raise you."

I chose to ignore him. "Josiah named me as his heir."

"No sons then?"

"No. Griffin came to find me, and I have been getting to know my dragon heritage this week. Tomorrow, I start the trials and then I shall decide whether or not I wish to take the throne."

My father stood and swept his wooden cup and bowl off his table in a temper. "Decide? What is there to decide? It is your legacy to rule. You are my son. A Rulefort," he bellowed. "It's in your very name."

I waited for him to shut up. "I am half-dragon, half-human, and my home is a happy one that has not been based here," I continued. "I intend to pursue the trials first to see if I am even able to rule. If I have the gifts and strengths needed, and then *I* will make my decision."

"I should never have slept with a human woman. That is my biggest regret," he spat out.

"No. Your biggest regret is that you have a half-breed son. That is what you mean. But, Father, even if you had bedded a dragon female, impregnated her, there's a possibility you wouldn't have had a son, like Josiah. Or you could have had a son like you, too self-involved to ever be able to command rule of a clan."

Joseph, as I would address him from now on, threw his weight at the cell doors which sparked and blasted him back. He screamed, and shouted, and raged.

"Let me out of here. You are fools. You cannot let this imbecile become king. We need a true dragon at the helm."

"I'm done," I told Griffin, and we left my father still throwing himself against the bars, despite the fact the magic and power blasted him repeatedly. He truly was in the grip of madness.

And as far as I was concerned, he never should be let out of jail.

"I'm guessing from his screaming that things did not go well?" Mum asked.

"He's still not of sound mind," I informed her. "Your decision back when I was five, still remains in his best interest. He needs to stay there, and you should just remember the good thing that came from the relationship. Me." I grinned and then stepped forward to hug her. "You're so small," I said.

"Yet big enough to still smack your arse if the need should arise," she said. It was a familiar routine, and that was exactly what I needed right now. A hug from my mother and a little light-heartedness.

"I'm taking Jason to the boardroom now. He'll be around an hour I would expect. There's nowhere there for you to wait, so I would suggest you call on Willow again. She could tell you about when Josiah did the trials maybe? What it's like for a spectator."

"Shouldn't I ask her about the trials?" I queried.

"It won't make any difference as yours won't be the same. The trials can never be repeated, or dragons would be able to study them and cheat the system somewhat."

"I'll go find Willow. I can remember the way," Mum said.

Griffin shook his head. "I will get Abe to accompany you. At the moment we cannot guarantee the safety of a human woman walking amongst dragons. You could be considered a delicacy."

I saw my mum audibly swallow. "Sounds good. Abe, I mean. Not me being served as a canape."

With Mum gone, accompanied by Abe, Griffin and I entered the boardroom. There was an enormous serving bowl of pasta on the table, the steam rising from it, and I took an inhale. Nope, still no smell. However, my mind remembered eating glorious bowls of pasta and my stomach gurgled in anticipation.

"Come, tuck in, before we start on this evening's agenda," Viper commanded. I didn't need asking twice. Us hungry dragons had the whole thing demolished in minutes. The door opened, and some women came in. They took away the empty pasta dish and brought in a huge tray of jam sponge pudding.

The dragons were all drinking beer, but I wanted to keep a clear head, so I decided I'd have a coffee. Though I mainly drank tea, right now, I needed the sharp hit of caffeine a strong coffee could give me. The jar had been left out from earlier, so I put the kettle on and spooned some into a large mug.

"I'll have one too," Viper said. "It is polite to ask others if they'd also like a drink."

Trust him to moan at me.

"Sorry. I'd assumed if you wanted teas and coffees, you'd have had the serving staff bring some," I explained.

"We have no need to trouble them for what we already have in the cupboard," he said, once more addressing me like I had no IQ.

I checked if anyone else wanted a coffee and wouldn't you know, everyone but Griffin said yes. Awkward fuckers. By the looks on their faces, it was Viper who'd whispered in their ears to all request one to wind me up. Well, I'd make them the best drink ever and then I'd try and get out of here as soon as possible because I wanted to go and see Charity, who actually liked spending time with me. I hurried to fix all the drinks, handed them out to barely a thank you, and sat down. When I ruled, I might make these fuckers lick my boots for the sheer hell of it.

"Could we start?" I asked Viper.

"Of course," he said.

I'd not expected him to be so agreeable and then Griffin whispered in my ear that as heir he would have needed a good reason to disagree with me.

While Viper droned on with the meeting housekeeping, I ate my jam sponge pudding and drank my drink. I could tell the dessert was sweet but couldn't discern its usual gorgeous taste. The sooner my smell and taste returned the better.

Viper took a sip of his drink and looked at it strangely. I watched as he spoke to those nearer to him and they took a taste too.

"What blend is this you've opened, Jason? It is very bitter, but weak."

"It's whatever was left out," I replied.

"Left out? Nothing was left out from this morning's meeting."

"There was a jar left out. That's what I used," I said tersely.

His face paled. "Could you get the jar, Jason?"

"Sure." God, was he going to complain I couldn't make a decent beverage now? He really did like acting superior.

I went to the small kitchen and picked up the glass jar containing the coffee, bringing it back to the table and handing it to Viper. "Doesn't say what blend it is. Label's been taken off."

Viper went a little green and began dry heaving. Some other dragons joined him. Turning to Griffin, I said, "What's going on? I've made coffee loads of times. I know how to make it."

Griffin snickered. "What's wrong is you've picked up the jar with your uncle's remains in it, Jason. You've given everyone a drink of their former king."

I looked at the jar, it finally dawning on me that it was like the others in the display cabinet, and then I realised I'd drunk some of my uncle's dead dragon body. Feeling myself going hot and clammy, I joined in with the dry heaving.

After it had been cleared with a dragon physician that no harm would come to any of us for eating a teaspoon or two of ashes, Viper announced that we should quickly do the ceremony to add my uncle to his final resting place with his ancestors and this was quickly actioned.

Then it was down to today's order of business.

"Firstly, I have added it to the agenda that in future, the ashes of the kings are placed in a jar and then in a ceremonial carrying vessel that clearly indicates the contents within," Viper said. All present agreed. Every time I looked at Griffin, he looked away, and put his hand over his mouth to 'cough'.

"Shall I bring the physician back, Griffin?" I queried.

He looked at me with tears in his eyes and shook his head as a strange noise erupted from him. The man was dying to laugh. As one of the only people not to consume dragon brew, he was clearly highly amused.

"Everyone here would happily hold you down and force you to drink some if you carry on," I added under my breath.

That shut him up.

"Okay, the final part of the meeting. The trial voting. The top ten trials were earlier displayed, and the clan voted on them. These results have been counted and verified and I have the final results in this envelope." Viper waved a gold envelope around. He was acting like he was on stage at an Oscars ceremony. He ripped open the envelope. "Trial one of three shall be a mud wrestle with current champion Kane Cosh."

Great. I was starting with a wrestling competition.

"Winner will be either points driven or KO."

"Coshed by Cosh. Fabulous," I sighed.

"Or ruled by Rulefort," Azar said, and I smiled at the first genuine support I'd received from someone on the council other than Griffin.

"The second trial," Viper continued. "A series of puzzles that a ruler should have no problem facing and solving."

"I gather he doesn't mean an implement of measurement," I said to the others, and some laughed. Viper was not one of them.

"Finally, Jason will be invited to put on a great ball. Here he shall be required to achieve a vote from the male dragons of over sixty per-cent to support his rule. And then he shall choose a consort from the women."

"Pardon?" I shouted out, standing up. "I don't bloody think so."

―――

Griffin walked me to the door. Once more he was in far too jovial a mood. "You drank your uncle, was told you'd have to fight the dragon's main wrestler, overcome a series of mental challenges, throw a ball, and win a vote, and the only thing you get in a tizz over is the easiest thing of all, choosing a woman."

"That's because I already have one. Who do these people think they are, telling me I have to choose from some other pool of women?"

"No one said Charity couldn't be there, Jason, did they?" Griffin asked.

"You mean they'd let me invite her and choose her?" My heart soared.

'Of course not, you dumbass, but I'm sure you can find a way to get her there. You have people at your disposal to help do you not? Witches, vampires, fae?"

It dawned on me then, that what he was suggesting was I got Gnarly to help me win. I'd been so focused on this being the dragon side of things, I'd pushed aside the fact I was half-human and my heritage was of the fell.

I decided then that I needed to confide in Griffin about everything I wanted to do. If I didn't have his support, then tonight I would consider walking away from everything.

"Griffin, about my rule," I said, and I told him all my plans.

CHAPTER TWENTY-ONE

Charity

When Jason finally arrived at my house, he looked weary. He scoffed down the pizza and brought me up to date with what had been a tremendously busy and emotional day for him. From discovering his cousin, to meeting his father, to accidentally drinking his uncle. Suddenly though, he beamed.

"I can smell your perfume!" My sense of smell is back. Yay. Ooh, let's go straight to bed, I want to sniff and taste you *everywhere!*"

"Down, boy. We've other things to do first seeing as you just told me you want Gnarly to support you in your trials and route to being king."

Jason had explained how things needed to change in response to how women were treated there, and he intended to be the one to bring the change, along with support from others. Griffin was on board and had told Jason that there were many others who felt the current ways were antiquated. While the trials were taking place and people were distracted, Griffin had agreed to sound out who was in support of a different structure; although as he'd pointed out, if he passed his trials and took the crown, Jason could do what he damn well wanted anyway. It just meant he'd probably be challenged straightaway by one of the men who believed women should be neither seen nor heard unless they were in the kitchen or in the bedroom.

"I got a book from Mya's library which I've been reading while I was waiting for you, and it corroborates everything Willow has said. It comes from years further back. From your great-grandfather's era I believe. It's more than time for change. The men have been seen to rule, but it's always been with the support of women at the back of them. Doing a lot of the legwork and never receiving any acknowledgement."

"It has to change, Charity, and as much as don't want to be in the middle of a clan changing disagreement, I can't leave them. I can't walk away from this."

I threw my arms around him. "I know and I love you for it."

We both tensed and went silent, until I thought *fuck it*.

I stared directly into his eyes. "I know it's only been a very short period of time, but I think it's been love at first sight, or maybe third sight, or fifth, but certainly, I most definitely have fallen for you, Jason Gradon Rulefort. The fact you are willing to go face what could be some very dangerous trials and other dragons in order to fight for women's rights... well, it shows me just how special you are."

He beamed. "I love you too. You could have become bitter and a manhater after what your husband and mother did to you, and instead you retained your compassion, looking after your brother and dating me. As for what I intend to try down at the lair, well, I was raised by one hell of a strong woman. It's time to let the Rulefort women have a voice."

With nothing left to say vocally, Jason carried me up to bed and we told each other everything again with our bodies. It was bittersweet as we couldn't know what tomorrow would bring. I just hoped Jason didn't get hurt, or worse.

CHAPTER TWENTY-TWO

Jason

She loved me! Charity loved me. I was the happiest man on earth, if I forgot about the fact I might get majorly injured or even die tomorrow. But that was tomorrow, and this was still, just about, today, so I'd make sure I had lots of sex and whispered sweet nothings to her. Then, if it was my last day on earth tomorrow, I'd at least made the best of the night before.

Early the next morning, Charity and I went out in search of whoever in Gnarly was prepared to come support me at the trials. Soon we were on our way, accompanied by my mother (of course), Chantelle, Mitzi, Kaf, Ginny, and Merrin. I'd drawn a line at volunteers after that, though I'd thanked the others who had wanted to come such as Dela and Nick, and Mya, who I'd decided would probably cause more harm than good, given that when we chatted to her she'd said, 'I'll keep an eye on The Book of the Dead on my app, and make sure to prioritise collecting your soul if you die. That is unless a designer dies at the same time. You understand that, don't you?' At that point Death caught my visual response and said Mya was best placed at the coffee shop, enjoying a red velvet cupcake and pink lemonade while keeping an eye on the app.

Having called for Merrin and Ginny last, we walked to the bottom of his field, and I had the entranceway opened for what could be the final time. I couldn't deny the thudding of my heart and my queasy feeling stomach. I just hoped I'd not made a mistake by bringing my family and friends with me.

We strolled down to the strong double doors, in my mind looking like a group of superheroes. The weather doors were opened, and Griffin and Viper stood on the other side. Viper did not look happy when he saw my party, but with a large sigh, he walked forward and shook everyone's hand and made introductions. "There are places spectators can sit. It is very full, but you can sit among the council. There is space there and you'll be safer."

I noted he said safer and not safe. Chantelle looked at me and put two thumbs up. She'd put protection spells on everyone. It was all we could do for now.

I was given a pair of shorts and told to get changed and then I was on my way to the first cave and trial to mud wrestle.

There was no going back now I realised as the cave opened and a giant naked man stood there, in front of a vast pool of mud, his dick erect and proud. As I saw his manhood and thought about it slapping against me as we wrestled, I felt sicker than when I'd consumed Uncle J.

"Where are your shorts?" I asked from the side.

Kane gestured to between his legs. "I'm showing you I have balls, my friend. Question is, where are yours?"

"Come find them for yourself," I said, hoping that by delaying things with chatter, a miracle would happen, and I'd somehow win this wrestling bout. The next thing I knew, I was in the middle of the mud with Kane sat astride me. I could feel his hard body part pressed right against me, the result of which was an inbuilt reaction to shout, "Get off me, you pervert," and to throw him off me. As I stood up, I found Kane at the other side of the cave, knocked unconscious from where his head had hit the wall as I'd thrown him.

I stood still, shocked and hoping that the guy would be okay. I'd not expected to launch him that far. I'd just completely forgotten that I was now in possession of my full dragon abilities. The doc entered and looked him over. As Kane stirred, he announced. "Kane is fine, just a little concussed." He left him and walked over to me, reaching for my hand and pumping it into the air. "Jason Rulefort is the winner."

I grinned. That trial had been basically effortless. Looking at the crowd watching, my eyes landed on Charity's. I could tell from here they were full of lust. As I carried on looking at the rest of the crowd there were lots more lust-fuelled gazes. Then I saw my mum's face and her gesturing wildly at me, like she did when she was annoyed with me. God, I'd won, hadn't I? Looking down at myself, I realised that while slipping in the mud, my own shorts had ridden down just enough that my cock was showing. Along with the fact I was generally slicked in mud, it was enough to bring out the horn in the dragon women as well as my own woman. I pulled my shorts up quickly however when my mum's face reminded me she was seeing it too.

Griffin approached and patted me on the back. "Well done. That went a lot quicker than expected. You didn't even change into your dragon."

I paused. "I could have changed into my dragon form?"

"Of course."

"Why was Kane not in his?"

"Not allowed unless you changed into yours."

"So I had no need to flash the crowd whatsoever?"

"Hey, it's helped you gain some more supporters, so don't knock it. Why do you think they nominated a mud wrestle in the first place? It wasn't to watch you fight."

I sighed. "How long until my second trial?"

"You can grab a shower and then it's straight over to the course. After this, you can go home and return tomorrow for the ball."

"Oh, that's cool."

"You've to pass these puzzles first."

"Oh yeah."

"And also, you've a ball to plan."

'Oh God, I forgot about that. So I've to arrange all the food and drink?"

"And the entertainment. Towards the end of the ball, the vote will take place to see if you become king."

"And if I don't pass the vote?"

"You'll go back to being Jason Rulefort, nephew of the former king, and will be welcome here as a family member, but the role of king will be back up for grabs. And, Jason, there are a number of men here who will do their best to sway your voters away from you."

"In effect then, the ball is actually the greatest trial of them all?"

"You're finally getting it," he said. "Now let's go get you showered and prepped for the next trial."

Frustratingly, I was allowed no contact with anyone but Griffin between trials, and so the cave was set up for the second trial while I got showered and the crowd stayed put. The doc was the only other person involved as an independent adjudicator, bringing in apparatus and making sure things were in order.

The doc addressed the spectators. "Thank you for gathering here to watch the puzzle trial. Jason will be presented with a series of three tasks. I now invite him in to solve the first." He gestured to me, where I was standing beside Griffin at the side of the entrance.

"Best of luck, Jason," Griffin said. Sighing, I made my way into the cave.

Inside the cave was a huge metal box with a padlock and a balloon attached to it. That was it. I looked around the box for a key and then decided the balloon would have the key in it and I needed to pop it. Lifting up the balloon, sure enough it appeared to have a key in it. I was just about to try to pop it, when I began to doubt myself. It seemed too obvious. However, there was definitely a key in the balloon.

I'd not explored every inch of the box because it was so heavy, so I began to feel at the surface of each side for any hidden pockets. Eventually, I used every bit of my strength to turn the box upside down and there on the bottom, taped on, was a key. Removing the key, I turned the box back to the right way up and undid the lock. It sprang open. Inside was a note.

Congrats on opening the box. Should you have popped the balloon you would have failed the challenge. Kings must thoroughly explore all information given before making a decision, not blunder into what appears to be the quickest option. You used your logic and you passed.
You will now move to the second puzzle of three.

I experienced a small amount of relief, but it was soon replaced with another feeling like a stone in my stomach as I still had two puzzles to go. Doc came in and asked me to read the note out to the spectators.

"Congrats on passing the first puzzle, Jason. I'll just bring in some items for the next one." Doc left again and I walked back to the now open box.

Inside the box was one hundred gold coins in a pouch and attached to the pouch it said *spend your money wisely*.

Doc returned carrying two small boxes which he placed on the floor. One said on it: *share with all*. Another said: *keep for yourself*. He then brought in a money box that had a chain wrapped tightly all around it, but underneath the chain you could see the box had the word *free* on it.

"Okay, Jason, please continue," he said and then he left. Again, I stared at everything. I immediately ruled out *keep for myself*, and was hedging towards *share with all*, but the chained money box still intrigued me. I lifted it and it was heavy, suggesting there was even more money inside it. Free money? Is that what the word meant? The chain covered the hole where you'd add coins. Keeping the money for myself seemed greedy, and trying to get more seemed greedy, so I picked up the coins and moved towards the *share with all* box. Then I stopped as I spotted the key from before. Who was the 'all' to share with? It wouldn't go far. Maybe I should take a chance and open the box? Minutes went by while I considered which would be the right choice and I began to feel my heart rate rachet up with the stress.

Then I remembered the lesson from round one, explore everything. I needed to look around the whole room. I paced the cave but found nothing. I'd avoided looking at the crowd as they weren't allowed to communicate with me, and I'd felt just seeing them sitting there would put extra pressure on me, but I decided I wanted to see Charity. Like she was my good luck charm or something. I looked out into the crowd of spectators. While they'd been cheering and screaming when it was the mud wrestle, now they sat still. Their eyes drank me in, but no one moved. And that's when I noticed that all their hands were by their sides, locked to the chairs. Huh?

I looked back at the chained money box. *Free.* Quickly, I used the key and sure enough it opened the box. Inside there wasn't money, there were keys, and a note that said **purchase these keys with the bag of coins**. I took out the keys, and then filled the money box back up with the coins.

Doc came back in, and I handed him the box. He handed me a piece of paper. I watched as all the crowd were freed from their shackles and they burst into a noisy round of applause and cheering, their arms once more in the air.

Thank fuck, I'd passed two of the three puzzles.

Doc came in and cleared everything from the room besides the key.

I opened the note.

Congrats once more on passing the second puzzle. Once more you showed that you consider all possibilities and 'think outside the box'. Thanks to you, those imprisoned are now free for the duration of the trial and will be awarded refreshments in thanks for their service during this puzzle.

Doc walked over. "Congrats, Jason, on passing the second puzzle. While we enjoy some refreshments you shall work on the final puzzle. He read out a piece of paper.

"For your final puzzle you have to simply work out how to leave the room. You have ten minutes." He handed me the paper and left.

Leave the room? Huh, so I guess we had a locked door or some kind of booby trap. I'd been left with the key, so it must fit the cave door. I went to inspect the door and there was no keyhole. Bugger.

The key was a red herring and time was ticking. I read the note again.

For your final task you have to simply work out how to leave the room.

I got hold of the giant door pull and pulled the door open. The clue had been there all along: *simply*.

Doc walked in. "Congratulations." He turned to the crowd. Jason Rulefort has passed the three puzzle tasks. You may now leave."

He handed me another piece of paper, which I opened and read.

Many congrats on passing the final of the three puzzle trials. Sometimes we have to act quickly and use our wits to make the right choices, and sometimes the simplest ideas are the best.

However, now it is time for you to prepare for the ball. Where you may have originally seen this as the easiest task, it is actually the hardest trial of all. For you have to win over the clan and look out for unseen challengers.

Good luck.

"Am I free to go now?" I asked the man. He nodded. "It is up to you what time you return tomorrow but the ball will open to all at four pm and you will need to be there to receive all guests. Here is a list of the minimum requirements for the event." He handed me yet another piece of paper, which when I opened it held a brief list saying food, entertainment, etc.

Thanking him, I moved towards Griffin who had stood by patiently waiting.

"You did it." He grinned.

"You doubted me?"

"Not so much now. But the Jason I met those six short days ago? Absolutely. The fact you care, Jason, stood you in great stead. Never change. Now go and see your mum and Charity. I know you're dying to."

"Thanks, man," I said, and I ran down to just outside the spectator room where my friends stood. I hugged my mum, before picking Charity up off her feet and spinning her around.

"I've aged about a hundred years, Jason," my mum complained.

"And no doubt seeing me naked freaked you out," I said.

"Huh?" Mum asked, just as Chantelle put her finger to her mouth and then winked. God, it must have really freaked her out if she'd had to be spelled to forget.

"Chantelle wiped it from everyone's mind, except hers and mine," Charity whispered to me. "I got quite turned on by seeing you all naked and covered in mud."

I smushed my mouth on hers. "I love you, Charity."

Our friends cheered. My mum whooped. "I thought it would never happen. Jason with a nice girlfriend."

I glared at her, but then became distracted when Charity said, "I love you too. Now are we going home?"

"Yes please," I replied.

CHAPTER TWENTY-THREE

Charity

When they'd said trials, I'd thought of death-defying, fire-dodging events, not a mud wrestle and a few puzzles. I wasn't belittling the trials. They'd been hard to solve, and Jason had done amazing. Plus, I was pleased he'd passed them as otherwise he'd have come to the end of his attempts to rule the clan.

Now there was the ball, and we had no idea what Jason would face there.

"It's very rude to zone out while covering me in Nutella," Jason complained. I'd been smearing it on his erogenous zones but had gone into a daydream and been circling his nipple for goodness knew how long. The mud wrestle had had me imagining a chocolate body paint session and I'd been pleased to remember I had Nutella in the cupboard, for in case Billy had wanted some on toast. He'd never eat it again if he knew what Jason and I were up to with it.

"Sorry. Just thinking about the ball tomorrow."

Jason stuck his fingers in the jar and smeared some on his left testicle. "These are the only balls you need to focus on for the next couple of hours."

I sucked it into my mouth and tried not to laugh at the fact it was named *nut*-ella.

Later, we showered and changed and met up with everyone at the bistro. Along with us, Ginny and Merrin, Fen, and Mitzi, we were joined by Della and Nick, Callie and her husband Lawrie, and Mya and Death.

Chantelle and Kaf were now working and had put us at a long table at the back.

"Okay, so I've been working on the buffet with Fen, and this is the cupcake I've devised," Callie said. "It's a pork belly blend, with a cranberry topping." She passed it to Jason, who stuffed the whole thing in his mouth at once. Chewing it, he made noises that really should have belonged in the bedroom. "Oh my god, this is heavenly."

"Excellent, that's a definite then. We'll get the others prepared tonight."

"I hope you know this is the only time I'll allow you to eat items in my restaurant that aren't from the menu," Connor said as he brought us some drinks over.

"Death eats things not from the menu, in the ladies sometimes." Mya winked. "If you catch my drift."

The table fell silent. Death picked up his phone. "Oh the app has called us, darling. Sorry to have to leave," he said.

"No, it hasn't," Mya protested, and then she studied his face. "Oh, you want me to be deathly silent again, do you? It's not my fault I'm quick-witted."

"If we can go through everything again one more time please," Jason distracted them. "So the ball will take place outdoors in the fields beyond Merrin's field. However, Merrin has kindly agreed to open up his part of the land for the occasion and will host upcycling events throughout the late afternoon and evening."

"It will be a good day to get some things shifted," he said. "I have my workshop in the morning and then this after."

"Shifted," Mya snorted. Death quickly shot her another glare.

"All food will be sent to Merrin's portal, and we can then easily get it down to the bottom field, as the vampire friends among us can work quickly to set things up. Same with chairs etc. We have

Merrin's spare chairs and tables, and my mum has organised that we can use more from the community centre."

Fen nodded her head.

"So music next," Jason said. "Is there anything in the community centre I can borrow?"

"I've got you covered," Death said, and we all turned to stare at him. "I've the whole shebang. Decks, everything."

"It's his new thing," Mya declared. "He says he's discovered a new love of music, but it's quite obvious he puts it on to drown me out."

"No, I don't. I've just found a new interest, that's all. Having a spelled soundproofed room means I can enjoy it to my heart's content without it annoying anyone else. He turned to us. "My favourite song is *Another One Bites the Dust*."

"Okay, so the DJ is sorted," I told Jason, nodding at Death who smiled at me. I felt like I needed to smudge myself, it was weird as fuck.

"You're scaring everyone again. Why can't you smile like a normal person?" Mya sighed.

"Because I'm supposed to be broody and scary. I'm Death. My face doesn't naturally align with glowing happiness."

"Aw, have you felt glowingly happy since being with me?" she said, grabbing his arm and smushing against him.

"Of course," he said giving her one of those horrendous smiles.

"Okay," Jason said. "Food, music, furniture, Merrin's upcycling event. Anything else?"

"We could give all attendees a gift," Nick said. "I'm sure I could persuade my father to let me have some of his surplus stock. Something like a decorative box with a lock and key maybe?"

"Perfect," Jason said.

With everything thought of, we ate and drank before saying our goodbyes and that we'd see each other in the morning at Merrin's upcycling event. It would be just one week since Jason had discovered his heritage. So much had happened in that short space of time.

Jason walked me home and we stood, my back pressed against the door as he kissed me until I was dizzy.

"I'll see you in the morning, girlfriend," he said.

"See you in the morning, boyfriend," I replied. "Hopefully, we can finally get those drawers done."

"I really want to get in your drawers," he said, before nuzzling my neck.

The window above us opened. "It's way past your bedtime, Missy, put the boy down and come inside right now," Billy shouted in a naggy-mother tone.

We laughed, said goodnight, and Jason went home.

"So what's the latest on the dragon king saga?" Billy said, coming out of his room and walking into the living room where I'd crashed out.

"Make me a cuppa, and I'll tell you everything," I pleaded. He rolled his eyes but headed off to the kitchen where I heard pots rattling.

He returned with a cup of tea for me, a glass of milk for him, and a half-eaten packet of biscuits. I grabbed a chocolate chip cookie and brought him up to speed.

"Wow, so tomorrow you could have a really good time, or it could go tits up and someone could, like, kill him," Billy pointed out unnecessarily.

"Kind of hoping the protection spells do their thing, but yes, it's not necessarily going to be all sweetness and light."

"Come on then. Put the drink down. We've something to do," Billy said.

"Huh?"

"How to be in tip top condition as a mermaid girlfriend. Hydration is key. Let's go swimming." He tapped into his phone and the next moment an angel appeared in the room.

"Billy, how many more times do I have to tell you to phone me for emergencies only? I am *not* a mode of transport," Kaf complained.

"It is an emergency. My sister might need to be badass tomorrow, so she needs a swim. Me too."

"What happens if you don't go in the water? Do you dry up like a prune?" Kaf asked me.

I laughed. "Nothing happens. I was just born in the sea that's all. Just like you can go in the sea, I can go on land. But my body does crave the sea as it's my natural habitat, and it will settle me ready for tomorrow. So if you don't mind taking us to the North Sea somewhere, I'd appreciate it. Just don't take me near to my old home."

"Deal," Kaf said. "I'll drop you off, and then I'll go hang at the beach front, and have a flirt with all the half-dressed women who'll be out tonight."

"Ooh, I'll hang with you," Billy said.

"You will come swimming with me. It was your idea," I told him.

His face looked like I'd kicked his puppy, bless him.

"Oh for goodness' sake, stay with Kaf then," I said.

Before long I was in the sea, my legs changed into my mermaid tail, and I stared down at the teal scales. Another thing Jason and I had in common that hadn't crossed my mind before! We both had scales in our alternate form. All my stresses melted away as I become one with the water. It was like filling my tank up, and by the time I emerged from the sea sometime later, I was buzzing and ready to face whatever happened tomorrow.

I found Kaf looking out over the sea and Billy stuffing his face with an ice cream.

"What happened to checking out women?" I queried.

"Rather have an ice cream," Billy mumbled through a mouthful of it.

"I was talking to Kaf," I said.

Kaf shrugged. "What's the point? I'm dead and they're not. They'd expect something to grow between the sheets but it being my wings might be a surprise."

"Well thanks for bringing me here. It was just what I needed."

He gave me a half-smile. "I can tell. You look... content. You must make sure you swim more often. However..." He stared at Billy. "I'll point out once more, I'm not your source of transport. Okay?"

"Just wanted to spend time with you. You're cooler than my other friends," Billy said.

Neither of us were expecting that statement and it made me see how much Billy needed a reliable male role model in his life. I hoped Jason being around would help, but in these early days I knew Billy wouldn't let himself fully attach to Jason, in case things didn't work out between us.

"Helllllpppp. God, please help." Shouts and screams came from further up the promenade. We all set off at speed to see what was happening and met a young male who looked around Billy's age, his face etched in panic.

"My mate's in the water. He insisted on a midnight swim. I told him not to go in."

Quick as a flash, Kaf dived into the water.

"Shall we go in too?" Billy asked. I shook my head. "Kaf has it handled."

I called for an ambulance, and we watched with bated breath until he emerged clutching the boy, both their heads bobbing on the surface of the water. I knew he'd have used his angel abilities, but his wings were hidden as he got to the edge and used the steps to climb out with the spluttering boy.

The ambulance tore down the promenade, lights and sirens flashing, and they took the boy from Kaf. There were tense minutes as we waited, but the boy turned out to have had a 'lucky' escape. It had been lucky all right. Rescued by an angel.

Once they were gone, I noted Kaf looking up at the sky.

"Beautiful, isn't it?" I said, looking up at the stars.

"Yeah," he replied, but he was grimacing as he said it.

"Oh. You're waiting to see if they beam you up."

Kaf nodded. "I just saved a life. Surely that's what I was put back here for? It's why I went up before, because I saved the lives of everyone who would have come after me with Portia."

I patted his back. "The reason will reveal itself when it's time, Kaf. Maybe you're here for a few things. They said you had lessons to learn, right?"

He thought for a moment, then nodded his head.

"Tonight, I usually would have flirted, but because of Billy, my mind was on looking after him, not on myself. I got him the ice cream and then once you came out of the water, we were on the promenade looking out to sea. If we hadn't been, you'd have met us somewhere else, and we wouldn't have been paying attention and heard the cry for help. We wouldn't have been here to help that boy and his friend."

"See. You're supposed to hang out with me. I'm teaching you lessons," Billy said.

"Nice try, but I'm still not your own personal taxi." Kaf ruffled the top of Billy's head.

"Come on," I said. "Let's get back. We have a busy day ahead of us all tomorrow."

'Can I have a few doughnuts first?" begged Billy. Seriously, nothing came between that boy and his stomach.

CHAPTER TWENTY-FOUR

Jason

It had been just one week since we'd last stood here in front of Merrin with our pieces of furniture. Now here we were again, but this time, instead of my mind being full of my new fledgling relationship with Charity, we were all pre-occupied thinking about what might come afterwards.

"You all look like you're here to be beheaded," Merrin complained. "Now if this was Jason's last day on earth, you'd want to make the most of it, so come on, let's have some fun." He then clutched his head, and we all panicked until he lifted it and said, "I see fun and furniture upcycling in everyone's future."

"I'm sorry. He's a work-in-progress," Ginny apologised, just as another vampire whizzed into view.

"Aria! Great to see you," Ginny said, flinging her arms around the pregnant vamp.

"Is it? Only a little bird told me that you have a new best friend and indeed I've hardly heard from you this week." She sniffed the air and walked up to Charity. "It's you, isn't it? The one who smells of the sea."

"Huh, would that 'little bird' be my brother?" Ginny asked. "And I saw you here two weeks ago."

Charity was looking a little unnerved by the vampire standing close and sniffing the air around her. I moved closer.

"Aria, this is my girlfriend, Charity."

"We already met when you were flirting with each other at the first upcycling. I did not know then that she would try to steal my friend."

We all jumped as yet another vampire whizzed in. "Good morning, all, I am Bernard." He pronounced it Barenaaaiiird. "Please excuse my sweet princess. She is becoming very protective of everything she holds dear. It is part of the pregnancy."

Kaf stepped forward. "When is the baby due?"

"Babies," Bernard explained. "We are expecting two and they are due at Christmas, so you know, only several more months to go," he said through a grimace. Bless him, you could see he was trying to smile, but clearly his wife was currently a handful.

"I'm staying here," Aria announced, and she moved herself next to Ginny near the front, giving my mum a fanged smile as she made her move up by dragging her by the hand.

That was it. She'd pissed me off, putting her hands on my mum, after already winding me up side-eying Charity. The next thing I knew, I'd changed, and I roared in Aria's direction. I didn't emit any flames. I was in control of my powers, but my animal was giving Aria a warning that I would protect my mum. Kaf had stepped forward anyway and placed his wings around Aria. He opened them back up when he knew it was safe.

I returned back to my human form and while I cupped my junk, Charity handed me a sheet used to cover the furniture which I quickly wrapped around myself.

"I would not have harmed her," I stated. "She just needs to know she's being rude."

"Still, it didn't hurt to protect her just in case."

"You're my hero," Aria said to Kaf, throwing her arms around him. "Bernard, did you see that. We must pay him to be my bodyguard."

Bernard looked about to strongly protest when Merrin clutched his head again.

"Oh, Merrin, we're sorry, okay. We'll start upcycling and having fun, won't we everyone?!" Ginny said in a firm tone.

But Merrin looked back up through bleary eyes.

"Shit. Did you really have a vision?" she asked him.

He nodded and looked over at Kaf. "It is why you are here. To protect Aria until she has the babies. Also, to be a guide to Billy. You will be here for a while yet."

"Fucking marvellous," Bernard said, as his eyes landed on his wife's delighted face.

Merrin stood up and clapped his hands loudly. "Okay, all. Last week a vision got in the way of my workshop. That's not happening this week, so if you're not here to design, it's time to leave. If you're staying, grab your furniture and let's begin."

As everyone did what he told them, I thought about how love had brought a newfound confidence to my friend, and he looked really good on it.

"They're done!" Charity announced as we looked at our upcycled drawers side by side.

"They are," I replied.

"Tomorrow once the ball is done and the drawers are dry, we shall put them in each other's homes and fill them," she said. She smiled at me, but the smile didn't reach her eyes.

Because we both knew that tomorrow never came and we didn't know what the future held.

I took her in my arms and kissed the living daylights out of her. People around us whistled.

"I love you," I told her. "It's not in my best interests to let anything untoward befall me right now."

"I know," she said. "If I didn't love you too, I'd give less of a shit if you got murdered."

"I'll wipe your mind if he gets killed, so you're not upset if you like?" Chantelle said as she walked past us both.

"Erm, no, that's okay. I'd like to remember I loved him, even if it all goes wrong," Charity replied.

I'd never heard anything so romantic in my whole life. I kissed her again.

Then we heard a noise from the bottom of the field and saw the large boulder moving once more. I could see a figure emerge and then a flare went up.

"That's Griffin," I said. "Come on. We need to get started prepping the ball."

It took some time, but eventually, the food and refreshments were laid out ready, with Callie, Lawrie, Dela and Nick dealing with the catering. Nick had also laid out the gifts next to where I would greet guests, Stan having donated a wooden Christmas ornament of himself for everyone in the end. Death was in position and already playing some tunes, Mya dancing beside him. My mum was overseeing everything, and guiding Stan, Mitzi, and Kaf to put out seating and a stage area with microphone, close to Death's decks.

Ginny and Merrin were being assisted by Aria and Bernard to run the upcycling workshops. Bernard's protests about his wife's safety had been drowned out by Aria's insistence that she was fine while the angel was in the village. Plus, Merrin had seen the babies be born anyway in a vision, so in the end Bernard gave in, as I guessed he did a lot married to Aria.

"You don't have to stay," I told Charity for the hundredth time. "Billy needs you."

"I think you'd better look at the people putting the chairs out again," she said, and as I stopped and paused, I saw Billy with my mum, Stan, and Kaf.

"We're a package deal," Charity said. "And we're both here to support you."

I kissed her. "Thank you."

"Okay, I'm off to get changed," she said. "I'll be back just before the start." She left and I walked over to Griffin, who'd been standing back, letting us get on with it, unable to assist by the rules of the challenge.

"It's looking good, Jason. I wish you all the very best," he said.

"Thanks. Now direct me to the ridiculous outfit I need to put on."

He laughed. "Viper is waiting for you," he said, and so off I went.

HOT AS SUCK

I knocked on the boardroom door until Viper's voice gave me permission to enter.

"Someone remembered what they were taught," he remarked.

"I wish my schoolteachers could see what a good student I turned out to be in later life," I quipped. "They wouldn't believe it."

"Your suit and robe are over there. You can change in the male bathroom," he directed, his face solemn.

It was going to be like that then. I wondered if it was Viper's dedication to things being done right, or him wishing it was his son about to put the coronation robes on that made him so serious.

Regardless, I picked up the outfit and entered the male bathroom where I proceeded to get changed in the less than glamorous surroundings.

I came out dressed in the velvet purple suit and silk orange tie I'd been given. The velvet orange robe fastened around that. I looked like I should be in Scooby-Doo, but these were the Rulefort colours.

Viper nodded approvingly when he looked me over. "Your uncle would be very proud," he said.

"Thank you."

He cleared his throat. "Right, let's go and face your third trial. I wish you the very best of luck. You have passed the trials so far and proved yourself to have the skills to lead despite your sometime flippancy. Now we get to see your endurance," he said, with no further explanation.

We went outside.

The sun beat down on me, and within seconds, wrapped in these thick velvet clothes, I began to sweat like a pig. I stood near the entrance of the cave ready to greet my guests as they came outside. Griffin stood at one side of me and Viper the other. I went to untie the robe. "What are you doing?" Viper whisper-hissed.

"Taking this bloody cape off. I'm roasting."

"Endure, remember?" he added.

That was the endurance test? Surviving overheating? Fuck me. I'd to wear this bloody costume all day? I thought I might meet my end in a battle for the crown with a renegade dragon challenging me to a sword fight. Not dealing with my own clothed sauna situation. *You're a dragon. Heat's part of it,* I thought to myself. I wasn't happy though. I was a t-shirt and jeans guy. Suits were for funerals. *Oh God, please don't let this be mine!*

One moment I was panicking, which was making me hotter, and then I felt a cool trickle going down my neck. Was I sweating that much? I felt at the bottom of my hair. Cool water? Settling my face on Charity's as she walked closer to me, she winked. I looked behind me and saw the trickle ran all the way from the trees where no doubt a small river ran. It was rising up the back of my robe but not soaking in and then overflowing down my neck to keep me cool.

"Thank you," I said.

"Just let me know when it gets too much. It will soak into your back and keep you cool. You won't look like you peed yourself and you won't look like a sweaty about to faint dragon either."

"Clever," Griffin said. Viper stayed silent and subdued at my other side.

"I suppose you're going to say it's cheating," I huffed to Griffin.

"Nope. You've assembled your team and they're doing their assigned tasks. Charity has shown initiative. Nothing wrong with that if it benefits the king."

"Well then—"

"—don't say it," Viper interrupted.

"Viper..." I began.

"We all know you were going to say something inappropriate. Don't even try to deny it."

"Spoilsport." I huffed.

"Showtime," Griffin stated looking at the cave entrance.

Dragons appeared and I began to move forward to greet them all.

Charity started to walk away.

"Stay," I said, but she shook her head.

"Do your duties. I will keep you cool, and I'll be just over there watching you." She pointed to some seats, one of which had Billy in it. He gave me a wave and a thumbs up. I did the same back.

I startled as a bird flew down and landed on my shoulder. Viper went to shoo it away, but I held up my hand. "It's my friend, Mitzi," I told him, stroking the feathers of the magpie, and then I greeted thousands of Rulefort dragons, managing to keep my cool and withstand the wearing of such thick clothes thanks to Charity's water trick. My neck and back stayed cool and wet, yet it never went into my clothes. She was one clever lady and I'd reward her for it later.

Around three quarters of the dragons had been polite, the others guarded, but none were openly hostile until I met a shaven headed, slim but extremely muscly young guy. "Welcome to the ball," I said.

"Welcome to your funeral, more like," he snarled.

I stepped back, a little startled.

"Thor, not now," Viper said. "Pay your respects to the potential future king."

The guy huffed, and said, "I'd rather shit my pants."

Mitzi flew up off my shoulder and crapped on his head. It wasn't his pants, but she'd done me a solid—or maybe it was more a liquid—on his head. It dripped down his forehead.

She flew off into the trees. I didn't blame her. The dude would probably be looking for her with a gun for the next hour.

"Go and get cleaned up, and come back with a different attitude," Viper snarled at him.

When Thor stormed off, he pulled me to the side. "I'm sorry about that. He's not been himself lately. I don't know what's going on with him."

"Don't worry about it. We all hit some rough spots in life. Just keep an extra eye on him during the ball, will you?" I asked.

"Of course. I'd be very surprised if he shows his face again though after that humiliation." Viper sighed and I felt for him. His son had just disrespected the potential future king, which was not the correct procedure for doing things. He'd feel embarrassed.

I greeted the final guests and then I proceeded to the microphone to officially declare the buffet open. It was time to enjoy ourselves.

Charity returned to my side. I couldn't keep a trail of water around me all afternoon and evening and she asked Ginny to turn the back of my top a little icy to keep me cool. My eclectic friend mix was working out fabulously, each having their own unique skillset. The dragons seemed to be enjoying themselves and no-one, so far, was giving the non-dragon folk grief. I guessed it would come down to the vote, where the clan members who were against anyone but a pure bred being king would have their say.

Death being in his element as a DJ was possibly the creepiest thing I'd ever seen, and it was at that point I worked out why people were behaving. Because of him. We were used to seeing him, but the dragons weren't. Death was in their midst, and as he called them over to dance it seemed they weren't willing to do anything but obey his command. It amused me no end and I decided to get Charity on the dance floor with me. "Give me a moment," she said, and she wandered off towards Death. I saw him nod and then she came back. The next song on was *The Doors*. The space in front of the DJ suddenly became packed with dancing dragons. It seemed *Light My Fire* was a firm favourite amongst the clan.

"This shall always be our song, okay?" I said, pulling her into my arms.

"Our song, I like that," she said, snuggling closer.

"Oh look, it's the half-breed wannabee with his non-dragon girlfriend," said Thor, who looked freshly showered and had unfortunately re-surfaced. Damn, I couldn't spot Mitzi anywhere.

Death stopped the song and gazed down at Thor, his face menacing. He pulled up his hood. Oh shit.

"I challenge you, half-breed," Thor yelled.

Viper came forward. "Thor, this is not the way of things."

Thor pushed him away hard. "Oh shut up, you stupid old man. I am so sick and tired of you telling me the way things go. What it says in the books of old. You would have us being ruled by a half-breed? And what if he marries this mermaid and has children? They would be mutants. We'd be ruled basically by non-dragons. I think not. So I will not wait and do things the usual way. Instead, I shall take the throne by force. He whistled and Andy came out of the cave, a gun held to his head by another man. I recognised the gunman as someone who had been guarding the jail cave my father was in. Did that mean? Oh God, no. Viper seemed to have the same thought at the same time. His face paled as he came nearer his son once more. "Son, no. Please tell me..."

"I said shut up," Thor screamed in his father's face.

He ran over to the microphone and looked at the gunman. "Do it."

The gun was smacked into Andy's temple. He sagged, but as it was turned to face his chest, he began saying an incantation.

"What's he doing?" I asked Viper, noticing Griffin was headed towards Andy.

"He's releasing all the charms of imprisonment from your father. He's setting him free."

"He's doing what?" I panicked, and as I looked around at the others present, I saw I wasn't the only one.

Another man ran out of the cave, and before I knew what had happened, he'd attempted to shoot Griffin. Griffin immediately changed into his dragon form, and as the other man did, I saw he'd been the dragon standing outside my father's jail when I'd visited. The one who'd remained in dragon form.

People were screaming, others began turning, and then there was a large thunderous rumble and my father emerged from the cave.

"I am the new king," he roared. "Pledge your allegiance or die."

CHAPTER TWENTY-FIVE

Charity

One minute we were dancing, the next war had broken out on the field. Here he was, large as life—Joseph Rulefort. An evil and self-serving dragon, now free to wreak havoc because of a dumb as fuck idiot who'd thought he was better than everyone else.

Thor looked across at Joseph and pulled a face. "What's he on about, being king? We agreed I'd be king, and he'd be my clan deputy. No one would dare go against us."

I turned to him. "You belittle me being a mermaid," I said. "Yet it is you who now threatens the survival of the Rulefort dragon clan."

He looked at me, going for an air of defiance, but his chin trembled. "He agreed I would be king."

"He's a psychopath. He would agree to anything you said if it meant you freed him, and here he is now, giving you all a choice. Choose him or die. You absolute fool," I spat out. Then I looked around at Death who was now in full possession of his Death mask. "And it looks like some will die, because my friend here looks ready to collect souls, does he not?"

Thor took one look at Death and soiled himself.

Viper had been watching us, and as Thor ran off towards some bushes, we both turned to see what was happening. I caught sight of

Jason making his way towards his father. We exchanged looks and then both of us ran to where they were.

"You need to keep back," Viper warned me.

"Why, because I'm a woman?" I asked.

"No, because you're not a dragon."

"Well I am," Willow said, standing by my side.

"The men will handle this," Viper said, as Joseph turned into his dragon and threw Griffin across the crowd, people running everywhere to avoid the large body hitting them. Griffin landed on his feet and bellowed a sound that almost split my brain in half.

And around us others started to change into their dragons, including Willow and a whole host of other women who'd joined her. Jason had changed and I stared at him again. Something I'd noted at Merrin's earlier now coming back into my mind. "Viper," I said. "How come Jason has one black scale?"

"I don't know." Viper's brow furrowed. "He didn't have that before. He was all silver with gold dust on them. It was Josiah who had black scales. How very strange. But I guess we can expect differences with him being part-human."

One of the dragons launched at Jason and in the blink of an eye found themselves sailing over the nearest tree.

"I don't understand what's happening," Viper said. "How Jason just did that. His strength is... increased."

"His strength is increased and one of his scales has turned black like Josiah's. Is it part of being an heir?" I queried. "Is there some familial way he now has his uncle's scale or is it a coincidence?"

"I've not come across it before, but it certainly seems like he has part of his uncle's DNA within him," Viper frowned, and then his face registered with a lightbulb moment. "The coffee," Viper said, grabbing hold of me. "We drank Uncle J. It might be that. Let me change. If it is, then I should have a black scale too." He became a dragon and sure enough he had a black scale. I nodded up at the dragon and then he was gone, into the bowels of the cave. I just hoped that whatever plans he had he did fast, because looking at Joseph, we didn't have much time.

Death stood beside me, and I shivered. Did this mean...? Shit. Who would look after Billy if I was gone?

"Charity," he said. "Jason's name is not yet on the app. I'll try to ensure it stays that way, if you will promise to take care of my decks so they don't get damaged. Only they're very precious to me."

"Sure, sure, you go do what you need to do," I said, watching as dragons tore at each other. It seemed there had been a secret rebellious faction led by Thor, and with Joseph now in charge they were fighting as part of his army. I was more than happy to keep myself behind the decks and fully intended to hide behind them for the foreseeable.

As I got down behind the music equipment, I tried to peek to see Billy and Fenella. My brother and Jason's *human* mum were out there somewhere.

"Sorry, Death, but they're worth more to me than your DJ equipment," I said, just as Mya landed in front of me.

"Vamp hearing, heard you," she said. "I got this, and he..." She pointed at Kaf. "Has who I believe you're looking for."

Kaf's wings were ensconced around something I couldn't see. "You coming, Charity?" he asked, and I went running. I couldn't be with Jason right now, but I could be with my brother and Jason's mum.

CHAPTER TWENTY-SIX

Jason

The ball had become a battleground, and now I came face to face with my father.

"Jason," he bellowed. We were dragons and yet I understood what he said, my mind translating his roars and growls. "It is not yet your time to be king, but you can come stand beside me as my deputy and heir. We shall rule it all. You shall marry your cousin when she comes of age and keep the genetic line strong."

A golden-brown dragon came to stand beside me, and she roared in my father's direction. "Your brother would be embarrassed by your display today, Joseph," Willow said.

"I stopped giving any fucks about my brother when he abandoned me for twenty-five years. But I do wonder who's doing that was really, because you always were the driving force behind him, weren't you, Willow? Anyway, I'll give you a choice. You can be my tart, or you can take my place in jail."

"Do not talk to my aunt like that," I snapped.

My father's tail swished and knocked me onto my side. "You will obey me, not defy me, *Son*. I'll treat your aunt as I see fit. As for your mother, she can spend the next quarter of a century without you and see what it feels like."

I got back onto my feet as Death walked towards me holding a microphone. He handed it to me. "To call for your supporters," he said. Then he walked over to my father. "I don't think we've met, I'm Death."

"Then I need to act fast," my father shouted. "Let's see if I can cheat you, shall we?"

He let out another cry. Willow turned to me. "The war cry. The battle for rule is about to commence." Many more dragons appeared at Willow's side. "We serve you, Jason Rulefort," they all chanted. I pressed the button on the microphone. "Choose your sides, Rulefort. Joseph Rulefort or Jason Rulefort are your contenders."

Over the next few minutes, more dragons joined, and others hovered in the periphery. A few joined my father's side.

But no one moved to battle... yet.

"Jason Rulefort, I challenge you for the throne. But I also offer you the option to instead join me. Be by my side and take the throne in time or die at my hands and I will birth another heir," my father said, an evil smirk on his face. There was no doubt in his mind that he wouldn't win, and he was likely correct. I was a half-breed dragon, against his full one, alongside his twenty-five years of his obsessive physical training.

Viper emerged from the cave. "Jason! Catch and drink the ancestors," he shouted, before turning into his dragon form.

A flask dropped at my feet. Drink the ancestors? Did he mean this had... ashes in it? But, why? What kind of sick prank was that?

"Look at my scale, Jason. Look at your scale," Viper added. "It's because of the drink."

Then I realised. I could become all who had gone before me.

Becoming my human self once more, I grabbed the flask just as my father's clawed hoof tried to smash it out of my way. But a wall of dragon protection had been formed around me. I quickly drank the disgusting drink, and then I changed again, and the other dragons gasped.

I didn't have time to admire myself or think what had happened to my scales, I just needed to act. I rammed into my father's dragon form.

He was strong, and though I could feel power flowing into me, it wasn't, unfortunately, an immediate powwow of power from the elders. We rolled across the floor, and I ended up on the bottom, pinned down by my father who looked like he was about to take a chunk out of my neck.

"Sorry it has to be this way, Son. I will mourn your loss," he said, just as I realised I had my father's dragon cock resting against my stomach. "Ewwwww," I roared. With a surge of power finally hitting alongside my complete disgust, I hurled my father across the field. He didn't hit just one tree. He sailed through around twenty of them, the last of which was a gnarled tree. It swung its branches back into him and my father sailed right back to my feet. Completely unconscious.

"Now what do we do with him?" I asked, just as Thor approached and stabbed a large knife straight through my father's heart.

CHAPTER TWENTY-SEVEN

Charity

While we'd been within Kaf's wings there had just been a peace, a stillness. As he opened them, he turned to us, and said, "I will stay with Billy, but Jason needs you both. He is safe, but he needs you."

We looked over, seeing now naked bodies being cuffed and dragged towards the cave entrance. The warlock stood making new enchantments, and at the front of the field there was Jason, standing in front of a slain dragon.

Had he killed his father?

Reaching for each other's hand, Fenella and I ran.

We found out what had happened while we'd been protected by Kaf. Death stood and told us that he had since passed Joseph's soul straight onto a demon soul collector. All that was left was the empty shell of Jason's father. Jason was on his knees in shock, and Fenella rushed towards him, placing her arms around him, and hugging him tightly.

Griffin and the rest of the council were dealing with the fallout. The voting had been postponed for the moment as the council needed to meet quickly. Viper had been in complete shock and led away by his wife. His son taken to jail.

There was nothing more I could do at this stage, so I returned to Kaf and Billy.

"I know you don't like being our taxi service, but on this occasion can you quickly whisk us home?" I asked.

"Absolutely," he said.

He dropped us right onto our landing. "You have my number if either of you need me for anything. I'm going back to the field to see if I can assist in any way."

"Please check Jason is okay. Keep an eye on him," I pleaded.

"Already on it," he said.

I had a feeling that in time Kaf wouldn't only be a brother to Connor. I had a feeling he'd become a brother to me too. The family of Gnarly would care for us for a long time to come.

Opening my portal door, I found my set of drawers in the room. That meant Jason's would be at his place too. I carried it to my bedroom, put it in the corner of the room, and then sat looking at it. It was a sign of hope for the future, and right now, I would cling to it.

I woke up later on my bed, wondering why I'd startled. Then I heard voices at the door. I sat up, rubbing the drool from my mouth, just as a knock came to my door.

Jason walked in, looking like he'd aged twenty years. "Can I just hold you?" he said.

I nodded, and climbing off the bed, peeled back the duvet. "Get in," I instructed.

We held each other close and dozed off. During the night after a few hours' sleep, Jason told me how the council had met. Thor was in a secure jail. Viper had wanted to resign, but Griffin wouldn't let him, instead suggesting he took an extended leave of absence.

Willow had been instrumental in assisting in Viper's place. She knew all the policies and procedures having been the silent partner of the recently deceased dragon king. It was arranged that Joseph would have a private cremation at midnight. Jason and his mum had been in attendance. Had said their goodbyes to someone they still needed to grieve, despite his actions. The vote had been rescheduled for tonight, and all had been dismissed. Stan had taken Fenella home, and Jason had come here.

To me.

And that meant the world.

CHAPTER TWENTY-EIGHT

Jason

When I woke, I felt as good as I could after a broken sleep following the previous day's drama. Being wrapped in Charity's warm embrace meant a lot, and we both smiled as we saw the chest of drawers in her room.

"I shall send some things through the portal later to go in there, and you can do the same," I said.

"Sounds good to me."

We made love and then showered, finally making it into the kitchen. Billy had left a note saying that he'd gone to college early as we were being too loud and he didn't want psychologically scarring for life.

That brought a blush to Charity's cheeks.

"Hey, he's eighteen soon, and then you can spend more time at my place, and he can have his own fun here. He'll not be complaining then."

"I do not want to think about my brother in that way, right now," she said. "It's scarier than your bedhead."

I smacked her playfully on the butt.

"Are you ready for the vote later?" she asked me.

"I sure am. And I'm hopeful that people will vote for me, given what happened yesterday."

"King Jason of the Rulefort clan," Charity said, passing me a coffee. "Can the first thing you do be to change the clan colours and move on from velvet?"

"Aww, don't you want me to role-play with you where I'm king and you're a loyal servant?"

"I'm afraid there'll be no fires lit if you wear that outfit again."

"Consider it gone. What would you suggest instead? A loin cloth?"

"Get out of here. I have work to do. Go to your future kingdom. I'll see you tonight for your coronation."

I quickly drank my coffee down, kissed her, and left. There was a lot to do before tonight.

At seven pm, after a day of intense negotiations in the council chambers, I once more emerged onto the field where I sat behind a long rectangular table, the rest of the council sitting beside me, as the crowds of Rulefort dragons emerged onto the field in front of us. When all were there, I stood up and spoke into the microphone.

"Rulefort. I thank you for your patience during the last week or so. You lost your faithful king and then discovered he had nominated a half-breed dragon as some call it, to inherit the throne. I stand before you today to say that I did not expect to want to take on that role, of being your king. I did not know my dragon side well and did not feel a man who had been brought up outside of the clan would be able to take over.

"But Rulefort surprised me. I found out that it wasn't really the king who ruled Rulefort. Not alone anyway. Josiah was supported by his council. Twelve amazing men who between them keep the wheels turning. But what you might not be aware of, is that most of the decision and policy making was not solely made by your king, but in large part was actioned by his wife, my Aunt Willow."

There were gasps and murmurs at this. Some men didn't look too happy, but the women were standing taller.

"That's right. When you came to ask for a larger cave, or a loan, it was Willow Rulefort who organised that for you, though her husband always took the credit as king. You owe Willow a huge thank you and debt of gratitude for what she did behind the scenes.

Of her service during the twenty-five years of my uncle's reign. But more than that, Rulefort has been making a large mistake for many, many years, and that is to not acknowledge its females. I would like you to all look at my aunt at this moment, and at the young woman at the side of her, my cousin Amaryllis."

Heads turned to look and then whispers ran through the crowds. "If you vote for me tonight," I said. "There will be no more hiding. I will give you my clear intentions. That I will rule until my cousin, the rightful heir, is over eighteen and feels ready to take over the crown. Then I will abdicate."

Once again there were shocked gasps, and chatter spread amongst the crowd.

"Of course you do not have to accept me. You can challenge me if you wish, just like Joseph Rulefort and Thor Hamilton did yesterday. But know I will take such challenges very seriously, especially if you are against females having equal opportunities here."

I hoped they'd all have a good long think about how my father had basically been shot putted through the trees when he'd challenged me; but whatever came up, I would face it. I looked at Amaryllis again.

I'd do it for her. For my cousin who deserved better than what she'd had so far in life.

"Eventually, the council shall have more females on its board, but for now I propose to have Griffin Wheeler remain as clan deputy, and for the rest of the council to remain as they were, with the exception of Willow Rulefort standing in for Viper Hamilton. When I'm more settled, the roles of the council will be reconfigured, but this is how I propose to start. Thank you for listening to my speech," I said, and I sat back down.

The crowd weren't allowed to cheer or boo. There was to be no clue to the potential outcome of the vote.

Griffin stood up. "Please form an orderly line and make your vote. We shall announce the result at midnight. Should you wish to challenge Jason, please hand in your written challenge to me before midnight."

And that was it. All we had to do now was wait.

I left my seat and headed into the crowd where my mum, Stan, and Charity stood with my aunt and cousin.

My mum was wiping at her eyes which were swollen and puffy.

"Oh, Mum," I said, giving her a hug.

"I've never been so proud, Jason," she said, before bursting into a fresh round of sobs.

"Could I have a quiet word, Jason?" Stan asked me, and my heart thudded wondering what he wanted to say. My mum had been through a lot since she'd met Joseph Rulefort and I'd make sure Stan knew that if it came to it, I'd stand down for my mum if she asked me to.

By midnight, my pulse was thudding everywhere you could detect it, and there were some places I hadn't been aware it could pulse. I just hoped my body feeling like a ticking timebomb wasn't an indication of my future. I took my place, this time standing at the side of the council table, because if the vote went against me, I would leave and Griffin would stay in charge until a new potential king was found.

The vote results were brought over to Chance. I swallowed hard, my throat dry, as he stood up.

"Dearest Rulefort. Firstly, there were no challenges presented against Jason Rulefort. Now onto the vote. He ripped open the envelope and time seemed to stand still.

"The votes cast in favour of Jason Rulefort. Ninety-one percent in agreement, six percent against, and three percent spoiled votes. We will now hear from the new king."

I'd done it. Oh my god!!!! I was king, and Rulefort was mainly in agreement to a huge change in the way it ran.

I stood with the council again and picked up the microphone.

"Thank you, Rulefort. I promise to do everything I can to bring happiness and security to you all. I know one thing that people were hesitant about was the potential dilution of the Rulefort dragon line. I would like to say that I have spoken with the warlock Andy, and a spell shall be made that means that any heir to the crown, regardless of their DNA, or percentage of dragon at birth, will inherit full dragon powers. Using some of the remaining ashes of those that went before us in the making of the spell, the future Rulefort dragon heirs will have the strength of all who went before them, and I can assure you, that's quite something."

Griffin took the microphone from me and addressed the crowd. "I now officially present to you, King Jason of Rulefort."

The crowd went wild and for a moment I felt like doing a little celebratory dance. I lifted my arms ready to wiggle and then I saw Griffin's raised brow and stopped. He nodded over to my girlfriend.

Charity had stood up and I watched her make a call on her phone. Then she approached the front and asked Griffin if she could borrow the microphone. The dragons went silent. Including women was one thing, but being addressed by a mermaid? I was nervous. What was she doing?

"Congrats, Rulefort on your new king. As a surprise and a thank you for you welcoming us to the ball yesterday, which as you know didn't quite go the way we'd planned, we invite you to celebrate with us again. If you'd just look over to where Merrin's is," she instructed. People looked over. "After this, we have food and dancing once more."

Then fireworks started from Merrin's property. Everyone cheered and the party began.

Charity and I went to stand beside Mum and Stan. Nick and Dela joined us, and I gave my best friend a hug. "Your best friend did good, hey? Became a full dragon, king, and got himself a gorgeous girlfriend."

"You did very good. However, I'm very happy to not rule a kingdom."

"You'll be Santa at some point, Son," Stan reminded him.

"I know. One day when you're too knackered to do the job."

"I'll have you know your dad doesn't get kn—"

"Who knows, one day I might have a fiancée," I interrupted my mum before she said something I'd need to burn my own ears off for.

"Steady on, Jason, it's only been a couple of weeks," my mum and Charity said in unison, and I guffawed.

"Got two of 'em at it now," I said, harking back to the day at

Merrin's just before he'd had his vision about the dragons coming for me.

"Jason," my mum said. "In all seriousness, I love Charity and trust you to make the right choice whenever that is. Because when you know, you know, and Stan and I wasted time." She turned to look at him.

"Stan?"

Her boyfriend was on one knee in front of her, holding out an open ring box.

"Oh my god," Mum squealed.

"Fenella Gradon, your son has now cast aside his surname and embraced that of Rulefort. I ask if you'd like to cast aside your own Gradon surname, by becoming Fenella Anderson, my wife."

"Yes," Mum shouted out in delight before leaping at Stan and almost knocking him over with her exuberance. We all gathered around to celebrate the engagement of my mum and my best friend's dad. Father Christmas would be my stepdad. I was going to get soooo many presents.

"What do you think to the New Year and a winter wedding, my darling? I get time off as you know following the Christmas rush," Stan asked my mum.

"I think that sounds pretty perfect," she said.

Eventually the celebrations fizzled out and everyone went home.

"Are you sure you're okay with dating a dragon king?" I asked Charity. "Because I don't know when Amaryllis will want to take over. I'm going to be busy, although, I shall delegate as much as possible."

"Do not put on your aunt. She had enough of that with her husband."

"Oh she doesn't mind as long as she's recognised for what she does. Says she can't wait to help shake things up."

"I'm proud of you, Jason. As for being busy, we both have jobs and responsibilities. I love my job and hated my ex-husband making me feel guilty for working long hours. We support each other in what we want to do, okay?" she said.

"Agreed, and what I want to do right now, is you," I said. "Let's go to mine and I'll look in your drawers."

Charity groaned. "Your jokes aren't getting any better."

"Are there any nice undies amongst the things you've sent through the portal?" I asked hopefully.

"Do I need to cool you down, Jason Rulefort? Because you know I'm more than capable."

"Nah, baby, it's time for you to get wet, not me," I winked, and grabbing her hand, I whistled and Kaf appeared.

"Just remember this is a one-off, King Jason," he muttered. "My celebratory gift. I am not a taxi service."

But he wrapped us in his wings and dropped us off outside my door anyway.

Just as Barb and Delores were walking past.

"Bloody hell, are you having a threesome now?" Delores shouted.

"They wish," Kaf said. "Ladies, allow me to ensure you both get safely home." He walked out to stand between them, bending his elbows so they could put an arm through his.

"As long as you're not planning to take us to Heaven. Well, you can, but not by killing us off," Barb quipped.

"Do you think Kaf's safe?" Charity giggled.

"He's on his own there. I have plans for us and they don't include rescuing an angel from two thirsty octogenarians."

"Oh yeah?"

"Yeah. So, c'mon baby," I said, pausing. Then Charity sang the rest of the lyric, before we went inside.

THE END

Can Bernard cope with having another man in such close proximity to his wife? Read on and find out in **Just My Suck**...

JUST MY
SUCK

CHAPTER ONE

Bernard

Author note: Everyone pronounces the name Baaairrnard at Bernard's insistence, except Death and Mya who pronounce it Burnud because it pisses him off.

August 2012

"My marriage sucks right now," I told my best friend Lawrie, before biting into a pink cupcake. My mood was temporarily lifted by the hit of O-neg hidden in the bun. I sighed heavily, my sigh half-despondent/half-tastebud heaven.

"I really don't need to know what you and Aria get up to behind closed doors," he quipped.

"Huh, I wish." I swallowed a mouthful of pink lemonade to wash down the cupcake and stared at him with narrowed eyes. "This is all your fault."

"What? How on earth am I responsible for the fact you're jealous your wife is being bodyguarded by an angel? You just feel threatened, that's all. Kaf's only here to make sure the twins are safely delivered. Snap out of it, mate."

I raised a brow. "Huh. I'd love to see what you'd be like if Kaf's next job was to guard Callie. I'm sure you'd be perfectly fine with the angel who's heavenly in not only spirit but physical body if he suddenly had to be around your wife twenty-four-seven."

Lawrie's eyes flashed red, and I gave him a 'told you so' smug grimace.

"Fair enough, I get your point, but I still don't see how you're now blaming me for it."

"Oh, let me think," I tilted my head and started touching my left index finger with my right one ready to make my first point. "Firstly, you took a woman on a date who you ended up siring and she became Queen of the Wayward. And what is Queen Mya's home? The mansion on the top of the hill just outside Gnarly Fell, where she resides with none other than Death himself, *my wife's* ex-boyfriend. By siring Mya, you tied the Letwine vampires to this bloody village and put me near that gloomy sod."

"I just realized Aria has a type." Lawrie stared at me pointedly.

My eyes narrowed further at him.

"Look, Gnarly is a great place, and I didn't exactly have a choice to become a father. It's not good for my image when a woman in her late twenties calls me Dad. Mya has far too much fun with it. Do you know what she said in front of someone in here last week? She said 'Daddy, do you remember when you took me on a date?' The woman next to her in the queue's eyes almost bugged out of her head. I had to say it was one of those Daddy/Daughter things like they do in America."

"I'll continue talking now, if that's okay with you, because this is about me right now." I'd come here because I needed to offload, to be heard. "Secondly, you marry a fae woman who owns a cupcake cafe, which becomes a cupcake café crossed with a bookshop while you're off enjoying yourself on honeymoon, and my wife decides she's going to work in it. She becomes friends with all these villagers, before thirdly, attending an upcycling workshop run by the artist Merrin, which fourthly, eventually leads to a dragon battle on the field nearby, where suddenly said artist declares the angel hanging around Gnarly is now the bodyguard of our twin babies. However, they're in my wife's belly so actually he's bodyguarding her. Therefore, given you started this chain of events it's all… your… fault." I huffed.

"You're so dramatic. All this sighing and huffing when you don't even need to breathe. Anyway, what's happened this time that's meant you're sitting with me in the cupcake café in the village you apparently despise?"

"I don't despise the cupcakes themselves. Go and get me another."

Lawrie raised both his brows at me.

"You owe me for all that's happening, and if you don't, I'll tell Kaf I think Callie's in danger, so he also comes hanging around here."

"And they thought I was the evillest vampire." Lawrie got up to get my bun and I watched him whispering to his wife, low enough so that even my vampire super-hearing couldn't make out what he was saying. But it didn't matter because no one could say anything right now to make me feel any worse than I felt already. I had twin babies due in four months' time, and what should have been the happiest days of my unlife were slowly becoming the worst.

All because of another man.

An hour earlier...

"*Bernard, I don't need another blanket. It's August. Not only that but I'm perfectly capable of getting up off the sofa and getting one myself from the blanket basket THREE STEPS AWAY.*" *Aria crumpled up the blanket and threw it back in the box in a hissy fit.*

"*Honey, don't let yourself get too vexed, it won't be good for the babies.*" *I stroked her back. "Let's get you back to the sofa to rest." I began to guide her to turn around in the direction of the sofa.*

"*Fuck off,*" *she spat, shoving me so that I almost ended up in the basket myself. My eyes widened as I took in her stance: hands on hips, jaw taut, eyes flashing with a red haze. I felt I needed to check it wasn't her who'd recently discovered she was a dragon, rather than Jason, because she sure looked like she was going to snort fire out of her nostrils at any given moment.*

"*I understand you have pregnancy hormones affecting you,*

darling, but was that absolutely necessary? I'm only trying to ensure you're comfortable."

"I'm sorry for swearing, but, Bernard, you're doing my head in." *Aria ran a hand through her hair.* "Everywhere I turn, there you are. It's been even worse since Lawrie got married. If I did breathe, I'd feel like I couldn't take one without you checking it was the right amount of inhalation. The babies are fine. I am fine. We have an angel living in the apartment next door to make sure they're fine. Merrin saw them born and healthy in a vision. You don't need to be a second's step away from me twenty-four-seven, so please go and find a hobby or some new friends or something and let me have some time to myself. Please! You don't need to be here."

She plonked herself back down on the sofa.

Now Aria's prickliness did not come only from the many moods of pregnancy hormones—she had often threatened to acquaint my arsehole with various implements when vexed—but what was different this time was the fact she'd just stated she didn't need me here. Not now we had angelic superhero Kaf in the apartment next door.

We'd been told we could extend our suite into the apartment next door when the couple who lived there left to travel, but it now housed the babies' new bodyguard. Dark blonde haired and baby-blue eyed, Kaf had been sent down from Heaven, delivered via Mya's attic in the Home of the Wayward, a couple of months ago, and he had been staying with his older brother Connor. But once Merrin had told us his vision, Aria went straight to our leader Edmond Letwine and asked for permission to move Kaf in. And though it was because of his angel duties, that didn't stop the other Letwine males from teasing me about it. About the fact my wife had asked for another man to live next door. 'Aria got a guy with wings, so she could swing', 'Did her cries of oh my god bring down a celestial being to check on her?' and so on... and on... and on. Of course, I didn't tell Aria any of this. I didn't want her getting upset or angry over vampire tittle-tattle.

But it had been frustrating to constantly have a hot guy checking on my wife. Watching her smile at him, and delight in his attention. The only thing that had kept me from melancholia was the fact that I was right there, at my wife's side. Ready should she need anything.

Want anything. Kaf was next door. He might be the babies' protector, but he wasn't their father.

But it appeared she no longer wanted me around her. I knew what the answer would be, but I asked her anyway. Got her to clarify, so I could make certain.

"Is there anything you want, Aria?"

"Yes, I want to be left alone without you all up in my personal space. For God's sake, Bernard, get out of the suite."

She turned her head away from me, so she didn't see me nod in return.

I'd do exactly what she asked and see if she even noticed when I was no longer there.

Needing thinking space, I'd gone to the café where Callie had shouted Lawrie for me. They lived above the shop. As I'd chatted with her husband, I'd noticed Callie's eyes flicker over me in concern. At least someone gave a shit about me.

"But the last time we spoke, Aria had been all about you being manly and possessive," Lawrie queried after I'd recounted my tale.

"Only because she'd been reading one of her possessive alpha books again and wanted to act it out. I don't think she sees me anymore as anything other than an annoyance. Once the babies come, I bet she'll push me even further away."

"She won't. She'll need you more than ever then."

"Yes, only to mind the babies, not because she actually loves me and wants me there." I stood up, having finished my refreshments. "Thanks for listening, Lawrie, but I know what I need to do."

Between his brows furrowed. "Go speak to your wife and tell her how you feel?"

I shook my head. "No. My wife wants me to get a hobby, and to leave her alone. I shall go find one. I will start in my birthplace, Paris."

"You were born in Leeds," Lawrie pointed out unnecessarily.

"My human birth was in Leeds. My vampire birth took place as you well know in a bathroom in the Eiffel Tower. That is where I will go now. To Paris for a while to consider my future."

"Surely there's a hobbies magazine to read that'd be much easier and less dramatic. Or go to the community centre. They run lots of activities there. Don't you think you're overreacting, just a little bit?"

"I'm not going to Paris just to find a hobby, my friend. My wife told me I was to leave. To give her time to herself. She is in a delicate state and so in order to respect her wishes I will give her that time. She has Kaf now anyway."

"Bernard, you're being ridiculous."

"Je ne suis pas ridicule."

"Yes, you are."

Walking around, I patted my best friend on his shoulder. "Au revoir, mon amie."

Before Lawrie could say anything further, I whizzed from the café, and appeared at the foot of the Eiffel Tower, making a few tourists blink twice.

I stood back, staring at the structure.

Paris was where things had changed for me. Where I'd died and been re-born immortal. Where I'd met my wife. It seemed only right that it would be the place I pondered my future.

And what I'd do if my wife no longer wanted me by her side.

CHAPTER TWO

Aria

With Bernard out of my hair and Kaf either next door or anywhere else he needed to be, I sighed with happiness as I laid on my sofa in all my full-bellied pregnant glory and just rested. No one asking me if I was okay. No one checking me over like I was a delicate bird's egg. Vampires didn't sleep much, but I'd needed more rest while incubating my babies, and I closed my eyes, knowing that *finally*, I could get some sleep.

The next thing I knew, my eyes opened, and the outside had gone dark. Looking at the clock on our mantlepiece, I saw it was four pm. Rain tapped, and wind rattled at the windows, explaining why it had gone dark so soon.

I stretched out my limbs, feeling so much better for a nap.

"Bernard," I called out. He must be in the bedroom.

There was no answer. That was strange. It'd been hours since he'd left the suite, and I'd fully expected that the moment I opened my eyes, he'd be there hovering on the periphery.

Getting off the sofa, I stood and stretched out once again. As one of the babies kicked, I stroked my stomach. "I know, you're hungry. You're always hungry. Let's go get a drink." I waddled into the kitchen and got myself two packs of blood from the fridge. It was important I kept my levels up. The fridge was extremely well stocked. Bernard had even got me a few different varieties for in case my tastes changed during pregnancy. Picking up my mobile phone which I'd left on the kitchen table at some point, I dialled his number.

The person you have called is not available.

That was weird. He took his phone everywhere in case I needed him.

Picking up my blood bags, I drank them down in succession and then I went back to the sofa. There was only one place he could be. I called Lawrie.

"Hey, Lawrie. Is Bernard with you?"

There was an awkward silence at the other end of the line.

"Lawrie?"

"Erm, did Bernard not call you?"

"Call me about what?" Typical, I was feeling fantastic and now clearly there was some drama happening. My mood began to sour. "What's going on, Lawrie, and just come out with it because I'm not in the mood for your nonsense. Have you seen him or not?"

"Yes, I've seen him. He came to the café to chat with me earlier this afternoon. He was very downcast."

"He's always downcast. That's his whole personality. I asked you to get to the point but you're still talking in riddles."

"How can I put this? If Bernard's misery was a staircase and he was usually halfway, he'd taken a couple more steps towards the bottom. He said you'd asked him to leave."

"Yes. So?"

"So, he did. He did what you asked him to do."

"Which was fantastic. I had a lovely sleep without him staring at me like some kind of crazed stalker. Now I feel lots better and thought we might go for a walk around the grounds together."

There was silence again.

"I swear to God, Lawrie, if you don't tell me what's happening, I'm going to whizz around to yours and let you find out how your own dick tastes in your mouth."

"Wrong threat to make. If I could physically manage that, my wife would love you for the rest it would give her own jaw, and I'd think it was already Christmas."

"Five... four... three—"

"He's gone to Paris."

"Oh." I paused for a moment. He'd taken himself off to the place he'd always called home before we moved to the fell. "Right. I advised him to look for a hobby, but because he was in a mood, he's gone to wander around Paris being all woe is me instead. Well, isn't that just typical. I'll just hang around here then until he comes back. Or, actually, I could go see if Kaf fancies a walk."

"He's not coming back, Aria. Not tonight anyway."

There was something in Lawrie's tone that made my back prickle with unease.

"I don't understand," I said, but I was starting to realise I would soon, and that I wouldn't like what was coming.

"Aria, when he came to the café, he said you'd asked him to leave. Said you'd told him to get out of the apartment."

"I did. He's been far too overprotective. Always there. He's driven me bloody crazy. I was at my limit today because I just wanted to be able to lift a blanket on and off my own body and walk without a hand at my back. But I only meant for the day. Please tell me he doesn't think I've actually asked him to leave, as in separate leave."

"He's confused, Aria. Since Kaf came he feels displaced."

At this point I wanted to scream in frustration. "God, not this threatened masculinity again. Kaf's been sent from Heaven to make sure our twins are delivered safely. Then he'll leave. It's not like I've taken on a second husband."

"Oh dear. I think Bernard's got the wrong end of the stick. You need to phone him or go find him and explain. He thinks you've tired of him and don't need him anymore. That you'd rather he was out of your hair."

"What an absolute dick. I'll give the moron a call and tell him to come home," I said while inside, my mind hatched an alternate plan.

"Be nice to him. It is bad for us males when we feel less of a man."

"Got it. Okay, thanks for letting me know, Lawrie. Enjoy your evening."

After ending the call, I put my phone down and laid back on the sofa. It wouldn't hurt for my dear husband to spend a bit more time in Paris. If he looked at his phone he'd see my missed call, and if he tried to ring back... I'd just not hear it for a while. In the meantime, I'd make the most of the time to myself. I switched the television on and found an episode of *The Big Bang Theory*. Bernard didn't like comedies. Enjoying myself thoroughly, one episode became a whole evening of television, and before I knew it, dawn had broken. I checked my phone. Bernard hadn't called me back so he must be ignoring me on purpose. Whatever. I went and crawled into our bed ready for some more sleep, and I star-fished my body into as much of the space as possible. There was a fleeting moment where I missed my husband's arm around my body, but then I remembered I could hog all the duvet to myself.

I'd call him again later and smooth things over. But right now...

Later that morning, I got out of bed and called Bernard's number again. This time he answered.

"You told me to give you some space, so I am doing. I'll come back to talk when I've had time to think," he said.

"Bernard, you idiot, I—"

He hung up.

Mouth open, I looked at the phone. "Fine, fuck you," I snapped at the screen. "You go and be all Morrisey's *Heaven Knows I'm Miserable Now* all over Paris. Meanwhile, I'll make the most of my new freedom and go and see my friends at the bookstore. How about it, babies? Special red velvets for all?"

I got ready and went to knock on the door of the adjacent apartment.

I heard Kaf's feet pad slowly over to the front door. He answered looking all bedhead, and sleepy. He was an attractive man, I could appreciate that, but my heart belonged to the miserable bastard who believed himself French.

"Morning, Aria," he said, yawning. "Sorry. I was working late at the bistro."

"Sorry to disturb you, but I just wanted to let you know that I'm going to the café this morning."

"Oh, okay. Give me a minute to get ready."

JUST MY SUCK

"No. No. I don't need you to come. I'm perfectly fine going on my own."

Kaf tutted at me. "You know that's not how this goes. Go sit downstairs in the large sitting room and I'll be down shortly. I'll not get in your way, but I will be nearby. That's my job."

"Give me strength," I said. "I'm a vampire. A full-blown killer. I can go and get a coffee on my own."

"Have you ever actually killed anyone?" Kaf leaned against the doorframe awaiting my answer.

"You're so annoying. Do you know that?" I harrumphed.

"It's been said to me before." He laughed. "I'll see you in five."

He was a man of his word and met me downstairs five minutes later. He'd tidied himself up and was wearing a white short-sleeved shirt and pale-blue jeans. Opening out his wings, he indicated for me to step forward. Despite the fact I could whizz around, Kaf always insisted he transport me anywhere when we were together.

"You do smell heavenly," I said, repeating the joke that was getting old between us now, but helped me feel more comfortable about being wrapped in another man's arms.

"Eternity for Men." He winked. "I mean what else would an immortal wear?"

With that he took me to the café.

Travelling in his wings was like how I'd imagine being wrapped in a cloud to be. It was soft and warm. You felt safe and comforted, and the movement was so gentle you didn't feel like you were moving much at all. In contrast, vampire movement could be sharp, jerky, and abrupt.

When I walked into the café, I felt, and no doubt looked, blissed out. What with all the rest and sleep, I felt amazing.

Smiling at Dela, Callie's sister, who was behind the counter this morning, I said, "Three red velvets please." Then I remembered my manners. "Oh, Kaf, what would you like?"

"I'm fine. I've arranged to meet Mya here to see if she's heard anything else from Heaven HQ. I'll hang around outside until she turns up."

"You mean you'll stand and watch all the women walk past in their skimpy clothes because it's a hot day," I teased. Kaf was a born flirt.

He left and I turned back to Dela. "Pink lemonade?" she asked.

"No, a really strong coffee please." Bernard had been restricting my caffeine intake since we'd found out I was pregnant, but he wasn't here now, so I'd enjoy one. I was going to have a strong coffee and a cupcake for me, and one on behalf of each twin.

"How are you? You're looking well, I have to say, but then so would I if I had two good looking men caring for me."

"It's just the one right now. Bernard's on a trip to Paris."

"He's left you alone?" Suspicion skirted across Dela's face. The bloody fae didn't miss a trick.

"Of course not. He knows Kaf is here. He's gone to collect some things for the baby. You know what he's like with Paris. The babies must know their heritage blah blah blah."

She laughed, seemingly satisfied with my response. "Bless him."

Dela glanced over at the book section. "Are you sitting in the book section near Ginny?"

I nodded. Ginny was Lawrie's sister and my closest friend. When I'd found out I was pregnant, she'd stepped in to work at *Books and Buns*. As I turned to look that way, she waved at me eagerly. I did miss serving at the bookstore. It had given me time not on my own, but time around other people, so that I'd felt like I had conversation when I got home. Books were an obsession to me and selling them here in the café had been a dream job.

"I'll bring your order to you when I've done your coffee. You go get a seat."

"Thanks." One of the most amazing things about being pregnant was the special treatment you got. People ensuring you were comfortable and spoiling you. Ginny was serving a customer, and so I sat down and got comfy, watching as Dela made her way over with my coffee, three cupcakes, and some mini chocolate brownies. "These go so well with the coffee. They're a treat from me."

"You're amazing. Thank you," I said, as Ginny came over, sat beside me, and helped herself to one of the brownies.

"Hey," I scolded.

"I'll get you another if you really want one after three

cupcakes." She rolled her eyes. "So, out with it. Where's the dust? In the vacuum cleaner? I thought your mood might tip over at some point, but if you've dusted Bernard then I'm not sure how we're going to explain that one away."

"I've not murdered Bernard," I said. "He's in Paris."

"The math isn't mathing, bestie. That man has been by your side throughout this pregnancy, like a piece of Velcro."

"More like a piece of plastic with static. You know where you shake your hand and no matter what you do it won't come off or it just moves to another part of your body?"

"Where is he? Where's Bernard?" she insisted.

"We're having some time apart," I teased, and I was just about to explain fully, when the voice of a vampire queen shouted out behind me.

"You and Bernard have separated? You'd better not try and steal my man, lady."

CHAPTER THREE

Bernard

I'd not felt the need to return to Paris for a long time. For me it was a place chock full of memories, some good, some not so good. But as I walked around the second floor of the Eiffel Tower, staring out over the city, I remembered how beautiful it was.

"Excuse me. Could you take my photo please?"

I turned to see a tall woman with a brunette sleek bob looking at me. She held a phone, which she was wiggling in my direction.

"Of course," I said, taking the phone and setting her in the frame just right, so the beauty of Paris was behind her. I snapped a couple of photos and handed it back. The woman swept through them and then smiled up at me.

"These are amazing. Thank you."

I shrugged. "I dabbled in photography years ago."

"Well, thank you. These are better than I imagined." The woman walked away, and I remembered a time from the past and a similar situation.

Six years ago...

. . .

"We're in Paris, the most romantic place on earth, and you're not entering into the spirit of things." I heard a woman basically hissing words at the man she was standing beside.

"I'm not here for romance, Aria. You know why I'm here. To work," the man answered, sighing.

I stared at them both. She was clearly desperate for him to see her in this beautiful city, and yet the man seemed disinterested. My years as a vampire meant I'd witnessed most things in life, including workaholics, which this man was if he was focused on work and not the stunning woman at his side.

This relationship wasn't going to work out. There was no real chemistry there.

I took in all the woman's features. Her cherry red hair, gorgeous green eyes, and absolutely perfect figure. Breasts that I imagined in my hands. Hips I would sweep my fingers down.

"What the fuck are you staring at?" she shouted, and I realised she was looking right at me.

I closed the gap between us. "Pardonne, ma cherie. It is not often I see a woman more beautiful than Paris."

She straightened then and flicked her hair. "Flatterer."

Her gaze swept around her, no doubt looking for her boyfriend, but he'd gone.

"You can do better than him. He is not interested in you. Not in the way you want him to be."

"Wow. You really have been watching us closely."

I shrugged. "I apologised already for staring, but to be honest my words weren't genuine. I'm not sorry at all. You deserve eyes on you, belle femme."

"You think I'm beautiful?"

"I think your beauty is beyond description."

I knew I should not be flirting with another man's woman, but something drew me to her, beyond her outside appearance. It was like the scent of her had reached my nostrils and lit up my entire body.

"You are too kind," she replied, holding out a hand. "Aria De Luca."

"Bernard Letwine."

Her eyes widened. "You're a Letwine vampire?"

I nodded, "And you are from the De Luca's."

JUST MY SUCK

The De Luca clan were a bunch of vagabonds, always trying to profit from others hard work. Aria did not fit with my image of one of them.

"I don't need to read your mind to know your thoughts, Bernard, for they are written all over your face."

"Then you know I am intrigued by you." I took the camera dangling around my neck and raised it. "May I?"

"You may."

She settled against the railing, her red hair billowing in the breeze, and I snapped a few photos.

The man returned and came to stand by us. His eyes alighted on the camera I'd just placed back down against my chest, now hanging off its neck strap.

"Aria, I'm finished here, and now have work elsewhere. Are you coming?"

She nodded. "Yes. It was nice to meet you, Mr Letwine. Enjoy the rest of your trip."

She took hold of the man's hand and as she did so, she let her mind guards drop. I felt the cold seep through me, smelled earth, and then the decay of death.

My eyes quickly alighted on the man who now stared at me with an empty, dead gaze.

Death himself.

I'd been flirting with the wife or girlfriend of Death?

I shivered and heard Aria laugh in my mind before I heard her words there.

'We will meet again. I want to see the photos you just took. There is no need to fear Death if you're already dead, don't you think?'

Her eyes met mine and then her and Death were both gone.

I spent the rest of the day snapping photos of Paris to show her when we met again.

Because I knew even though I shouldn't, I would find her once more.

It was inevitable.

CHAPTER FOUR

Mya

"I'm going to meet Kaf at the café. Ooh that sounds quite poetic, doesn't it?"

I received a Death stare.

"Yes, Mya, after years of reading the works of Keats, Wordsworth, Blake, Poe, etc from the many poetry books in the turrets, meeting Kaf at the café sounds like Pulitzer Prize material."

I stuck my tongue out at my broody, moody boyfriend.

"You got any plans today?"

"Thought I'd go and collect some souls. Oh, hang on." He placed a finger on his lips. "I'm going to meet the near deads in their beds."

"Oh ha bloody ha. Go on. Get to work."

"You might like to do the same, given there are still wayward souls in the building."

I nodded. "I will later on but seeing as Heaven spat an angel out in the attic a couple of months ago who's still here, I'm off to supervise my charge. I know what it's like to suddenly end up somewhere unexpected."

"Fair enough. And I'm sure you'll not in any way catch up with friends while you're in the café. Or talk books. Or eat cupcakes..."

I silenced him with a kiss.

"You can't always stop me from talking with kisses you know?" Death put his cloak on.

I raised a brow and he sighed. "Okay, yes you can. That and other things. Have a nice day."

"You too," I said and this time *he* raised a brow.

"You really do need to think more before you speak, Mya. A nice day... turning up and people realising they're dying whenever I appear. Yes, it's always such a party. People welcome me with open arms, and we have a laugh and a joke before I extract their soul."

I kissed him again. "Go on, suck off," I told him. Having a portal to Heaven in the attic, and one to Hell in the basement meant I had to even out cursing versus being nice. Not the easiest of tasks with my personality to be fair.

With Death finally gone to work, I got myself ready and whizzed over to the café to meet Kaf.

"Kaf at the café," I said, as I greeted the angel, who was checking out Chantelle's butt as she walked past with a latte.

"What about it?" he said.

"Never mind." Clearly, the men around Gnarly had no sense of humour.

I followed him into the café but became distracted as I saw Aria chatting with Ginny. Aria was my boyfriend's ex. Now, since she'd announced her pregnancy, I'd felt a lot better about being around her, and in fact, we did share a love of books. But habits were hard to break and my first response every time I saw her was to get the green-eyed monster. I mean the woman was staggeringly beautiful and somewhat of an enigma since Death wouldn't talk of his past relationships and didn't want to know about mine either. He said only the future mattered. The only thing he'd ever said was that he'd worked out she wanted The Book of the Dead rather than him.

Then I heard her words.

"We're having some time apart."

"You and Bernard have separated? You'd better not try and steal my man, lady," I yelled out. Everyone in the café's heads swiftly turned in our direction.

Aria groaned and flicked some of that gorgeous hair as I made my way towards her. "I don't want your man. How many more times? I didn't really want him when I had him."

That should have helped but it just made things ten times worse. That she didn't even value what she'd had.

"Death is absolutely amazing, and he wanted to date you, and you didn't even appreciate him."

"Would you rather I'd loved him like crazy and still pined for him now?" she retorted.

"You don't, do you?" My lip wobbled.

"For Christ's sake, SHUT UP," Ginny yelled. As we were stunned into silence by the sheer decibel level of her outburst, she turned to the café and apologised to the customers whose ears would now be ringing.

Ginny gestured for me to join them.

I looked at Kaf.

"I'll go and stand outside for a bit longer. Give me a shout when you're ready," he said, before turning and walking back out of the café.

Ginny pointed at an empty seat at the table. "Sit. Then once we've ascertained what's happening you can go on your way."

"God, you're bossy." I did what I was told though.

"Right, Aria. What's this about you and Bernard having time apart?" Ginny's face creased with concern.

"I was joking." Aria had the decency to look at the floor a little embarrassed. "He got the wrong end of the stick yesterday when I asked him to bugger off for a bit, and he went to Paris."

"Oh, thank God for that," Ginny said. I also felt very relieved.

"I have to say though, it's been very nice having the apartment to myself. I watched what I wanted to watch on the television last night and star-fished in the bed."

I sighed in appreciation. "Yeah, as much as we love them, a night on your own now and again is nice."

"Anyway, Bernard won't talk to me yet, so he's wandering around Paris all forlorn, thinking I don't want him anymore. I'm not in a physical state to be traipsing around France after him, so for now I'm making the most of the peace and quiet."

"You mean Bernard doesn't know that you don't actually want to kick him out?" Ginny double-checked.

"I just told you. He won't talk to me."

"Aria, sometimes you are a complete idiot. What if Bernard throws himself off the Eiffel Tower or something?"

"Well, he'd just fly to the bottom, wouldn't he?" Aria said. "He'll be fine."

"Bernard should be here, not in Paris." Ginny picked up her phone and dialled. "Lawrie, get your arse down here into the café. You're needed ASAP."

Spotting three red velvet cupcakes on the table, along with five small brownies, now I felt Aria wasn't coming for my man, my mouth watered. The next second, there was nothing there. Aria had eaten the lot, in seconds.

"My babies and I need sustenance after expending all this emotional energy," she said. "Also, I think I deserve some books to be sent to my apartment from your turrets, given you basically accused me of wanting to steal your boyfriend."

I sighed. "Sorry. I'll send you a few later. I've read a really good one by—"

"—Oh please, what am I needed here for?" Lawrie drawled, interrupting us. "Please don't tell me it's to change Mya's nappy because she's full of shit again."

"Always a pleasure to see you, Dad." I gave him the middle finger.

Ginny tugged on his arm to get his attention. "You need to go to Paris, find Bernard, and bring him back. He's not talking to Aria, and so he's out there thinking she wants a divorce or something, when really, she just wanted an hour of peace."

"Well, maybe an evening of peace," Aria stated. "In fact, if he wanted to spend a few days in Paris…"

"Fetch him back now," Ginny ordered.

"Or now," Aria said, sighing.

"Is he being that much of a pain?" I whispered while Ginny spoke with her brother.

"You have no idea."

"Just lose yourself in a book and forget he's there."

"That's the thing. I've not been able to read because Bernard is never away from my side, and he talks incessantly. I can't concentrate on anything," she confessed.

And just like that, the fact that someone was being prevented from doing one of the best things on earth—reading—meant that I was offering my former sworn enemy an escape at my house. The one where her ex also lived. The one I was paranoid she might try to steal back.

"Why don't you come over to the house sometime, and choose the books yourself? There's a lovely chaise longue in the main library. Kaf could bring you. We could chat favourite recent reads, and then I could leave you to read and relax for a while."

"Oh my god, that would be amazing." Her eyes lit up and she gave me a genuine smile. Once again, I was knocked sideways by her beauty. "Probably not tonight because Bernard and I need to talk and straighten some things out, but maybe tomorrow? I'll call you and make sure it's convenient."

"Okay." I got up and gestured for Kaf to come back into the coffee shop.

"So what was all that about?" he asked.

"It seems that Aria is getting annoyed with Bernard being up in her personal space all the time. They had an argument and Bernard thought when she told him to get out, she meant permanently. Lawrie is about to go to Paris to fetch him back."

"There's never a dull moment in Gnarly, is there?"

"Nope. But you need to keep more of an eye on them, because you're supposed to be protecting Aria and yet you had no idea any of this was happening."

He looked away for a moment, pondering my comment. "I'd feel it, Mya, if there was anything amiss. Petty squabbles don't resonate with me. It's just unimportant in the scheme of things, unless like with the dragons it turns into a battle that threatens lives."

"Fair enough."

Lawrie walked past then. "Dad," I shouted. "Can you get me a present from Paris to make up for not being around until my twenties?"

"I'll get you a dummy, sweetie. It might keep you quiet for a minute." He scowled at me before walking back behind the counter and disappearing through the door that led to the kitchens and the stairs up to their apartment.

I smirked then turned back to Kaf. "So how are you then? Adjusting to being back on earth?"

"I guess. I mean I have much better digs now I'm at the mansion, and I get to spend time with my brother, but..." he sucked on his bottom lip.

"But what?"

"But I feel not right. I'm here, but for other people. Can I date? Can I have a bit of a 'life' while I'm here, or should I be tunnel-visioned in helping others? Its just people are living their lives, and to be honest, I'm a bit bored, and a lot jealous as I didn't get to live mine. But do I have a right to be bored when I'm an angel? I'm sure I'm supposed to be above such feelings."

"I'll ask later when I despatch some more souls up there," I assured him.

"Appreciated."

Aria wandered over towards us. "I'm ready to get back, Kaf. Lawrie has gone to get Bernard, so I need to be back home ready for when he turns up."

"We're done here," I said. "I'll be in touch, Kaf."

He nodded.

"I'll see you at yours at some point soon, Mya," Aria said. "Looking forward to a change of scenery and a read."

Kaf looked bemused.

"Actually, I'll just call at the ladies before we travel," Aria told him. "Otherwise, someone down on earth might suffer an unexpected small rainstorm from my bladder."

"Don't say it," I warned Kaf.

"You've invited the woman you're jealous of for dating your boyfriend first, around to your house where she'll no doubt meet said boyfriend, in order that she can escape her own husband for an hour."

"I said you weren't to say it," I grumbled.

CHAPTER FIVE

Bernard

I'd wandered the streets of Paris and enjoyed Duck a l'orange at a brasserie on Place de Palais Bourbon, along with a few bourbons to accompany it and an exquisite piece of Tarte Tatin for dessert. Then I'd booked myself a room at the Shangri-La, overlooking the Eiffel Tower and the river. It was the ultimate in luxury and yet I'd wandered around in a state of utter grief, knowing my wife didn't want me around.

When I'd seen the missed call, I'd decided to ignore it. I wasn't ready to hear any words that might tear my soul apart further. Yet then I sat and tormented myself that she didn't call again. Wasn't regretting her words.

I had a fitful sleep, and when I woke, I drank a few espressos and sat on the sofa of my duplex suite staring out at the tower where my life had changed not once, but twice. The first time had not been so pleasurable as when I'd first met Aria.

Feeling like my mood couldn't get any darker right now, I decided to immerse myself in a memory of times past. Now I liked to lie and say I'd been changed for two thousand years, but the truth was I'd been turned when thirty years old, the year the Eiffel Tower had been built, in 1887. It showed no one took any notice of me that it hadn't yet been pointed out that the tower wasn't built two thousand years ago, and so at least one part of my story was a lie. Either my age or my turning. Only Aria, and Edmond Letwine knew the truth. That my turning was the most boring and pathetic in vampire history.

One-hundred-and-twenty-five years ago

I was a boiler maker for the Leeds railways and had gone to work that day like I had any other. I still lived with my mother, who was only interested in my wages rather than me. I knew I'd been an error. She told me often enough. But while I had no wife of my own, I was happy enough to ensure my mother and I were fed and healthy.

There was a new guy there that day and I'd been told to show him what to do. He did nothing but ask me questions about myself, and I hated it. I wasn't a sociable person; I was a loner and much preferred to just get on with the job.

My answers were as short as possible, and I waited for him to get the message of my disinterest and stop annoying me.

"Have you ever been away from Leeds?" he asked.

"No."

"I've just returned from Paris. They finished building the Eiffel Tower there."

Now my ears perked up, because the tower was a staggering feat of engineering and I'd been following the building of it as much as I could.

"Is it as brilliant as they imagined?" I asked him.

"Better," he said, and he proceeded to tell me all about it. How many engineers it had taken. What it was like to walk around it. Now I was enraptured in a way I'd never felt before. Sure, I'd had an interest in the building, but the way he described it had me entranced.

Of course, later I would learn about compulsion. Back then, I just thought he'd awoken an interest within me.

Later that night, I went to meet Ernest Letwine at a tavern. My mother was not impressed, saying I was on the road to Hell. Her words turned out somewhat true.

After far too much ale, I found myself staring up at the Eiffel Tower.

JUST MY SUCK

"Wh-at. How?" I staggered, looking up at the building. Being here wasn't possible. I'd clearly been slipped some absinthe or something. Sitting on the ground, I just went with the flow and marvelled at the tower, taking in its ironwork.

A moment later, I suffered another bout of dizziness, and then found myself on a viewing platform. "Jesus." I lost my balance and was caught by Ernest. "I don't know what's going on. I'm not well."

"Yeah, let's get you to the bathroom," he said. "You look a bit green." I let him lead me to the conveniences.

All I remembered after that was pain. Lots and lots of pain before the world blacked out.

When I came back around, I was somewhere else entirely. The Letwine mansion, where Edmond Letwine told me my sire had been staked after Eiffel Tower staff had heard my screams, and I'd been picked up from a shallow grave, thrown out like trash because a new attraction didn't want the negative publicity of a murder having occurred in the bathroom.

I'd been fixated with the place ever since. The juxtaposition of a building of great beauty being connected to a time of great trauma.

My phone rang again. Glancing at it, I saw it was Lawrie.

"Hello?"

"Where are you?"

"Paris."

"Ha bloody ha. I mean whereabouts in Paris. I can come over and scent you, but it's far easier if you just tell me."

"Why do you want to know?" I asked enquiringly.

"I've got bored of Callie and thought I'd come hang."

"Oh, brilliant. We can moan about women and visit a casino. We can gamble and get very drunk."

"I'm joking, you idiot. I've been sent to come and get you, because you've got the wrong end of the stick. Your wife's not thrown you out. She just wanted an hour to herself."

I remained silent while I replayed our conversation in my head. There was a possibility I'd overreacted. However...

"That may have been the case, but her mannerisms demonstrated a deeper frustration with me."

"Where are you?" he repeated.

"Duplex suite, Shangri-la," I confessed.

A moment later he was there. Lawrie stood taking in the sophisticated elegance of my room.

"No one could say you can't sulk with style." He came to sit on the sofa beside me. "You need to come back, Bernard, and sort things out, before you actually end up making things worse."

Picking up the telephone at the table beside me, I ordered a further espresso. Lawrie rolled his eyes.

"This is where my best friend listens to me," I pointed out.

"Get me a latte," he sat, part turned around on the sofa, and I did the same at the other side after adding his drink to the order.

"Tell me what's going on in that head of yours, Bernard. Do I need to contact Dr Milton?"

I shook my head. "Aria's always had a temper as you know, but this was different. She'd completely had enough of me. She's having my babies and I felt I was her protector, her provider. For once, I stepped into the role—or should I say attempted to—of what I felt a father-to-be should do: to comfort my wife, provide for her every need. But she doesn't want it, or if I'm honest, need it. She's never needed me, and I think that's the root cause of what's going on with me. If she doesn't need me then she can easily rid herself of me, can't she?"

"Aria loves you. That's why she's with you. It doesn't have to be anything beyond that."

"What if she's falling out of love with me?" I panicked. "She'll have the babies to occupy her soon. There's a gorgeous angel living next door. She's one of the most beautiful women on earth. She could have anyone."

"She chose you."

"Over Death. I don't think that was too hard a choice."

"You're always so hard on yourself, mate. There's no need. You need to come back and talk to Aria."

The refreshments arrived then, and we quieted until the staff member had left.

"After this, we're going back to Gnarly. Your wife does need you, and you need to be near your babies."

"Why? I know they're okay. It's Kaf's job to protect them. Merrin's seen them born."

"As things stand. I know from how I ended up with Callie that things can change. She was in The Book of the Dead, but she lived. Merrin's had a vision. It doesn't mean it can't be changed, does it? If there are outside influences that change the course of history? I mean, were we set to be vampires all along, or did we once have a human future that was derailed by the Letwine vampires?"

"Thanks, Lawrie." I patted him on the arm.

"You're welcome." He smiled.

"You utter fucking cretin." I leaned forward and gave him a thick ear. "Now you've got my mind pondering a million different worries that something might happen to my unborn children."

"Ow. I was only trying to help."

"You've succeeded in one thing," I told him, standing up and drinking down my espresso. "I'm definitely going back home now. Because while I think destiny is just that and it can't often be changed, I cannot rule it out, and so I do need to keep an eye on my wife and children."

Lawrie rubbed his ear.

"I'll finish my own drink while you get organised. After you've checked out of the hotel, we'll go back to Gnarly."

"Okay, but can I go back to yours first? I don't want to go straight to see Aria. I need to think of what I want to say to her."

"We'll go to the café. You can have another espresso while you ponder. And Callie and Dela can see you're back then."

"They'll tell Aria."

"So be it, mate. You're not hiding away in my flat, because your wife will come at me, and she's scary without pregnancy hormones, never mind with them."

"Fine."

It wasn't really. I would rather have spent more time in Paris contemplating things while walking around art exhibitions, and feasting on culinary delights while reading morose literature, but I did have to confront this situation with Aria, choose whatever the outcome was. We'd hit a bump in the road, and I didn't think it was just her pregnancy one causing us to need new directions.

"Oh, thank God, you're back," Callie said, as we arrived back at the shop.

"Why? Has my absence caused Aria a huge regret?" I asked.

"Erm, I meant Lawrie, because the café's got extra busy."

"Oh."

Did anyone ever need me? I thought. *Really?* I didn't recall a time lately when anyone did.

Lawrie went off to help and I got an espresso and sat down at a table on my own.

Though I'd intended to think about my own issues, I ended up listening to Fenella and Stan who were at the next table. Fenella was Jason, the Dragon King's mother, and Stan was Father Christmas. He'd recently proposed and they were getting married in the New Year.

"I just think we're going to have to change the date of the wedding," she said, sighing.

"But there'll never be an occasion when we have lots of spare time, darling. The Santa store works all year round, you have the launderette, and I have the DIY store. My only real break is in the New Year."

"And it would be perfect, if it wasn't for the fact we'll be absolutely pulled out just before then. How can I deal with last-minute details or any problems that arise when it's Christmas? Christmas must always come first."

"Well, I'm fed up of it always coming bloody first," Stan said. "I've a good mind to hand it all over to Nick."

"No, no." Fen touched his wrist. "You love being Father Christmas, and anyway, I've not yet had chance to be Mrs Claus."

He looked at her then with such love and tenderness. It reminded me of everything I'd done to make sure mine and Aria's wedding was incredible.

I got up from my seat and stood by their table. "May I join you?

I couldn't help overhearing with my superior vampire auditory skills and I think I may be able to provide my services."

Fen stared at Stan for a second and then shrugged. "Sure, Bernard, pull up a chair." I was touched that she pronounced it my way rather than how Mya and Death said it. I pulled my chair round and sat down with them.

"Am I correct in assuming that your schedules for arranging the wedding are conflicting with Christmas somewhat? In that it will be very difficult to co-ordinate everything, especially in the last-minute run up?"

"You are very correct," Fen said. "Though I wish to marry Stan as soon as possible, I think next summer would be a more appropriate time."

"But I want us to see in the New Year as newlyweds," Stan grumbled.

"I arranged mine and Aria's wedding," I told them. "It was incredible if I say so myself. Intimate, romantic, and well executed."

"Wow. And Aria didn't mind?" Fen enquired.

"I consulted with her about everything except the honeymoon destination. She just didn't have the hassle of it. I took that off her. I could do the same with you. I find myself, while I await the birth of the twins, at a bit of a loss of something to do. I'm getting on my wife's nerves, and she has the angel around anyway. So what do you say. Would you like a wedding planner? We could have an initial meeting to discuss things, and if you're not interested then no harm done. But if you are impressed with my ideas, then you could employ me."

Fen looked at Stan.

"It's up to you, darling, but if it means I get to marry you on the first of January I'm all for it."

"What about the fact you'll be a new father by then? Won't that interfere with arranging the wedding?" Fen asked.

"Not at all. I will have everything ready by then, and when I need to work, Aria will just have to do without me. She says I'm under her feet all the time anyway. She can't have it all ways."

"Okay, if you're sure. I'm sure between us we can figure things out anyhow," Fen said. She held out her hand and I shook it. "Gosh,

I forgot how cold you vampires are," she added, extracting her hand and blowing warm air on it.

"I might be cold in body but I'm so very warm in heart, Fen. I look forward to discussing things further with you. Is there a time that's good for you?"

"How about my house, tomorrow afternoon? I can go through the few ideas I've had so far, and we can take it from there? Three pm?"

"Perfect." I rose from my seat. "Good day, Fen, and to you, Stan. I look forward to creating the wedding of your dreams."

I walked over to Lawrie who was behind the counter. He finished serving a customer and approached me.

"You look a lot happier," he noted.

"I am, Lawrie, and I have you to thank. If you hadn't brought me back here, on this day, at this time, I would not have overheard Stan and Fenella talking about their problems with fitting in wedding planning."

"Erm, okay," he said. "And that's good because…?"

"I have offered. I'm going to be their wedding planner and create the New Year wedding of their dreams."

Lawrie scratched his head.

"But what about the babies, mate?"

"Aria can look after them if I need to work."

"I meant, what if they're late? What if they decide to come on the day of the wedding? You can't be supervising the wedding and at your wife's side."

"It'll all work out," I insisted.

"I hope for your sake, you're right," he said, shaking his head at me. "Or their dream wedding could become your nightmare."

CHAPTER SIX

Aria

I was relaxing on the sofa by the time my husband returned from his travels. I didn't know what mood he'd be in when he came back: embarrassed after getting the wrong end of the stick or playing the pouty-and-put-out card for me making him misunderstand. The one mood I'd not really expected him to have was the good mood he appeared in.

"I'm just going to get a shower, Aria, only Lawrie didn't give me much time," he said. "Hello, my babies," he added near the direction of my stomach on his way past.

I figured I had around two minutes left to myself before his superspeed shower was complete and he was back by my side, so I closed my eyes and enjoyed the silence. It went on... and on... and on...

Looking at the clock and seeing that over thirty minutes had passed, I got off the sofa and went in search of my husband, who I now presumed had disappeared off somewhere again, or had accidentally staked himself somehow with a toothpick.

Then I noticed I could hear a strange sound coming from the direction of the bathroom. It couldn't be... Bernard was *singing*.

The words of *It's beginning to look a lot like Christmas* were a tad strange to hear in September, but not as strange as my husband being happy and musical.

I pushed the bathroom door open and stood beside the shower cubicle.

"What's going on?"

"I'm having a shower," Bernard replied, pointing to the showerhead. "Is everything okay?"

"You tell me." I stood with my hands on my hips. "You've come home and you're acting all weird. Smiling and singing. Have you been possessed? Do I need to call an exorcist?"

Bernard laughed again and continued to soap up his body. It'd been ages since I'd seen him naked in such a way and I let my eyes roam his flesh. He was slim, but strong, with defined pecs, biceps, and toned thighs.

"You're looking at me like I'm food and you're starving, darling," he said, adding a cheeky wink.

"I don't like this, Bernard," I said, trying and failing to stop my eyes from hungrily wandering his body. "You're not acting like my husband. I don't know whether to fetch Kaf or not."

"I'm not entertaining a three-way," he said. "But if you want to get in, you can."

He let the water sluice the soap suds off his body and gave me a full view of what I could expect to entertain me. It'd been a while as I'd not been in the mood lately—all hormonal moods and feeling uncomfortable with my ever-growing tummy.

I'm not proud of the fact that I decided possessed or not, I was making the most of this Bernard. I stripped off my clothing and entered the shower cubicle.

As I did, I noted that I felt a little nervous. I could barely make eye-contact with my husband, and it wasn't just because I couldn't stop staring at his cock.

Pulling me towards him, the warm water began to pour onto me too, wetting my hair. The jets hit my shoulders and the back of my neck in just the right place to feel soothing.

"I'm sorry I've been so clingy of late, Aria," Bernard said, pushing my hair behind my left ear. "Being away for that short time made me see how I've been losing myself slowly. I know I've been annoying, but rest assured, I will not be in your hair as much from now on. Metaphorically speaking," he said, stroking his hands through my hair again.

"I'm sorry you thought I meant for you to leave and never come back," I replied. "I love you, you idiot."

Bernard swept his head down so that his mouth captured mine. His hands came to my breasts. "I love how full and round these are," he said, gently massaging them in turn. My senses alighted as his hands stroked across my stomach swiftly and then his fingers began to stroke between my legs. "Oh, yes," I cried out.

Moving me against the wall, he filled me, gently moving inside me until I was screaming out his name.

Afterwards, he washed me and then himself, and we climbed out of the shower, dried off, and went to relax on our bed in spa-style towelling robes we'd been bought by Ginny last Christmas. Ginny loved all the finer things in life and so her presents were always something luxurious.

Whereas usually he would wrap me in his arms on the bed and curl himself around me, Bernard was leant up against the headboard, hands behind his head.

"I know I was only away for a short time, Aria, but something changed. Seeing the tower reminded me of us at the beginning, and then when Lawrie came to find me, I asked him to take me to the café first, rather than straight here. I just wanted a little extra time to think."

"I did try to explain, but you cut me off," I said.

He inclined his head towards me. "We needed this, Aria. Yes, I misinterpreted your words, but there was some truth in them. You were getting increasingly frustrated with me, and I've had time to think on that while in the café and in the shower. Since Lawrie met Callie and moved out of the mansion, I've been a little lost and that's meant I've been around you more. I see I've been morose, sulking, clingy, and while I've always had a penchant to turn sombre, I'd lost all my joy in life. For myself, that is. I've been looking forward to the babies, been protective of you, and felt that was my role. When Kaf came I felt like I had lost another part of myself, because I should be there for the babies."

"You are here for the babies. Kaf might be an extra layer of protection, but he's not their father."

He nodded.

"I get that you want to be there for me, but it's been twenty-four-seven, and I've felt like I can't breathe," I confessed. I held up my hand as I saw his mouth open. "I know I don't breathe; you know what I'm getting at. You've just been there, all the time, like you possessed my own shadow or something. Even though you're my husband and I love you, I do need some time for myself."

"And you shall have it, my darling, because you are looking at Fenella and Stan's new wedding planner," he announced, flourishing his hands and grinning.

"What?"

"They were talking in the café. They want a beautiful wedding, but don't have the time to arrange it with all the Christmas stuff, and everything else Fen does for Gnarly. I mean, she's got even more on her plate now she's the mother of a dragon king. I volunteered my services. So I have a job and shall be going out to work and therefore you will have time for yourself. Our own wedding was so beautiful, it suddenly made sense. I know it's around the time of the babies being due, but I have a feeling it will all work out."

I saw then why he'd looked so happy. Because he'd found a new purpose. A new job, but one that he was exuberant about, and our wedding had been spectacular.

"Oh, love, I'm excited for you. I just know you'll do a fabulous job, and while you're out I'll have time to read, which I've really been missing."

"See, it's all working out. And I won't say a word if you buy a zillion books from *Books and Buns*. Whatever makes you happy."

"Oh, I shouldn't need to. Mya said she would let me borrow from the library turrets," I informed him.

"Wow. That's very kind of her. She's been better of late, hasn't she, with you? Not as paranoid."

"Yes, she finally seems to be getting the message that there's nothing between me and Death. I've tried to explain that there never really was. And then once I was having the babies, she seemed to accept that even more."

"That's good then. That you can see the woman without her glaring at you unnecessarily."

"She even invited me to the turrets to go relax there. Said we could chat books for a while and then she'd leave me to relax if I fancied a change of scenery." I didn't say 'to get away from you' as I didn't want to ruin the moment.

Bernard snorted. "That's funny. Nice, but funny."

"Why is it funny?" I tried to keep the irritation from my voice at his scoffing.

"Like, it's great she's being nicer, but as if you'd go to your ex-boyfriend's house to hang out when you've this amazing suite."

I folded my arms across my chest. "I'm going tomorrow night."

His mouth dropped open. "Pardon?"

"I'm going tomorrow night. To the Home of the Wayward. I'm going to choose some lovely new books, chat with Mya about her recommendations, and then I might come back, or if I fancy it, I might put my feet up on a chaise in the library and read there for a while."

"And what does Death think about this?"

"I don't know. Mya invited me, not him. It's her house as well as his and the libraries belong to her. Jenny made Mya the librarian. I doubt I'll even see him."

"Good. I don't want you hanging around with your ex-boyfriend. It's weird. I hope you don't think we're all going to be friends and double date, Aria."

Suddenly the temperature in the room went from warm to icy.

"That's fine. If they invite us out for dinner, I'll go on my own."

"No, you will not."

"Is that no, you'll come after all, or no you're telling me I'm not allowed? Because you're not in charge of me, Bernard Letwine."

"I'm well aware of that, Aria. You're my wife, not a pet." He sighed. "Look, I'm trying. I've been suffocating you and I know I need to give you space but meet me halfway here. It's hard enough for me to think of my wife being near an ex, but for us to get all friendly? I'm not there yet, and I doubt very much Death is either. He might have found out your true feelings afterwards, but at the time he thought I stole his girlfriend. When I saw him at Mya's fake funeral, it was clear he was still not ready to move on."

"That was before he and Mya fell in love. He couldn't care less now."

"You know that for a fact, do you?"

"Well, no, but he's madly in love. This is ridiculous, Bernard. I just want to go relax and read a book for a bit."

"You can read here."

"No, I can't. Can I? Because you sit staring at me, asking me if I'm okay every five seconds, and I can't concentrate."

"Fine, Aria. You go to Mya's. Or to the café. Or anywhere else you feel you need to go. Once the babies arrive, I'm sure we'll be too busy to argue about you having time to yourself, so go have your freedom. I won't stand in your way. There's my new career to concentrate on, so I will focus on that."

"Are you being sarcastic, or moody? Is your 'fine' that one women reserve for when they're anything but?"

Bernard sprung up off the bed and began pacing. "What more do you want from me, Aria? You say you want to relax a little and for me to be out of your hair. Your wish is my command. Enjoy your time. But you won't find me being all Brooding Bernard. I'm going to arrange this wedding and enjoy myself, and I'll take some time for me before the babies come."

"So I can go to Mya's?"

"Like you said, I'm not in charge of you. You can do whatever you want."

I should have been happy, but an unease swept through me because clear in his words was the implication *and so will I*. And I realised it had been a long time since Bernard had done his own thing and I didn't know how to feel about that.

CHAPTER SEVEN

Bernard

I was beyond frustrated now. It didn't seem to matter what I wanted; my wife wasn't interested in taking my feelings into account. She would just do as she liked. Well, fine, and yes, I meant it in the way that's not fine at all. The way that's 'you do that then and see where it gets you' kind of 'fine'. Obviously, I wouldn't say that to Aria as I didn't want staking, but I would go and do what I wanted. It was time for me to go back and remember the Bernard's of the past, and to work out what future Bernard would be. I wanted to be the best father imaginable and so it was time for me to put myself second. The babies would always come first, but the carrier of them, my dear wife, could have the me-time she wanted now. In spades.

I spent the rest of the day prepping for my meeting with Fenella tomorrow. I went into London and bought new stationery, all the latest bridal magazines, and made some mood boards, and set up spreadsheets. By the time I'd finished I was dead excited about my upcoming meeting with Fen.

Aria had spent her time mainly on the sofa reading. It's what she said she wanted so I hoped she enjoyed it.

One thing I knew for sure. It was usually me who bowed down in any argument, but this time it wasn't happening.

"Would you like to come for a walk around the grounds,

Bernard?" she asked me after several hours, her head popping around the office door. "I'm very well rested and now I'm almost boggle-eyed after all that reading. It looks a lovely evening."

"Why not," I replied. "I've got everything ready for my meeting with Fen tomorrow. Just give me a minute to put everything in my briefcase. I'll be out shortly."

She left the room and I smirked. She'd come to me.

"Just think. In a few months we'll be out here pushing the babies around," Aria said, as we walked in the gardens. She took a route away from the statue of her that had been erected when her pregnancy had been announced. Vampire pregnancies were rare, and we'd been inundated with visitors. In the end, Merrin had created a sculpture of Aria that other vampires could visit and stroke for good luck. It protected both Aria *and* the visiting vampires, believe me.

I beamed with happiness thinking about having two children. With vampire fertility being so hit and miss we'd not dared to long for one child, never mind being blessed with two. We just thought if it didn't happen, we'd go the usual route of applying to adopt a child who'd been sired by a rogue vamp. That happened occasionally and those children needed a lot of love and support.

The babies decided to kick then. Aria grabbed my hand and held it to her stomach. We gazed at each other; all arguments forgotten as we marvelled in our good fortune.

The next afternoon, I was due at Fen's at three pm, but I'd had an idea before then, so I called in at the café and asked for Lawrie.

"If you need advice on relationships, I'm flattered, because my wife is completely and utterly satisfied in all ways of the word, but there are counsellors at the Letwine mansion to save me from being bored of listening to people's problems, so I suggest you go there," he said, much to Callie's complete and utter disbelief.

"That's not what I'm here for," I said.

Lawrie preened and ran his hands though his hair. Callie

elbowed him, hard. "Not near the food. Go get a pink hairnet if you're standing around here."

"I'll be but a moment. Bernard has clearly come to tell me how amazing I was yesterday, and I think you should hear it. See how lucky you are."

"You'll be lucky if I don't take a marshmallow kebab and stake you with it," she replied.

He sighed and came out from behind the counter. "She's just up for some angry hate sex, I reckon," he winked. His fae wife didn't have his super-hearing and for the sake of his future undead life I was grateful.

We sat at an empty table.

Lawrie drummed his fingers on the tabletop. "So....?"

"I wondered if you fancied a night out?"

He nodded. "Sounds good. I can come to The Vampire's In(n)."

I shook my head. "No, I'm expanding my interests and horizons. So I thought I'd come here to Gnarly and we could call in at the bistro to start and then take it from there."

"Take it from there? What has got into you lately? Are we going on a pub crawl?"

"Yes. I think we should invite all the men. Letwine vampires and your Gnarly friends and have a fantastic night out. In fact," I said, warming up the idea. "It can be Stan's bachelor night. He'll be too busy nearer the time, so let's have it as soon as possible. I'll check in with him when I've been to see Fen."

"Count me in. Will there be strippers?"

Callie was behind him at that point clearing a table.

"Or a lapdancing club?"

I was trying to warn him with my eyes, but Lawrie just burst out laughing. "Your face, Bernard, I can hear and scent my wife behind me. It's you I'm winding up, not her. Is she looking suitably angry though?"

"Nope, your wife is just rolling her eyes," Callie said. Lawrie turned to her smiling. "Lawrie, honey, if you want to hang with strippers or at a lap dancing club, you go for it. Just don't forget that Fen will be having a hen do and that we'll be up to all sorts." She winked at him then and I watched his eyes flash red.

"You're just not amusing," he said to her.

She giggled, thoroughly amused even if he wasn't, and I'd bet my life that Fen's party would end up a lot wilder than Stan's.

"Are you staying for a drink, Bernard?" she asked me, and I shook my head. "No, thank you. I'm off to Fen's now to discuss wedding arrangements."

"I wish I could have seen what your wedding was like. Lawrie said you went all out?"

"I did," I said, remembering the day fondly. "It was at the Letwine mansion, and I had the place looking magical. It was the height of summer and the evening we married was beautifully warm. I'll be creating the opposite for Fen and Stan's winter wedding. I'm just so excited about the whole thing. It's given me something new to think about."

"I can't wait. We'll be being invited so I'll get to see this one."

Lawrie worried at his lip. "Callie, you thought our wedding was okay, didn't you? I mean, we just went to Vegas."

"Lawrie, our wedding was perfect. I'd have married you anywhere as long as you were there," she said.

"*Dela*," Lawrie shouted at the counter. "You'll have to run the place yourself for a bit with Ginny's help if necessary." He grabbed his wife and in seconds they were gone.

"Bloody possessive vampire males," Dela huffed. "No respect for anyone else."

"Sorry, it's our biology," I said to her. "Anyway, I'd help you myself but I'm off to see Fen."

Fenella invited me into her home, as she needed to. It was true a vampire had to be invited over a doorstep. Most vampire folklore was just made-up nonsense, but that particular rumour was true. Otherwise, there wouldn't be many people left on earth as my kind would have helped ourselves like an all you can eat buffet.

Sitting at her dining table, I looked at the empty space, apart from two coasters, and two place settings, with a tray in the middle with scones, and red velvet cupcakes.

"Would you like a pink lemonade and a red velvet while we chat? I popped in at the café earlier."

JUST MY SUCK

"Yes, please, that would be lovely." From what I knew of Fen, the person who organised all the events in Gnarly, I'd expected her to have her own mood board on the table and a file full of ripped out papers.

"Where are all your own ideas for the wedding?" I asked her.

"Truth? I'd only had a few and decided to scrap those and start afresh today. Let's get some cake and I'll let you in on a secret, and why I'm so very glad you've appeared like my own... I was going to say fairy godmother, but you're my vampire godfather."

I didn't tell her that would be someone hired to serve up justice. It would ruin the whole vibe where I was wanted and appreciated.

Fen made herself a coffee, put my pink lemonade in front of me, and I selected a cupcake while she got herself a scone, jam, and clotted cream.

"I've found myself not able to plan for the wedding, because my last relationship went so spectacularly wrong that it took me years to finally trust another man." Fen's head lowered. "I love Stan with all my heart and feel more for him than I ever felt with Joseph, but it went so wrong before. What if I've misjudged again?"

"Misjudged Father Christmas?" I said. "I think we can safely say not only does he love you, but this is the guy who makes wishes come true at Christmas for everyone."

"But does he?" she said softly. "It's a question I've never dared ask."

She was confusing me now.

"Huh?"

"The naughty children. They're always told they won't get presents. Does Stan deny some children a Christmas?"

"Only Stan can tell you that."

"I know." Fen sighed. "But if he tells me he does, then I don't know what that will do to my feelings."

"Fen, you need to be able to talk to Stan and deal with any of these issues before we arrange a venue."

"I know," she said glumly. "Thank you, Bernard. You're telling me what deep down I already know, but I wanted to run it past you. I know you're from outside the village, but I've watched you. I watch all visitors who come into Gnarly. Initially, to protect the place, and then I grow fond of you all as you join the Gnarly family so to speak."

I felt all warm inside at her saying I'd joined the family.

"Look, Fen. You do need to talk to him, but I was thinking of setting up a bachelor party as soon as possible for Stan. It was one of the things I was going to discuss today. So how about we set that up and I can also see Stan's feelings for you myself. Gain an outside perspective."

"Thank you. I'm sure my gut is right that he's the love of my life, but I thought that once about Joseph." She slammed her plate down on the table. "Damn that man. I'd buried him deep inside, and then he had to resurface and then die. Now Jason is among all the dragons, and I can't run away from the past anymore."

"None of us can, Fen." I patted her hand. "Mine comes up all the time, but we do learn to let it affect us less. The key is to replace the bad memories with good ones." I told her about the Eiffel Tower. "So you see, it's still a place that can bring me trauma, but it's also where I met my wife. The key to your future happiness is to face what happened in your last marriage, and then have the most amazing wedding to the true love of your life, and that's what I feel Stan is, Fen."

She grinned. "I really hope so. I will talk to him later, about everything."

"And can you confirm a date suitable for holding the stag do please. The sooner the better, so it's not in the run up to Christmas."

"Let me call him now," she said.

I waited while she chatted, and she turned to me with a raised brow. "Is tomorrow evening too soon?"

"Nope, tell him it's a date," I said. "We'll be starting at the bistro. I'll call him later with a time."

She did and ended the call.

I fished my vision boards out of my briefcase. "Okay, Fen. Let's start with what venue you have in mind and work from there. Also, though we'll loosely discuss dresses today, I will make an appointment for you to try some and come with you. Feel free to also invite a friend, although they'll need to be okay with vampire travel."

"I might ask Charity or Dela along," she said, "but we can get into London and meet you there."

"We're not going to London," I said. "We'll be going to Paris."

CHAPTER EIGHT

Aria

I was feeling extremely well rested. After we'd returned from our walk, I'd been left to read some more. Bernard had ensured I had my quota of blood, more now that I was growing two babies, and I was feeling very mellow.

Seeing as he was busy meeting Fenella to talk about her wedding arrangements, I decided I would spend the day getting the nursery more organised, interspersed of course with more reading. Later, I was off to the turrets to choose some more books, which was exciting now it looked like I was going to get plenty of time to do so.

I pushed open the door of the nursery and had a look at the story so far. We didn't know the sex of the babies and so the walls were cream. I'd been concerned about any wooden items, so there were a lot of wicker baskets and a wicker blanket box. Ginny had made us a wooden one, bless her, but I'd put that in our guest room. I didn't want any splinters of wood anywhere near my precious babies.

Placing my hands on my stomach, the babies seemed to sense the warm and wriggled slightly. I marvelled at the miracles in my tummy, feeling so lucky. We'd bought some clothes and toys and I flicked through the rail of new-born clothing, getting all teary at the smallness of it. Who'd have thought Aria Letwine could get so soppy!

I spent the next hour removing price tags from the clothes and getting them ready to be laundered. I didn't trust myself to not shrink them, so I decided I'd go to see Fenella at the laundrette tomorrow and ask her advice about how to keep baby clothes in tiptop condition. Bernard usually did all our laundry, but I wanted to do these myself.

Selecting a holdall, I placed the items carefully inside, once more revelling in their cuteness. It was hard to believe that in a couple of months there would be actual babies wriggling inside them.

Walking over to a mobile hanging over one of the bassinets, I turned it, listening to its musical lilt. Butterflies exploded in my tummy and the babies wriggled again. This was what I'd needed. Some time to gather my own thoughts and walk around the babies' space and begin to imagine the future. No disrespect to my husband, but anytime I came in here when he was around, he'd appear too and start his own conversations. Did we need more blankets? Should we put a bed in here? He threw out so many questions, I didn't have time to process them and think of what I really did need. Now I was alone, I sat on the nursing chair in the room, and had time to go through what I imagined a day in the unlife of a new vampire mum would be and made a mental list of some things I needed.

Bernard arrived home later that afternoon looking happier than I'd seen him in a long time. I was also feeling content after my peaceful day. It was doing us both good to have a little time apart.

"How did your meeting with Fen go?"

Bernard sat down in the chair adjacent to me. "Very well. We've come up with a general theme for the wedding—fresh starts. You know, New Year, new marriage, letting go of the past etc."

"Very appropriate for the time of year," I replied.

"And also, we set up Stan's stag do. It's tomorrow, beginning at the bistro. So I won't be in tomorrow evening."

"Why so early? The wedding's not for three months." As soon as the words were out of my mouth, I realised the answer. "Oh of course, Father Christmas will already be getting busy."

"Indeed. So tomorrow it is."

"Look at us getting all sociable. I'll be setting off to Mya's at seven."

A shadow of frustration flittered over my husband's face, but he refrained from saying anything. It still annoyed me though. What also annoyed me was he didn't ask how my own day had been.

"I removed the tags from the babies' clothing and I'm going to pop to the launderette tomorrow and ask Fen to show me how best to wash them," I said.

He waved a hand in dismissal. "Oh, I'll sort all that," he said, in his usual way. "You'll be busy nursing them; I'll do the cleaning up work."

"I want to know how to do things myself, Bernard." I would have cursed under my breath in frustration were it not for a vampire's incredible hearing skills.

He paused for a moment and then nodded. "Fair enough. If the wedding comes up in conversation, I would appreciate it if you could please refrain from adding any of your own opinions, if you will. This is my project with Fen after all."

"Noted," I said, while inwardly I thought, *petty twat.*

"Okay, I'm going to go to the office and put all my project things away and update my spreadsheets. I'll see you when you're back from Mya's. Have a nice time," he said through gritted teeth.

"I will."

By the time I arrived at Mya's I was pleased to be out of the house. I knocked on the large outside door of the mansion. It was answered by a wizened man with a wooden leg who closed the door in my face.

I knocked again.

He opened it a fraction. "Yer not welcome ere, yer wretched urchin. I've not fergotten what yer did to my boss."

"Spence." Mya's voice came from behind him. "I've invited Aria here tonight to look at and borrow some books. If I can look past her past with Death, so can you."

He bared his rotten teeth at me. "I'll be watching yer, and so will Jenny. Especially around the book. Although, I'll give yer one advance warning," he said. "You touch that book and yer'll risk those babies. It knocked Mya out and she's far stronger a vampire than you."

I attempted to reassure him. "I come in peace, Spence, just to borrow some fiction romance books. I'm a reformed character since I became a Letwine vampire."

"If you think the De Luca's aint been watching yer, yer more stupid than I thought. And I thought yer were very stupid, wi how yer treated Death."

"Get back to the second floor. That's an order." Mya pointed upwards.

He rolled his eyes but went on his way.

"Sorry about that," she said. "Come in and we'll go straight to the library."

For a moment, I thought I'd made a mistake in coming here. As I walked through the entrance it took me back to six years ago and the last time I'd visited. A past where I'd been a very different Aria indeed. Aria De Luca. An Aria that I may have attempted to put behind me, but that Spence remembered very well.

Six years ago

"So this is where I live," Death said as we stood at the foot of the hill. We'd been dating for a week, and he genuinely thought we'd bumped into each other in the corridor of a London hospital. Of course, in reality I had been stalking him like prey for weeks. My sire, Tiana De Luca, wanted The Book of the Dead, a tome so powerful given it shared news of how and when death would occur. She craved the power it wielded and dreamed of all she could potentially do with it. I had been ordered to seduce Death himself and find an opportunity to get the book for her. And if Tiana De Luca ordered you to do something, you did it.

"What a beautiful home," I acknowledged. It was gothic: black and turreted and set against the sky with its high position. We flew up to the top and Death opened the door and invited me inside.

That had been his first mistake. If he had revoked the invitation each time, I'd have never been able to enter without his knowledge.

JUST MY SUCK

Not that I'd ever managed to get near the book anyway. Spence had made sure of that. The bastard had never let me out of his sight when I'd let myself back in following that first date... but I was getting ahead of myself in my memories, and I returned to that first visit.

The floors were a black and white chequerboard of a pattern. Death took me through to his sitting room, another dark room with scarlet carpets and thick black drapes and invited me to take a seat. I looked around but there was nothing of interest for me to see here. This wasn't where the book was kept.

We chatted and I brought the conversation around to reading. I genuinely loved books anyway, having been brought up by well-read parents before I'd been turned, and Death had told me about the turrets in the mansion. He'd only been in position for a few years, his past a mystery to him. No memories of any life he may have led before that time.

"May I visit the turrets sometime?" I asked him.

"Of course. How about now?" He was so agreeable. I actually felt guilty of taking advantage of him. Still relatively new to his role, Death's life was black, and he saw me as a shade of grey. A chink in the darkness. Still somewhat like him, a member of the dark side, but with me came hope of an ally in the void, and maybe even more of a connection. I saw how his eyes looked at me: attraction, but most of all, vulnerability. One which I intended to exploit. He was a good-looking man, of that there was no doubt, but I preferred blondes, truth be told.

And so we went upstairs. But not to his bedroom, to a secret door on the second floor, which when opened gave access to the main turret filled with books and cared for by a mysterious librarian.

As I stared at the hundreds, maybe even thousands of books, I knew The Book of the Dead could well be hidden among all these tomes. I would need to return when Death was otherwise engaged.

Still, I spent some time requesting different books to look at from the librarian. I had to communicate via writing in a notepad left on a desk there, so the place remained silent.

The collection was incredible. A mix of true literary greats and first editions, along with a mix of other, more modern tales. Death allowed me to borrow a romance book, and I figured that gave me the perfect reason to enter the library again on Tiana's mission for me.

That night I allowed Death to kiss me before I left. His kiss made me feel nothing. His yearning for connection made me feel guilty.

"I think we'll continue this non-conversation upstairs," Mya said, and I came out of my memories. I still stood in the hallway.

"You pushed through my guards?" I asked.

"I'm very strong, and you allowed me in," she said. It was true. I'd seen no point in denying Mya the memories I felt she was bound to ask me about anyway.

"I feel better, knowing you never really liked him," she said. "That's silly though, isn't it? He still liked you."

"Your issues of jealousy will cause you problems until you accept we all have a past," I told her. "The man is in love with you."

She nodded. "Come on. Let's get you all comfy and sorted with some books."

I followed her upstairs. As we headed towards the turrets, I could feel that Spence was in the shadows, watching me.

CHAPTER NINE

Aria

The library hadn't changed much since the last time I'd been here, except maybe there were a few more piles of books around, needing to be put away. It was still painted bright orange and had comfortable velvet couches.

"Do you miss working at *Books and Buns*?" Mya asked me as I stared around, once more taken aback by just how many books were in here.

I turned to face her. "I really do. It was nice to be around other women and have a little time to myself."

"Do you think you'll return after the babies? Part-time maybe?"

"No. Ginny is so happy working there, and if I can just get a nice balance with my husband, I'd like to be a stay-at-home mum."

"But you don't want a stay-at-home dad?" Mya gestured to the chaise in the room, and I sat down. She sat beside me.

"I really don't. Not just because he'd drive me insane, but because I wish for my husband to find his own joy. I have reading. As you know yourself it's an escape. Bernard has had nothing of late. He's lost his way. Now he's helping co-ordinate Fen and Stan's wedding, I'm hoping he sees a potential new career. Slowly, over the years of us being together he's narrowed his world."

"Fen's excited. She's been telling everyone about how he's taking her to Paris to look at dresses. It's good to see her like that.

She's always taken care of everyone else. Now she's being taken care of."

My mouth dropped open. "Oh my god, Mya, that's it. Bernard has a need to take care of people. As long as that need is satisfied, he'll be happy. And soon he'll have the babies. That's why he's driven me crazy. It's something deep within him. And do you know what? I think it goes back to his turning. His mother forced him to care for her, and even though she wasn't a kind woman, he always felt guilty that she was left behind." I briefly told her how Bernard had been turned. "You'll keep that to yourself though, won't you? I think Bernard would be pissed off if he knew I was sharing personal stuff with others. He's very private."

"Of course. Death's the same. Every time I mention us having sex while we're out in public he gets really annoyed with me. Yet he's quite happy to let people know I nickname him Big D. Men, huh?"

"Indeed," I said, "and also, congratulations." I winked.

"You never had experience of the big D then?" she asked nervously.

"Nope. Just a few kisses that I honestly had no interest in. Like you read in my mind, I was only with him to get to The Book of the Dead."

"And Spence stopped you?"

"Yup. Him and the librarian. I let myself back in after my date with Death and he followed me around. I didn't take him as a threat as he was a spirit, but I soon found that he and the librarian could use books as missiles, and I quickly got out of there."

"You'll be glad of that."

"Is it true the book knocked you out?"

Mya nodded. "I was in a temper and tried to push it off my desk. That was all. I flew across the room, hit the wall, and the next I knew I was coming around from unconsciousness. The book commands respect and reverence. It is more powerful than us all. The De Luca vampires would never have been able to get hold of it. The most powerful species in the world put together don't hold as much energy as that book. It holds the future of all species within its pages."

"Wow. I had thought of asking to see it, but do you know what, I don't think I'll bother," I said.

Mya went on her phone. "You can see an illustration of it on the app." She showed it me. "It's very old and extremely creepy looking. Took me a while to get used to handling it, though a part of that is because I thought it might attack me again."

I said nothing because the truth was that I had eventually seen the book, but I dismissed the thought from my mind in case Mya decided to read me again. I could block but she was immensely powerful and could possibly push past it. I turned my thoughts back to the books.

Mya looked settled on the chaise longue, and I allowed myself to relax. There was a footstool, and I pulled it towards me and put my feet up.

"Are you okay? Need anything?" she asked.

"Nope, this is perfect," I said. "Who'd have thought we'd end up spending time together like this?"

"Not me, that's for sure." Mya laughed.

"You and Death have almost been together a year now, right?"

She nodded. "Next month, yes."

"Death and I were together a few weeks, and that's together as in I hung around and had dates with him to try to get to the book."

"I'm getting that now. He still liked you though, Aria. Found you attractive. Wanted to date you."

"He did, but then I'm pretty hot." I laughed and it felt good. "Many men have been attracted to me, Mya. It's surface shit. And I have vampire allure in spades. That's why Tiana wanted to use me. Death wasn't a human to be mind-controlled by suggestion, but he was new enough to not realise I still had an effect."

"You mean your vampire allure may have called to him as well as the fact you're hot?"

"Could be. But all that matters is now, Mya."

"You're right. And right now is about finding you some books to take home and letting you and those babies have a rest, so, as the librarian now, please tell me what kind of books you'd like to peruse."

And that was what we did for the next thirty minutes. Then Mya left me to curl up on the chaise and read.

A couple of hours later, I found Mya and said my goodbyes. She gave me a message for Kaf, and armed with seven new books, I returned home.

To find Kaf sitting beside Bernard on the sofa. The two of them chatting like best friends.

Well, that was an interesting turn of events.

"Did you have a good evening?" Kaf asked, getting off the sofa and moving to the chair. I sat beside Bernard after putting my books down on the coffee table.

"Really good, thanks."

"The babies okay?" they asked in unison.

I rolled my eyes. "One of you fussing at once is bad enough."

"Tough," Kaf said. He pointed to Bernard. "Husband: it's his job to fuss." Then he pointed at himself. "Angel: put here to protect babies. My job to fuss."

"I guess I should be honoured you at least allowed me the freedom of visiting Mya."

Kaf looked shifty.

"You followed me, didn't you?" I sighed.

"It's my job. I made sure you got there safely. Mya took over from there, and then I followed you back, getting here a few seconds before you."

"I can't wait to have had these babies and be free," I said.

Kaf cackled at that. "Free, after having two children at once? Oh, that's hilarious. You do crack me up."

"Is that the time? I think you need to leave," I said grumpily.

Bernard stood up as well as Kaf. "Not you," I yelled.

He shared a look with Kaf. "Worth a try," he said, and they both burst out laughing.

"Oh, it's like that, is it? Becoming all chummy now, and picking on your watch?"

"I'll see you tomorrow night," Kaf said. "Obviously, I need to keep an eye on the babies, but I should be able to manage to fit a quick drink in to help Stan celebrate his last nights of freedom."

"He's not going to prison. He's getting married," I stated.

The two of them shared another look.

"Piss off," I told them both, grabbing one of my books and refusing to look at either of them again.

The next morning, I set off to the launderette. Pushing open the door, I breathed in deep. The smell of fresh laundry was incredible, and my olfactory senses took it all in.

"Bernard said you were popping in," Fenella said, walking out from behind the counter and coming to hug me. I was not a hugger, and so I basically defrosted in her embrace, from frozen statue to a limpet. Her hugs were sooooo good.

"Why am I not surprised that my husband called ahead, rather than letting me just go about my business?" I huffed.

"He was making sure I'd be in. Sometimes it's Jason who's on shift, and he felt you'd rather see me. Not that Jason is here much now he's a dragon king."

"Uuugghhh. It's even more annoying when he's done the right thing," I whined.

"He said he was getting on your nerves. That's why he offered to be our wedding planner."

"He's gone from my sexy protector to my over-protective suffocater," I told her.

"Oh dear. I have the absolute opposite problem at this time of year. I don't see enough of my other half, unless I go help him at work, and that's not exactly ideal when I already run my own business."

"What will happen when you're Mrs Claus?" I asked. "Surely, you'll have to commit to the Christmas business then?"

"I honestly don't know," Fen answered, and I noticed how tired she looked. "I'm supposed to, and I'd like to, but I've run the launderette for so long... I always thought Jason would take it over, and he doesn't intend to stay the dragon king longer than necessary. But I'm not sure he wants to run a launderette business. Anyway, take no notice of me. I've much to think about and that's why I'm glad your husband is helping me with the wedding at least. That way I might enjoy it, rather than seeing it as another chore."

I put a hand over my mouth. "Fenella! Your wedding will not be a chore. It shall be the happiest day of your life. Bernard will make it the day of your dreams, and Stan will take care of the night." I winked. "And Bernard said I wasn't to interfere, but what about we take a little trip to London to sort out the night attire?"

"That would be lovely, but I don't want to be dragging a heavily pregnant woman around with me."

I waved her off. "I shall shop too. For things after my babies are born. It will be nice to experience a little decadence."

"Well, that would be lovely, but you make sure you run this past your husband. I don't think buying my wedding night trousseau is on his to-do list, but you never know with his attention to detail."

"We could go this evening, while they are out on the stag do. The shops are open until ten pm now. I will clear it with Bernard and let you know."

"Ooh okay. Maybe I can get something a little extra for when Stan gets home tonight too!" Fen grinned. "Now, let's have a look at that bag of baby things you've brought. I'm a long way off grandchildren myself, so let me coo over all these lovely things."

Fen instructed me on labels and was honest with me about the fact that as babies make mess with puke (of which ours would be red), I was better separating things into clothes for 'best' and the everyday, throw in the washing machine items. She advised I bought a few more red bibs and babygrows, and muslin cloths for my shoulder. By the time I left I felt much more confident about things.

I was just considering popping to say hello to my friends in Books and Buns when a shadow crossed me, and I saw a blast from my past head down the path between the end of the shops and Stan's.

It couldn't be...

But as I followed the trail, despite my brain yelling for me to whizz home, I turned the corner and came face to face with Tiana De Luca.

"Wow, someone's been busy," she said looking pointedly at my stomach.

"How are you here?" I asked.

"How am I here? Well, I whizzed here, dear daughter. But that's not what you mean, is it? You mean how did I manage to escape Hell?"

I swallowed.

"The thing is, when you sent me to Hell, you upset the apple-cart so to speak. A human got sent to Heaven to even things out. And Heaven and Hell have been busy with this anomaly. Trying to work out how to fix it. They cast out the angel, and then they cast me out too. The difference was, no-one noticed me escape the basement at The Home of the Wayward because I could whizz straight out."

My mind tried to process everything she was saying.

"I've spent a little time, finding my feet, and now I'm back," she said. "And you and I... we have unfinished business, don't we, daughter? I'll be in touch," she said, and she whizzed away. Leaving me standing there shaking.

CHAPTER TEN

Bernard

Aria had been quiet since her return, but she'd told me she was okay, and I left it at that, since otherwise we'd be having another row about me fussing. She'd arranged to go shopping with Fen later, so I took it as being another pregnancy mood. One of many.

I was excited about going out. It had been ages since I'd gone out socially, and this was not only a chance to hang out with my best friend, but also a chance for me to mingle more with some other species from the Fell. It would do me good.

Arriving at the bistro half an hour early at seven thirty, I walked inside to find a gentleman trying to get the waitress' attention.

"Chantelle, stop pretending like you don't see me," the guy hissed. "Or I'll do a spell so I'm all you see."

She looked behind him to me. "Bernard! Good to see you. Let me show you to the large table I've set for you at the back of the bistro. Connor will join you shortly. He's just finishing getting ready." Connor was the owner of the bistro and Kaf's younger brother.

I followed her to the table and found the guy who'd been trying to get her attention came with us too.

Chantelle took my drink order, carried on ignoring the man, and then left. He held out a hand to me.

"I'm Saint. I own the pizza parlour here in Gnarly. I've come to help celebrate."

"Ah." I shook his hand. "Good to meet you... but I have to ask—"

He sighed. "Chantelle and I had a few dates back near Valentine's Day, and then things went wrong. We weren't talking and now she's acting like I don't exist at all."

"Oh dear," I replied.

Saint shrugged. "It is what it is. Tonight, we're here to celebrate the one and only Father Christmas having found his true love. My own lack of a love life shall be pushed to the furthest reaches of my mind."

"We shall have a great night," I reassured him. "I'm Bernard, and I'm organising the wedding."

"So I hear. Marvellous thing you're doing, so that the two of them can concentrate on Christmas. And with two babies due too. You're a braver man than I."

"And they say men can't multitask." I held up my hands. "I shall show people that isn't true at all."

"A baby in each arm, as you direct people to the left or the right, hey?" Saint said.

"It'll work out. What's so difficult? As long as they're fed, changed, and happy, they can stay with Mummy while Daddy goes out to work."

Saint looked at me for a second too long, which was unnerving. Then he leaned closer. "I'm not supposed to use my magic for such things, but if you have to bring them along and need me to freeze them, let me know. It's only a temporary thing. For God's sake don't ask Chantelle to do it though, unless you plan on calling one Elsa."

"Erm, thanks," I said, but then other guests began to arrive, thankfully ending this strange conversation.

It appeared I was woefully unprepared for the reality of Santa's stag do. Things had gone well at first, with Lawrie, Jason, Merrin, Connor, and Kaf arriving, before Stan himself walked in with his son, Nick. More villagers then turned up: the rest of the men from Gnarly, most of whom I'd never met. The bistro began to get crowded, and I saw Chantelle bite on her lip while looking over at the table.

Connor turned to me. "Few more than we were expecting, Bernard. How many more are coming?"

"I only asked around a dozen. I'm not sure where the others are coming from," I admitted. Watching, I saw Chantelle asking people to begin queueing, and then she made her way over.

"Bernard, I can't let any more people in. Health and safety on numbers. What do you want to tell them?"

I ran a hand through my hair, feeling a little lost. My plan had been drinks and food here, and then drinks in London, but now I had queues forming outside to celebrate.

"Stan?" I asked. "Did you invite a few more people to your do?"

"I did." He grinned. "Couldn't help myself. Joy's infectious, right, and I'm Santa. Love making people smile, so I asked the rest of Gnarly, a few family members, and also the elves."

I froze in place for a moment. "Th-the elves?"

"Yeah. Feel bad I forgot, to be honest. Can't leave my staff out, can I?"

"And how many elves do you have here in Gnarly?"

"Erm, couple of hundred."

I looked around the restaurant and at the door. Stan's eyes followed my gaze.

"Oh, er, should I have not done that?"

"Just need to engage my back-up plan," I said, with a lot more conviction than I actually had. What the hell was I going to do? Chantelle was still standing waiting for my instructions.

"Move things to the park," a guy standing to my right said. That was weird, I'd never even noticed this guy arrive.

But he was correct. The park would fit everyone in it. It was just what to do with everyone when they were there.

"I'll get my staff cooking up a batch of pizzas," Saint told me, clapping me on the shoulder. "I'll see you at the park shortly."

"Thank you," I told him.

"I've a lot of beer in the cellar coming up to its expiry dates. I'll donate that," Connor added. "Lawrie, you can move fast. Can you help me get it to the park?"

"Sure."

"I can start a bonfire," Jason said. "With just my breath," he added, shoulders back and chest puffing out.

"Okay, let's do this. Venue change. We're off to the park," I told everyone. Only when I turned to thank the man who'd suggested it, he wasn't there, and I couldn't even recall what he'd looked like. I put it down to the stress of the current situation and got up to get things organised.

Thank goodness for mild weather. We all arrived at the park and gathered around, and everyone looked in my direction. What the hell was I supposed to do with everyone now? This had not been in my plans at all.

"Pizza will be on its way soon," I said to the two hundred-ish strong crowd. "So, just grab a beer as they arrive and relax. We're all here to wish the big guy, Stan, an enjoyable stag do, known as a last night of freedom, although he's not actually getting married until January, and so let's have some fun."

"Yay," said all the elves in unison and they all ran at Stan, giggling, and carried him off into the trees.

"What's going on?" I asked everyone left.

Nick was the only one not shrugging his shoulders. "Elves are naughty. And you've just told them to have some fun. So that's exactly what they're doing. Subjecting my father to some stag night shenanigans. Could be a strip club, who knows? But I can hear giggling from the woods, so shall me and you take a trip there to find out?"

I nodded. Lawrie looked around the rest of them. "We will stay and begin to enjoy the beer and pizza." What he was saying to me was he'd keep an eye on things back here. Which was good as I needed to whizz me and Nick further into the trees and hope Santa wasn't enjoying a lap dance rather than Lapland.

"Nick, please help," said a female voice.

"Shit, that's Dela. What's going on?" Nick panicked, dashing towards a large wooden home. I'd not realised anyone lived out here.

She had her hands over her eyes. Meanwhile a slim brunette

JUST MY SUCK

was holding her stomach while laughing and pointing. I followed her finger and saw Stan naked as the day he was born, his white flabby arse cheeks getting as red as his face. He was tied to a tree. The elves were laid on the ground giggling.

"Elves. Not funny," Nick scolded. They all looked at the floor. "Okay, it's a bit funny," he said, "but no more stag do party tricks. Go and get some beer and pizza now." They all happily went on their way. Nick walked over to the tree and picked up his father's clothes before untying him. I walked over to the women.

"Sorry about that. Not used to elves," I explained.

"No one needs to see their boyfriend's dad's naked arse. No one," Dela complained. The woman, who introduced herself as Dela's mother laughed. Once he was dressed again, Stan and Nick came back over.

"What's happening? I thought you were going to the bistro and then into London. Did the elves get lost?" Dela asked.

"Too many of us," I explained. "I slipped up."

"No, it wasn't you, son, it was me," Stan said, huffing. "I got a little carried away and invited the elves and then I got carried away... to the woods. I'm so sorry, Dela."

"I'm used to seeing your ruddy red cheeks... just usually the ones on your face," Dela said, before she burst out laughing. "Anyway, what's the plan now then?"

"Do you have a good music system?" I asked.

Thanks to Dela's iPod and some speakers that stretched outdoors, we were able to get some party tunes on and moved the party up to the park and woods nearer Nick and Dela's home.

Saint arranged a magical spell that meant no harm would come to either Dela and Nick's, or Sheridan's homes and possessions, and we warned people that any rubbish was to be put in the bins provided around the park, especially noting the recycling points. With that the beer and pizza were enjoyed and then everyone boogied.

Stan sure had some moves and he taught us all a few routines.

Dela came out with some refreshing home-made lemonades and waters, and some freshly baked cookies she'd rustled up fast.

I went up to Lawrie, who'd sat on a tree stump. He was so still he looked like he was modelling for GQ.

"Aren't you going to dance?"

"Don't be ridiculous. I'm going to sit here until it's time to go home. Is it time to go home? Please?"

"No. Not yet."

"I agreed to come to the bistro and to London. I did not agree to doing the hokey cokey in the middle of Gnarly Park. And those elves just put something 'in' they weren't supposed to. Are you even keeping an eye on them?"

I sighed.

"If it wasn't for the community of Gnarly coming together tonight, this whole stag do would have been a disaster, Lawrie. Saint did the food, Connor the drinks, Dela the buns and the tunes. What if I can't arrange their wedding? What if I miss something and mess it all up? I should have known Stan would invite the elves."

"Mate, Stan was in the wrong. He should have told you how many people he'd invited. You've been hired to do a job and you're working with Fen, not him. Just ensure Fen is aware that her husband-to-be needs keeping in line. That's her task, not yours."

"But if the wedding goes wrong, that's not what people will think. They'll blame me."

"Bernard," Lawrie stood up and took me by the shoulders. "It's time for you to stand up for yourself. Plan the wedding, and by all means try to think of contingencies. One thing you can learn from this evening is to have back-up plans. But that's where your responsibility ends. His voice lowered. "Your mother was not your responsibility. It was the other way around. Aria is not your responsibility, she's your wife. Stan and Fen? Not your responsibility beyond arranging the wedding as they wish it. After that it's on them. The babies *will* be your responsibility. They'll count on you, and I know you'll be an amazing father. And that's what this is really all about, isn't it?"

I'd have answered but a strange musical sound rose above the dance music. Through the trees I could see the distinct shape of an ice cream van.

"Come, come," Stan said. "Let's go get an ice-cream from Knight."

We formed an orderly queue. I was next to Stan and once we were at the front, he indicated I should go first. The man serving the ice cream looked so familiar, but no matter what I did, I couldn't place him.

Stan asked for a chocolate Feast.

"Thanks for coming, Knight, and for providing the ice creams."

"Anytime, Stan, and I'll try to make the wedding. Though it depends."

"I know." Stan patted the guy's hand. "It'll end soon, I'm sure."

We walked away and I was going to ask Stan about... something. But I couldn't remember what. I stared at the ice cream in my hand.

"Where did this come from?" I asked Stan.

"A friend of mine," he said. "A dear friend of mine." His eyes stared into mine. "You don't remember seeing him at all?"

I shook my head.

"Nightmares fade," he said. "Otherwise, we'd be haunted all day."

"Huh?"

"Knight Mare fades," he mumbled again under his breath. I put it down to too many beers and changed the conversation.

"Hey, Stan. I have a question for you," I said. "At Christmas, what really happens with the naughty kids? Do they not get presents?"

"Of course they get presents," he scoffed. "Obviously, we tease them that they won't get any because we want to do our best to get them to behave, but we always come through for them in the end."

"But surely that means they don't change?"

Stan shrugged. "Some never will, but for some they get their gifts and feel they can't have been so bad then. They feel hope. That present an indication that someone (ie Santa) is looking out for them. To not deliver a present would reinforce a negative. You'd be amazed how much it gives some children a confidence and happiness they'd not had before."

"Fen's very lucky to be marrying you," I told him.

"Nah, I'm the lucky one," he replied. "Come on, let's go dance," he said, heading towards the music.

CHAPTER ELEVEN

Aria

Six years ago

"You've been dating Death for three weeks. Surely, you've learned how to get hold of the book by now," Tiana snapped.

"It's not that simple. Do you think we're the first people to think about stealing it?" I snapped back.

She grabbed me by the hair and pulled me up towards her. Eyes roaring with red fury, fangs bared, I thought I'd finally gone too far.

"I need that book. To be able to see who dies and exploit it. Offer to change things for those who face their demise. So see that you get it for me by the end of this week, or I'll get rid of you and find someone who can help me." Her inference was clear. Get it or regret it. She was going to stake me if I didn't.

Tiana left and I slumped down onto a sofa, placing my head in my hands. I was no further forward in gaining access to the book and from what Spence had warned me, faced extinction that way too. Either way, I lost, but in trying to get the book I at least had a chance, so that was what I'd have to do.

My phone beeped with a text.

Death: I won't be able to meet you later. I have business to do at the Eiffel Tower.
Me: I'll come with you.

Death: It won't be very romantic. I'm soul collecting.
Me: I still want to come.
Death: Okay. Second Floor. Eight pm. Don't be late.

He didn't sound keen on me being there, but I might find out some more information about the book. Also, I might as well enjoy seeing as many beautiful cities as I could, given that it felt like I was on borrowed time.

At eight, I found Death waiting where he'd said he'd be. He turned to me and smiled. He was becoming a little more confident now in my company.

"So some poor person is meeting their end here? You have to feel sorry for them, don't you?" I said to him.

"I can't give you the reasons why I'm here, but it's something that Death himself needs to oversee," he said.

I sighed. "I don't see why you can't share the details. Don't you trust me? What do you think I'm going to do? Go to the press?" I rolled my eyes.

Death pondered for a moment.

Staring at the view, I changed the subject. "Isn't Paris just so pretty? I think next to London, it's possibly my second-favourite city."

He followed my gaze. "It is very easy on the eye," *he said, and as I turned to face him, he blushed slightly. I didn't need to read his mind to know he thought the same of me too.*

But again, I knew I just didn't feel the same way. I wondered how long I could string Death along until he made moves I'd have to reject, which would bring everything to a halt.

"I need to go collect the soul," *Death told me.*

Once more I looked out at the view across Paris, toying with the chain around my neck. If only I had more time. Could spend days here visiting the sights and the boutiques, enjoy the delicious food and drink. Maybe even have a taste of a Parisian or two. Just a nip. I felt a heavy weight in my chest, and my sight seemed to dull, the view becoming less important. I needed to hit out and Death just happened to be the only one around.

"We're in Paris, the most romantic place on earth, and you're not entering into the spirit of things," I spat out.

"I'm not here for romance, Aria. You know why I'm here. To work," Death answered, sighing.

If the relationship hadn't been fake on my side anyway, this would have been the final straw.

"Just go," I said quietly.

He did.

And that's when I sensed I was being watched. My eyes alighted on the pale-blonde haired vampire currently looking me up and down like he was taking my measurements for cloning.

"What the fuck are you staring at?" I shouted. I'd had enough now. I was nothing more than Tiana De Luca's puppet. I may as well head back and take my chances with The Book of the Dead.

The vampire approached me. He was extremely good looking.

He did a mock bow. "Pardonne, ma cherie. It is not often I see a woman more beautiful than Paris."

That accent. He was Northern and yet his French sounded polished. Maybe he'd moved here?

We chatted a little more and I found out he was a Letwine vampire. From another London clan, in his case based in Chelsea.

I was enjoying myself, even posing for a photo or two, as the man had a camera around his neck. Then Death returned.

"Aria, I'm finished here, and now have work elsewhere. Are you coming?"

I looked at the vampire male. Maybe coming here today hadn't been a waste of time after all.

I nodded. "Yes. It was nice to meet you, Mr Letwine. Enjoy the rest of your trip." *I let the vampire see who I was with. The shock on his face was apparent as I let the images of Death fill his mind. I spoke mind-to-mind.*

'We will meet again. I want to see the photos you just took. There is no need to fear Death if you're already dead, don't you think?'

And that's when I knew that somehow I had to survive whatever was coming.

Because I'd never believed in love at first sight before today, but I certainly believed it now.

Knowing Death was out getting another soul, I travelled back to his home.

Spence met me on the second floor once more. "No good can come of this, Aria. Just let the man down gently and sling yer ook."

"I can't," I told him.

His yellowing eyes narrowed on me. "Why?"

"You must have encountered trouble at sea, Spence. Blackmail, corruption. Had to make choices that made you look bad, but gave you no choice?"

"Why do yer think I'm telling yer not to do whatever it is you're clearly here to do."

"Because I don't have a choice," I said truthfully.

"There's always a choice," he replied. Spence tapped the side of his temple. "God gave yer this to think with, so think. Look for an alternative," he said.

"Where's The Book of the Dead?" I asked him.

He let out a heavy sigh, a grim twist set upon his lips.

"I'm gonna show yer around, lassie," he said. "Then yer on yer own."

Spence showed me what Death hadn't. The interview rooms where the wayward found out their fate, the attic, the basement, and finally, Death's own room where his bed and desk were, the book itself casually resting upon his desk like it were nothing special.

Walking towards it, I reached out, all thoughts of attractive vampire males forgotten as the book called to me.

Touch me.

I did. I picked it up and it allowed me to look within. The old leather was soft against my hand. Sitting down on the chair in front of the desk, I placed the tome back down and began to open it. The pages were blank.

Damn it.

Ask me.

Was the book actually communicating with me, or was I losing *my sanity? Was it playing games with me, or genuinely letting me look?*

"Please show me the death of Aria Summers," I asked.

The pages flipped over in front of me, and an entry appeared on the page.

Aria Summers.
Age thirty-one on demise.
Single.
Lives in Farnham, Surrey
Works for family business, produce soap, skincare, bathing products etc.
Family background: Father, mother, two elder brothers.
Friends: Best friend Clarissa. Known since school.
Personality assessment: Resents having to work in the family business, but it's expected. Rebels against authority of any kind. Becoming distant from best friend who now has a family. Yearns for adventure.
Interests: Geography, walking.
Date of death: August 23rd, 1986.
Circumstances behind death: After a quarrel with the family at dinner, Aria goes for a walk, and decides to go into the park to sit on a swing to consider the future. From there she is dragged into the bushes and turned by the vampire Tiana De Luca.

There it was in black on aged paper. A small piece of my history. I'd had an outburst. I still remembered clearly shouting at my parents that I did not want to work there any longer in the family business. That my life was shit. Still single in my thirties, I'd been enjoying a major pity party for one. The frustration was actually with me, but that's not how it had come out. A hormonal rage that I would regret until the years made the memory fade. Either that, or I just pushed it to the outer edges of my mind as what good did revisiting it do? You couldn't rewrite the past.

"Do I die again soon?" *I asked the book.*

Another entry showed.

Aria Summers.
  Age fifty-one (thirty-one). Vampire since 1986.
  Single.
  Lives in Tower Hamlets, London.
  Works for Tiana De Luca: extortion, blackmail, thievery.
  Family background: Father, mother, two elder brothers.
  Friends: None.
  Personality assessment: Wants love. Desperate to find a solution to her current difficulties.
  Interests: Geography, walking, Paris.
  Date of death: August 23rd, 2006.

The irony that I was fated to die on the same day of a different year, and worse, that day was today. I'd not even realised it was the anniversary of my death until now. I'd been too focused on my current circumstances and the fact the book had revealed itself to me without harm. The words flickered in and out on the page, and as they faded, something strange began to happen. They alternated with another death notice.

Tiana De Luca.
  Age: one-hundred-and-six (Twenty-eight).
  Single.
  Lives in Tower Hamlets, London.
  Vampire Leader of De Luca clan.
  Family background: All deceased.
  Friends: Nil.

Personality assessment: Power hungry. Will stop at nothing to get her hands on The Book of the Dead.
Interests: Death, destruction, power.
Date of death: August 23^{rd,} 2006.

So that was the choice then. Clear here to see. Her or me. I remained seated on the chair, even though I knew at any point Death might return. I was frozen in place, needing to think. The book had shown me my options. Now it was for me to work out how I made sure I survived. Thoughts of everything I'd been shown raced through my head.

And then it came to me.

It was a long shot, but it was definitely a chance to get rid of Tiana De Luca. And if I managed that, I wouldn't waste any more of my life. I'd finish with Death, and I would seek out Bernard Letwine, for he was only in Chelsea, not far away at all.

I thanked the book. It could have been tricking me, for I had no place being there, but something deep inside me left me to think that wasn't the case. That this path was pre-determined and my actions would result in one death or another.

Making my way to the room that I felt held the answers, I closed the door on Death's bedroom. Spence was outside the door.

"I know you don't care about me, but I also know you do care about him. For that reason, I need to tell you my plan," I said. "Just in case things go wrong."

Spence sighed. "I'll listen to yer, but only for him, missy. Only for Death."

I nodded and brought him up to speed.

CHAPTER TWELVE

Bernard

I was drunk. Rip roaringly, amazingly drunk. It felt fabulous. Lawrie was now sitting on a park bench while I laid down on the grass. I giggled again.

"Jesus Christ, Bernard. I think it's time you maybe called it a night."

"Not until everyone goes home," I said to him while gazing up at the stars. "I have to be the last to leave."

"I've told you three times now that everyone has gone home."

I sat up quickly. "You have?" The world swam and I laid back down.

"Yup," he said, "and that's why Groundhog Day is happening, because you lay back there, remember something funny and forget."

"Oh my god, when the elves wrapped Santa up and said they were going to deliver him back to Fen. But he'd burst out of the paper so all that was left was a bow on his penis." I clutched my sides with mirth.

Somewhere in the midst of laughter I heard my best friend sigh and then laugh.

The next thing I knew, I was staring at Kaf in the doorway of his apartment.

"Huh? How did I get here?" I asked.

Kaf's top lip curled up at the corner.

"Oh dear. Put him on the sofa and I'll let Aria know he's here."

"I'll do that," Lawrie said. "You just take care of him. He's not used to drinking and enjoying himself."

"When did you get home?" I asked Kaf.

"Bernard, I only stayed an hour. I went to keep an eye on Aria with Fen, remember?"

"Ooohhh yeah, they were going lingerie shopping." In seconds, I felt the evil roll through me. My eyes alighted on Kaf who took a step backward.

"Did you witness my wife in her undergarments?" I snarled.

"No, I did not. I stood outside the store. And you, who would be witness to your wife's undergarments, as she was planning to be wearing them when you got home, are sadly not capable of making the most of her efforts. Do you know how lucky you are? I've had a message from Heaven that I'm not here to date, but to work. How sucky is that?"

I lost my fury and my happiness. "What? My wife is waiting for me, dressed for seduction? I must go to her."

The angel stepped forward and wrapped me in his wings and the last thing I heard was, "Sorry, mate. I'm counting this as for the both of yours protection." Then it went black.

I opened an eye and found myself staring at an unfamiliar ceiling. Sitting up quickly, it took a minute for my vision to catch up with my brain. Kaf sat in a chair in the corner of the room reading a newspaper.

"Good morning, Bernard. Would you like me to accompany you to your apartment now, so that you can get your breakfast blood?"

I felt my brows come together. "Huh? Why do you need to come with me?"

"Aria bought sexy underwear to greet you with when you got home. You were so drunk your best friend figured it was safer he left you here with me and warned your wife about your predicament. Do you want to be alone with her, or would you like a sidekick so that you won't get side kicked, or arse kicked, or any other kind of injury that a hormonal pregnant Aria might decide to bestow upon you."

I didn't need to consider his words.

"Please come with me," I begged. "I'm scared."

After throwing some cold water over my face, I walked with Kaf towards his front door. "I guess I just passed out last night then?"

"You were ninety-five percent there. My angel wings sorted the last five percent."

"Huh?" I had no recollection of this whatsoever.

"I wrapped you in my wings and used my powers to send you straight to sleep. You went out like a light."

Part of me felt awkward I'd been wrapped in his arms, the other was annoyed that I couldn't remember it. I wondered if it felt like a fluffy blanket to have an angel's wings wrapped around you all to yourself.

"Want a cuddle?" Kaf quipped, having clearly read my mind.

"Not right now, but if Aria's in a mood, keep the offer open," I replied.

After walking into the apartment, I found Aria on the sofa in the living room reading. She looked up, but there was no anger on her face, just a sadness. I flew over to her and dropped to my knees.

"I'm sorry, my love, for the state I got myself in last night. I hope I didn't disappoint you too much that I didn't come to the bedroom and see the efforts you had gone to for me?"

"It's fine," she said, in that not fine way. But again, she wasn't angry Aria, or tetchy Aria, or re-arrange your manhood Aria, she was just... morose. In fact, she reminded me of me.

"Are you okay, sweetheart?"

"Yeah," she replied. "Must just be the baby making me tired. I'm just going to read and rest today."

I picked up her hand, "Do you want me to cancel taking Fen to Paris? I can stay here with you?"

She shook her head. "No, Fen is beyond excited about this. You must not let her down. I have Kaf nearby." She shot him a look which was much more herself. "He's shown how good he is at taking care of people last night, so he can make sure I'm okay today."

My eyes met Kaf's.

He sighed. "It's fine with me. If you feel up to it, go off and enjoy Paris with Fen. She was excitedly talking about it last night."

"Once I've had my O-neg I'll be perfectly fine," I said, though I wasn't completely convinced. Maybe I'd have two just to make sure.

It was while I was in the kitchen that it came to me that I'd said the wedding wouldn't interfere with anything and I'd manage to juggle the babies alongside it, and yet here I was leaving my wife, who looked entirely fed up, behind with the angel, while I took another woman to Paris.

I threw the blood packet across the room.

"What's up?" Kaf's voice came from the doorway.

"Other than it's not a bottle so my efforts were like presenting a deflated micro-penis in a King Cock competition?"

"Yep, other than that," he said, opening the fridge door and getting a packet of blood and then starting to assemble a pot of coffee.

"I should be doing these things." I said.

"You do, ninety-nine percent of the time," Kaf pointed out. He leant against the kitchen side. "Bernard, you've got to stop beating yourself up all the time. I'm here for a reason. I was ejected out of Heaven, and I have no idea what's ahead of me. No idea at all of why I was turfed out and if I'll get back. None of us know the future, well, except Merrin gets a few ideas, and one of those is he knows your babies arrive healthily. What else matters? You're not going to Paris on a holiday. You've kindly offered to help Fen and Stan with their wedding. You're allowed to leave your wife's side. Stop assessing everything and making yourself miserable. Our human lives were short, Bernard. I've yet to meet my 'one', never mind start a family."

As he looked at the floor, I felt guilty then.

"You're right. I need to loosen up a little."

He nodded. "Go and find Fen's dream dress and make her day, knowing that your wife is at home resting. I'm basically a housemaid if you think about it."

I shook my head. "No, Kaf, you're a friend," I said, and we both smiled, a moment passing between us. An acceptance of the situation and from me a new understanding that Kaf wasn't having it easy either.

Kaf turned towards the kettle to sort his coffee, and I picked up my blood packet, drank a second, disposed of both and left.

"You look incredible," I told Fenella as she modelled the wedding dress, the fourth one she'd tried. It was a midnight blue wrap-over top, with a slight A-line skirt, and it had a lacy overcoat that was covered in a white snowflake design. It was utter perfection, and as she swished her skirt Fen glowed. She'd already been in a state of complete happiness since I'd reassured her about the naughty children, but now I think she'd give Kaf a run in the glowing stakes.

"This is the one, isn't it?" She stared at herself again in the mirror, turning this way and that.

"One-hundred-percent." I clapped my hands. "Now, let's sort some matching shoes and a little clutch."

An hour-and-a-half later we had the whole ensemble including a tiara with imitation sapphire jewels.

"Charity is doing my hair, so I'll contact her when I get back and we can practice some hairstyles," she said. Charity was her son Jason's girlfriend and Gnarly's hairdresser.

"Perfect," I said. "Now allow me to first treat you to a new signature fragrance for the wedding. It shall be my gift to you, and then let's do lunch."

We sat inside a bistro where we both ordered steak and chips and a glass of red wine. We'd left the dress behind with the designer for a few alterations to the length of the skirt etc.

"Thank you for all this, Bernard," Fen said, her eyes twinkling with joy. "I thought everything was going to be hurried, and I wouldn't get to enjoy it. You're making an old woman very happy."

"Be off with you, old," I scolded. "You are in your prime."

"I'm fifty-five," she said. "Definitely past that."

"Nonsense, fifties are the new thirties," I said. "You've no young babies anymore and you're about to be a newlywed. Kaf let me know you and Aria both bought some very pretty undergarments yesterday." I winked. "Though I didn't get to see my wife's because I was too inebriated."

"You and my fiancé both." Fen laughed. "Stan walked in with a bow on his dick, said he'd got me a present, and then proceeded to faceplant the bed where he fell asleep. I kind of expected it though to be honest. Plenty of time for nice undies with us going to be newlyweds."

"I'm much older than you," I said. "Although eternally thirty-five-ish."

"Does it get tiring?" Fen asked. "Being immortal?"

"I'm beginning to think there are ups and downs whether you're immortal or human," I answered truthfully. "We have counsellors for if we find things difficult and we can go and have a rest, a long sleep. But at the moment things are good. No, actually, great," I answered honestly. Because it was occurring to me more and more that Aria and I were so fortunate right now, with babies coming and the protection of an angel. We'd also been given the apartment Kaf was currently in to extend into by our leader Edmond. Then I remembered how fed up Aria had seemed.

"Was Aria okay when you went shopping?" I asked Fen. "Only she seemed a little down today?"

"She's probably just tired," Fen acknowledged. "I thought she didn't seem quite herself, although I don't know her that well really. I put it down to the fact that she'd done quite a bit that day. I know she's been sorting out the nursery and the babies' clothes, then she came with me. We had a laugh choosing the undies, but when she forgot I was looking, she did look tired. It's good she's resting up today."

I nodded while enjoying a bite of my rare steak. The blood oozed from it like a freshly opened vein. It was delicious.

I noticed Fen was staring at me. Then I noticed my fangs had descended.

"Sorry. Just a really amazing juicy steak," I said.

"No, I'm sorry for staring," she replied. "It's just that I know you're a vampire. You transport me here with that whizzing thing.

JUST MY SUCK

We talk about it, but it isn't until I've seen you around the blood that it's really, really dawned on me that you're a *vampire*, and I'm a human woman. I must really trust you, and from a woman who has major trust issues around men after Josiah, that is praise indeed, Bernard."

"Why, thank you, Fenella, those kind words have made my day," I said, while thinking that this day really had so far proven to be amazing. I'd started what I think they called a 'bromance' with Kaf and had begun to accept his help. Fenella was so happy about her dress and had now said she trusted me when she had trust issues. I grinned at her in sheer happiness.

"You might want to think about not having blood dripping from your mouth when you smile," Fen giggled.

I held up a finger, took a drink of my wine, and then opened my mouth.

"Better?" I asked.

"Slightly. I get the whole red wine thing now," she said. "Now tell me more about being a vampire," she ordered.

So, I did. Feeling comfortable in the company of the woman who'd done so much for the place she lived, I told her all about my turning and how I'd first met Aria, and for the first time in a long time, I let myself enjoy the moment without worrying about anyone else.

CHAPTER THIRTEEN

Aria

I'd not wanted to disappoint Fen and so I'd kept our shopping date. I think I'd managed to be good company and it wasn't like I knew her well anyway, so I didn't worry too much. If anything, it helped to keep my mind off having encountered Tiana. The last thing I'd wanted to do when I got back was actually put sexy lingerie on, so it was a relief when Bernard ended up being that drunk he'd no idea I'd not done it anyway. It also meant that I'd been able to think about things some more without having the man who knew me better than I knew myself nearby.

"What's going on, Aria?" Kaf said, taking a sip of his coffee.

"I know why you're here," I said simply. "With regards to me and the babies," I added. I didn't want him getting his hopes up that I knew more about him than I did.

So I let Kaf know about my bumping into Tiana and how she'd told me that Kaf had been ejected because she had.

"So I went to Heaven in some sort of yin/yang for Tiana being in Hell?"

"Apparently so. I'm sorry that my actions had repercussions for you."

He wet his lips. "Don't be sorry. My death wasn't down to you. And I've been told they recognised me as the angel known as Cassiel and that's why I went to Heaven, so I wouldn't take this

Tiana's word for it." His gaze probed. "She definitely said it was me?"

I nodded. "She said they threw her out and 'the angel' out."

Kaf finished his drink, deep in thought.

"I think we need to go see Mya," he said. "All this is tied into the Home of Wayward Souls. We need to figure this out together."

Thirty minutes later we were sitting in Mya's living room with the lady herself, who flung herself down on the sofa limply.

"Death's going to go insane that another one escaped."

"You mean it's happened before?" Kaf asked.

"Yeah, a while back a demon escaped, but Jenny, the ex-librarian said it was because he had things that needed dealing with in Gnarly itself."

"That's it!" I said. "It's the same for you and for Tiana. I tricked the system into taking her into Hell, and it wasn't my place to do so. Whether I like it or not, she's to continue her undead life here until The Book of the Dead decides."

"What do you mean, you tricked her?" Mya said. "I think before we go any further you'd better get Kaf and I up to date on everything that happened between you and Tiana De Luca.

I nodded and did just that.

Six years earlier

"Hey, Death," I said, appearing on his doorstep with Tiana beside me. I'd told him my sister was visiting and that she liked reading. He'd been more than happy for us to visit the library.

Spence was hovering outside the door and when Death got called away, he asked Spence to make sure we were both okay and that he'd show us safely out.

"What er yer really doing here?" he snarled, once Death had departed. "And who's she, cos she's sure not yer sister."

"Why don't you worry about the fact you need to see an

orthodontist at your earliest convenience and you keep your damn nose out of who I am and why I'm here," Tiana flashed him with a red gaze.

But if she expected Spence to back off, she was mistaken. The man grinned, showing off all those rotted teeth and the spaces in between.

"I'm sorry, do you mistakenly believe you're a match for me? A ghost pirate versus an extremely powerful vampire?" Tiana scoffed.

"No, not me," Spence admitted. "Your hissy fits don't bother me though. Yer sound just like one of me wenches when I cast em adrift. I'll leave you to attempt whatever it is yer think yer ere to do. Good luck." With that he walked away.

My stomach turned over, because I knew one of the two of us didn't leave this house. The question was... who?

"So what now?" Tiana demanded, her patience clearly at its last.

"Now I need to do some work on the computers. I need to trick the book and then it's yours. Do you want me to explain further?"

"God, no. Boring. If it means the book ends up in my hands, then just get on with it."

And that's what I'd relied upon. That Tiana De Luca was power hungry and lazy.

She followed me into the interview room, and I powered up the laptop. I opened up a questionnaire.

"You need to play along. This is how we get it. You answer the questions. You must be truthful though. The book will appear to complete the process and then we grab it," I lied.

"Fine." She waved a hand dismissively.

"Can you confirm the following details?" I asked, querying her name, date of birth, where she used to live. Everything about her.

"So the reason you are in this room today is because the house and book need to decide if your death was good or evil," I stated.

Tiana looked at me then, tilting her head, and I thought she was going to ask me what the fuck I was playing at. But instead, she just smirked.

"Good and evil," she exclaimed. "At first, I thought myself a victim, but actually it was good I died, because then I got to be an evil vampire queen. One who will control life and death itself."

I finished inputting and checked the algorithm. It asked for my decision, and I chose Hell.

"Okay, come with me," I said. "This part's done."

"I thought you said the book would appear?" Tiana stood, with a hand on each hip. "You'd better be giving me this book, Aria, or you can say goodbye to your existence."

"It's downstairs. That's it. It's there. I've tricked the system and you'll be able to get it," I told her. "I've done what you asked. I dated Death to find out the secrets and now all you have to do is lift the book, say an incantation and it's yours." *Everything I said was a lie, but when you were desperate to continue your undead existence it made your words believable.* Tiana huffed but followed me downstairs.

And there it was, on an ornate table carved with evil symbology.

"How do I know it will respond to me?" she said.

I took her hand and said the words of the incantation I'd completely made up.

> "From Death to Undeath,
> This book seeks someone new
> Just call it, command it,
> Unto you."

"Show me you're mine," Tiana ordered. "Show me my death."

Spence had told me it was the thing that everyone asked it for first and he'd been right. In front of Tiana, the pages flicked across, and she dashed over and lifted up the book.

Big mistake.

Because she saw the entry written across it. That her death was today. I pressed the button that called up the demons, and Tiana's horrified gaze was the last I saw of her as the portal opened and a demon collected her.

She was gone. I'd done it.

Or rather, **we'd** *done it.*

Spence stepped out from his hiding place in the corner of the room.

"Now you promise me that you leave him and that we never see you around here again," he said.

"I will break up with him in such a way that he will know there is no return for us. For what it's worth, Spence, I am sorry."

"It's not worth anything," he said, his words hitting me hard in the gut. "You're an evil woman who would use Death in order to save herself.

"It's done now," I said. "You won't have to see me again."

Spence huffed with derision. "All actions have consequences, and I'm sure this will be no different. But I made my choice in helping you. I did it for him, and for the house, and the book. If the book hadn't agreed with what you did it would have hurt you. I don't know what it means that it let you touch it, that it played along, but that's not for me to query. I am but a lodger here. Now please leave."

I rubbed my fingers down my nose and slid them off my chin. "So there you go. That's what I did. How that ties in to Kaf, I don't know. All I know is that Tiana's back and she's really, really pissed. She's also determined to have the book."

"Let her have it then." A rip appeared in the air in the room and a man stepped through it. Hood up, face of Death in place.

"Bloody eavesdropping again," Mya snapped. "How many times have I told you that it's really rude to use portals to disguise the fact you're nosying at me?"

Death just smirked at her. Then he looked at me. "Aria."

"You've heard everything I just said?"

"Yes."

"Shit. I'm sorry."

"For what?" he said. "There I was thinking you just cheated on me with Bernard, but no, actually you didn't want me at all. Just the book. At least I know the truth now."

"The actual truth is that I set it all up. I arranged to see Bernard that night knowing where you'd be."

"How could you..." Death turned around and fixed Spence with a glare. "You again?"

Spence just shrugged.

Mya leaped up. "Do you want me to kick any of their arses for what they did?" And just like that Death dropped his angry façade, sweeping Mya up into his arms.

"No. I'm glad Aria didn't want me. I'm glad Spence helped her finish things. If it wasn't for these things, I wouldn't have met you."

Then he kissed her, and it showed me beyond doubt that he was as head over heels for her as she was for him, and I was glad, because he deserved it.

"So now what?" Kaf asked.

"Now we get you and the vampire in a room with The Book of the Dead," Spence said.

"How did I know you were going to say that?" Kaf huffed.

"You are most definitely a key part of this, Kafziel," Death said. "For you were both cast out. Mya, please set up the interview room and replay Kaf's death. See if you can spot anything of note. Kaf, go with her."

They got up and did so. While she was away, Death asked us to stay, and he went to get changed.

My babies wriggled inside me, and I placed a hand upon my belly. Spence looked at me. "You doing okay then? Babies okay?"

"At the moment. But that's why Kaf is here. Well, one of the reasons. To make sure things stay that way."

"This house," he began. "People always see Death, or now, Queen Mya, as the figurehead of Purgatory. It's what the Home of the Wayward and the book need people to see. But all of it works together, I'm sure. Because a puzzle is easy to solve if all the pieces are obvious and given here is an access portal to Heaven and Hell, it can't be that simple."

"Otherwise it would be overrun with people trying to trick it?"

Spence nodded. "Evil spirits wait here, and more hang around the basement waiting for the new recruits. Jenny and I know we are some kind of guardians for the place, but all I can do is follow my gut instinct. That's why I helped you that day. I saw you in the room able to handle the book and so I knew it had a task for you."

"To get rid of Tiana?"

"No. To get rid of you."

"Huh?"

He raised a brow. "Do you think that book saw you as a consort to Death? Someone who could take on the role of queen?"

I sighed. "No."

"It allowed you to temporarily get rid of Tiana until Mya got here and you became pregnant. Fate dealt her hand, and so the book reverted the anomalies. That's what I think anyway."

"Spence, I think you're right."

"I didn't like how you treated Death, but it all worked out for the best, and I'm glad you're happy now and wish the best for you, Bernard, and the babies."

"Thank you. I'm glad you found Jenny."

At that point footsteps sounded out, coming downstairs, and closer to the living room. Mya walked in.

"Everything okay?"

"We found out the connection between Kaf and Tiana."

"Oh yeah?"

"She's the serial killer who ended his life," Mya said.

CHAPTER FOURTEEN

Kaf

I followed Mya into one of the interview rooms and sat down, remaining quiet while she logged into the computer.

"Please show me the supporting information and death of Kafziel O'Keeffe, which took place on August 23rd, 2006," she ordered. The screen went blank for a moment and then a video appeared. Mya paused it and turned to me. "Are you sure you want to watch? I'm happy to go through it myself... it's just you might notice important details I could miss."

I moved my chair next to hers. "I'll watch too. It's fine. You can't change what happened and if it gets too much, I'll close my eyes."

Mya patted my hand and pressed play.

On screen, the woman I'd known as Portia, appeared. She was talking to her father in the car sales showroom.

"You're becoming careless, Tiana," the man roared at her. Yet she didn't flinch. "Too many bodies are being found drained."

She rolled her eyes. "No one tells me what to do, Carlos, especially not my deputy. You seem to forget you're not really my daddy, you're my employee."

"I bring in a lot of money to the De Luca clan, not only with the legitimate car sales, but also with the bootleg blood bank we have going."

"And where do you think that blood comes from?" Tiana glowered.

The man paused. "You said you robbed the blood warehouses."

A wicked laugh erupted from her throat. "I do, and I also add in a little extra from my own collections."

The already pale man I'd known as my boss, paled further. "I'm selling blood from your victims? What if someone traces it?"

"God, for a vampire, you are so very boring. Where's your sense of danger, excitement? Running so close to the wind that it whips your cheeks. It's a good job you have a great business brain, or I'd have got rid of you long ago." She tilted her head at him. "So if I were you, I'd be a good little daddy and make as much money for your dear daughter as possible."

With that she left him and walked out onto the forecourt where I was cleaning down a new Mercedes we were about to put out for sale.

"Morning, Portia," I said. Watching myself made me feel uncomfortable. Where I'd thought I'd looked cool and impressive, giving her my cocky smirk, I could see now what she saw. A man who was a little bit nervous, and keen to impress.

"Morning, Kaf. How are you today?" she enquired. Sometimes she'd flirt with me and other times she'd be dismissive. I thought she'd been playing a game of treat me mean to keep me keen. Now I saw she'd been toying with me. The vampire with her prey.

"Well, I'd be better if you'd just date me already and stop playing hard to get." I rubbed the cloth over the car, so it flexed my bicep. Watching it now, I felt so pathetic. There was me, back then, thinking she'd be staring at my body with lust in her gaze. She'd been taking in my body all right, but it wasn't my physique she was interested in, it was my O-neg.

"I've told you already that my daddy won't let me date guys from work. He says he doesn't want business mixing with our personal life, but I think he just sees you as beneath me," she teased, running a finger along the side of the car through the suds.

"I think he doesn't want you beneath me," I flirted back. "Come on, Portia. Be a little rebellious."

She sucked on the inside of her cheek. "Fine. One date."

I grinned; triumph etched across my features. "At last. Where would you like me to take you, and when?"

"Tonight, and I have to keep a low profile, so how about we have a picnic at the park?"

I scoffed. "A picnic? Let me take you to a restaurant."

"That's my offer. Take it or leave it," she said, walking away.

"Okay, okay. A picnic it is. What should I bring?"

"Just yourself. I'll get your details from the personnel files and text you later." She left and I leaned against the car looking like the cat that had got the cream, when really, I was a mouse near a trap, the cheese held in a picnic basket.

As the scene switched to the place of my demise, Mya pressed pause and turned to me. "You good?"

I nodded my head. "I had no idea she was a vampire. No idea at all."

"She hadn't needed to enthral you because you were already attracted to her. Had you worked there long?"

"About three months. We'd been flirting for a month maybe. She didn't pop in much, but when she did it'd made the day more interesting. I feel so stupid now, watching it."

"Mine's no better, Kaf," Mya said. "If I looked back, I'd see a bookseller accepting a date with a vampire after which Death asked her for reading recommendations."

"Really?"

"Yup. It's not until we die that we realise just how fragile human life is. We fear silly things like flying in aeroplanes when in reality every step of our life weaves us across paths lined with unknown outcomes. There's much to be said about mindfulness and living in the moment."

"Or in our case, unliving in the moment."

Mya laughed. "Yup. Ready to watch more?"

"Go for it," I replied, and I sat back again to face the screen.

This time the picnic area appeared on screen, and I saw Portia there before I'd arrived, placing down the hamper she'd brought and setting out blankets. When I finally got there, she smiled at me and now what I'd thought was attraction in her gaze, as she flicked her honey-blonde hair, revealed itself as thirst. We ate strawberries and drank champagne, and chatted amiably, getting to know each other better.

"God, I'm looking at her like a lovesick fool. I wasn't used to champagne, it made me groggy fast," I said.

"No, Kaf," Mya said, "she was enthralling you here. Every lick of her lips has you watching her, and she keeps making eye contact with you. It looks like she's interested, flirting, but she's pulling you under. Maybe the champagne softened you up, but you were under her spell."

Eventually, I slumped against a tree trunk and asked Portia to order me a taxi home.

"Don't worry. You're not going home," she said.

"I really need my own bed. Sorry, Portia, I've never had champagne before." My head rested against the trunk, my eyes closing.

"Don't worry, Kaf, I'm going to take good care of you," she replied.

Mya and I sat and watched the next scenes that I'd played in my mind over and over. How I saw the glint of a carving knife. How she removed my phone from my pocket, not knowing about our overprotective mother and the burner phone with its emergency message. How I'd pressed send on my second phone when I realised what was about to happen wasn't anything good. This was the point when Connor got my message that gave him my exact whereabouts and said I was in danger.

But it was too late. A blade slit across my neck and a vampire drank her fill. She didn't drain me. I guessed because she was being wary of what Carlos had said, but she marvelled, her eyes sparkling like rubies as she watched me breathe my last.

By the time Connor reached me, it was too late, and Portia/Tiana was long gone.

"When I went up to Heaven, they told me Portia would be caught, imprisoned, and would murder no more. I thought they meant she'd been caught that night."

"She was, because after that date she met Aria here," Mya explained. "Heaven kept you as they recognised you as one of their own. Hell had Tiana."

"But why would we get ejected now? Six years later?"

"Who knows? And we may never get to know. The ways of Heaven and Hell are beyond us. They've decided it's time to correct the anomaly where Tiana was sent to Hell through trickery and not the correct route. My guess would be that it's as simple as this is how it should be."

"How do you do this? Work out who goes where? It's a heck of a responsibility."

Mya nodded. 'It is, and I gain more skills every day. Like now, I see that if I do make a mistake, it's likely Heaven, Hell, the book, or the home will have me correct it anyway. I'm beginning to see I'm part of a system now. This is actually settling something inside of me, Kaf. Giving me more confidence in my role as Queen of the Wayward. I don't decide their fate. I just decide on their next move."

"That makes sense. And now we have to decide what the next is for Tiana De Luca."

Mya nodded. "Let's go join the others and get them up to speed."

"Tiana murdered you?" Aria said, her eyes wide. "Just before I sent her to Hell?"

I nodded. "Yup. I had just gone to Heaven and I'm guessing that's the reason Tiana actually got through the portal at that time. Not because you'd managed to work out how to 'trick the system' as such, but because she'd just done a heinous murder and was to all intents and purposes dead."

"Wow. This all blows my mind," Aria said.

Death coughed to get our attention. "This brings me back to my original comment when I stepped through the portal. We now need to reacquaint Tiana with The Book of the Dead. She won't rest until she has it in her hands, and so that's what we do. And we let the book do its thing."

"Send her back?" I queried.

Death shrugged. "I've no idea. Just as none of us know our fates until they befall us. But that's the next step. So how do we do that bearing in mind she's not going to come here voluntarily when she just escaped."

"I have to take it to her," Aria said. "If the book allows me."

"That's far too dangerous," I protested.

"But that's why you're here, Kaf. Don't you see? To protect me and the babies, and also to confront the person who murdered you. It's all come full circle."

As we all glanced at each other: me, Aria, Kaf, Death, and Spence, we all murmured in agreement.

"Not today," I said. "We've already been through enough. Aria, you need to tell Bernard what's happening, and feed up or something. I want to chill in my apartment and get my head straight after everything I've just seen. Tomorrow, we'll come back here and see if the book allows you to take it, and we'll go see Tiana. Do you know how to find her?"

"She's my sire. If I allow my guard down, I'll know exactly where she is," Aria replied.

"That's it then. We reconvene tomorrow and see what happens," I said. Everyone agreed, and yet it was clear that none of us wanted this to be the way forward. We were all too apprehensive about what came next.

CHAPTER FIFTEEN

Bernard

It was late afternoon when I returned from Paris. I dropped Fen at the laundrette and then I decided to pop into Books and Buns for a delicious coffee and cupcake before returning home. Dela was behind the counter.

"Bernard! How goes it after last night's shenanigans?" she asked. "Lawrie told me about the state you were in."

"What happened at the stag party shall stay at the stag party," I winked. "But let's just say that I needed two drinks this morning, and I'm fancying a coffee and cupcake this afternoon. Could I also have three to take away for if Aria fancies a snack."

"Of course. What coffee would you like?"

"Americano please."

"Coming right up."

"I did want to ask you something else, Dela. It's only an idea and I don't know if Fen and Stan would be interested in it, but I'd considered applying for a permit for them to be married in the park. That way if Stan accidentally invites a few hundred extra guests there'd be room. You live out there. Do you think it could work?"

"Oooh, absolutely," Dela's face went dreamlike. "You could string lights between the trees. There's the old bandstand. That would be the perfect place for the ceremony, and you could even have some music of some kind on there afterwards—like a choir or something." Then her expression dulled. "It's just the weather. It could be bitterly cold for guests."

"Hmmm, you're right. It's perhaps not the best idea. Fen isn't keen on a church service either."

"What about the community centre? It has a huge garden at the back that the summer fetes are held on. Even better, since Fen sits on the committee it shouldn't be too difficult to get permission. That way you have an indoor space and an outdoor space."

"That could work! Thank you, Dela. I'll chat with Fen and see what she thinks to the idea." I did a little fist pump. "I'm so excited about this. They're such a lovely couple. They deserve a beautiful day."

I sat and enjoyed my coffee and cupcake and made updates to my notes about the wedding. Then when I left, I walked back to the launderette where I found Fen looking red faced, a customer in front of her tapping their foot.

"I'm so sorry, Sheila. I'm just not sure where Jason's put your coat. Give me a minute."

"Okay, Fen. I have only got a minute though. I'm due at the dentist."

Seeing that Fen had quite a pile to go through, I stepped through and behind the counter. "What is your full name, my dear? I shall look too."

"Sheila Gregson."

I went into the room behind the counter and with vamp speed found the coat placed behind three others at the back.

I returned and presented the coat to the customer with a flourish. "There you go. Thank you for visiting 'Suds Law', please call again." I beamed at Sheila in what I hoped was a charming manner. She smiled back and left.

"Are you okay?" I asked Fen.

She shook her head. "Not really. Jason's so busy with dragon business that he's doing it while here, as in his paperwork etc. He's taken his eye off the ball and every time I return the place is a mess. But I can't tell him off because it's not his fault he inherited the crown."

She gestured behind her. "Look at it all. I don't know what needs doing and what's been done."

"Come on," I said. "With my speed we can get through this in no time."

I swear you're some kind of guardian angel. Your wife is very lucky to have you *and* Kaf."

The launderette was back organised, and I appraised all my fine work. "I don't suppose you also want a job here, do you? Being here when I can't? It's only a couple of days a week at the moment, but from the beginning of November it would be full-time." She waved her hand. "Ignore me. I'm being silly. As if with the babies you can spare the time to work here. You're already doing enough with the wedding."

"I should be okay, up until the babies' birth." My eyes looked around the building. It smelled amazing, and I'd quite enjoyed doing the organising. Plus, it gave Aria more space just like she'd asked for. "Why don't you show me the ropes now, and then I can help out on the odd occasion and see how it goes?"

"Are you sure?" Fen's forehead creased with concern.

"I shall run it past her indoors, but I think it'll be fine."

"It would be such a help. We get such a lot of laundry and dry cleaning here with being into re-use and re-cycle. The twins at the second-hand store have been having to do their own shop's laundry as I've just not had capacity of late."

"If I come, we should be able to expand capacity as long as there are enough machines. My speed is a very fortunate effect of my vampirism."

"They could have done with making Santa and the elves vampires. Christmas might not need to be an all year round system then."

"It would certainly take less time. Especially if they drained all the children."

Fen's mouth dropped open.

"Kidding!" I laughed. "People are always so quick to believe we're all evil, bloodthirsty creatures, but most of us use blood banks now."

"Thanks so much, once again, Bernard. It's really appreciated."

"Oh..." I said loudly, startling Fen once more. "Totally forgot what I'd come in for. Dela suggested you might hold the wedding at the community centre. What do you think?"

"Hmmm. It'd need a good clean and tidy after all the Christmas festivities and the New Year celebrations, but I know you can deal with all that quickly with your speed, so yes, why not? I'll book it into the diary. I know no one has New Year's Day booked. They're always too busy getting over New Year's Eve. With that in mind, the wedding had better be later in the day. Shall we say three pm?"

"Perfect," I replied. "You book it and I'll work on some plans on how to make it amazing. You'll have to give me permission to enter so I may take a look around."

"You have all the permission you need," she said.

With that I said my goodbyes and I whizzed home.

My wife was on the sofa again when I returned, once more reading.

"Goodness me. Have you actually not moved today?" I asked her.

"I did say I was going to rest all day," she snapped. "What do you suggest a knackered pregnant woman growing twins should do? Train for a marathon?"

"I'm sorry," I said. "It's just I've been so busy today." I rattled through all the things I'd achieved. "So is that okay with you? If I work at the launderette on the odd occasion and see if I like it?"

"Yeah, whatever," Aria replied dismissively, staring back at her book. I was so excited and yet she didn't seem the slightest bit interested. She wanted me to get a life, and now I was, even that didn't make her happy. It must be the hormones.

"Now obviously, usually I would attend to your every need, but I know that's annoying you of late, so I'll go get some blood and spend the evening on the computer. I need to update my spreadsheets and do our own accounts. Would you like anything before I go?"

"Nope, I'm fine. I'm still tired and not in the best of moods, so it's probably better if you give me a wide birth."

"That's what you'll be having if the babies come out at the same time." I giggled.

A glance colder than Siberia met me.

Then I remembered that last night she'd been lingerie shopping.

"Oh, by the way. I am really very sorry for being drunk last night and having to stay at Kaf's. I should have kept myself in check. I heard from Kaf that you had a surprise for me which I wasn't present for. Just to let you know, I have no plans for any further evenings out and so feel free to model your purchases when you like."

"You're allowed to enjoy yourself, Bernard."

"I know, but I also don't like to let you down. I love you. You and my dear babies."

She smiled then. "I know and we love you too."

I hesitated. "Though I'm enjoying finding new activities and I'm feeling a lot more settled within myself, my priority will always be you and the children. If you need me, you call me. Now and forever."

Aria's eyes teared up then and she swiped the pink drops off her face angrily. "Oh my god, my bloody hormones. That's one thing I'll be glad to see the back of after birth." She turned to me. "Can you go to your office? I don't want you seeing me like this. This weak and pathetic blubberer is not me."

"Of course, darling. Just shout if you need anything," I said and I went through to the kitchen to get my blood for the evening.

Aria didn't shout for me and when I finally left the office, she was asleep in our bed. But she looked settled, and that was all I cared about. I climbed in at the side of her, and at some point during the night she snuggled in closer to me. That's when I thanked the universe for my wife, babies, and new opportunities. I was the happiest I'd been in a long, long time.

CHAPTER SIXTEEN

Aria

Deceiving my husband was the hardest thing, but despite Kaf's protests, I'd decided not to tell Bernard about Tiana. Kaf was there to protect the babies, and if Bernard went there, Tiana would stake him in seconds out of spite just because of my love for him. And that was the only reason that Kaf eventually gave up trying to persuade me otherwise.

'You protect my babies. I'll protect my husband', I'd told Kaf. 'That's how this goes'.

Bernard and I had enjoyed a lovely breakfast together. Guilt had made me extra amenable, and I blamed being soppy on my pregnancy hormones once more so that he didn't become suspicious. Once Bernard had set off to visit the community centre, and then to see Fen for more launderette training, I let my mask slip and sunk down onto the sofa in despair. I had no idea what was going to happen today, but it wasn't going to be pleasant for at least one of us. All I could do was hope that our belief in the book, the Home of the Wayward, and Heaven and Hell was rightly held.

A baby kicked out. I rubbed where the foot had hit and felt another wiggle beneath. A ferocity that even I had never known before flooded my system.

My babies.

I would die for my babies. But more...

I would kill for my babies.

Tiana De Luca might have been the boss of me in the past, but she wasn't the boss of my present and future.

Kaf called for me.

"I'd say it's not too late to change your mind but given you've either grown a triplet overnight or you're trying to disguise hidden weapons, I'd say that's a waste of time."

"Huh. Is it that obvious?"

"Uh-huh," he replied.

"I'd usually strap a blade to my thigh, but I can't chuffing reach anything past my huge tummy these days. Plus, I don't want anything too near the babies." I began unwrapping my extra layers and pulled out a rolling pin, a paperweight, a heavy book, and a very protectively wrapped cupcake.

I threw everything on the sofa, then unwrapped and began eating the cupcake.

"I'm sure the evil vampire Tiana would have quivered faced with a book on pregnancy," Kaf said with heavy sarcasm. "Were you hoping to distract her with a photo of a birth canal?"

I stuck my tongue out at him, probably revealing a few cupcake crumbs. "I'm ready now," I said, the bun having disappeared down my throat in mere seconds. I was getting hungrier by the day and could easily have eaten another few. "Let's get through to The Home of the Wayward and see if the book wishes to play ball."

A tense looking Mya and Death waited for us.

"I know we're facing an unknown outcome, but can we at least try to look positive?" I asked them.

"That's not why Mya has a face like a smacked arse," Death said. Mya narrowed her gaze at him.

"Oh?"

"Believe it or not, despite the fact I told my girlfriend I was pleased things happened how they did so that we ended up together, she has taken it upon herself to be annoyed that it was you who made the decision to end our," he did open quotes, "'relationship', and not me. Therefore, she is annoyed with my past self, the one who existed before I even knew she did."

"Oh, Mya," I said. "The man is completely and utterly in love with you. You're being ridiculous. You've got to let the past go."

Mya's eyes filled with tears. "It's too hard," she said.

"I don't know why. We barely dated and it was all false on my part."

"And I've already told you that I know my feelings for Aria were nothing at the side of what I feel for you," Death said with a desperate sigh.

"That's not what's too hard, is it?" Kaf said, and I knew Mya wasn't herself because she resisted making a joke about his sentence.

She shook her head and then she ran off out of the room.

Death and I looked at Kaf.

"I'm guessing her human life wasn't the best. She can't believe anyone loves her for her, and she's trying to find reasons to either work out it's all a lie or to push you away. It's her default mechanism for all the times she's suffered before. That's my guess anyway. You'd have to ask her if my intuition is right."

Death nodded at Kaf. "I think that's exactly what this is. One of the things that made me consider Mya for the position of Queen before I ever developed feelings for her was the fact she had no one. Her family didn't care about her. Barely anyone turned up to the fake funeral we held and the relative that did was just seeing if she'd left any money."

"Go after her," I said.

"I will in a moment, but first, let's see what happens when you touch the book," he said, pointing to the coffee table where the book revealed itself.

"If I am able to take you with me to see Tiana De Luca accompanied by Kaf, please could you turn some pages," I said aloud.

The book flipped open and quickly flicked several pages before setting on one.

I walked over and it showed me an entry.

And I knew then that everything would work out okay.

"We're good to go. The book has told me all I need to know," I said to Kaf. "It's time for me to contact Tiana."

I phoned the number I'd kept in my contacts despite hovering over the delete button many times.

"Well, well, well. If this is you calling with excuses, I suggest you end the call and reconsider," she said.

"I have the book," I told her.

There was a silence.

"If this is another trick to send me to Hell, I won't be playing. You come to me this time at my house. You place it in my possession and then we're done. Any funny business and I'll kill your babies. Not you. I'll let you suffer knowing the loss of them both."

A shiver travelled down my spine that anyone could be so evil as to leave a woman with that amount of pain and suffering, worse than any other form of torture.

"I only have one item on my agenda and that's to get you out of my life," I said.

"I'm here and ready when you are," she said. "See you shortly."

Giving Kaf a nod, he let his wings appear and wrapped me within them. We landed near Tiana's home, and Kaf released me, staying out of sight. "I'll be outside, keeping watch."

"Thank you."

"Are you sure about this? Can you not tell me what the book said?"

"No. You're going to have to trust me."

"Okay. Good luck, Aria. I just hope this all works out because I don't want to have to face Bernard or my conscience if it doesn't."

"It's going to be fine," I said, and I pushed open the door and went inside.

I was used to the grandeur of the Letwine Mansion and so walking inside this small house with its cracked walls and peeling paint was a culture shock. It looked like since her return, Tiana was not the top dog she'd once been. A rat scuttled across the floor and the scent of its family's urine filled the air.

Following the scent of Tiana herself I pushed open her sitting room door.

She sat on a chair that looked like a throne. I wanted to laugh because it seemed so pathetic. Tiana sat there and I saw her for exactly what she was: an opportunist, a thief, someone who had got where she was by desperation. Something I now recognised in myself. That survival instinct was what I'd never really considered, even on my turning. I didn't know the strength of it until I needed my unborn babies to survive.

"Aria. Why, look at how much you've grown," she said, her eyes focused on my stomach.

I went to reach inside my coat.

"Halt. I don't think so. How do I know there isn't a stake in there about to head my way?"

"You come to me then. The book is in a bag hung from my shoulder. Open my coat and you will see the bag."

"You do it, but go slowly," she ordered.

I did as asked, revealing the shoulder bag.

"Place the bag down on the coffee table," she added bossily.

I not only placed the bag down but I let the book slide out of it so she could see it was there.

"There's just something too easy about all this," Tiana sighed. "It's not real, is it?"

The book flicked open, and she headed towards it. Then she gasped. "That's my human death. Show me Aria's," she ordered. The book flipped its pages once more.

"If you are real, let me see more of your power," she ordered it. The book burned through the coffee table and dropped onto the carpet. Ripples of electricity buzzed through it. The smell of burned wood permeated the air, yet the book remained undamaged.

Tiana's eyes lit with fascination. "It's real," she said. "How did you get it to obey you?"

"I promised to care for it," I told her. "You can't control the book, but if you care for it, it will allow you to use it. That's the key," I said.

"Hmmm. Transfer it to me."

"And then we're done?"

"Yes, yes. Once I have the book you can go live your pathetic attempt at happy families."

My palms folded into fists that I wanted to smack her in the jaw with, but instead I focused on getting this over with. "Almighty Book of the Dead," I said. "Please listen to Tiana De Luca and allow her to touch you." The ripples of electricity ceased. I gestured for her to pick it up.

Hesitantly, she reached down and gingerly touched a fingertip to the front. Then once she saw it hadn't reacted, she greedily scooped it up.

"Show me the death of Carlos De Luca," she ordered, and the book flicked open. She turned to me with glee on her face.

"Here it is. His death caused by me. All I have to do is show him he's fated to die, and it can only be changed if he bows to my whims. I shall rule the De Luca clan once more," she announced. Then she turned to me. "Now, what to do with you. As if I was going to let you leave."

A knock came to the window and Tiana swung around. But of course there was no one there, because Kaf appeared right beside her.

"Hello, Portia. Or should I say Tiana."

She gasped. Kaf's wings were clearly visible.

"Y-you. I killed you." Her eyes were wide. Panicking, she stared at the book. "Show me the death of... of..."

Kaf scoffed. "You don't even remember my name, do you? I was nothing but a toy. Another victim of your cruelty. It's Kaf," he told her. "But that book won't tell you about me. This one would though." He brought out a copy of the Bible. It shone with a bright white light that lit up the whole room. "My name is also Cassiel. I'm an archangel."

Faced with an unpredictable outcome, Tiana reverted to type. Desperation. She dropped The Book of the Dead, and swept around in my direction, reaching for me at the same time she reached for a stake. What she didn't know was while she'd been distracted, my husband had appeared. He struck his own stake straight through her heart. A shriek and then only dust remained, floating down and covering the book. It flicked its pages in annoyance to clean itself.

Reaching down, I picked it up and hugged it. "Thank you for showing me that my very annoying husband has still been spying on me, throughout the time he's supposedly been giving me my own space," I told it while also staring at Bernard with a half-smile on my lips. "That way I knew exactly what would happen here today. Now let's get you back where you belong," I said.

"Are you talking to the book or to me?" Kaf said. He was shimmering brighter than ever.

"I think you'd better go and visit your brother, Kaf, while you can," I advised. I placed the book down on the coffee table ready to return it to my bag and then I reached for him and hugged him. The goodness just soaked through him and into me. His arms embraced me, and I felt such love, not romantic love, but love of the earth, the universe.

"Hey, it's my turn," Bernard demanded, and I was about to roll my eyes at his jealousy at me being in another man's arms, when he moved me to the side and hugged Kaf himself.

"Charming," I said good-naturedly.

"Be good to each other," Kaf said. "I hope they'll allow me to visit from time to time to see the babies. I was told I'd be keeping an eye on Billy, Charity's younger brother, so I don't think I'm completely done in Gnarly. Just maybe on a break for a while." He disappeared.

"We drop this book back off and then we go straight home. Don't think I won't be having a word with you about putting yourself in dangerous situations," my husband scolded.

"Yes, and I'll be having a word with you about being overprotective," I said.

And then we narrowed our eyes at each other before we burst out laughing.

CHAPTER SEVENTEEN

Kaf

As soon as I walked through the door of the bistro that my brother owned, my facial expressions must have given the game away because his smile fell straight off his face and tears welled up.

He was preparing for opening for lunch but gave excuses to his kitchen and gestured for us to go up to his flat above the restaurant. The minute we were through the door he took me in his arms in a hug that threatened to break my bones.

"Please tell me you're not leaving," he said, his voice trembling. "I can't lose you again, bro. I can't."

"It's okay," I reassured him. "Sit down and I'll explain."

He let go of me and we made our way over to his sofa, taking opposite ends. I explained what I'd been doing and how Aria and Bernard's babies were now safe. "I feel called back to the Home of the Wayward," I told him. "I think they'll take me back up to Heaven, but I also think that there will be times I have to return. I know I've to look out for Charity's younger brother, Billy, and so I don't feel my time in Gnarly is done."

"I hope not," Connor said. He rubbed tears out of his lower lashes. "I've got used to having you around. I mean, I never thought I'd see you again. But you came back. Though I grieved for you, I never got over losing you. For you to return and now have to go again. It's just cruel, so I will pray over and over that you get to come back and I'm not even religious."

I arched a brow at him. "You can't say you're not religious to an archangel. I mean what else do you need to see to believe other than your own dead brother returned as one of God's own?"

Connor nodded his head. "Fair point."

I stared around the flat. "You're going to be lonely without me. What you need, bro, is the love of a good woman."

He laughed. "Yeah, forgive me if I don't take the advice of someone who got murdered on a date."

I joined in with his laughter. "Fair point," I parroted back.

"Okay, so the restaurant can do without me today. Let's have one final day together before you go back to the Home of Wayward Souls," Connor said.

"Sounds good to me. What are we going to do?" I asked him.

"As much as we can fit in," he replied.

We played pool, had beer, ate burgers. We went to the cinema to watch Resident Evil: Retribution in Leicester Square and then we walked around London for a bit. The night drew to a natural close and I saw the wistfulness appear on Connor's face again as we reached his flat.

"I'm not saying goodbye because it's not," I said, and then I let my wings come out and I just left. It wasn't going to be easy, whichever way I did it, so I decided to just go.

The next moment Mya was opening the door of her home.

"They're waiting for you," she said.

"I know. I feel it within me," I replied.

Following her upstairs to the second floor, I then climbed up into the attic, Mya following me. Sitting upstairs was a fellow archangel, Raphael.

"You've had quite the adventure," he acknowledged. "But now it's time to come home for a while."

Where I expected to feel sorrow at leaving Connor behind, instead Raphael's light seemed to seep into me slowly, filling me up until I became something other. A being with love for all: my brother and all other.

"Thank you, Mya," I said.

"We'll miss you," she replied.

"He'll be back before you know it," Raphael winked.

Then he reached for me and with a flash of light we were back above, into a place beyond description.

CHAPTER EIGHTEEN

Mya

November 11th, 2012.

Since I'd become Queen of the Wayward there had never been a dull moment. Yet some parts of it, I got used to. Like having Death as my boyfriend. The alternative would be to go crazy. But watching one archangel come to collect another. Well, that was something to behold indeed, and I hoped it would stick with me for a while before my brain accepted it as part of my usual new world.

Today marked one whole year since I'd been offered the 'choice' of whether I died into nothingness or became Queen. It had passed in a flash. It was also approaching the date where the Gnarly curse had been lifted, meaning residents could fall in love and stay in love.

And then I'd fallen in love myself.

In reference to the fact it was a year since we began living together, Death had arranged for us to go out to dinner at the bistro. I was looking forward to a nice meal and then hopefully some sexy shenanigans when we got home. To that end I put on a sexy red lacy bra and matching panties before slipping on a tight black dress over the top. My Louboutin's completed the look, but only I knew that the soles matched my undies.

Or so I'd thought.

"Ooh, I say, the man's in for a treat tonight. Me and Jenny will keep an eye on the wayward for yer, so yer can have the night to play."

I whipped around. "Spence. What the fuck are you doing in my bedroom?"

He grinned and gave no apology for the fact he'd invaded my privacy. The man was a rogue.

"I've been knocking and shouting fer ages. You've got yer music on that loud, they can probably hear it down in the village."

I huffed, turning the volume down on the remote.

"Anyway, why are yer yelling that loving him is red? Surely loving Death is black?"

"Hang on while I just phone up Taylor Swift to complain about the colour she chose for her new single," I answered with heavy sarcasm, but as usual it just went over Spence's head.

"I came to tell yer that Death got called away, so he said he'll meet yer at the bistro at eight."

Folding my arms across my chest, I huffed. "Sucking typical. I hope he's not late. I've been looking forward to our night out."

Spence shook his head and looked at me like I was a pile of steaming horse shit. "Someone else is probably looking forward to their evening, only to find out they aren't having one." He fell on the floor playing dead.

"One year I've been putting up with you. One whole year," I told the ghost laid on the floor. He cracked an eye open and gave a wicked cackle.

"Ger on with ya. Ya know ya love me."

The bistro was shut. What the actual fuck? There were no lights on. The door was closed and here I was standing outside, dressed to the nines for an anniversary dinner that marked my death. Who celebrated popping their clogs with a pop of a champagne cork really.

"Fuck my life," I said out loud.

"You're dead," a husky voice said from behind me.

I swung around to find Death standing there. He wasn't dressed in his work outfit. He was wearing a dark denim coloured shirt, a pair of black slacks, and a black tie. He smiled at me, his gaze triumphant, and I didn't know whether I wanted to get annoyed at his smug trickery or snog his handsome face off.

"You weren't called away to work at all, were you?" I said, as soft lighting slightly lit up the interior of Smokin' Hot. Connor and Chantelle opened the restaurant door and stood looking at us expectantly from the doorway.

"Nope." He grinned again, took hold of my hand, and walked me to the restaurant entrance. As we walked through, I saw that a table was set in the centre of the room, lit by candlelight. It was the most romantic thing that had ever happened to me across both my dead and undead life.

"Please follow me, while our chef returns to the kitchen," Chantelle gestured ahead. We did as asked.

As we approached the table, Death pulled out my chair for me, and once I was seated then sat down himself. Chantelle placed two glasses of O-neg in front of us.

"On the house," she said. "I will bring your starters over shortly."

"I ordered for us both, so that they could have everything prepared," Death explained. "Mya, you look incredible tonight."

Smiling at him, I gave him another once-over. "As do you."

Reaching across the table, he took hold of my hand once more. "Mya, I know you weren't really given much of a choice on this evening a year ago, but I want you to know how happy I am that you chose to come to Gnarly. I'm aware it's not been easy to adjust to being undead and to handle wayward spirits and curses, but time and again you prove yourself. I know the Book got what it wanted, but the by-product was that so did I. I love you, Mya."

"I love you too," I said honestly. And had I drunk champagne rather than blood, I would have popped a cork then for my own death, because I realised that despite its ups and downs my undead life had brought me more love and joy than my previous life ever had.

"You're it for me, Mya," Death said. "I need you to know that I've never felt like this about anyone else, and so..."

Right then if I'd been alive my heart would have stopped. Was he about to propose?

"Owwwwwwwwwwwwww," someone screamed out, and I shot

up out of my seat and hissed. My eyes felt like they were burning in their sockets they were obviously so red. Now crouched on one of the neighbouring seats, stalking out the location of the sound, suddenly the lights switched on.

"Surprise," Lawrie said drolly and half-arsed as other Gnarly Fell residents appeared through the doorway at the back of the restaurant.

The next thing I knew, an extremely pregnant woman was carried in by her husband. "Can someone help me get us to Chelsea?" Bernard panicked. "I don't want to whizz us, and have a baby fall out on the way."

I snorted, having returned to my normal self. "What are you saying about Aria's vagina, Bernard. Is it that loose?" Death gave me a glare.

"There's no time for me to go anywhere," Aria yelled. "Someone help me with these babies. They're coming *now*."

"But they aren't due until Christmas," Bernard said perplexed.

"Oh, honey, I must be mistaken by the excruciating pain across my stomach, and the fact I feel like I've pissed myself. Do you want to go check outside that it is amniotic fluid I lost, and while you're there find your fucking bollocks and brain cells?"

Bernard startled. "They're coming now?"

"That's what I said, dipshit."

Bernard promptly fainted.

Pandemonium reigned. Into the restaurant came my best friend Callie, Dela and Nick, Fen and Stan, Ginny and Merrin, the twins, and Charity and Jason. They all stood around looking lost as the surprise party had become a surprise babies' appearance instead.

I stared down at Aria, who was panting through another contraction.

"It's a good job I've finally decided to like you since you interrupted my anniversary dinner."

"Bite me," she spat back.

The contraction eased.

"Sorry," she said.

I patted her arm in reassurance. "What do you need to get these babies out safely?" I asked.

"Dr Breen. She's the one who's been keeping an eye on me. Her number's in my phone. She's a vampire." She passed me her handbag. "I know this was a surprise party, but you have to admit I went over and above for you." She looked over my shoulder at Death. "Sorry, though. I hope I didn't spoil things."

"Not at all. I was just about to say 'surprise' when you screamed," he stated.

They were looking at each other so they didn't see my utter disappointment. God, I'd never even been bothered about getting married and yet now I was gutted that Death hadn't been about to propose? *Get it together, Mya,* I told myself sharply. There are babies to be born. And looking around me, people to be organised.

I got out Aria's mobile, found the contact info and spoke with the doctor. She appeared within a minute. While she attended to Aria, I gathered up everyone else. "Party's over, folks. Sorry. I really appreciate you all coming, but as you can see there have been other developments."

"Not to worry, love," Fenella said. "We can get together again anytime. But before we go, we just want to say you've made such a difference to our lives, Mya, sweetheart. If it weren't for you, none of us would be with our loves. Thank you for choosing us." Walking over she kissed my cheek. "We love you, Mya. Death told us you've never really had a family who cared. Well, we want you to know that you have now."

"Including the best father anyone could ever hope for," Lawrie added.

A groan from Callie followed. "As modest as always," she said, rolling her eyes.

Everyone came up and hugged me and then they left, and it was just me, Death, Bernard who had now recovered and was by his wife's side, and Dr Breen. Chantelle had gone home, and Connor had said he'd be round the back if needed.

"Are you okay if we leave?" Death asked the doctor.

"Yes, me, mum and dad have it from here," she said.

"I'm going to be a dad," Bernard said, going a little green.

Death patted his shoulder. "Bernard, you've got this," he said, and he pronounced it Berrnnaird. It was enough to shock Bernard out of his panic.

"Y-you said..."

"I know. I think at this stage, as you prepare to become a father, and as I leave with the best thing to ever happen to me, that we leave the past in the past and just embrace the future, okay? Now, your babies are coming and it's time for you to step up for them. It's no longer about you and Aria, Bernard. It's about your family."

I swear Bernard grew two inches taller as he relaxed at Death's words.

"You're right. I need to step up."

"Jesus fucking Christ. I'm sitting here with my innards on display, pushing out not one, but two babies, while you two declare your undying love for each other. Wipe my brow with that face cloth, Bernard, before I crumple it in my hand and shove that and potentially a barstool up your arse so you might have an inkling as to what I'm currently going through."

The fact Aria's pussy was on display in front of Death made me go green then. Jealous green.

"Oh for fuck's sake, Mya. Death hasn't looked, but if he had it would be the first time he'd seen it. Get the fuck out so I can have my babies. I'm sure you've better things to do with your anniversary evening."

"Yes, we were going to have a surprise party before you made it all about you." I stuck out my tongue. "Good luck, and I'll see you and Bernard tomorrow. Don't even think about telling me I'm not allowed to visit. I'll just shove my way in like you have my party."

"It's Berrnaaaird," Bernard said.

"Shut up," we both shouted at him, and then we laughed.

"Huh, that didn't quite go as planned," Death said as we walked towards the boulevard exit.

"Does anything?" I replied. "Are we walking back?"

"Yes, it's a lovely crisp evening. Let's have a romantic stroll," he suggested, once again taking my hand.

"It's certainly an evening to remember," I told him. "Soon Aria and Bernard will have their babies and I got to see that I now have my own family too."

"You do."

JUST MY SUCK

"So really, although it went wrong, it also went a lot right." I squeezed his hand.

"You're now calling him Bernaaaird too then? You said Bernard back then."

"It was my last one. Time to put all of that in the past like you said."

Death staggered, mock wiping his brow. "Did you just... just... agree with me?"

"Don't get used to it."

We walked a little further on. "It's such a rare night to see the stars so clearly in the sky, isn't it?" I noted as we began ascending the hill. The moon was almost full, and it made me think of Aria and the swell of her belly. I told Death that.

"I know we won't have that. It's Death and taxes, not Death and babies, but that's okay, as long as I have you," I said, letting my guard down for once.

"Hang on, my shoelace came undone," Death said.

I whirled around. "I'm declaring emotions here and you—" I ceased talking, my mouth open. Death was in front of me, on one knee, holding out a ring box.

"Y-you said to Aria you were just going to announce my surprise party."

"That's all Aria knew about. She didn't know I intended to propose."

"Ohhhh."

"Is it okay if I do that now then? Kinda in the middle of something and you bring up Aria. Is she always going to be between us," he teased before winking.

Walking in front of him, I dropped onto both my knees, so I was looking him in the eyes. Those beautiful browns.

"Mya Malone. Will you marry me?"

"Yesssssss, but..."

"But what, woman? You are so infuriating. Just accept my proposal."

"I don't want to get married for ages. I just feel at the moment there's still a lot for me to learn about Gnarly and I don't want to take the edge of Fen's wedding."

"Mya, I couldn't care less when we get married. I just want to put a ring on your finger, so you know I love you and no one else but you."

"So it's because I'm insecure?"

"Just put the man out of his misery already and say yes, wench, or yer will have me to answer to," an annoying ghost said.

"Yes. Yes, I'll marry you... one day," I said.

"Whahhoooo," Spence cheered.

I side-eyed him. "Me and you will be having words about your turning up everywhere you shouldn't be."

"Looking forward to it. Love it when you get all feisty. Then Jenny loves it." Winking, he strolled off back up the hill.

Turning back to Death, I held out my hand and he placed the bright red ruby on my wedding finger. It was shaped like a blood-drop. "It's beautiful," I said.

"As are you. Today you've made me the happiest man on earth."

"Oh dear, what about the fact you're supposed to be all brooding?"

"I'll get back to that tomorrow after I fall over an abandoned Louboutin."

I looked at my ring again. "Are we really doing this?"

Death sighed. "Mya, it's okay if you don't want to get married. Just tell me. As long as we're together, it's fine."

"No, I do. I really, really do. It's just hard for me to let myself go fully, you know? But I'm getting there. One day I will stand there and become Mrs..." I remembered then Death didn't have a surname.

"Mrs De-Ath?" Death suggested.

I nodded. "Works for me," I said. Leaning forward, my lips touched Death's and I let all my real feelings out into that kiss. The fact that I was scared to let someone fully in, but he was the one, for sure.

"Let's go home," I said after breaking the kiss.

"I'm not sure I can get up. My leg's numb from being in this position so long," he said.

I pulled down the front of my dress, giving him a flash of red, lacy bra. Suddenly, he wasn't worrying about a numb leg, his mind was focused on another part entirely.

CHAPTER NINETEEN

Bernard

"Thank goodness, he's gone," Aria panted after her most recent contraction.

"Yes, it's not really the best birthing experience to have your ex-boyfriend here," I agreed.

"That's not what I meant, Bernard. Thank goodness, Death left." It was then I realised that the relief on my wife's face came not from the end of a contraction but because while he remained behind she'd been frightened.

And it had never even crossed my mind.

I squeezed her hand.

"Our babies will be born safely. I promise you," I said, though really I could do no such thing. But I did believe it. Merrin had seen it so, and there were no signs of concern on Dr Breen's face.

"Okay, Aria, on your next contraction I think we'll have baby number one out. Get ready to push."

Sure enough, the most gorgeous creature exited on her next screams and then made her own.

"It's a girl," Dr Breen announced, handing her over to me. I stared down at the tiny creature in my arms and felt a wave of love like I'd never experienced before. Aria looked up at me, euphoria in her gaze, but then she winced. "Baby number two doesn't intend to be too far behind."

Aria pushed some more until a baby boy appeared. "Okay, Mummy, you can hold your boy first. It's only fair."

The doctor passed our son to Aria.

After the delivering of the placenta and a few other checks of the babies, Dr Breen arranged for transport to take us home. While we waited, I passed our daughter to her mum and picked up my son.

"Hello, Alain, my son," I said, giving him the name we'd agreed on. It meant handsome.

"Hello, Cherie," Aria said to our daughter. Her name meant cherished one and it was the first thing I'd called Aria when we'd first met. Both names were of French origin.

I placed our son beside his sister and gazed adoringly at my wife and babies.

"I've never loved you more," I told Aria.

"And yet, you'd put a stake through my heart before it went through either of our children's," she said. "I feel it too. Such immense love and happiness. Bernard, thank you for making me your wife."

Leaning down, I placed a gentle kiss on my wife's lips.

"The transport is here. Let's get you home, cleaned, and settled," the doctor said.

Connor came out from the kitchen. I'd totally forgotten he'd been hanging around in case he was needed.

The man looked like he'd been stuck in a ghost train: petrified.

"Congrats," he said, shaking my hand. I probed his mind and found his guards down.

I never want sex again after hearing those screams. Jesus Christ. Let them get out of here so I can drink myself into oblivion and try to forget that noise.

"A vampire will clean up in here and leave it as you desire," Dr Breen said to Connor. "We thank you for letting the Letwine babies be born here and owe you a debt." She looked at me.

"Yes, Aria and I do owe you," I told Connor. "So let me know if we can repay you in any way in the future."

"It's fine. Just glad the babies are here," he said. "Kaf did his bit and now I've done mine." His smile was half-hearted, but then I missed Kaf, and he wasn't my kin.

JUST MY SUCK

I hugged him. At first, he stiffened in my arms, but then he leant into the hug.

"Thanks. Let's call that the debt settled. I needed that hug more than you know."

"Okay, thanks once more," I said, and then I escorted my wife and babies to the ambulance taking us home.

A few days later

Being a vampire, my wife had soon recovered from the birth, and we had been slowly finding our way around the beginning days of parenthood. Aria was feeding both babies, and so I made sure Aria was fed and then watched the babies so she could have a read and rest up.

Alain and Cherie were four days old and cards, presents, and visitors had poured in. The first had been our leader Edmond, closely followed by Ginny and Merrin, and then other vampires from the clan. My best mate Lawrie had practically been dragged in by his wife.

"I suppose they are quite cute," he said. "Though I prefer how my child came: fully independent."

"Excuse my husband's manners," she said. "You know how he is."

"I like what leads to babies," he whispered in her ear. Of course, we could hear his whispers. Knowing this, Callie went bright red and slapped him playfully.

"Behave yourself."

"Absolutely not," he'd said and whizzed her home.

We'd also endured a visit from Mya, who had tried to focus on the babies, but couldn't stop showing off her engagement ring.

Eventually, we'd seen the most important people in our lives and called a halt to anyone else. We wanted family time. Time alone, just the four of us.

"Do you need anything?" I asked Aria.

"Only for you to stop asking if I need anything, sickhead."

"Huh?"

"I can't swear now we have babies. I'll have to use an 's' instead like Mya does."

"Are you okay then if I go over to the laundrette and see if Fenella needs help there?"

"Abso-sucking-lutely."

"Thank goodness. I'm about to go bat...sit."

"Bye. We love you. Call at the café and bring us some cupcakes, Daddy," Aria said.

I took the hint and left, and rather than think it an insult, I took it as good progress that Aria felt she could handle things.

Fenella shook her head at me as I walked into the launderette and announced I was there to help. "Goodness me, Bernard. No, I don't need you right now. Go and rest up in the café. You must be exhausted," Fenella said. But she was the one looking exhausted.

"We're vampires. We're adapting and doing okay. I need something to do that's not getting shouted at by my wife, which is what would be coming if I stayed. Now, you tell me what to do here and then you go to the café and have a rest. I'll compel you if I have to," I warned her.

"You're an absolute love," she said, seeing sense and grabbing her coat and bag while quickly telling me what I needed to know. "With a month to Christmas, it's getting so busy, and I'm just not the age for burning the candle at both ends. It's okay for Stan with him not being human."

"Fenella," I suddenly had a thought that I needed to run past her. I wasn't sure what she'd think of it, but I had to ask.

After I'd said it, she looked immediately deep in thought. "Leave that with me," she said. "I need to think on it myself and then talk to Jason and Stan but thank you. I might just take you up on that," she said.

A week later, I took over ownership of Suds Law.

CHAPTER TWENTY

Fenella

Though we hadn't been officially married yet, I'd been able to do a run-through of life as Mrs Claus thanks to Bernard's offer.

I thought I'd miss the laundrette, but as soon as I'd signed the business over, I'd felt free. It had been the beginning of my life in Gnarly. A place I could work and take my baby. That brought in money in the place that had looked after us so well after the disaster of my first marriage and provided a needed service to the people I adored. Maybe that's why it seemed so fitting for me to let it go as I embarked on a new marriage, a new career, a new beginning.

Jason, even when he gave up the throne eventually to his cousin, would still be involved in dragon politics. He'd become so much more confident of late, and his romance with Charity continued to blossom. He had his own life to lead, and I doubted taking over a laundrette was on his list. He'd been on board with all of Bernard's suggestions. I'd been surprised.

Bernard was flourishing. As a father and as a businessman. He was another man who'd grown in confidence in front of my eyes, and I knew Aria was pleased he'd gained some independence. She'd told me in the café over a coffee and cupcake while I'd had cuddles of both babies. They both idolised those children, and Aria had just agreed to take over the book club at the community centre. It was once a week on a Friday and meant she'd be able to get out and chat about books with her friends. It would give her some me-time.

Standing in front of the mirror I took in my pale face and added a little more blush. I wanted to be a blushing bride not a snow queen. But snow it had, just a dusting, making the outside of Gnarly look magical.

Both Jason's girlfriend Charity, and Nick's girlfriend Dela were with me today to help me get ready, but I'd just come into the bathroom to have a moment. So much had changed of late, and before I signed up for my happy ever after, there was just one thing I wanted to do alone. I high fived myself in the mirror.

"Girl, you did good," I told myself. "Now, go get your man."

Bernard had done an incredible job, despite his last-minute nerves of something going wrong. The centre was dressed up like a Winter Wonderland, with fake snow inside, and the real stuff outside. With the theme of fresh starts, there were flowers just coming into bloom in large vases around the place. In the main hall, there were full seats at either side of an aisle, and at the top waiting for me was Stan. He grinned and I could see his rosy-red cheeks from here.

"You ready, Mum? If you've changed your mind, it's not too late. I'll turn into a dragon, you can climb on my back, and we can get out of here?"

"I've not changed my mind."

"Good," Jason said. "Because Stan is a good man, and I know he'll continue to make you happy."

I grinned at my son. "Let's do this."

Not long after that Stan and I were declared husband and wife.

"You may now kiss the bride," the registrar said.

Stan swept me in his arms and tipped me back, awarding everyone a look at our 'movie-star' kiss. They all applauded.

Stan stroked my cheek once I was back upright.

"I love you, Fenella Anderson, my wife," he said, making my tummy turn over with happiness.

"And I love you too, husband," I replied.

"Shall we get the photos done, so we can tuck into our wedding feast?" he asked.

"Always thinking of food," I teased.

He shook his head. "I'd ditch it all to get you back to ours and see what's underneath that dress," he teased back. I playfully slugged him in the arm.

"Ow," he yelped.

"Oops, sorry, I forgot my strength," I said.

"Be gentle with me tonight, won't you darling?" he quipped.

"May I extend my sincerest congratulations," said a deep voice from behind. We turned and looked at Edmond Letwine.

"Thank you," we said in unison.

"Thought I'd come forward first to give you the usual spiel about looking after my daughter or else." Edmond bared his fangs.

Stan lost some of the ruddy colour in his cheeks.

"Just joking." He snorted. "That never gets old."

He pulled me into a hug. "Don't forget, even though you've decided to be an Anderson, you are a Letwine now, Fenella. We will always be here for you."

"Thank you," I replied. He let me go and walked away, revealing Bernard behind him.

I flung my arms around him. "Thank you for our beautiful wedding. Who could have known where this journey would lead us?" I exclaimed.

"Yup. From wedding planner to brother," he contemplated. "You don't regret making that choice, do you?"

I shook my head. "Not at all."

When Bernard had asked if I wanted to be turned, so that I'd have strength and longevity to be with Stan, I'd needed time to think. Selling the laundrette had been an easy decision, the delay only due to having to run it past the rest of the council. But to become a vampire wasn't only my choice. Stan and Jason had been encouraging though, saying anything that meant I was destined to be around longer and be stronger was fine with them. So I'd gone over to the Letwine mansion where Edmond had sired me, giving me an instant extended family of many, including Bernard as a 'brother'.

"Okay, let's go eat," I announced. "Well, drink for us," I winked at Bernard.

During the wedding meal, my husband stood and clinked his glass with a spoon. Everyone went quiet and turned to face him.

"I would like to propose a toast. Thanks so much to everyone for coming to join my *wife* and I here today. Gnarly is more than just a home to both of us, it's a family, and lately that family has been extended to encompass the Letwines." He nodded over at where Edmond, Bernard, and Aria sat, a baby in each parent's arms.

"As many of you know, I was in love with Fen, from a distance, for many years. I'm sure you all know why—"

"Her cracking rack?" Lawrie heckled, earning a sharp elbow from Callie.

"I'm not going to lie, that's on my list." Stan grinned. "But I was talking of her selflessness in always looking after others. Well now, dear wife, you have me to take care of you."

I smiled up at him, feeling love overflowing for the man I knew would never let me down, and just like that, a weight lifted from me, and the past disappeared forever.

Stan came to the end of his speech. "So if we can raise a glass to my new wife, Fenella," he said. "We can certainly say that Santa definitely pulled a cracker."

I groaned as everyone else laughed.

EPILOGUE

Connor

Three weeks later

The new year had been a challenge. Suddenly the restaurant went quiet after six weeks of chaos. This January was proving even harder without my brother being around. He'd said he'd be back, but he couldn't know that for sure, could he? It might well be that I never saw him again.

Chantelle was looking at a message that had just come through on her phone. She stomped her foot.

"Problem?"

"Nothing I can't deal with. I just need a new love interest."

The door pushed open then before I could ask further and Mitzi walked in. Mitzi owned the saverstore in Gnarly. She was a magpie shifter and there was something about her, namely her lack of manners, that just rubbed me up the wrong way.

"Is Kaf around?" she asked.

"How can you not know he went back up there?" I pointed up at the sky. "You run the convenience store, surely you get all the gossip?"

"If I knew that I wouldn't be here asking if he was around, would I?" She sighed. "Damn it, he was good company on a flight. It gets boring flying solo sometimes, but I don't like other magpies. They want what I want, and some are faster than me."

"Well, he's not here, so if that's all."

"Connor," Chantelle warned, her tone pulling me up on my attitude. "Mitzi, can we get you anything? A drink or lunch?"

"No thank you. I know when I'm not wanted. Your personality sucks, do you know that? It's hard to believe you and Kaf are brothers. He clearly got all the good stuff."

My eyes narrowed at her, but hers were even smaller and intimidating.

Bloody bird eyes.

"Yes, he did. But like I said he's not here. Took his good stuff up there where he belongs, leaving me here. So you're stuck with my personality whether it sucks or not."

"God, I pity the person who ends up with you. If anyone ever does, that is."

I grabbed hold of Chantelle and pulled her closer, kissing her full on the lips. The girl was too stunned to speak, rubbing at her lips. Then she looked out of the window. Saint from the pizza parlour was staring. He turned on his heel and stomped away.

I was undeterred. Chantelle was just staring at me, clearly trying to come to terms with what I'd just done. There was no choice but to continue and hope for the best.

"Chantelle is my girlfriend, and she has no complaints. Do you, honey?"

Cogs whirred and I saw Chantelle come to a decision. "None whatsoever." She turned to Mitzi. "You don't know him like I do. Connor's a good guy too."

As Mitzi opened her mouth to say something further, there was a loud crash from upstairs.

"Someone's in my flat." I panicked. "How can anyone have got up there?"

We listened, frozen in place with fear, as footsteps began to clump down the flat's stairs. I grabbed a rolling pin, and Chantelle a pan and we stood either side of the door.

My brother walked through, his wings batted the pan and rolling pin away.

"You liar," Mitzi snapped at me before turning to Kaf. "Your brother told me you'd gone back to Heaven."

"I had, but something has just occurred that means I've been sent back down. Someone here has just placed themselves in danger." Kaf turned to look at me and Chantelle.

I remembered how Saint had looked at Chantelle. Something had been going on between the two of them, but there was clearly a problem.

"Is it about that Saint bloke?" I asked, Chantelle's eyes going wide.

"Nope. Brother, I'm here for you," he said.

"Erm, welcome home?" I queried. What the bloody hell had I done?

THE END

Connor finds himself tangled in a wizard's webs of mischief when he agrees to fake date Chantelle in TOO MANY SUCKS.

Get it here: geni.us/toomanysucks

For more on my paranormal romcom, join my mailing list and receive the short story prequel to **The Supernatural Dating Agency** series, *Dating Sucks*:
geni.us/andiemlongparanormal

ABOUT THE AUTHOR

Andie M. Long lives in Sheffield, UK, with her long-suffering partner, her son, and a gorgeous Whippet furbaby. She's addicted to coffee and Toblerone.

When not being partner, mother, or writer, she can usually be found wasting far too much time watching TikTok.

SOCIAL MEDIA LINKS

Andie's Reader Hangout on Facebook
www.facebook.com/groups/1462270007406687
(come chat books)

TikTok
@andieandangelbooks

WANT MORE OF ANDIE'S PARANORMAL?

PARANORMAL ROMANTIC COMEDY

Sucking Dead
Suck My Life – also available on audio.
My Vampire Boyfriend Sucks – also available on audio.
Sucking Hell
Suck it Up
Hot as Suck
Just My Suck
Too Many Sucks
Sucking Nightmare

Supernatural Dating Agency
The Vampire wants a Wife
A Devil of a Date
Hate, Date, or Mate
Here for the Seer
Didn't Sea it Coming
Phwoar and Peace
Acting Cupid
Cupid Fools
Dead and Breakfast

WANT MORE OF ANDIE'S PARANORMAL?

Also on audio and in paperback.

The Paranormals
Hex Factor
Heavy Souls
We Wolf Rock You
Satyrday Night Fever

Also in paperback. Complete series ebook available.

PARANORMAL ROMANCE

Paranormal Fairy Tale Re-Tellings
Caging Ella
Sharing Snow

SINGLE TITLES

Filthy Rich Vampires – Reverse Harem
Royal Rebellion (Last Rites/First Rules duet) – Time Travel Young Adult Fantasy
Immortal Bite – Gothic romance

Printed in Great Britain
by Amazon